Divinity Road

To Jean-Louis, Munia, Nicky, Joe, Ella, Patrick, Awat, Kate, Mike, Milan, Tom, Inge, Ataullah Khan, Jim and everyone else who helped in one way or another. And of course to you, Elaine. Thank you, thank you, thank you.

Divinity Road

Martin Pevsner

Signal

First published in 2011 by
Signal Books Limited
36 Minster Road
Oxford
OX4 1LY
www.signalbooks.co.uk

A catalogue record for this book is available from the British Library.

ISBN 978-1-904955-79-5 Paper

Quotations in this novel are taken from the following:
The Meaning of the Holy Qur'an (Tenth Edition), Abdullah Yusuf
Ali, Amana Publications, Beltsville, Maryland, USA, 1999
The Holy Bible, Collins, London, 1952

Production: Jennifer Krebs
Cover Design: Brianna Corbett
Cover Images: javarman3/istockphoto; Brianna Corbett
Printed in India by Imprint Digital

PROLOGUE

So this is how it will be.

I will arrive at the airport by taxi. I will be dressed in a charcoal suit, white shirt, blue tie, black leather shoes. They bought the outfit yesterday morning and I put it on for them when they got back. They examined me carefully, made me walk up and down the room, finally nodded their approval. The shoes pinch but I did not tell them.

I will pay the taxi-driver with two one-hundred rand notes, pocket the change. I have a third note if the taxi driver tries to overcharge me. Apart from the money and the mobile phone, I will carry nothing on my person except the locker key.

From the taxi rank, I will head straight into the airport, turn left and head for the left-luggage lockers. I will find locker number three-four-three, open it with the key, take out the briefcase.

I will follow the departure signs, check in at the desk. I will hand over my ticket and passport while they confirm my booking. The airport will be air-conditioned. The counter staff will be cool, indifferent.

Once I have checked in, I will wait exactly thirty-five minutes before going through immigration. To kill time I will visit the airport boutiques and drink a cup of espresso. Then I will brace myself and pass through the gates.

I will place the shiny maroon booklet on the counter of the cubicle. The immigration officer will take the document, flick through to the page with the photo, scan it through some computer system, look up briefly to match face with picture. He will give me a fleeting but professional glance, then slap the passport back on the counter. The passport will be clean, its owner seemingly composed, showing none of the tell-tale signs of suspicion that the officer will have been trained to spot. As I bend to pick up the briefcase, the officer will already be looking beyond me to the next in line.

After immigration, the next hurdle will be security. I will pick up my briefcase with my left hand, the passport with my right, walk straight ahead following the line of travellers. If all has gone to plan, there should be three security checkpoints, each manned by a pair of officers. I will go for the checkpoint on the left. The officer I'll deal with will be expecting me. I will know it is him because he will have something wrong with his mouth, a cleft lip or similar deformity that has been operated on, half-repaired. I have seen a photo of him. He will be mixed race, greasy-skinned, cool in white short-sleeved shirt and navy slacks, his ID badge hanging from a thick, black lanyard.

His job will be to ensure the safe passage of myself and the briefcase. That is all I know about him. It is all I need to know.

After that, it will be plain sailing. Through to the departure lounge, wait for the flight to be called, make sure I have the boarding card ready. The flight attendant will smile at me and I will smile back.

And then we will be gone.

The end of my pain.

The end of my story.

This is how it will be.

GREG 1

Woosh! Like a deep sea diver breaking water, ripping through from the shadowy depths, the relief of the familiar, the escape from the unfathomable, he surfaces into a kind of semi-consciousness. He knows he's returned from an uneasy place, but he can't remember what or why, only that his apprehension is justified.

He's still only aware of physical sensation in the loosest sense, a feeling of wholesale trauma to his entire body so cataclysmic that it has resulted in neurological shut-down.

One part of his brain registers a vague sense of anxiety, a knowledge that something has happened that is so awful that there may be no pieces left to pick up.

But the shock to his system has numbed the pain and the blow to his head scrambled his thoughts and so he's able to shelve his doubts, surrender to this foggy upheaval with calm resignation. It is an acquiescence made easier by a hazy belief that what he is undergoing is not shared by any significant loved ones.

Yes, there are loved ones, he knows that with absolute certainty, they exist in some other place, though he can't for the moment think who or where they are.

So his overriding feeling is one of submission. Physically he's temporarily out of order, circuits broken, wiring fried. Mentally he's drugged on brain chemicals, befuddled by trauma to the head. There are no coherent questions flashing through his mind, no Am I dead or alive? no Is so-and-so OK? no What should I do next? He floats on a wave of passive acceptance until...

Woosh! He slips back into the murky twilight of oblivion.

⌘

Again the cavernous obscurity, the bursting into light. This time he's more receptive, the shock-induced, pain-killing adrenaline has long-since receded. He's lying down, that much is clear. On a hard surface, an uneven surface. His eyes are closed and he doesn't yet feel disposed to open them. All in good time.

He has no idea how many minutes or hours have passed since he last dipped into consciousness, or indeed since whatever devastating event occurred to bring about his current predicament. As he lies there on the rutted, unyielding surface, the journey from the comfort of ignorant stupor to the burden of wakefulness nearly complete, he can feel each bodily sensation returning, the nerve endings switching on like an electrical circuit – click, click, click – the pain receptors powering up after a period of inactivity.

The change is sudden and brutal, from dulled anaesthesia, through angry discomfort to the present sensation of jagged, furious, all-consuming pain.

He has a sudden bad feeling about what he has woken up to, makes a half-hearted effort to will himself back into his soothing coma, but the hurting is too great.

He becomes aware of a sound, a low sporadic groaning. It's chilling and pitiful, and he is about to force open his eyes to investigate the cause of this suffering when he realises that the moans are coming from his own mouth.

The pain is like a wild-eyed, whip-wielding dervish, howling and slashing mercilessly. He tries to isolate the different sources, running a mental ruler down his body. There's a throbbing in his lower abdomen, just above his groin, as if someone has given him a tremendous kicking. The left side of his face from cheekbone to temple feels as if it has caved in. He wonders idly what could have caused such trauma – a hammer blow? a roof-top fall? a car accident? – but as yet has

4

neither the strength nor inclination to investigate further. He pictures a crumpled skull, tufts of bloodied hair glued to flaps of shredded skin, oozing brain matter. He's too frightened to reach up and touch himself.

His head is throbbing viciously, the principal refrain in an all-encompassing symphony of the aching, the sore, the tender. As yet he's done little more than shift his body in microscopic movements, but it's enough to know that it has taken a massive battering.

He becomes aware of a particular source of discomfort, a sharp stabbing from behind his right knee. For the first time, he makes a proper movement. He discovers that his right arm is hanging by his side and he sends it down to investigate the hurt. He pictures ruptured ligaments, crushed cartilage, but discovers that the source of the discomfort is external, that his knee is pressing down on a sharp stone. He shifts off the stone and the stabbing gradually recedes.

Time to open his eyes. Another effort, but in so doing, he registers two more facts about his circumstances that have so far eluded him. Firstly that he is outside. It is not so much the rocky soil he's lying on that gives it away, but more the outdoor smells – the scent of dust and heat and unknown herbs – and an almost imperceptible breeze. Secondly that the temperature is fairly high, that he's somewhere warm.

And so he opens his eyes and these two truths are confirmed. He looks up at a cloudless sky. His vision is at first blurred and shifting, the result, he suspects, of whatever damage has been done to his head. But it soon settles down and for a few minutes he makes no effort to look around, is content to gaze upwards at the heavens. A realisation that he is still alive, that he has survived something ruinous, brings relief.

He tilts his head slightly and sees that lower down towards the horizon the sky turns from azure to a deep savannah orange, licks of golden flame heralding a sunrise. Sunrise, yes. Not sunset. The air's too fresh, not balmy enough, the dusty soil at his fingertips not warm nor dry enough for dusk.

He can put it off no longer. He needs to get up and

realises that this may prove more of a challenge than usual. He's aware, too, that he needs to empty his bladder urgently. The throbbing in his head won't subside.

I'd better get up. I don't want to piss myself.

Just wait a bit longer. Just stay exactly where you are. You're in limbo. You're safe. Once you get up, you'll have to confront whatever world you find yourself in. And I have a hunch it's not going to be a picnic. So what's your rush?

But I'm going to piss myself.

OK, OK. Have it your way. But don't say I didn't warn you.

And then like a punch to the stomach the memory rises out of the quagmire, and he remembers how he got here. And all at once he's back in the plane, headphones on, flicking through his ipod for something lightweight, some Louis Jordan perhaps, or Count Basie, aware that the bony, thirty something black woman sitting next to him doesn't like him, something in her tight-lipped smile when he asked her to let him get past to his seat, then her sigh the first time he had to edge past the other way to get to the toilet. He remembers the secret relief at her rejection as it closed off the possibility of banal airplane conversation.

He remembers what was on his mind, a problem with a painting he'd been working on (where?), a head-and-shoulders profile of a young girl (who?), a difficulty with the tonal values of her face.

And then he remembers what happened next. Just as he finds the Louis Jordan, the muffled blast of the explosion, the jolt of the plane, the drawn out seconds afterwards, the first screams, the twisting of the aircraft, the rushing air. Then the shaking, the plummeting. Someone flies past, spinning down the aisle. The man next to him in the window seat muttering something in Xhosa or Sindebele, a prayer perhaps, but it's all muffled by the deafening roar. The man directly in front trying to rise, shouting in panic, struggling, too shocked to deal with his seatbelt.

And then, ipod still in hand, he turns to the woman

in the aisle seat, the one who doesn't like him, and looks up at her face, the fine features frozen by fear, her eyes bulging, lips pulled back in a rictus of terror. And as the plane twists into a nose dive, judders and jerks, he puts out his hand to steady himself, holds onto his tray flap, then feels the woman's right hand reach out to his. It's an unconscious reaction, a desperate need for human contact in the face of imminent death. She squeezes, and he remembers his shock at her strength, her nails digging into his flesh. Jesus, that hurts, he thinks. He looks down at his enveloped hand, her claw-like grip. She's digging deeper and his eyes begin to water. Shall I say something? he thinks. Or just pull my hand away?

And then, from one instant to the next, the lights go out on his world.

His mouth is parched, his tongue a desiccated sponge. He tries to run it across the roof, over his teeth, but it feels unwieldy, an alien and unresponsive object. His earlier determination to get up seems recklessly ambitious. By lying absolutely still, his eyes clamped shut, he has reduced the waves of pain to a dull throb, the angry demands of his bladder to a niggling ache. Not yet.

Everything is muzzy, soggy mush. He has a sudden picture of the contents of a breadmaker churning the spongy dough in preparation for baking. It's set up on a kitchen table, white formica, somewhere familiar, looking out onto a cold wet garden landscape. Somewhere far away, a past life.

Where?

He pictures his brain as a broken computer, an endless sequence of zeros and ones, damaged by some malevolent virus, a logic bomb or ruthless trojan, the connections snapped, the memory busted.

Work with what you've got, he tells himself. He tries to concentrate on the image of the breadmaker, to mentally pan away from it. He sees the kitchen laid out around him, whitewashed brick wall, stained wood kitchen units, fridge adorned with magnetic butterflies. There's a silver microwave, half-filled cat bowl on glazed lemon floor tiles, a set of shelving cluttered with radio, scattered CDs and tattered recipe books. The breadmaker hums gently in the background.

Where?

He's tired again, weary from his efforts. His second wind has been and gone. His temple is throbbing from the blow, stinging from what must be a cut or graze. His teeth ache. Perhaps I'll just have a short rest. Again, he surrenders to his body.

Minutes pass as he floats in a halfway house of confusion, but soon he stirs, returns to the here and now. What happened there? he asks himself. Did you give up? He's thirsty now, would give anything for a sip of cold water. Come on, he tells himself. Be strong.

He works himself back into the kitchen and looks out through the sliding glass door. Outside, the garden is gently neglected, the beds accommodating both shrubs and weeds, the lawn strewn with bats and balls, a plastic wheelbarrow and overturned see-saw, everything wet with overnight drizzle. The sky is leaden.

He turns away from the garden view and as he does so, he realises that he's no longer alone. And there they are, standing at the entrance to the kitchen. She's looking at him, smiling, flanked by both of the children.

Who?

His eyes are still clamped shut, all the better to concentrate on the pictures in his head. One moment he's outside the front of the house, peering up at the rust-coloured brickwork, flaking sash windows. The next he's catching flashes of other rooms in the house – higgledy-piggledy bedrooms, jumbled lounge, mucky basement art studio – but it's all still unfocused, simultaneously familiar yet distant.

He's reached an impasse, so he backtracks, returns to the airplane. The terror of the descent is still vivid, but now he remembers other details. The dry, powdery roll and square of rubbery cheese in his meal tray; a picture of buffalo in the glossy in-flight magazine; the sleek, mixed-race stewardess re-filling his coffee cup; the churning of his post-meal indigestion.

And beyond that, a crowded air terminal, a harassed stranger in tailored pinstripes scanning the flashing departure board while shouting into a mobile phone, a stoical woman with braided hair and African robes clutching her bawling infant to her waist. A long queue at passport control, the apathetic immigration guard, then the security officer, hare-lipped and uniformed. And before that, a snatched beer in the airport bar with...

Who?

With his friend: tall, rangy, black-skinned, smiling sadly. Embracing him as they say their goodbyes. A memory tinged with pain, a sorrow shared. With a final remark, they separate and he makes his way through security to the departure lounge.

What's his name?

Retracing footsteps, fleeting images of the preceding days, sunny and colourful, music and beer and children and laughter. But melancholic, too. An image of a church. A funeral. Women crying, men looking sombre. A coffin. Child-sized.

Where? Who? What?

Pull yourself together. Come on, Greg.

Greg?

And then, from frustration to enlightenment, it's as if someone has recopied one of the lost files to his damaged hard drive. He opens his eyes wide, blinks, dazzled by the morning sun.

He's Greg. She's Nuala. They're Sammy and Beth. The house is in Oxford, England.

The airport is Johannesburg. His friend is Farai. The funeral was for Farai's son, Robbie.

Now the funeral is over. He's on his way home.

An explosion. The plane falls out of the sky. He crashes.

Exhausted by mental labour, slapped by a wave of dizzy nausea, he closes his eyes, yields to his weakness, sinks into the relief of a blackout.

⌘

This time he's stronger, though the pounding in his temple remains unabated. The tenderness in his abdomen seems, if anything, to have worsened. Some hours have passed. His intuition tells him that it's mid morning. He wants to open his eyes but in his present position, lying flat on his back, the light's too bright. I can't put it off any longer, he thinks. It's time to move.

His right arm is bent into an 'L', the hand resting on his stomach. The left one lies straight by his side, the fingers brushing his thigh. Cautiously, warily, he flexes his fingers, rubs thumb and forefinger together, experiments with a fist. Then, with great deliberation, he allows his right hand to glide up from his belly to his chest, past his chin and cheek. He approaches his temple gingerly, his fingers probing gently, expecting the worst, is relieved to find nothing more serious than cuts, bruises and dried blood.

I need my eyes, he thinks. There's no question of opening them while facing the sunlight. Even with his eyes closed there's a burning orange behind his eyelids. I'll roll over, he thinks. He braces himself, bends his knees slightly, brings his right arm across his torso and turns his body so that he is in a kind of rudimentary recovery position, resting on his side with his face sheltered in the crook of his arm. The ribs on his right side have taken a beating and he shifts to accommodate the pain. Finally he finds a less awkward position and allows himself a few minutes' respite.

Despite the stabbing in his ribs and the all-over aching, he's aware that his last manoeuvres would not have been possible had anything been broken, and for that he feels some sense of comfort.

For a split second his mind seeks to grasp the magnitude of what he has experienced – and survived – but the implications are too overwhelming, so he concentrates on getting his eyes, now sheltered by his arm, to adjust to the light. He forces his eyelids open, blinks, closes them again. Waits. Repeats the process, each time keeping them open for a few seconds longer. Little by little his vision returns until finally he can look steadily at the ground, focuses on the sandy grains of soil, the two off-white pebbles.

He becomes aware again of his bladder's irate call. He still feels that the challenge of standing up is too great, so he shifts his body so that he's on his side, facing downwards, the ground sloping away. He fumbles with his trousers, pulls out his penis and relieves himself from his horizontal position. He watches the liquid snake in rivulets through the dusty soil.

So far, so good. Piece of cake. Time for a look round.

He accepts this suggestion quite breezily, hasn't made the connection between the atrocity that's put him there and the scene he might expect to find when he surveys his surroundings.

So when he shifts his head so that he's no longer looking straight down, but is now peering ahead, at ground level, he's completely unprepared for the upper torso, severed at the waist, that's lying six or seven feet away, blocking his line of vision. He blinks, freezes, appalled but unable to drag his eyes away.

He stares for some seconds at the butchered corpse, the spray of blonde hair, the cream silk blouse, the mush of shredded flesh and severed bone. The head's turned away so he cannot see her features, the expression on her death mask.

New waves of shock roll in. As he levers himself up onto his knees and slowly gets to his feet, an observer could easily mistake his dazed, robotic manner for casual and leisurely. Then he sways, catches himself, and the illusion is broken. In his stained indigo shirt and baggy, bloodied trousers, he looks vulnerable, beaten.

He turns full circle, surveying his environment. The scene is so brutal, the carnage so overwhelming, that at first his eyes edit out the horror, take in only the physical layout of the location.

He seems to be standing at the foot of a steep hill dotted with rocks and bushes, a version of the kopjes he knows so well from his southern African past.

The kopje's behind him, in front the landscape slopes

gently down for several hundred yards to a broad, arid plain speckled with thorny trees, termite mounds, scrawny shrubs. Beyond that, in the faraway distance, a range of hills rises up through the blue-grey haze. He concentrates, peering, scans the flat terrain for evidence of human activity – a village, a cattle kraal, even a temporary dwelling – but sees nothing but untouched nature. He feels a chill of loneliness.

A chill of loneliness, but nothing more. Artist though he may be, today he cannot weigh up the sights that meet his eyes in terms of form and shape, tone and perspective, doesn't wonder where the optimum vantage point would be to capture the panorama, the best time of day. Today he will not visualise his palette, the burnt sienna and yellow ochre, the cobalt blue and viridian green. For the moment all he sees is his own isolation.

And then, almost as if the filter has been removed from his vision, he becomes aware for the first time of the full extent of the devastation that surrounds him. For a few fleeting seconds he takes it all in – the pockmarked terrain, the strewn aircraft wreckage, the debris, the bodies – and he stands there, tall but broken, and tries to make sense of the mayhem. Simultaneously, like a tripped fusebox flipped back into action, his other senses come alive, and he's aware at once of the stale sour taste in his mouth, the sticky grime of his fingers, the buzzing whine of blowflies, the reek of aviation fuel mingled with the sickly stench of death.

But it's too much, a sensory overload. He rubs his eyes with his grubby hands, teeters, weighed down by the desolation around him, weakened by the battering he has received, by dehydration, by the rising temperature.

Unable to take in the totality of the destruction, he seeks escape in detail. Dropping his gaze, he registers three or four playing cards strewn at his feet – a queen of hearts, a two of diamonds, the others face down. He looks up, spots a stunted tree to his left and staggers towards it. He keeps his eyes to the ground, circles the twisted body of a young boy, a black leather handbag, a mangled camera, a tan lace-up shoe.

He's sweating, his head's pounding, and when he spots a floppy green hat, the kind worn by Afrikaaner farmers and safari guides, he picks it up, dusts it off on his trouser leg, then pulls it down over his head. When he reaches the tree he squats down in the shade, allows himself a few moments to gather his strength.

A painting looms up in his mind, skeletons attacking human beings, a scene of pillage and massacre, but he's still dazed and it takes him some minutes to identify it, the ghoulish vision of Bruegel's *Triumph of Death*. He seems to remember a poster on his wall as a child, hours spent gazing at the painting's macabre detail. And he realises why he's thought of it now, not because the scene around him today reminds him of the painting itself, more that his present environment brings to mind how he would imagine Bruegel's scene would look the next day, when the murdering, marauding skeletons have departed. Yes, what he's surrounded by, he realises, is *Triumph of Death: The Day After*.

The flies are bothering him, circling his head in endless aborted landing patterns. He swats away at them feebly. He's aware of his tremendous thirst, an overpowering need to find water. He looks around. In a semi-circle sweep of twenty yards in front of him he can see three, four, five bodies, an empty blue canvas holdall, a pair of gleaming trainers, a meal tray, a pair of headphones, several cartons of cigarettes, a row of seating, a stuffed giraffe, two glossy magazines, an arm, severed at the shoulder. There's a bumbag, three or four blankets, a jagged piece of fuselage, a walking stick and a gutted suitcase, its contents spewed out – a scattering of underwear, a bathbag, leaking toiletries, an alarm clock, toothpaste, paperbacks, the front casing of a busted radio.

Spotting a plastic water bottle, he staggers back up on his feet. He stumbles over to the bottle and picks it up. It's almost empty but he sucks greedily at the inch or so of tepid liquid. He needs more and so, driven by dehydration, he looks around for a likely source. It's the first time that survival instincts and rational thought have joined forces.

He looks around at the crash site again, awed by the scale of the devastation, the amount of debris, of carnage. He tries to recall what kind of aircraft it had been, its size, but his memory is hazy. He always experiences flying as a blur, like being sucked through a tube at speed. Had the plane been full? He remembers seeing a few empty seats, but the scene around him suggests that a vast army of travellers have descended from the skies, that the plane had been immense.

He takes in the three principal sections of the aircraft scattered down the slope at roughly ten, twelve and two o'clock, the first about twenty yards away, the other two slightly more distant. He decides to investigate these first, heads for the closest, zigzagging his way between body parts and baggage.

It's part of the main section of the fuselage, a great tubed segment containing two rows of seats, overhead lockers, flooring. Four corpses are still strapped in, surrounded by a plague of whining flies. The first, a middle-aged black man with powder-snow hair, looks calm and serene, eyes closed, his head pressed back against the headrest as if catching forty winks. Next to him, two white schoolboys sit primly in blazers, shorts and long socks, their heads twisted forward grotesquely. Behind, the next two seats are empty, the third occupied by a silent, staring Asian man dressed in sober suit, white shirt and charcoal tie.

Greg approaches with caution, as if frightened of waking his fellow travellers. When he spies the water bottle tucked into the mesh netting pocket at the back of one of the schoolboys' seats, he reaches down gingerly, extracts it, twists off the cap. It's a half-litre bottle, almost full, and he drinks it off in one go. To escape the swarm of flies, he retreats, then heads towards the second section of fuselage.

On the way over, he passes a scuffed leather satchel, a woman's padded jacket, pens, lipsticks, a CD of gospel music. He skirts several bodies, each time rousing swarms of darting flies. Everywhere, there is smashed glass, the shards catching in the sun, the ground a bed of diamond lights. He catches the sour smell of whisky, the pungent scent of perfume, smashed

14

duty-free stock, he supposes. But more dominant, always, is the stench of blood, of flayed flesh, of human waste.

This time the wreckage seems to originate from that section of the plane where the flight attendants prepare meals and where the toilets are situated. As he approaches he sees with relief that there are no bodies, though the reek of excrement is powerful.

Next to the segment of the plane lies a twisted metal trolley, the kind used to bring around the drinks, and one of those sleek, stainless-steel compartmentalised containers used for storing the hot food. Among the array of shattered glass, broken plastic cutlery, empty juice cartons and smashed trays, he sees a couple of bottles of water, which he extricates, and some small sachets of roasted nuts.

He examines the third section hastily. Despite quenching his thirst, he's still weak and giddy, nauseous from his physical and mental ordeal. On the way, weaving between luggage and unidentifiable wreckage, he has to circumnavigate more corpses, more body parts.

He notes that this section was part of the storage hold, and that a fair amount of the luggage seems to have come down to earth intact. He glances at the topsy-turvy pile of suitcases, backpacks and holdalls – a mountain of leather, plastic and canvas, floral, striped and tartan – and shrugs.

He needs to rest, so heads back to the shady spot under the tree, lowers himself onto the dusty soil, drinks another bottle of water and tries to formulate some coherent thoughts. Without him noticing, the pain in his head has altered from a pounding rhythm to a needling drill.

What next?

Some fucking paracetamol wouldn't go amiss.

Focus on the bigger picture.

My head hurts.

My heart bleeds. Take a look around you, you ponce.

And all at once it hits him that the scattered bodies parts about him recently belonged to living creatures, that the bodies had names and identities and, with a flush of guilty shame, that some of those bodies may still be alive, that he has been so wrapped up in slaking his thirst that he hasn't even bothered to go round and check them for signs of life.

After all, you survived. Why couldn't one of them have too?

He hauls himself to his feet, makes his way unsteadily to the nearest corpse, changes his mind, decides to make a systematic sweep starting to his far left, make sure he misses no one, gives everybody a fair chance. It's like a pact between the living and the dead. Only they're not dead yet, he reflects. They remain in some floating limbo, waiting to have their status confirmed.

His legs are stiff and bruised, scratched in a hundred places, his ribs raw and angry. As he stumbles towards the furthest corpse, he becomes aware that the stink of decay in the air is growing more pronounced.

The first body is that of a young woman, perhaps twenty-five, an African with espresso skin and horsey features. Her lips are drawn back, her teeth exposed in a grimace, her eyes wide open but empty. He reaches down, touches her face and closes her eyes. There's an airline blanket lying next to her which he picks up and places gently over her head.

He can remember the next two bodies. The first, an elderly white, an outdoor man to judge from his ruddy features, has clearly broken his neck. The second, the mixed race air hostess, has had her skirt and blouse ripped from her in the crash, is dressed only in panties and bra, looks as if she is sleeping. It is only when he lifts her head that he sees that the back of her skull is missing, that grey, oozing brain matter is exposed. He lays her back on the ground and fetches a blanket to cover her face, another for her bare body.

After that his sweep of bodies becomes a blur, this one missing a leg, that one's features unrecognisable, the next almost decapitated. For each casualty, he makes sure the body is covered up, its eyes closed, its modesty preserved.

An hour later, sweating, nauseous, shaking from his exertions, he returns to the shade.

He is the only survivor.

On his travels, he has picked up another bottle of water and he sips from this as he recovers from his ordeal. The heat is stifling, the stench worsening. He takes off the floppy hat he's been wearing and douses his hair with water. It provides a few moments of relief.

So what's the plot? When do the cavalry arrive?

Depends where we are. Depends whether they know.

'Course they know. Black boxes, flight transmitters, all that stuff.

Yeah, well, maybe. Might not be so easy to get here. It's not exactly Henley-on-Thames, is it?

So where are we then, smartarse?

Dunno. Think about how long we were in the air. Think about the flight path.

He closes his eyes, tries to visualise a map of Africa, to trace a line from South Africa northwards, to calculate time in the air and translate that figure into distances.

Congo. Or maybe the bottom half of Sudan. Maybe even further north. A long way from home, anyway.

And then he remembers his mobile phone. It's still in his breast pocket, flat, silver and sleek. He takes it out, checks whether it's working. It's apparently undamaged, but he can't get a signal. He gets up, limps over to the nearest body, a male flight attendant, takes a deep breath, bends down and begins rifling through his pockets. He's examined four bodies, tried out two more phones, before he accepts that he's not going to communicate electronically.

Back under the shade he feels restless. Despite the heat, the shock, the gore he's witnessed, he feels the first pangs of hunger.

If I'm going to be here a while, I'd better sort out some food.

He heads back to the section of fuselage that contained the meal preparation area. Amongst the remains of the chicken trays and dessert pots, he finds some portions of processed cheese, three or four rolls, a box of cellophaned crackers, packets of peanuts, a stash of undamaged water bottles. He empties a plastic carrier bag lying nearby and fills it with the provisions. In the earlier sweep he'd come across other scattered food – some sweet biscuits, more crackers and peanuts – and he limps off to fetch them, adding them to his bag.

On the way back to his tree, he comes to an abrupt halt. On his previous sweep, away next to a section of the aircraft's wing, he'd noticed an old-fashioned rucksack with what looked like a tent strapped to the frame. He totters over, retrieves the bright orange baggage, carries it back to his base.

As he side-steps one of the bodies that he's recently covered in a navy-blue blanket, he notices an almost imperceptible movement from beneath the fabric. He stops, bends down, pulls back the blanket more in hope than expectation.

The body, that of a middle-aged woman, is lying face up. She looks Middle Eastern, short black hair greying at the roots, thick eyebrows, olive-skinned, faint downy hairs on her upper lip, a large brown mole on her chin. Her mouth is slightly open, her lips and teeth stained with fresh scarlet blood. And as he crouches down and peers at her face, a small pink bubble forms between her lips, then pops feebly.

Jesus. She's alive.

He racks his brains for hazy, half-forgotten first aid directions. Don't move her. Don't give her anything to drink. Call an ambulance and reassure the casualty while you wait for its arrival. He almost smiles.

He swipes away a cloud of flies, considers what to do.

If I get the tent up in the shade, she can rest there. It'll keep the flies off her at least. I'll have to carry her over and she'll just have to take her chances.

Despite the damaged ribs, the bruised legs, he hurries back to his tree and sets about erecting the tent. It's an amateur effort, the tent pegs refusing to penetrate the unyielding soil, but he eventually gets it raised. He returns to the woman and tries to pick her up but in his weakened state he can't manage. In the end he clasps her under her armpits and drags her to the tent, pulls her inside, lays her gently on the bed of blankets he's prepared. Apart from the bloody bubble, she shows no other signs of life.

Disregarding his earlier directives, he fetches a bottle of water, tries to pour some into her mouth, but most of it trickles down her chin. He feels for a pulse, cannot find one, yet he's sure she's still alive. He zips up the flap of the tent, sits down outside it.

The heat's reached its zenith and the fetid odour is becoming increasingly difficult to bear. He pictures the stomachs of the other bodies swelling, notices the clouds of flies thickening. He cannot relax, his senses overwhelmed by the stench, the relentless buzzing.

So you're just going to wait it out, are you?

You got a better idea?

Well, you might want to consider making a move.

Really? What about the cavalry?

Yeah, well, they might come. But in the meantime, this is no picnic site, is it?

True. Still, I can put up with the stench. It's not going to kill me.

Maybe not, though it's what it might attract that's more the problem.

What're you talking about?

Dead bodies. Carrion. Hyenas, lion. Think about it.

Here? You sure? He looks around doubtfully. He's suddenly aware that most of the day has gone, that it's only a few hours until sunset. The thought of spending the night here alone is terrifying.

Chin up. Someone might turn up at any moment. Still, just to be on the safe side, it wouldn't do any harm to have another look around, see what you can find that might be useful if you do have to leave. Pack a proper bag. Better safe than sorry, eh?

And with that, he's up on his feet, sets about emptying out a backpack he'd noticed wedged between a section of wing flap and a thorny shrub close to the section of storage fuselage.

He slings it over his shoulder, sets off on yet another scavenging mission.

It takes him an hour to fill his bag. At one point, when he finds someone's first aid kit, he stops to take some aspirin, swabs the bloodied side of his face with cotton wool doused in disinfectant, washes off the worst of the grime and gore from his various cuts and scratches.

Soon after that he strikes gold. Away near what may once have been the cockpit, he finds a green plastic box marked *Emergency Survival Kit*, cracked but still intact. He extracts a compass, a heliograph, a safety whistle, a folding knife, first aid dressings and some waterproof matches. He adds his mobile phone to the bag, more for talismanic reasons than from hope of making contact, and a handsome pair of binoculars that he recovers from a leather holdall. He's also packed the supply of food including a packet of dried fruit, some biltong and a tube of boiled sweets. The backpack's still only half full, and he fills the remaining space with more bottled water. By the time he's finished looting, his battered body is utterly exhausted.

Back in the shade, he checks on the woman, then makes a pillow from a rolled up blanket, lies down on a second blanket next to the tent and closes his eyes. He knows he must rest before attempting further physical activity.

Later, he stirs. His clothes feel soiled and he suddenly wonders whether he can find his own bag in the storage. He'd travelled light – it'd been a last-minute decision to travel to the funeral – and he'd taken only a small canvas holdall. Back amongst the wreckage, he climbs onto the pile of bags, begins to sort his way through it.

The large metallic case is lying next to his holdall, so when he first sees it he ignores it, focuses solely on retrieving his own possessions. It's only when he's picked out a pair of khaki trousers, an olive, long-sleeved shirt, some clean socks and a pair of trainers, stripped off his filthy gear and re-dressed, that his attention returns to the case. It's oblong, stainless steel, heavy, over a metre in length and protected by two elaborate-looking combination locks. His eye is caught by the fire-red

PROHIBITED ITEM stickers plastered on the front of the case, the yellow SPECIAL ITEM tape wound around the handle.

He hauls the case out, drags it back to the tree and tries to force the locks with the penknife. Sweat runs down his forehead, stinging his eyes. The buzzing of the flies, the stabbing pain in his head, the obstinacy of the locks all combine to turn his curiosity into fixation, his exhaustion into rage. He gets up, hunts the ground for a suitable rock, carries it back to the shade. He begins to pound at the locks with all his strength.

For a full five minutes he attacks the locking mechanisms. The casing becomes scratched, dented, loses its smart shine, but the locks remain firm. Blisters are forming on his hand. He stops, looks up, notices the first streaks of dusky orange on the horizon as the sun sinks gradually behind the faraway hills, feels a squeeze of panic in his bowels at the prospect of the approaching night. In the distance, off where the furthest debris has landed, he watches something large and dark swoop down from the sky, land next to a body and approach it in great hopping movements. It takes him a few seconds to recognise the vulture.

He channels the panic into fury, redoubles his efforts and, when he least expects it, the casing opens and the first mechanism surrenders. Encouraged, he begins work on the second lock. By the time it, too, yields, the blisters have been rubbed raw and his hands are slippery with blood. He opens the case.

He's unprepared for what he sees, but feels a sense of satisfaction that the contents justify the effort put in to reveal them. He finds himself looking down at a sleek, elegant hunting rifle encased in rich black velvet. There are two slots sunk into the velvet for the small, trim magazines, a flap revealing an empty pocket for ammunition. He takes out the rifle, runs his hand along the flat wooden stock, the cold black barrel, the smooth curve of the telescopic sights.

He recalls a visit to Ireland to visit Nuala's relatives, her farmer cousin taking him out shooting with a shotgun, another episode of target practice with a small .22 rifle used for lamping rabbits. He senses that the weapon he now holds in his hands is vastly more powerful, and he feels a surge of adrenalin as he weighs it in his hands.

He picks up the magazine, sees with disappointment that it is empty, reasons that gun and ammunition have perhaps been kept apart for safety reasons. Maybe somewhere among the cargo there is a separate package of rounds.

And then he recalls a small steel case he'd spotted earlier near the food preparation section, another box covered in the SPECIAL ITEM tape. His first instinct had been to investigate, and he'd bent to remove the bundle that lay across it, recoiled in horror as he recognised it as part of a severed leg. Revulsion had replaced curiosity and he'd moved on.

Now, though, he backtracks, locates the silver case quickly, forces himself to nudge aside the half-clothed limb, brings the case over to his tree and sets to work on the lock with his rock. He feels driven, works to a rhythm, his efforts more efficient. Within ten minutes the lid buckles, the hinges snap open and the top and bottom separate to reveal two boxes of ammunition.

Next he attempts to load one of the magazines. There's a sense of urgency in his actions, a need to protect his charges against scavengers, but it is this impatience that slows his progress, causes him to fumble with the shells, to misunderstand the system of loading the magazine, to attempt to fix it back-to-front to the underside of the rifle. In the war films it all looks so straightforward, he thinks. The soldier slots home the magazine with an expert fluency, the magazine itself is always fully loaded, seems to have an inexhaustible supply of bullets and rarely needs changing.

He begins to panic and this clouds his judgement, muddles his systematic approach to mastering the weapon. Sweat's running down his forehead, burning his eyes and turning his grip slippery. Take a deep breath, he tells himself. Calm down.

He works through trial and error, a process of elimination. It takes him over twenty minutes, several false starts, before he gets the magazine loaded and fitted into the underside of the rifle. When he looks up he sees the original vulture he'd spotted has been joined by ten or so others, that more are looming out of the sky, spreading out, working away on several of the furthest corpses. He raises his rifle, aims and pulls the trigger.

Nothing. The trigger is jammed and at first he fears he's made another mistake with the magazine. He closes his eyes and tries to visualise footage he's seen of gun fire. He pictures a cocking action, a bolt being slid back, something to direct the first bullet to the chamber. He examines the rifle and sees a likely-looking lever. He twists it upwards, draws it back and forward, returns it to the position. He aims again, his finger finds the trigger and he squeezes.

A second failure. Then a flash of déjà vu, and he remembers about safety catches,• turns the gun over in his hands until he locates it and slides it to the off setting. He raises the gun a third time, taking aim again. The trigger feels stiff under his finger and for a second, as he squeezes, he thinks there's still something wrong.

The blast is deafening in the stillness of his seclusion. The kick of the weapon is shocking, far more vicious than he'd expected. His shoulder feels battered, pummelled, he knows there'll be bruising, another injury to his poor broken body.

And the blast, too. How can something so sublimely elegant make such a thunderous, hellish noise? His ears are ringing, he's deafened. He looks down at the rifle and marvels at its potency. A painful experience, yes, but heady, too. The rifle's strength and the sense of protection it offers are intoxicating.

He looks up and sees that he's missed the vulture, but that they have all panicked, taken to the air, circling. Even as he takes this in, the first one, emboldened by hunger, swoops back down to resume his feasting.

For a few minutes, consumed by a compulsion to shoot that he justifies as a need to test out the firearm, he fires at the birds, reloads the magazine, fires again. His eardrums feel shattered, his shoulder begs for relief. Gradually, the firing mechanism becomes familiar, though his shooting is no more accurate, and for every vulture he hits, five more seem to appear.

He realises that he's fighting a losing battle, that he's become the sole spectator of a ghastly, gruesome picnic. He cannot see in any detail what the vultures are doing, but pictures the pecking and ripping and tearing. He feels his stomach heave in revulsion.

I can't stay here. I've got to move.

What about your rescue? What about the woman?

He stands up and for the first time looks away from the debris, the sloping plain and up the other way. The kopje stretches ahead, steep and rocky. It's difficult to gauge how high it is, he can't see the summit from his position at its foot, but it now feels like a place of safety, a vantage point away from the carnage, the stink, the gory horror that is unfolding.

I can't do any more for the woman. I'm not even sure she's still alive. At least in the tent she's safe from scavengers. Her only hope's a rescue team. Her fate's in their hands, not mine. Anyway, I'm not going far, just up the kopje. I can keep an eye on her from there.

He picks up his backpack, adds the box of bullets to a side pocket and hauls it up onto his shoulders. Finally he grasps the rifle in both hands. He takes a few steps up the slope, then changes his mind. There's something in his canvass holdall, something he had forgotten that he knows he must take, so he puts down the bag and rifle and scrambles back to the fuselage wreckage. He finds his bag, throws out his clothing, shoes, a soapstone statue given to him as a farewell gift less than twenty-four hours ago, extricates the sketch pad at the bottom, returns to his backpack and slides it inside. Now he's ready.

He pauses only once more before he begins his ascent. There, at the foot of the hill, his eye is caught by a brightly coloured object, a small plastic keg. He picks it up, notes that according to the front label it's supposed to contain two white handheld flares for night-time distress signalling and two orange smoke signals for day-time emergencies. But the canister feels too light and he sees at once that the top has come loose and the contents have gone astray. He scans the vicinity for the missing flares, reasons that they could be anywhere or nowhere, winces with irritation. He's aware how crucial the distress signals could be but feels too exhausted to start a new search. He tosses the keg behind him.

Ten minutes of steep climbing brings him to a level section of granite and shrub. The air here is fresher, less polluted. He turns and looks down at the crash site. The first body to be attacked is now enveloped in a churning, squabbling sea of vultures. It is a sickening sight and the urge to press on, to put more distance between himself and the vampire banquet below is irresistible. He thinks again of the Breugel painting.

A further ten minutes and he's back on a steep stretch, clambering between boulders. He's weary, his muscles crying out for respite, when he finds himself on a flat bed of rock concealed behind thick bushes. He takes off his pack, about to sink to the ground when he notices that behind him the rock stretches into what looks like the mouth of a cave. Clutching his rifle, he takes a step or two towards it cautiously, automatically equating caves with wild animals, but it is shallow, no more than a couple of metres deep, and empty.

Perfect. This'll do for the moment. I'm away from the bloodbath, but if anyone does come to the rescue, I'll be able to spot them easily.

Yeah, and if any animal wants to mess with you, they'll have to get past my friend here. He grips his rifle with grim determination.

He takes the blanket out of his bag and spreads it out in the floor of the cave. He's about to reward himself with a rest when he's struck by an idea.

Not thinking of putting your feet up, are you?

Well, actually…

You've got work to do. It'll be dark in an hour or so. How are you going to signal your position if they send a plane over? And what about wild animals? What's the one thing they're scared of in the bush?

Fire?

Right. Now get off your backside and fetch some firewood.

OK, OK. Give me a second. I'm feeling pretty ropey, you know.

He's collected three or four good dry sticks, a handful of kindling, when he sees it. He's bent down too quickly, feels a wave of dizzy nausea and lifts his head to let it pass. He glances down the hill to the crash site, then raises his line of vision beyond, to the plain stretching off into the sunset. And there it is, still a mile or two away but approaching fast, the clouds of dust left in its wake. A vehicle, a landcruiser or pickup – it's still too far away to distinguish clearly – is heading towards the wreckage.

Towards him.

AMAN 1

Beginning a journal seems a timely idea now that I have arrived here in the United Kingdom. It is not that I fancy myself as a literary animal or foresee its publication leading to fame and fortune. It is more to do with the family I abandoned, my dear sweet wife and my precious children. Of course I pray that we will be together again one day, and together we can read my words, follow my adventures, laugh and joke and cry together. But if I do not see you again, if God forbid we are never re-united, I know you will have questions. The journal, then, will be the answer to your wheres and hows and whens and whys.

Mind you, if this journal were to be valued by some literary agent as a work of genius, translated into English and French and Russian, published by some esteemed New York firm, I would not complain. I can picture a fabulous screenplay turned into Hollywood blockbuster. Or perhaps Bollywood. Yes, that is more like it, a Bollywood saga complete with dance routines and rousing song. I see myself played by Salman Khan, your role given to Rani Mukerji. It will be an instant success, a tale of good over evil, a passionate testament to the power of love.

There is a second justification for writing this diary: it looks likely that I will have plenty of time to kill while I enjoy Her Majesty's hospitality and my case is processed. It will be a form of therapy, a way of fleeing the locked doors and barred windows, an escape from a confined present to a freer past. Because, of course, I cannot write about my daily existence without explaining how I came to be here.

Where to begin? Not that fateful Eid evening three

years ago. I must dig deeper. Our wedding? No, still further. A hastily sketched background is called for, a swift hop, skip and jump over my infancy, adolescence and bachelorhood, just to provide some context.

Yes, the more I think about it, the more I am aware of how little I have told you about my life before we met. You, my darling, were always the talker, the divulger of your thoughts, your inner life, your past. I have never been much of a communicator, never great at putting feelings into words. So you only know the basics of my past, the superficialities of what makes me tick. I pray I gave enough away to reassure you always of my love for you. But beyond that, I fear I have told you little. Well now is my chance to make amends.

So, a brief perambulation through my early years, a leisurely stroll just like my family's regular six o'clock passeggiata along Harnet Avenue, central thoroughfare of Asmara, the heat of the day relenting as my father would nod and greet acquaintances, occasionally stopping to shake hands and exchange a word or two with a few of his more favoured friends as they too accompanied their families on this early evening ritual.

Some families would indulge themselves, stopping to buy macchiatos and pastries at one of the numerous cafés, beautiful examples of art deco colonial architecture that I only learned to appreciate after I had left the city. This was needless frivolity in my father's eyes, particularly when we had such delicious home cooking waiting for us on our return. So we would amble along with the crowds of families, past the Catholic cathedral, turn around at Sematat Avenue, then head back towards Fenkil Street. Once home, my mother would hurry off to the kitchen to supervise the final stages of the evening meal, leaving us children – my elder brother, two younger sisters and myself – to kick off our shoes and settle down in the dust of the back yard to continue our games and jokes and squabbles.

Our mother's shout, some twenty minutes later, was our signal to call a truce and head for the communal room. We would sit round the table while Fatuma the maid, her face shining from kitchen efforts, passed around a bowl of water and hand towel. Father washed his hands first, then my brother and I. My mother would go last, of course, too anxious to ensure that her family's needs were met to contemplate her own physical requirements.

And then it would be the usual feast of earthly delights, a scramble to break off the still-warm injera, dip it into the delicious kitcha, perhaps a bowl of steaming zigni spiced with berbere, a fragrant, meaty tsebhi, or an aromatic alicha birsen curry. My father liked it best when my mother joined us for the meal. He would ask her about her day, listen attentively to her funny stories of market shopping or neighbourly gossip, relate the events of his taxi-driving labours, the fares he had taken, conversations he had had.

Sometimes my mother might make an excuse, disappear off into the kitchen – she had very erratic eating habits – and father would turn to his children to question us about our school day. He had a great thirst for education, having been deprived of his own by family obligations – the eldest in his family, he had left school aged ten to add an income to his family's finances and help support his younger siblings' schooling – and he would ask us for the smallest minutiae of our day's learning, listening with absolute absorption.

When we had finished eating, Fatuma had returned with washbowl and father had wiped his bushy moustache with his carefully folded handkerchief, we would go back to our backyard activities. My mother would disappear back into the kitchen, father would head out to the mosque to meet his friends, as much a social ritual as a religious one. My sisters would take their places on rush mats plaiting each other's hair, while my brother, always the most earnest and self-righteous member of the family, would sit himself down armed with the green, leather-bound family *Qur'an*, his mouth working silently as his fingers ran along the Ayat of each Surah

And I? Even in those early days I had an interest in art and architecture, was in awe of the majesty of buildings, intrigued by the process that could turn four walls and a roof into something rich and powerful and glorious or, equally, ugly and inhospitable. So even then I would steal into the kitchen to sharpen my pencil with one of the chopping knives, pocket the scraps of rough paper used by the market women to wrap up vegetables and spices, brought home by Fatuma and then discarded. These I would recycle for my sketches, drawings modelled on photographs I had seen of the wonders of Islamic architecture, the mosques and palaces of Istanbul and Isfahan, Damascus and Cairo, Fès and Agadez. These juvenile masterpieces were displayed all over the house, stuck up on the whitewashed walls in every room, evidence of my perceived talent and the pride my parents felt for me.

So you see, my childhood was a time of happiness, of family love and parental care and support. By the time I was nineteen my early dreams of becoming an architect were made concrete by my remarkable school-leaving exam results. With a scholarship guaranteed, I was all set for a rosy future, my plans mapped out for me: a degree in architecture in Egypt, then a job in my Eritrean homeland or, more likely, Addis Ababa, one of the new generation of east African professionals set to lead the region from its colonial past to a bright new dawn of technical and cultural self-sufficiency.

A month later my father was dead, victim of a heart attack at the age of forty-five, and I was driving his taxi, my educational ambitions turned to dust.

I am being called for breakfast. It seems a good place to pause, marking as it does the end of adolescence and the beginning of adulthood. That is, the period before I met you, my angel.

⌘

I am back in my cell, my stomach churning from the unfamiliar diet I am subjected to here: dry, cold toast, tasteless as cardboard, lumpy lukewarm porridge, soggy cornflakes. To protect my digestive system, I eat little and stick to the sweet milky tea.

So where was I? Oh yes, the catastrophe of my father's death. By that time, my brother had a year to go at teacher training college, both sisters still at school, a considerable household with no income, so I made the obvious choice. After all, my father's taxi was sitting outside the house. It was a straightforward decision. One day I was queuing for a student visa at the Egyptian Embassy, the next I was ferrying the great and the good of Asmara between the Medebar Market, the Great Mosque and the Governor's Palace, hauling my compatriots to and from the airport or train station.

And I did not resent my state of affairs. As you well know, I was not, have never been particularly religious, more out of ignorance than considered thought. I left that to my elder brother. But I suppose I accepted my father's death and my changed circumstances with a quiet fatalism. After all, I loved my family, and felt a filial obligation to protect my mother. I suppose that my golden mapped-out future was still an abstraction for me. You do not miss what you have never had.

So I became a taxi-driver, stepping into my father's shoes, even inheriting some of his regular clients. At home, things changed gradually. My mother never really recovered from my father's death, survived him by three cheerless years during which she rarely left the house, ate almost nothing, leaving the running of the household to Fatuma and my sisters. She finally succumbed to her broken heart half-way through the month of Ramadan. Meanwhile, my brother finished his studies and got his first posting in a school just outside Mendefera. My elder sister got married, the younger one found a job as a secretary in the Ministry of Education.

Eventually I tired of treading water. I began to ask myself whether I wanted to live out the rest of my life in Asmara. I had a sudden urge to spread my wings. I reasoned that Addis Ababa, capital city, political powerhouse, headquarters of the Organisation of African Unity, could surely accommodate another hard-working taxi-driver. I could speak basic Amharic, the result of a friendship with the children of our Ethiopian next door neighbours. I had it all planned: I would drive by day, sending monthly contributions back to my unmarried sister who had taken over the running of the family home. Then in the evening I would enrol on some courses, revive my abandoned educational ambitions, starting with some kind of diploma in draughtsmanship, and work my way up gradually.

With this plan in mind, I packed up my belongings, loaded them into the back of the taxi and set off for Addis Ababa and, though I did but know it, for you, my flower.

Now I must stop. Kalil, my cellmate here, has promised to teach me some English and it is time for my daily lesson. I will leave you with another memory from childhood, an episode that came back to me recently. I am eight or nine and my father has given me a few coins as pocket money. It is late afternoon and I am hungry so I head for the neighbourhood street vendors, following the aroma of the sweet, deep-fried dough balls. I buy half a dozen from one of the women, clutching the package to my chest. Still some distance from the family home, I come across a group of street children, bare-footed and feral, and in an instant I am surrounded, pushed to the ground, relieved of my precious treasure. I still hear their triumphant laughter in my ears as I arrive back in the house, dusty and defeated.

The story is prised from me over supper. My brother is unsympathetic and calls me weak, telling me I should have fought for what was rightly mine. My mother offers a vague, slightly anxious smile. My father tells me that it is wrong to fight fire with fire, that you should fight fire with water. Repel evil with that which is best, he says, then adds, *Al Mu'minun*, the name of the Surah in the *Qur'an* from which he is quoting. He tells me that the boys that attacked me were living on the streets without help or support and that we should pity them. He says that if you treat people like animals for long enough, they will eventually start to behave as such, that it is not their fault. He points to the *Qur'an* in the glass cabinet and tells me to seek support within those pages, to let the gentle words soothe me. He takes it down, flicking through the pages to find what he is looking for, a particular Ayah that I came across recently in my reading, an instruction for a good Muslim to:

> *Spend of your substance,*
> *Out of love for Him*
> *For your kin*
> *For orphans*
> *For the needy*
> *For the wayfarer*
> *For those who ask*

He was a man of peace, never harmed a soul, not even with words. Never laid a hand on any of his family. I have always tried to follow his ways, my dear, as you well know.

⌘

Well, that is my lesson for the day completed. It is not easy, I can tell you. Kalil himself admits that his English is rudimentary at best, and our only textbook is a bilingual version of the *Qur'an* that I received on arrival at this centre, a donation published in America. I fear that our linguistic instruction is at the mercy of the translator. Still, beggars cannot be choosers, and my father would be happy to learn of my religious piety.

Let us return, then, to Ethiopia, to my cramped room, my initially inept attempts at taxi-driving in an alien city, my gradual establishment of a new life away from my beloved but sleepy Asmara in this sprawling and confusing metropolis.

My first few months there I was all at sea. My taxi licence and first month's rent ate up most of what savings I had taken with me. More often than not, I got lost while delivering my clients. Sometimes it would be the passenger who would direct me through the confusing labyrinths of Addis. But I persevered, frequently spending my free time in my vehicle, an old Peugeot 504, driving around the city, familiarising myself with each district and setting myself challenges to re-locate addresses I had previously been given and got lost finding, forcing myself to make these streets my own. I began to feel the layout of the city, the government and educational sector in the east, the commercial central sector, and the downmarket western sector with the Mercato, the central mosque and the industrial sites. With the extra outlay in fuel, my monthly profits were pitiful, but my own needs were minimal and I still managed to send home a little each month end.

By the end of my sixth month I was beginning to feel more at home there. I was working long hours, a morning shift from six until noon, then back to my room for a bowl of shiro, that chickpea porridge we Eritreans are so fond of but which you, my darling, could never develop a taste for. After a couple of hours' sleep, I would go back for a second shift until midnight. There was no question of attending night school at this stage, though I continued to read my architectural books, to sketch and dream. My Amharic was becoming more fluent, and that helped reduce my sense of alienation. I suppose in my quiet way I was content.

And then I met you. It started one morning at seven. You were outside the post office on Churchill Avenue near Adua Square trying to hail a taxi to your first lecture of the day at the University. As I was later to learn, you were in the final year of your teaching degree. I stopped to pick you up but did not really want to take you all the way to the campus as I was planning to head out to the airport, a much more lucrative proposition. But one look at your full lips, your slender neck, those laughing eyes and flashbulb smile and all thoughts of financial profit flew out of the cab window. I was hooked.

Of course nothing happened on that first journey. You barely registered my existence, answering my gently probing questions about your studies with a vague detachment. You said later you were worried about a test you were due to take that day, but I think in truth I simply made no impression on you. When, as you paid the fare and made to leave, I asked you what your name was, you hesitated, as if waking from a day-dream and realising for the first time that you were in someone else's company, then shrugged and answered with a non-committal but not unfriendly smile. I felt fully alive for the first time since my arrival in Addis.

I soon worked out your routine, planned my morning

shift pattern around your pick-up, cursed if another taxi driver took your custom and worried if you did not show up. Our conversations deepened gradually and little by little I worked my way inside your consciousness until you, too, began to see me as more than just an object in your daily life. I remember the first time you asked me about my background and I told you about my aborted study plans and my passion for architecture.

For my part, I had already learned a lot from my casual questioning. I knew you were from a well-to-do Christian family, that you had ambitions to teach children, that you liked home grown jazz, devoured African history books, that you could speak some French and English.

My breakthrough came that first morning of the student strike, you remember. I had picked you up and we made small talk as we headed towards the campus. I could see something was up as we crossed Sidist Kilo Square and approached the southern gates of the Guenete Leul Palace. The roadblock was a new addition to the thoroughfare and the soldiers looked menacing, so I reversed and pulled up in front of the Yekatit 12 Hospital. Well, I said, looks like no school today. You smiled and shrugged. A holiday, you answered. Whatever am I going to do with myself? You raised your eyebrows and made a show of looking perplexed, but at that moment I knew you were deliberately offering me an opening, and by God I took my chance with both hands. Trying my best to remain outwardly casual, though failing miserably I am sure, I pretended to pause for thought. How about a sightseeing tour of your hometown? I suggested. I will show you the architectural wonders of the city. Another shrug from you. But no violent reaction, no outraged rejection. So I took that as a yes.

We started with Africa Hall, passed the Filwoha Springs and Giorgis Cathedral on Churchill Road, the Menelik Mausoleum, Trinity Cathedral, the Grand Palace. We took in the Tiglachin Monument, the Freedom Tower, the churches of Menbere Leul Kidus Markos and Meskia Hazunan Medhane Alem. We stopped outside the Entoto Mariam Church and the National Theatre, drove past Arat Kilo. At each building, I would describe what I was seeing, what made it special, what I would have done to improve it, how it made me feel.

And then it would be your turn, and you would fill in the history of each site. From you I learned that it was Queen Taytu's love of the Filwoha Springs that persuaded her husband to establish Addis as his capital, that Giorgis Cathedral was built to commemorate the victory over the Italians at Adawa, that the Menelik Mausoleum housed the tombs of many of the Ethiopian emperors. That the National Museum accommodates Lucy, the three-and-a-half million year old female fossil so important in tracing human evolution. I learned the story of Zerai Deres' martyrdom at the Lion of Judah Monument, of the massacres carried out by the Italian Vice-Roy Marshal Grazziani commemorated at Yekatit 12 Square. Finally, you pointed out which of the city's squares were used to display the bodies of the Dergue's victims during the Red Terror.

By twelve o'clock we were both tired and hungry and I suggested going to the Mercato for lunch. On our way to the market, we passed through Abune Petros Square with its imposing memorial and later, as we ate injera and wat at a cheap roadside café, you told me the story of the bishop it was named after, a martyr executed by the Italians in 1937.

When I finally pulled up outside your house, we became shy again, as if we had only just met. I suppose it was the ambiguity of our relationship, the transition from customer to friend not yet complete. I told you I thought the strike would continue the following day. You agreed. There was a pause, then you thanked me politely for the sightseeing tour. I panicked, already anticipating the emptiness I would face the next day if I did not see you. Stumbling, stuttering, I managed to cough out a suggestion that we meet in the morning, that I take you to see if the campus was open, that if it was not... I ran out of steam then, too timid to suggest another 'date'. But to my surprise you too seemed keen on the idea. Yes, as you told me later, you felt something for your nervous, stammering Eritrean taxi-driver, didn't you? For the time being, though, neither of us could admit to our feelings. We were both sheltering behind the routine of our daily taxi ride together, saw it as the means to maintaining our contact.

That night I could not sleep, my mind replaying the events of the day, our conversation, every word you had spoken, analysing our exchanges for hidden meanings, signs that I had made a favourable impression on you. Lying on my bed, closing my eyes, I recaptured the earnest way your upper teeth played with your lower lip when you were listening intently, the furrows in your brow as you recounted some significant event in Ethiopia's colonial past, the explosion of laughter in your eyes when I managed to say something that you found witty.

And if that first date had gone well, the next day was even more of a success. Thank God for militant students, I thought, as we turned into Sidist Kilo Square and caught sight of the police roadblock. This time I had come prepared with provisions and an itinerary. In the boot I had a flask of coffee, a rug and a package of pastries. When I suggested that we head out of the city to the mountains, I thought for a second you would say no. But your face lit up and you nodded enthusiastically. Let's go to the Church of Entonto Raguel, you said. It is at the top of Mount Entoto. It's the place where Menelik was crowned. I will tell you all about its history and you can tell me why it is a beautiful building.

So that is where we went, you guiding me through the outskirts of the city while I basked in the warmth of your presence. It was a marvellous day, perhaps the happiest of my life to date. You remember the glorious weather, sunshine but cool up in the mountains, the picnic of coffee and cakes, the growing pleasure in each other's company? A magical time, the flower of our love budding but not yet in bloom.

They are calling us for lunch. Yesterday there was only plain rice, no stew to accompany it. One of my fellow detainees, a young Somali, complained about the poor quality of the food. The prison officer looked at him with such venom I thought he would strike him. Well, if you don't like the menu, Kunte Kinte, he said very slowly and loudly, so that we could all understand, you can fuck off back to your own country. Where does such anger come from? Why does he not understand that most of us would much rather be back in our motherlands if we believed we could live a peaceful life there without fear or hunger, that being here is not a choice but a necessity, a matter of life or death?

⌘

Back to my journal, my belly churning from the swill. I have decided to reduce what I eat, given that the food is so unappetising and does not seem to agree with me. There are plenty of fellows here who are grateful for my helping. Just as the inactivity seems to rob me of my appetite, so I witness others getting fat through boredom. We each react differently to our burdens.

Well, where was I? Yes, I had taken you on my journey through the wilderness of my solitude to the moment when we connected. On a superficial level, after that it was all plain sailing for the next ten years, wasn't it? Courting, marriage, the move back to Asmara, the births of our children. The summer of our love.

But of course it was never that easy. Our relationship was an explosive shock to your family, I was from the wrong class, the wrong religion, and our move back to my homeland was less a positive step than an escape.

Back in Eritrea among my people, it was your turn to be the alien, our union frowned on despite your conversion to Islam. But we persevered, working hard to create a healthy home environment, careful to lead blameless lives. I drove my father's taxi night and day, built up our savings and made plans to buy a plot of land in Kahawta. But it was you who made the true sacrifices. You threw yourself into your cultural and religious re-education, learning Tigrinya for everyday conversation, Arabic for your *Qur'anic* classes, recruiting my sister to teach you our cuisine, my aunt to show you our city, the best market stalls, cheapest shops, determined to make new friends, to fit into our society. You never complained about your exile, the rejection by your family, the loss of your friends. The times I felt low, I thought of you and your spirit inspired me, my love.

So as I struggled to build our financial security, you fought for acceptance, toiled to put down roots. And little by little our efforts were rewarded. You had graduated before leaving Addis and had even done a term's teaching at that primary school in Keraniyo, the one with the Sudanese head teacher with all those gold teeth and those odd spinster twins who had been teaching there forever and a day. Now, in Asmara, you were determined to continue with your career, to play your part in the community and in contributing to the household finances. I remember your first day at your new teaching job, that pitiful school in Sembel, the dilapidated classrooms, doors off hinges, the missing window panes, the ever-hungry children. It must have been demoralising at times, but you never gave up and always made the best of the situation. And after the birth of each of our own children, after the maternity leave, once you felt they were happy and healthy, you always went back to your job, to your other children at that school.

So there we were, ten years of growth. A cheerful home, two people in love, blossoming children, the respect and affection of family, friends and colleagues around us. We felt secure, invulnerable, our home an impenetrable fortress. And then, in the course of a single fateful evening, our citadel laid siege to, overrun, laid waste. The fragility of happiness.

You remember the evening, don't you? A day of national celebration, Eid ul-Fitr, the end of the month of fasting. The streets of Asmara heaving with crowds dressed up in their finest, the usual stream of families enjoying the passeggiata along Harnet Avenue, the stalls and cafés and restaurants buzzing.

You at home with the children, supervising their efforts to decorate the house, preparing a delicious family feast of Eritrean specialities you had taught yourself over the years: the lamb's tongue sember, the spicy zilzil keih, the milder derho alicha.

And me out in the taxi, despite your protestations that on this one day of the year I should take a break. Up before the muezzin had made his early morning call to prayer, a full day's work behind me already, ferrying the jubilant to their relatives or further afield, to the bus terminus, the train station, the airport. Returning home through the crowds at five, deciding to give in to your pleading and spend a precious evening together. And then, minutes after getting through the front entrance, no sooner had I kicked off my shoes, the knock at the door, the neighbour's daughter bringing news of the onset of her mother's labour, the plea to take her to hospital. So shoes back on, reversing out of the driveway, the women groaning in the backseat, her sister alongside me up front urging me to put my foot down.

And then the drop off outside the maternity ward entrance, the sister's fumbling with coins and notes, my refusal to accept payment for such a noble mission. I remember thinking, that's it, now home to my loved ones. I recall feeling excitement for my neighbour's family, but also relief that I was not about to embark on a night like theirs. After all, we already had our children. Our family was already complete. Already perfect.

But before I could pull away from the hospital, I found myself blocked by a young white woman frantically trying to flag me down. She was smiling, mouthing something at me, an appeal to take pity and give her a ride I supposed, her face so pink it looked as if it had been scrubbed with a wire brush. I hesitated, picturing your disapproval as your feast grew cold and the disappointment of the children. But it went against my nature to turn down a fare, so I shrugged, pulled up beside her and waited as she climbed in alongside me.

I go train of Massawa thirty minutes, she began in breathless, halting Tigrinya. Please help quick. Then added, as if to clarify, Please railway station thank you.

And there it was. In accepting the challenge to reach the station before the departure of her train, I was sealing my fate. Of course, I cannot blame her. What is she guilty of? Slack timekeeping? An over-ambitious itinerary for the day? As we set off for the train station my speed was, I have to admit, a fraction higher than usual, but I was not distracted, my mind focused on navigating through the Asmara traffic and crowds of pedestrians.

I was just negotiating my way across Bahti Meskerem Square when I hit the boy. I swear he came out of nowhere, sprinting onto the road, his head turned back, chuckling as he ran clear of his chasing friends, his mind empty save for the thrill of his game, oblivious to the dangers of the road.

Witnesses backed me up. It was a glancing blow to his side. I had seen him at the last second, braked and swerved. The impact was not enough to kill him. It was barely forceful enough to cause more than heavy bruising, but he fell awkwardly, spinning round so that his arms could not cushion his fall, so that the first contact with the tarmac was his head. It was this blow, a split second's trauma to his skull, that did for him. By the time I had pulled up and raced to the boy, a crowd had gathered around him. Already blood was seeping from his nostrils, a trickle from his mouth. His friends stood around, silent and shaken, while we waited for the police and an ambulance. I stumbled back to the car to collect my documents and found the white women had disappeared. I think I knew the boy would die as soon as it happened, I remember the feeling of certainty as I was driven to the police station in the back of the patrol car. As I found out an hour later, he never regained consciousness.

I have never gone into so much detail about that catastrophic evening. It has always been taboo, marking as it did the end of our carefree life, the beginning of our downward spiral. The rest you know, of course. Not just the legal cost – my trial and three-year prison sentence for careless driving and manslaughter – but the less tangible consequences. Our attempts to settle the accidental death with the victim's family through compensation payments. The realisation not only of the power and influence of the boy's family, but of their relentless desire for vengeance. Their refusal to accept our efforts at mediation. Their unyielding, ruthless campaign against you and the children while I was incarcerated.

I will not speak of my experiences in prison. Suffice to say, I felt, still feel, tremendous guilt for my crime. That whatever pain and misery I suffered behind bars was entirely justified as settlement for what I had done. After all, there was a mother sitting alone somewhere in Asmara grieving for a son she would never see again.

No, I felt no self-pity. I took my punishment as a form of redemption. But what they did to you and the children, my love, was nothing short of mental torture. And if the purpose was to tear our lives apart just as I had torn theirs, then of course they were triumphantly successful.

It started very quietly, didn't it? I remember you telling me during one of your monthly prison visits that a stranger had sidled up to you in the market and whispered in your ear that your house was being watched, that one of your children was to be targeted for an unpleasant accident. You were too stunned to speak, dropped your shopping bag in shock, and by the time you had bent down to pick it up, the figure had vanished into the crowd.

A few days later, you opened the front door first thing in the morning to find the dead dog disembowelled on the porch. A stone was thrown through the front window one evening the following week. More threats, incidents of intimidation, men approaching our children, silently drawing a finger across their throats, neighbours telling of loitering strangers, night visits warning them not to associate with us. Little by little we became social pariahs.

And then came the message from the boy's family, delivered verbally to you by an uncle one evening twelve months into my sentence. Only the life of one of our children would ease the loss of their son, no other compensation would be acceptable. Perhaps it was a serious threat, perhaps just an upping of pressure to drive us out of Asmara for good. Whatever the case, it was enough to galvanise you into action. I remember your last visit so clearly, the strain etched painfully into the lines of your face, your eyes puffy from lack of sleep. We agreed that you would take all our savings and drive the taxi back to Addis. It would be a hazardous journey for someone who had only just picked up the basics of driving, though I thanked God for our perseverance in the ritual of our Sunday morning driving lessons.

And that, my love, was the last time I ever saw you. You sold up our household goods, gave away what nobody would buy, packed the rest into the taxi wedged between children, then set off for your home city. You continued to write, of course, wonderful stirring letters that gave me the strength to bear the pain of our separation. You wrote regularly, though the unreliable postal service meant that some months I would receive nothing for weeks, then four letters in as many days.

You wrote of your attempts to re-build a life in Addis, your efforts at mending relations with your family, their rejection of you and your 'heathen' children. Setting up a new home, just a modest room in a poor district of the city, paying school fees, new school uniforms, repairs to the ailing taxi, all ate away at our savings. Frightened by the threats to the children, you were unwilling to return to teaching and to leave them alone for any length of time, so you bought a sewing machine and set up a tailoring business from home. As always, you showed courage, spirit, enterprise. My love and pride were never stronger.

There were many obstacles to overcome, but your steely determination and good spirits prevailed, and over the next eighteen months you forged a new life for yourselves. And then, when least expected, the axe fell again. Another evening visit, another stranger at the door. The message, that the boy's family had branches of the extended family living in Addis, that they had got wind of your move there, that the situation had not changed, the old threats still applied.

In the last letter I ever got from you, written in the early hours of the following morning after a night of sleepless worry, you outlined your plans. You would not risk the safety of the children by remaining in Addis. You had debated moving to a neighbouring country, Sudan perhaps or Kenya, but decided that more drastic action was needed to prevent any further threat to their lives. So you proposed selling up everything and using the money to pay a trafficker to smuggle you all overseas. It did not matter where – Canada, the USA, Great Britain, Germany. That would in any case be in the hands of the smugglers. Once you had set yourselves up in the new country, you would then contact me via my brother – I would have been recently released – and I would join you in the new home. Typically, you wrote with such enthusiasm for the scheme that you made this escape seem like the brightest of opportunities.

I had no choice but to bide my time and serve my sentence. The final months – the period following your supposed departure from Africa – were a constant battle to avoid plunging into depression, all my strength concentrated on refusing myself the easy slide into self-pity. The boy was dead, the mother anguished, and you and the children had embarked on a perilous journey. What right had I, the perpetrator of this upheaval, to complain? I embraced the penance.

As each week passed with no news from you, I felt the black hole of fear inside me grow.

The day of my release, I could not help but hope that somehow you and the children would be waiting for me at the prison entrance as the gates swung open.

In fact I spent the first evening at my sister's, lay sleepless during the early hours, had packed my few clothes into a holdall by daybreak and was inside the taxi minibus en route for Addis before my sister had even stirred.

I deserve no pity, seek none. So I will give you nothing but the bare facts in describing the next three months, my relentless search in Addis for clues as to where you might have gone to. It was an odd time, a period of uncertainty and paranoia. I was trying to seek out the smugglers who had offered you their business, and my attempts to make contact with them were met with hostility. At the same time, I became increasingly conscious that I myself was being watched. I realised that the tentacles of the boy's family were still spread across Addis and that spies had become aware of my return and were monitoring my every move.

What I learned about your flight was confused and contradictory. Through persistence and bribery I was introduced to a middleman who admitted setting you up with a group of Somali traffickers, but the group itself seemed to have disbanded or moved back to Mogadishu. One man I spoke to, a kat-chewing Yemeni, seemed certain that you were to have been taken overland to Sudan, then flown to Germany or Britain. Another lead, a businessman who had known my father, believed the Somalis' favoured routes were always via Libya or Egypt.

One evening, returning to my tiny rented room deep in the Addis slums after another fruitless day's investigations, I was crossing a quiet street when a car parked ahead of me pulled out at speed and swerved across the road. I looked up and threw myself out of its path a split second before it hit me. Needless to say, the car did not stop. It was, at best, a warning.

My enquiries were getting me nowhere. At around this time, I received the news that my brother had died of meningitis. The attempt on my life was the final straw. I contacted an uncle in Asmara and begged him to lend me some money. He agreed to send me $8,000, less a gift of love than a pay-off to disappear. There was nothing left for me in Asmara. The family home had been sold, both my sisters were by now married, their husbands afraid of contact with me, the family outcast.

So I went back to my trafficking contacts, this time in search of business, not information. Suddenly they were much more amenable. They took $5,000 of my money and promised me a problem-free journey to Germany. The route was more or less as the Yemeni had described yours. False papers and a truck providing a smooth ride to Khartoum. Then a new passport and plane ticket to Frankfurt, where I would claim political asylum. In my mind I imagined myself following in your footsteps, believed myself to be drawing ever nearer to my precious family.

The journey was a disaster from the outset. The

departure was inexplicably delayed by two days, so that by the time I got the signal one chilly morning to make my way to the car park of an abandoned warehouse on the outskirts and clambered on board the truck, I was a tangle of nerves. The truck, loaded with flour, wheezed and clanked as it pulled out onto the road. I glanced at my fellow passengers – a father and young son, two young men who I later learned to be brothers, a teenage girl and her aunt – and sensed in them the same anxiety that I felt.

We crossed the border at Kurmuk, but rather than turn a blind eye, as we had been promised, the Sudanese border guards pounced on us. They seemed almost to have been expecting our arrival, arrested the driver, confiscated our papers and locked us up in police cells. The next day we were loaded up into a military truck and driven north, up to a remote area on the border with Eritrea, where we were abandoned in a refugee camp they called Kilo Sitta Wa Eshrin. It was a hellish place, squalid with little food to go round. The Sudanese soldiers in the vicinity were a brutal rabble and because many of the residents were Eritreans escaping military service, the Eritrean army would sometimes raid at night, kidnapping any young men they came across. I survived a week, then bribed a Sudanese soldier to give me a lift to Kassala. From there, another few dollars paid for a hitched ride into Khartoum.

I thought, briefly, that my luck was turning. I should have known better. I bought some Sudanese identity papers from a Lebanese market trader. He suggested I head for Libya, where I could live illegally without too many problems from the authorities while I earned enough to set me up in Europe. I was told that from the Libyan coast I could buy passage on a boat crossing to France or Spain or Italy.

I travelled up to Dongolla with a series of bokasi, the pickup taxis that cross that vast country. I had been given a contact name by my Lebanese friend, and through this man, I secured another boksi ride across the Libyan Desert. It was a gruelling experience, my memories now a blur of heat and thirst.

Crossing the border, a repeat of my earlier disaster. A patrol of Libyan soldiers came across us by chance, and once again I suffered the indignity of arrest and transportation, this time to a detention centre named Misratah.

It was another hellhole, the inmates a mixture of Ethiopians, Eritreans and Somalis, men and women, the elderly down to the new-born, packed seventy to each windowless cell. We had blankets for beds, overflowing toilets, meagre rations and dirty water, no medicines to treat the cases of malaria and diarrhoea and TB. The guards were sadists, the weekly drip drip of physical abuse culminating each Thursday in an orgy of drink and violence, women inmates dragged from their cells to be raped, any attempt by their male counterparts to halt this torture met with teargas and beatings.

Six weeks of this purgatory. Every few days the guards would line us all up and read out lists of names of detainees to be deported. Sometimes, filled with the thought that I was following in your footsteps, I felt a fiery determination to fight on, to complete this journey regardless of where it eventually took me. At other times, when the task of locating you seemed altogether hopeless, I felt resigned to a return to Asmara and to the vengeance of that unforgiving family.

Together with two fellow countrymen, I began to plan my escape, a hazardous breakout involving decoy fires and the scaling of a fence topped with razor wire.

Fortunately, our getaway was actually far more straightforward. Like me, one of my co-conspirators had his remaining wealth – in his case, three gold rings – sewn into the seam of his shirt. Afraid of the risks involved in my escape plan, this man, an army deserter from Beylul named Hassan, simply approached the most corrupt-looking of the guards and offered him the rings for our freedom.

The guard did not hesitate. The following Thursday he placed the three of us in a separate punishment cell for some invented infringement of rules and that night, after the other guards had collapsed into a drunken stupor, he unlocked the door, guessing that our escape would be covered up the following day by his shame-faced, hungover colleagues.

The following weeks are hazy, days hiding out in orange groves, nights walking the highways, skirting the towns, scavenging just enough to stay alive. Hassan had the name of a contact in Benghazi who organised passage by boat to southern Italy and then sealed lorry runs to France and Britain, so it was to that city that we headed.

One night, sleeping rough on the outskirts of Benghazi, Hassan and our other companion went to buy bread. Whether they were caught by the police or simply abandoned me, I never saw them again. I had the name of the contact and of a restaurant in the sprawling market, the Souq al-Jreed, and after a day of discreet enquiries, was finally introduced to the trafficker.

I still had two thousand dollars left, and all of that went on my new identity papers and getaway. Though in hindsight it was money well spent, at the time it felt as if it was torture that I was buying.

If the voyage on the fishing trawler was an awful three days of nausea and suffering, in comparison to the lorry journey that followed, it was a pleasure trip of sumptuous luxury. Locked in the back of the lorry along with twenty or so fellow Africans, I passed the endless hours in complete darkness, the air fetid with sweat and human waste, the continual motion and lack of light creating a sense of total disorientation. How many days and nights did the journey take? Which countries did we pass through? After a day or two I could barely differentiate between sleep and wakefulness, let alone answer such complex questions.

But I was getting closer to you, my darling. So when the back of the lorry opened for the last time and we emerged, dazzled by the light and still nauseous from the Channel crossing, onto the potholed tarmac of a lorry park on the outskirts of some English coastal town, the loss of nerve I experienced was tempered by my belief in your proximity.

I stood on that tarmac, rubbing my eyes and blinking in the sunlight, watching the other new arrivals slink off, some alone, others in twos and threes, all anxious to slip away and protect their new-found freedom.

From talking to these fellow-travellers during the interminable journey, I had gathered two essential pieces of information regarding my status in this country: firstly, that if I did not apply for asylum with the authorities immediately on arrival, I would have no recourse to public funds, would not be allowed to seek legal employment and would therefore face homelessness and starvation; and secondly, that according to EU law, if the authorities could prove that I had arrived here from another 'safe' country – in my case France, I supposed – I could be deported to that country on the basis that I should have claimed asylum there.

Standing on that tarmac, watching the last of my fellow-travellers disappear, I dithered, unable to square my fear of police, born out of my Sudanese and Libyan experiences, with the urge to throw myself at their mercy and set my application for asylum in motion. And of course I shilly-shallied to the end, finally handing myself in at a police station in Brighton, but only after four days of sleeping rough and aimless wandering. Cold, filthy, hungry, the loss of freedom seemed at the time a small price to pay for a hot meal and warm bed.

And from there to here, my love, was but a short hop. The police could not locate a Tigrinya-speaking interpreter, and even with the half-hearted assistance of an Arabic-speaking one, the confusion caused by my language problems and my genuine ignorance of the route I had taken to Britain raised immediate suspicion. Two days after handing myself in, I found myself here at Glynbourne House. I feel suspended in time and space, my existence in limbo.

And you, my love? Am I closing in on my beloved family, drawing ever nearer, tolerating these short-term inconveniences for the sake of our long-term future together? Or is this, as I sometimes fear during those bleak early hours before daybreak, just a long and lonely wild goose chase?

SEMIRA 1

Dear Kassa

Well, it must be after midnight. The heating is off and the flat is icy so I am wrapped up in two thick sweaters. Winter here is no joke, I can tell you. Nothing can prepare you for the numbing cold. Yanit has been asleep for hours. She is feeling anxious about her first day at school tomorrow and switching off is her way of coping, I suppose. She spent the evening immersed in a book, lost in its fictional world. It will be tough for her starting a new school mid-year, straight into a Year 4 classroom, but I have told her just to be herself, that friendships will come, insh'Allah.

Abebe is in an easier position since he is starting in Year 1. As his teacher explained, there will be a number of other new children starting in his class tomorrow. Being that much younger, he feels none of Yanit's anxieties, only excitement at the prospect of an end to these months of boredom and at the thought of all that school offers – games and playmates and organised entertainment. The buzz of expectation has kept him awake long past Yanit's bedtime, but he too has finally succumbed.

It is such a relief to finally have a place of our own. The flat, two bedrooms, kitchenette, lounge and bathroom, may not be a palace – compared to Africa, everything is cramped in this small, overcrowded island – and I know it is only temporary accommodation, but it certainly beats the madness of the hostel we stayed in when we first arrived here after our dispersal. Oh, Kassa, those were crazy times. Women and their children crammed together, everyone's fuse shortened by exhaustion and despair, no outlet for the tension, no escape,

Yes, this flat is only temporary, but who knows what that means in real terms, so I have decided to make the best of it and treat this corner of Bristol, a suburb they call Lawrence Weston, as my new home. I do what I can to lay down roots. I take Yanit and Abebe to the nearby parks and the local library. We do our shopping at the Ridingleaze row of stores or sometimes venture further afield, to the ugly Broadmead shopping mall to browse, or for the sake of our souls, to the vast grounds of Blaise Castle where we can spread our wings, fill our lungs, run and scream and fight and laugh.

For all these months I have watched our lives unfold, a helpless observer. It is difficult to express how I have been feeling, Kassa, but close your eyes and imagine that Abebe and Yanit and I find ourselves lined up on a dry dusty plain, standing with our arms straight down by our sides like soldiers on parade. Imagine that we then realise that we are part of some giant children's game, that we are the skittles and these infant monsters towering above us are about to launch colossal bowling balls at us, that we are paralysed, waiting to take the full impact of these missiles, that they will cannon against us, sending us spinning off in unforeseen directions and that there is nothing we can do to prevent this bombardment. Can you imagine that, Kassa? Well, that is how I have been feeling.

So I yearn for permanency, for some stability in our lives and perhaps this letter, this words-on-paper process, is also part of my attempt to fix our existence, to make it more real.

I hope too that you will appreciate this account of our lives since we separated, Kassa, you whose passion was always the story in all its forms – the yarn, the fairytale, the myth and legend – you whose nose was perpetually buried in one novel or another, whose notebooks were filled with your own creativity, plays and tales of domestic discord, family betrayal, political machinations, broken hearts and unfathomable courage. Perhaps you will read our story and it will inspire you.

So where do I begin? Let us start here in Bristol and

then go backwards. This city, I read from a local history book, my first borrowing from the library, has a population of over 400,000, was always a major urban centre, a wealthy commercial port, but only really made a name for itself with its involvement in the Atlantic slave trade in the eighteenth century. During that period, I discover, more than 2,000 ships were fitted out here, responsible for the transport of over half a million slaves during those ghastly but profitable years.

But let me take you back to our arrival, cold and wet and filthy, crawling out of that lorry somewhere south of London, our first contact with the authorities at the police station, the first days at the hostel. The initial shock at the women there, glazed and mute through surrender; or irritable, vicious-tongued, their tempers taut with tension, the slightest look or word a pretext for a venting of fury. And their children, feral with neglect, twitchy with boredom, sweeping through the rooms like packs of wild dogs.

And back we continue, ever further. Back to the dark, vile journey across Europe that brought us here across the Channel, no idea of our precise itinerary, only vague snapshots of signposts and advertising hoardings spied during the snatched toilet breaks, clues indicating a route from Turkey that may have passed through Bulgaria, the Balkans, Germany and Belgium.

And if we take one more rearward leap, we are again in the back of a lorry, dusty days and nights carrying us from Ethiopia through Sudan to Egypt. Weeks of waiting in Cairo, then up to Alexandria and the boat crossing to Turkey.

And then, between these two hellish journeys, somewhere in Turkey there is a black hole so deep and dark that I cannot, will not, must not attempt to penetrate it. Not now, not ever.

But that is not the only chapter of my story that I will not touch, my dear. The first chapter, our life at home, I must also by-pass. That whole world, my studies, my job, my marriage, my friends and, dare I say it, my family, the ups and downs, the mirth and misery, I roll it into a ball, box it up in a locked case, stow it under my bed. Besides, most of it you know already, of course. No, I will start my story in the here and now, the bright positive present.

Bristol is a strange city, a gateway to the countryside, a split personality, half cosmopolitan and half peasant; half Old England, half ethnic melting pot. A walk through the town is like a stroll through modern British history, the words from my library book made real: I see maritime commerce in the floating harbour and the tobacco warehouses; I pass through breezeblock Broadmead rebuilt after the devastation of German bombing; I admire the engineering feat of Clifton Bridge, what my library book refers to as a proud legacy of the Industrial Revolution; I observe another legacy, this time of colonialism and Empire, in the ethnic diversity of the inner-city districts; and finally I am struck by the elegance of the mansions and palatial townhouses of Clifton, built with the blood of African slaves, men and women and children torn from their families, their communities, by circumstances beyond their control.

I was with my solicitor today. With him, I walk a tightrope between truth and deception. My passport and our identity papers disappeared into the hands of the traffickers before we had even left Ethiopia. To give my real name, my authentic story, is to reveal myself to the world, open up the possibility of my discovery by that Asmara family and their boundless tentacles, to put Yanit and Abebe in danger. While our true identities stay hidden, we remain safe. Yet, as the solicitor told us when we were first interviewed after our arrival, any hope for our asylum case here rests on the plausibility of our story, and lies are always harder to maintain than the truth.

I had given this a lot of thought during our journey and in the end I decided it would be too risky to reveal the blood feud story. Instead I have created a political prisoner for my husband's persona, fabricated a history of persecution. Much of what I told them was true – Ethiopian woman weds Eritrean man, our marriage and move to Asmara, even his imprisonment, though his misdemeanour has become political. And historical events are on my side – growing government repression in

Eritrea has made my story more believable.

The case is backed up further by the interpreters and language experts assessing my linguistic competence in Amharic, Tigrinya, Arabic, as well as Yanit and Abebe's language abilities. And of course when the children were interviewed separately, they could also confirm their father's imprisonment, though they are vague about his so-called crime. You remember, don't you, that they had been too young to understand what he had done? We had only told them that he was being jailed unjustly, hadn't we?

Our names, too, are another half-truth. I have reverted to my grandfather's name here. You remember that it is our custom for children to take their father's first name as surname when they are born? To avoid identification, I have given Yanit and Abebe my own family name as theirs. I have drilled them since our arrival, it is what they use at school, and they accept it without question.

Today, the solicitor runs through the story again. There is still no court date, but I am told my presence is not required. Our future is decided in an unknown place by strangers who have never met me.

A further task completed since our arrival in the UK was to seek help from the Red Cross and its international tracing service. At the interview I told the truth, the full story of our misfortune, all the details I could muster, nothing withheld except our real family names. Now there is nothing to do but wait and pray...

It is late and I am tired. It is comforting to have re-established contact. I will let you know how Yanit and Abebe get on at school. It goes without saying that they miss you, just as I do. Give my love to Gadissa, you are both always in my thoughts.

⌘

Dear Kassa
Who am I trying to fool? I cannot remember all the details of

my last letter, only the tone, a casual catching-up of news like two old classmates whose lives have meandered in opposite directions but who feel that their friendship is sufficiently significant to warrant these informal updates.

I am sure this was a deliberate stance on my part, my darling, a desire born out of necessity, a survival instinct, an inability to face the true nature of our connection.

Even now, you can see how I hide behind euphemism. Our 'connection'? It is pathetic, I know, but for now that is all you are going to get. Indulge my tone, tolerate my voice, endure my trite twitterings, they are but the sweepings of my soul, seeping leaks from the hole blown through the centre of my heart. I am sorry, my sweet, but that is all I can manage for the moment

So where was I? How to describe our life here? Transitory, I think, sums it up adequately. Last week I was a Lawrence Weston resident perched on the north-west edge of the city. Today I am an inner-city dweller, forced out of my temporary accommodation and scrambling to find a property to match my housing benefit allowance.

With no time to pick and choose, I find myself jumping at the first opportunity, the downstairs flat of a converted terraced house near the local primary school in St Paul's. The accommodation is OK, a little drab and damp. Unfortunately the couple upstairs seem at war with each other, with their children, with the world at large, so there are verbal fireworks every night, a constant background of angry conflict.

It was hard for Yanit and Abebe to leave our life on the estate. He was enjoying the structure of the classroom and she had begun to make her first friends. I debated keeping them on at that school but getting them from St Pauls to Lawrence Weston every day using public transport was just too daunting so I signed them up for this local school, a stone's throw from our front door.

It is a nice surprise to see so many black faces around and it is a more vibrant environment than the estate. But I already have my reservations about this community. During daylight hours the streets and shops seem safe and the people friendly and open. I have already joined the Cheltenham Road library, have identified a favourite local grocer's and a halal butcher.

But when night falls I sense the danger. The street that leads me out of the neighbourhood, by day congested with pushchairs and schoolchildren, is lined after dark with girls plying their trade. Cars prowl and cruise, their boom-boom-boom music mingling with the clamour of pavement squabbles and the wail of police sirens. We stay inside after sunset, ignore the couple upstairs with their endless quarrels and bury ourselves in television and books.

A further development to report. At the children's school I saw a flyer pinned to the notice board advertising government-run English classes. I plucked up the courage and went along to register, and here I am, back in the world of study, a part-time English language course, what they call ESOL, two mornings a week close to the city centre. And no sooner have I signed up than the teacher announces exams at the end of term! My poor old brain can barely keep up. I wish you were here to help me out, you were always so good at English, the teachers forever blowing your trumpet!

No news on our court case.

No news from the Red Cross.

Our love to Gadissa. You are always in our hearts.

⌘

Dear Kassa

And so it continues, our roundabout journey through life. Another change, this time voluntary rather than enforced. One evening last month the usual street sounds, shouts and screams, the squeal of brakes and sound of shattering glass. Only this time the following morning a knock at the door, a policeman politely enquiring whether we had witnessed the stabbing of two youths on the pavement right outside our house the previous night, one young boy dead, the other in intensive care. I saw the yellow police incident notice placed just outside my garden gate, fancied I could still see the dark brown traces of blood on the pavement, and realised I could no longer live there.

The decision has been made easier by Yanit's unhappiness at her new school. She has never settled and does not seem to have made any friends. And nor, for that matter, have I. Arriving to collect the two of them each afternoon, I was struck by how sad many of the parents appeared. They seemed hollow-faced and edgy. Perhaps I was just experiencing the alienation of an outsider. Whatever the case, I did not feel that I belonged.

So back to bag-packing, to notice-giving and house-hunting, to scraping together a deposit from what little remains of my savings. Our new home is another converted terrace, this time right in the heart of Easton.

Again, the process of nesting, the discovery of amenities, where to buy fruit and vegetables, halal meat. A new library to explore. The closest school is as ethnically diverse as the last one, but somehow the atmosphere seems less aggressive. The local Muslim cultural centre runs an after-school club and I have enrolled both children for that. Outside the house there are still the night-time sounds of a world gone mad, still the police incident notice boards, but somehow here I feel safer.

I continue my English classes. My fellow students are from all walks of life and every corner of the globe. I arrive late for each session, breathless from the cross-town rush. I sit at my desk, pen in hand, scribbling new vocabulary into my notebook and feeling like a little schoolgirl. My brain is not as flexible as it once was and stubbornly refuses to accept new ideas without a fight. But I persevere and to my surprise I passed my end of term exam. I have the certificate to prove it. You would be proud of me, my dear! Still, no respite. The teacher has registered us for the next exam level, so my nights are spent toiling over my homework. I am ashamed to say that sometimes I go begging to Yanit for help!

She is much happier here. She plays with Fatima,

the daughter of our Pakistani neighbours, and she has the beginnings of a circle of friends at school. Abebe has adapted, too. He takes after his father and gets on with everybody. Both of them are doing well with their schoolwork. They get praised by their teachers for their industry and enthusiasm, for their helpfulness. Can they really be so untouched by our journey? Or is the damage so deeply buried that for the moment it is undetectable, concealed like some slowly mutating tumour? Worries, worries...

All this change, all this anxiety, it has aged me beyond measure, my dear. I am sure you would have a job to recognise me, what with my wrinkles and greying hair. Yes, that beautiful head of hair that you used to help me plait has begun sprouting grey and I have bought my first ever colouring product, and I am not yet thirty-seven years old!

No news from the Red Cross.

Look after yourself. Look after Gadissa.

With all my love

⌘

Dear Kassa

Will it never end? Goodbye Easton, hello Hartcliffe. From colourful inner-city to windswept estate, it seems we have come full circle. The house is not too bad, a quiet road. They tell me many years ago there was a tobacco factory here, a thriving, busy community. Now there seem to be so many people wandering around during the day, young and old, men and women, that I wonder whether anyone has a job or goes to school.

For me, the usual process of discovery, a new library, new shops to explore, new bus routes to negotiate to take me to my English classes. A new college also, as the old site was too far from here, perched as we are on the southern edge of the city, so I have transferred to the Bedminster campus, one bus ride away. Sad to say goodbye to my old friends, my thoughtful teacher, but if Yanit and Abebe can put up with this constant chopping and changing, then so can I.

I do feel for them, the guilt has never been stronger. Blossoming at school, neighbourhood friendships, the beginnings of a social life. Then these fragile roots torn out, another upheaval, more dislocation.

It is bad enough for them as it is, what with having to cope with so many bewildering puzzles in their lives. Confusion upon confusion! The challenge of language here, for example. Consider their linguistic history. Think about what they have had to cope with: born into a Tigrinya-speaking environment but with Amharic spoken at home and Arabic in the mosque and *Qur'anic* classes. Then thrown into an English-speaking world, though with most of their neighbours in Easton speaking Urdu or Bengali or Punjabi. It is more Babel than Bristol, but they cope, automatically fit their language to the context, and seem to thrive in all of them, as if somehow each one complements and supports the others. You would be amazed to see Yanit's nose buried in a thick English novel, to hear Abebe chattering away to his friends using the latest slang. Oh silly me, I am starting to cry! What an old fool I'm becoming...

But that inner-city chapter has now ended and I am not too confident that this next one will be as much to their liking. Gone are the playmates, the mixed school, the halal butcher, the mosque, the Asian shops and Muslim centre a stone's throw away. This is a different kettle of fish, black faces most definitely in the minority, a tough, white, working-class world.

But we beggars cannot be choosers, as I tried to explain to tearful Yanit when it came to breaking the news to her. The lease came to an end, the landlord wanted to sell the property, and after three months of increasingly frantic house-hunting, I had found nothing we could afford with my housing benefits.

As a result, made homeless, we found ourselves placed by the council in emergency accommodation, in this drab but clean house in Hartcliffe. It is the most space we have had, not only the usual two bedrooms, but a proper lounge, a full-sized kitchen and our own piece of garden behind. The downside of this new location is the road we are situated on, a cul-de-sac next to a field. Even an outsider like myself can see it is a problem site. Neighbours' gardens are filled with discarded fridges, sofas, bags of rubbish. The field is the nightly meeting place for drug dealers, joy riders, gangs of intimidating youths. As always, we batten down the hatches after dark, find escape in our homework, our books.

We continue to maintain some of our old ties. We still make the trek to St Mark's Road for the children's *Qur'anic* classes. Once a fortnight I take Yanit up to visit Fatima, taking the opportunity to stock up on meat and vegetables and spices in the Stapleton Road stores. But in truth, the page has turned, a new chapter has begun. It is up to us to make the most of it.

My solicitor phoned on Tuesday to tell me we have a date for my case on the first of the month. We can only pray.

No news from the Red Cross.

To you and Gadissa as always we send our purest love. There is never a day, an hour, a minute when we do not miss you. When I say you are always in my thoughts I do not only mean that I think about you a lot, that there is a frequency to the number of times I recall, reminisce, reconstruct, speculate. No, what I mean is that whatever I do, the filling of a kettle, the visit to the baker's, the queuing for the bus, the brushing of my hair, every activity is flavoured by your absence, spiced by my loss, poisoned with the virus of our separation. Every knock at the door, every car horn beep, every time the phone rings, my heart skips a sweet-sour beat. That is what I mean.

GREG 2

His first reaction is to stand up, drop his rifle and run, screaming and waving, down the hill. He takes a step and checks himself. Some instinct, a voice in his head, whispers to him to stay put, to return to the flat ledge of rock concealed behind the bushes, to be patient. He crouches down, scrambles from boulder to bush, taking care to keep himself hidden. He reaches his refuge, digs out the binoculars from his backpack and lies down flat behind a thick bush.

He watches the approach of the vehicle through his binoculars. As it reaches the crash site, it slows, weaving between the debris and scattering the regiments of pillaging vultures. The creatures are only momentarily put off and soon return to their feast.

The vehicle pulls up about fifty metres from the tent. Through his binoculars he can see that it is some kind of pick-up converted for military use, a heavy-calibre machine gun manned by a shaven-headed youth in khaki battle fatigues, the weapon welded to the vehicle's bodywork. The driver, sporting a flat peaked cap, is dressed in a similar outfit. The back of the pick-up is crammed with six other African men, all armed, several dressed in ill-matching army garb, others in loose robes and wound cloth headgear. From a distance it's difficult to distinguish detail, but two of them look no older than teenagers.

The cavalry, he thinks, but there's a small question mark in his mind, enough to stop himself from rising to his feet and waving.

The soldiers clamber out of the vehicle and the leader,

short and slight despite his camouflage uniform and military boots, barks an order, points to various points around the theatre of death. Casually, he lifts the automatic rifle he's holding and fires several bursts into the nearest group of vultures. The birds squawk and flap in panic, the unscathed ones taking to the air leaving three or four carcasses strewn around the crash victim they had been gorging on moments before.

The commander reminds Greg of someone he can't quite place. He strains to recall and is about to give up when the memories slot into place and the connection is made: it's the head teacher at the small rural school in Zimbabwe where he first worked as a volunteer all those years ago, a petty man whom the other local teachers had nicknamed Pol Pot due to his bullying style of management.

Greg watches as two of the soldiers approach the body. For an instant he thinks they are going to cover it, return to it something of its dignity, but is shocked to see one of them bend down to remove its watch. Already two other soldiers have located the wreckage containing the store of baggage and are emptying the suitcases, removing electronic equipment and other valuables.

He watches as one of the youths grapples with the body of the air hostess, pulling off her necklace, watch and bracelets. Another soldier whoops with joy as he pulls a handful of banknotes from a besuited corpse. The youth has now moved on to an elderly woman lying near the section of a wing, struggles to remove some rings from her swollen fingers, pulls a machete from his belt, puts his foot on the lifeless arm to steady himself, slashes down on the fingers two, three times, then bends to pull off the bloodied jewellery.

It is a systematic and cruelly efficient looting. Every so often one of the soldiers fires his rifle at the vultures to gain access to a body, but the birds are only fleetingly deterred. For some minutes Greg watches the ruthless progress of the marauders, but when one of them uses his rifle butt to extract the white farmer's gold teeth he can bear it no longer. He looks out to the empty plain, to the mountains in the far-off distance and the dying embers of the sunset sky, trying to cleanse himself of these visions of brutality.

A line flits into his head, 'deliver us from evil', and in his disorientation and exhaustion it takes him a minute to trace it back to the Lord's Prayer. He thinks of Nuala, of a future reunion, and wonders where his deliverers are, the rescue parties, the planes and helicopters, wonders what in God's name he's doing here in this horror movie and how he will ever escape.

He's been feeling a growing giddiness, and now with a lurch he identifies the source of this queasy unease, a feeling that he's been press-ganged into some hideous game, a game whose rules he does not know. Or perhaps there are no rules. Maybe he has to make them up himself.

Meanwhile, Pol Pot has been standing around idly, occasionally shouting an order, firing a burst of his Kalashnikov at the scavenging birds. Greg watches as he wanders over to the tree, zips down the tent door and pokes his head inside. He bends down and disappears into the interior.

Maybe he'll help her.

Minutes pass. When he emerges, he's pulling up his combat trousers, buckling his belt.

Jesus, no. It can't be...

Pol Pot barks something and through the binoculars Greg can see that he's smiling, gesturing towards the tent. The three nearest soldiers join him, begin arguing, jostling each other for position. The leader says something and points to one of the men in flowing robes who shouts in triumph, then bends to enter the tent.

No way. No fucking way, he whispers.

And here it is, he realises, the moment when he has to make up the rules all by himself. He scrambles back along the ledge to the cave, retrieves the hunting rifle and checks that it's loaded. He trains it on the tent entrance, aims through the telescopic sights and waits. He estimates that he must be a hundred metres or so away and hopes that it's still in range. A flashback, a childhood memory of Greg playing with his neighbour's airgun, the boy's father, ex-services or territorial army, lecturing them on body position and grip, breathing and trigger pull. Greg remembers his odd mantra: Squeeze the trigger gently, lads. Squeeze it like a baby.

Now he ceases to consider the consequences of his actions, that he's about to give away his own presence here, and, as the robed man scrambles out of the tent a couple of minutes later, the smile of satisfaction on his face, Greg pulls the trigger.

Another deafening blast, another stabbing pain in his shoulder as the kickback hammers home. This time he hits his target. The man is thrown back into the tent, and after a few seconds of shocked silence the soldiers are thrown into a frenzy. Greg presses himself to the rocky ground, listens to the screams, the shouting and the bursts of automatic gunfire below. When he looks up a minute later, peering through the thorny undergrowth, he can see that the soldiers have gone to ground, hidden behind wreckage, shrubs, the pick-up. Only the vultures seem unperturbed.

He wonders to what extent precisely he's revealed his location. They must surely know that he's somewhere up the kopje, but can't have identified where exactly.

Sit tight or make a run for it?

Greg's aware of the speed of nightfall in Africa, realises that he's observing that swift transformation at this very moment, guesses that dusk will give way to darkness in half an hour or less. The temperature's dropped suddenly and he shivers.

Be patient, he answers, and huddles down to wait.

⌘

Cutting through the pitch-black gloom of the evening, the low voices of the militia below are easily discernible. He fears they'll mount a night advance up towards him, hoping instead to hear the sound of an engine starting, a vehicle pulling away and receding back across the plain, but he's disappointed. He wishes that they would at least build a fire to signal their decision to stay put during the night. He's too frightened to sleep and remains crouched on the ledge clutching his rifle, tuned to the slightest sound from below. He waits.

As the minutes turn to hours, his thoughts eventually wander. In the immediate aftermath of shooting the soldier, he'd been too shocked to consider his actions, too focused on his own survival, on keeping his location a mystery. Now, with time on his hands, the full impact of his deed hits home and his head reels. Jesus Christ, he thinks. What have I done? I'm just a soft shite from Oxford. A week ago I was wielding a paintbrush. A day ago I was eating groundnuts and sipping a cold bottle of Castle. Today I killed a man with a hunting rifle, put a bullet through his chest. I fucking killed him.

He crouches and waits, every sound magnified a thousand fold, every rustle, every murmur. He pictures the men gathering below and imagines he can hear their whispers, their stealthy steps. They might at this very moment be stealing up the kopje towards him. He remains braced, engulfed in the tense agony of fear and indecision.

At midnight he can stand it no longer. If he stays put, he'll still have to face them in the morning. He heaves his backpack onto his shoulders, clutches his rifle in both hands, edges his way off the ledge and heads up the slope towards the summit.

His progress is excruciatingly slow, every footfall tested for potentially noisy twigs, every step hindered by knee-cracking boulders and needle-sharp thorns. Twice he finds himself face to face with a sheer wall of rock and has to backtrack to find a less perilous route. It takes two hours of exhausting climbing to reach the peak. He stops for a brief rest, gulps down some water, urges himself on, aware of the need to put distance between himself and the soldiers before daybreak.

If anything, the descent is even more demanding than the climb. The soil is pebbly, the stones as slippery as marbles, constantly threatening to upend him. His calf muscles scream from the effort of braking. By the time he reaches the foot of the hill, dawn is breaking and through the murky obscurity he can see that the terrain on this side of the kopje is less arid, more scrubland but with a thicker covering of vegetation. He's desperately tired, aching and bruised and scratched from his blind escape, but knows he must force himself to keep going. He gathers what strength he has left. His body, battered by the crash, seems irrevocably damaged, and his mind, traumatised by the shooting, feels no less broken.

He walks on. At one stage he thinks he can hear the low hum of a motor engine. He stops and strains to listen. Silence. He crosses one dried river bed, then another. He halts to drink, to make futile attempts to use his mobile phone, to pull out some dried apricots that he chews on as he stumbles along. He tries to picture the soldier-bandits, to second guess their plan of action. He reckons that the booty at the crash site will be too great a pull to waste time on a man hunt, imagines their pick-up loaded with loot, the remaining soldiers high-tailing it out of the area. Still, he can't be sure, can't risk being found, and fear of their reprisal spurs him on. He wonders who they are, what they represent.

Hours pass, the sun rises and the temperature soars. The throbbing in his temple and the stabbing in his abdomen form the beat to his marching rhythm. As he tramps through the inhospitable bush, he falls into a kind of numbed trance, his legs moving automatically, his mind retreating into a half-slumber. Every so often he jerks awake, stops to check his bearings with the compass, to make sure he's not walking in some giant deadly loop that will bring him back round to the plane and the soldiers.

From time to time he finds himself forced out of his stupor by the physical pain. He thinks again of Nuala, wonders if they've broken the news to her yet, pictures the phone calls, the TV footage. It's too awful to contemplate. By sheer force of will he conjures up an image of their kitchen at home, a peaceful breakfast scene, the children with their cereal bowls, Nuala spooning tea leaves into the blue china teapot, the toast popping in the toaster. It is this picture that he forces to the front of his mind as a spur to drive him forward.

By nine o'clock his clothes are soaked with sweat. Perspiration stings his eyes, runs down his nose, drips onto his shirt front. Despite the shade provided by this area of denser vegetation, the sun is ferocious. He sinks down into the shadow of a termite mound and eats a couple of stale rolls with a square of sweating cheese. When he gets up to relieve himself against a large rock, he notices that his urine is pinkish, laced with blood from some internal injury, the result, he assumes, of that blow to his abdomen.

He's about to hitch his rucksack back up on his shoulders when he hears the drone of a light aircraft. He glances up, tries to peer through the foliage of a tree and looks around for a clearing from which to signal his presence. Dropping his bag and rifle, he sets off at a trot, wincing at the abdominal pain and ignoring the weariness in his aching legs. He remembers the empty distress flare canister and curses his bad luck.

Hey! I'm here! Here! he cries, his voice cracked and hoarse from heat and dehydration. He remembers the heliograph in his bag and considers running back to retrieve it from his bag. But he knows already that it would be a futile gesture, that he's too late.

The plane passes overhead while he's still under tree cover. He catches a glimpse of a small, twin-propeller aircraft, but by the time he emerges from the wooded area onto the flat, dry savannah, it is receding rapidly into the distance. He stops, waves, shouts, his attempts at signalling turning first to obscenities, then to pleading. He ceases his yelling only when the plane is a dot on the horizon.

Retracing his footsteps, he recovers the firearm and bag and heads back towards the savannah. Using the compass to take his bearings, he notes that he's heading due north. The display on his ineffective phone tells him that it's ten o'clock, and he decides to walk for as long as he can, take a break during the worst of the day's heat and then hike some more towards the end of the afternoon. He sets himself a target of a two-hour march before he'll find a shady place to rest.

As he walks he tries to assess his situation. He realises

that up until now, his every action has been reactive: the search for survivors, supplies and essential equipment to satisfy his basic needs for human contact and sustenance; his retreat up to the hill cave to escape the carnage; his flight up the mountain and beyond to get away from the soldiers. Now, he tells himself, he needs to become proactive, to set himself goals, come up with a plan.

The armed men he's met are clearly accustomed to acts of extreme violence, opening up the fearful possibility that he's in some kind of war zone. Still, he thinks, that's just an assumption. For the moment he just needs to press on, find a town, a telephone, make contact with the nearest British embassy.

He closes his eyes and pictures the chain of events he desires, the hum of an engine in the distance, a pick-up truck slowing down, a lift in the back crouched down with sacks of grain and trussed up chickens, arrival at a police checkpoint on the outskirts of the city, handshakes for the sole survivor, a hotel with bath, cold drinks, hot food. Then a flight home, the airport reunion. He imagines Nuala's fierce embrace, the children's endless questions. He feels himself choking and chases the thoughts away. Far from providing him with comfort, they've served only to remind him how alone he is, how small and insignificant and isolated, how far he is from where he wants to be.

It's almost exactly noon and he's already been scanning his surroundings for a suitable resting place for some time when he notices a cloud of greasy grey smoke, more haze than a solid plume, way off beyond a ridge of rock a mile or so ahead.

For a moment he's rooted to the spot, torn between hope and alarm, but he dreads his current vulnerability more than any unspecified danger. Twice he's been bent double from the onset of shooting abdominal pains, twice he's been hit by waves of giddiness that he's sure are linked to the blow to his head. He's still peeing blood, feels himself weakened by the physical trauma he's experienced, knows he needs medical intervention. He's running on adrenalin and fear but knows his tank's nearly empty.

He stumbles on towards the lip of the ridge. As he crests it, he pauses to examine the terrain ahead through the binoculars he's hung around his neck. He can see the rocky ground sweeping down gently for a couple of hundred metres, then flatten out for a kilometre or so before giving way to small, barren hills. Half way along the flatland he can make out the source of the smoke clearly. What was once a small village, six or seven huts, a thorn tree and cattle kraal, is now empty, just smouldering ruins. He scans the site slowly, checking for signs of human life, but it is deserted.

It takes him twenty minutes to reach the village, a further five to inspect the huts, check for sure that they are uninhabited and find a suitable place to rest. The roofs of the huts have all been burnt away, the ochre walls scorched black by flame. One of them, the cooking hut he presumes, is littered with shattered clay pots. A fire has been lit outside it, perhaps to destroy what could not be carried off, and it is this, smouldering gently, that had first caught Greg's attention. He glances briefly at the wide circle of embers, distinguishing between the charcoal remnants twisted sculptures of unidentifiable melted plastic, fragments of scorched cloth and something which could once have been bone.

Several of the huts are still smouldering but of the others he chooses the cleanest. He leaves his bag there, then carries his blanket, rifle, crackers and a bottle of water over to the tree. He settles down, sips at the water, chews the crackers. He returns to the hut, retrieves his phone, tries again to make a call, then digs out his sketch book. He holds it for some minutes in his hands without opening it, seeking within it some distraction from his present predicament, then limps back with it to the tree.

He lies still in the shade gathering his strength, too weary to do more than hug the book to his chest. When he eventually opens it, he forces himself to skip the recent photos of Nuala and Beth and Sammy that he's slipped in the front cover for protection – he's not strong enough for those yet – and stops at the first of his sketches.

What he's looking at is a pencil drawing, a scene of dunes infinitely stretching, perpetually shifting, the swirling undulating patterns in the sand created by wind and time. It's based on a postcard, a photograph of the Grand Erg Oriental, the Tunisian Sahara. And it's this postcard, sent by Nuala on holiday in North Africa over ten years before, that has played such a crucial role in his life.

Ten years ago. He'd still been an art teacher at that time, too timid and insecure to imagine himself as a full-time artist even though he'd harboured such ambitions since childhood. But the postcard had struck a chord, set off his imagination, and from it he'd produced first one painting, then a series, a collection of desert scenes that had formed the basis for his first solo exhibition, Sand Seas, the first stepping stone that would lead to his professional career as a painter.

Gazing at the sketch, he conjures up a mental picture of the postcard and this sparks a series of associations, memories of a significant time in his life, a crossroads in his relationship with Nuala, a reminder of a moment when their bond moved from live-for-the-moment pleasure to long-term commitment. For it was after this Tunisian holiday that Nuala had agreed to marry him.

And so in the years that followed, in deference to that postcard, he's made a habit of starting each new sketchbook with a desert scene, a ritual like a cat marking his territory.

As his mind turns to Nuala, he experiences a stab of pain, and so flicks through the sketches that follow in an attempt to distract himself. The drawings are the fruits of his South African stay. He's been harbouring a vague idea to turn them into a collection, perhaps contrasting these African images with corresponding ones from Oxford. But now, surrounded by the brutal devastation, the idea seems absurd and he wonders whether there will ever be another exhibition.

He glances at the first sketch, a market scene, an attempt to represent the turmoil and chaos as the township shoppers mingled with the hawkers and traders, the page a scribbled maelstrom of activity. It was Farai's wife, Rose, who'd taken him to the marketplace to buy mealie meal and vegetables. After all, she'd said, the living need to eat. Looking up from the sketch, he pictures her grieving face and feels a biting loneliness. He turns the page quickly.

The second sketch depicts a patch of Rose's back garden cleared for vegetables, a few straggly maize plants. The third a full-length study of one of Farai's neighbours, an elderly woman, sitting shelling nuts on her stoep. He recalls the smooth crack crack crack as she removed the nuts from their husks, her delicately-lined face, her questioning eyes, seeing with annoyance that all these features he has failed to capture to his satisfaction. He turns the page in frustration.

The next three sketches are of a teapot and cups he'd drawn in Rose's kitchen, then a beerhall scene inspired by a farewell drink he'd had with Farai and his cousin, and another draft he'd made of a couple he'd observed at the club they'd gone to afterwards. The feeling of bonhomie they inspire seems so recent yet so far away.

The last sketch is a head-and-shoulders portrait of Farai and two of his offspring, Edward and Albertina. The image of family togetherness in the midst of their bereavement is poignant, and his train of thought takes him from Farai's family to his own, to Nuala and Beth and Sammy. In trying to find a few moments of relief from his current trauma, he realises he's returning to memories of what he has at least temporarily lost. It's a bitter-sweet sensation. He closes his eyes and the pages turn and he feels something close to comfort, something close to an ache.

Pull yourself together. He snaps the sketch pad shut and returns it carefully to the depths of his backpack.

He dozes, wakes, then falls into a deeper sleep. He wakes again at sunset, retreats to the protection of the hut.

He's just debating whether to hike on for a few hours or spend the night where he is when he hears a child's voice followed by the sound of an adult's rebuke. He picks up the rifle and peers through the door of the hut, careful to keep the bulk of his body concealed.

The woman's in her thirties, he guesses. She's wearing a colourful but ragged dress, a pattern of orange and lime green swirls, a matching wrap around her waist, a headscarf falling to her shoulders. The children, both primary school age, one boy, one girl, walk by her side. He's naked save for a pair of filthy shorts, she's wearing a torn pink frock. They are all bare-footed and empty-handed.

The mother pulls up by the fire and looks around hopelessly. She's muttering, her voice soft yet poignant. He reads the anguish in her gestures, sensing that it must be her home that she's fled. He tries to picture this environment as peaceful, harmonious, domestic, and wonders where the rest of her family is, who has survived, who will not return. The children's faces are stony, etched with exhaustion. He feels his presence at this scene of mourning as an intrusion. When he can bear it no longer, he clears his throat loudly and steps out of the hut.

The woman's reaction is instantaneous. She snaps out a command, turns and begins to run. It's only after she's taken several paces that she realises the children have not moved, are frozen in place. She stops, confused, turns, repeats her previous instruction, but the children, whether through fear or curiosity, remain stationary. The woman's maternal instincts win out over her terror. She takes a step back towards the young ones.

Greg is suddenly aware that he's holding a rifle. He lays it on the ground, lifts up his hands, palms open, makes no move to approach.

It's OK, it's OK. I'm not going to hurt you, he says. Don't run.

His gesture and the tone of his voice have the desired effect. No one moves. Taking this as a good sign, Greg lowers his hands.

Don't move, he says. I'm coming right back.

He backs off through the hut door and emerges a moment later with a bottle of water, uncaps it, then steps unhurriedly towards the three figures, the bottle held out in offering. At first no one moves. Then, in a lightning movement, the boy reaches out, snatches the bottles and begins gulping down the tepid liquid. The woman, grim and stern, barks a few sharp words and the boy stops, hands the bottle to his sister who takes two gulps then offers it to the woman. She gestures for her to return it to Greg. He shakes his head.

No, go on, you have it, he says.

The daughter holds it out to her mother, says something soft, soothing. The woman, her face still a mask of fierce defiance, takes the water and helps herself to a small sip. She hands it back to her daughter and gives another command, this time in a gentler tone. The daughter hands the half-empty bottle back to Greg.

Late afternoon is giving way to evening. Greg gazes past the figures at the horizon, the darkening skies streaked with the dying sunset orange. Meanwhile, the woman, now more composed, has spoken to her children again and they've disappeared.

This is your home, isn't it? he says. I'm sorry.

She looks at him, gauging his intentions from the softness in his voice, the pity in his eyes. She's still too traumatised by the events of the past day to wonder much about this white stranger. She still feels wary, but she knows her options are limited and besides, her exhaustion is overwhelming.

They've gone to fetch firewood, the children. This is my home. You can stay here tonight if you want. We have no food, I'm sorry.

Greg listens to her voice, tries to read meaning into the unfamiliar words.

I won't hurt you. It's late. I need to stay here tonight. I hope that's OK with you. We can stay together. He has a thought. Perhaps we should get some firewood. He gestures towards the smouldering fire.

The woman looks around her. The initial shock of her encounter is passing and she becomes aware of the full extent of her misfortune. She remembers the events of the attack, the life she had prior to it, what she has lost. She begins to weep.

They came at dawn, she sobs.

Are you hungry? I've got some food in my bag.

I'd woken early. Rasheed, the boy, he'd been complaining during the night about a stomach ache, so I got up before dawn to make a medicine.

I'm sorry. I'm forgetting my manners. My name's Greg. Greg.

I woke Munia, told her to go out and look for the plant we use for stomach problems. I'd seen some growing up by that hill over there. She gestures vaguely. Her weeping has stopped as she relives the events of the morning, but her voice is raw with emotion.

I've got a bit of cheese left, some crackers...

I heard the horses coming. I knew what it was at once. We live in fear of them, expect the attacks, but when it happened...

I think there might be another roll somewhere, though it'll be pretty stale by now. Still, it's better than a kick in the teeth, eh! He gives a half-hearted chuckle, an attempt at levity.

I didn't know what to do. I was torn. She begins to cry again.

I'll go and fetch it, shall I?

I grabbed them, told them to follow me. We ran and ran.

I was in an aircrash. You know, an airplane. He sticks both arms out at right angles, mimes a plane, a crash, looks up expectantly.

I left my husband, my sister-wives, their children.

I survived. Christ knows how. Amazing, eh?

Everything gone. The goats, our grain stock, all our things.

I'm just trying to get home now. I'm heading for the nearest town, anywhere that's got a telephone. He mimes holding a receiver.

And Omar, my little Omar! I've lost my little Omar! She looks around distractedly, as if expecting him to suddenly appear.

I've got a family at home. In Oxford. That's in England.

Omar! My Omar! I'd left him on my mat. He'd been grizzly all night. Teething he was, giving me hell. I just put him down while I sorted out the fire, put a pan of water on to heat up. I left him, me his mother. How could I do that?

My wife's called Nuala. I've got two kids. Just like you.

I left him. I killed him.

The boy's called Sammy. The girl's Bethany. I've got some photos in my bag. Would you like to see them?

I killed him. My own son.

She sinks down onto the ground, buries her head in her hands. He looks at her helplessly, tries to think of something useful to do, decides to fetch the food.

When he returns he finds her in the same position. His conversation has dried up. The mention of his family has rendered him silent with homesick melancholy. Her hopeless lethargy is infectious.

It's nightfall by the time the children return. Munia appears first, a pile of sticks stacked on her head. She's followed by Rasheed who is dragging a section of dead trunk. Greg produces his waterproof matches and they soon have a fire going where the earlier one had smouldered. They sit around it, passing around water, pieces of dried fruit, crackers. The woman and her children are initially dubious about the crackers, the cheese, but they are hungry and soon the food is gone. They sit in silence for a while. Greg is suddenly aware that the fire, though a warming comfort, is also a signal to outsiders.

Greg, he begins again. My name's Greg. He stabs his own chest, repeating his name several times. The others look on blankly. Munia's the first to catch on, repeats his name, then points at herself, says Munia, points at Rasheed, enunciates his name carefully. Greg repeats each name several times. For the first time, the children smile.

And you? he asks the woman. She hesitates, wonders how much she should trust this man.

I am called Asrar.

I am called Asrar, he repeats. The boy laughs, the girl

stifles a giggle.

No, Asrar. Asrar. That's my name. Asrar.

It's his turn to catch on now. He smiles.

Asrar, he pronounces carefully. Asrar, Rasheed, Munia. He points at each of his companions as he names them.

Greg, says Rasheed, pointing.

⌘

It's an interminable night for Greg. His day-time napping prevents him from sleeping now, as does his ailing body. Besides, he's worried about their exposed position, the campfire, wonders how Pol Pot and his followers are faring. He sits away from the fire, cradling the rifle in his arms, and tunes his ears to his surroundings.

The two children are soon slumbering, the blanket he's given them wrapped around their frail bodies. Asrar's sleep is more broken. She groans, tosses, calls out. Once, she thrashes so violently that she wakes herself.

Greg presses the cold barrel of his gun to his forehead. His headache seems to have shifted from temple to somewhere deep inside his head. His abdominal pain, too, has spread to his lower back. What's he got down there? he wonders. Liver? Kidneys? His knowledge of vital organs is vague, but he's certain something fairly significant is amiss.

His train of thought moves from a focus on his injuries to their root cause. His recollection of the final moments in the aircraft is still muddled, but for the first time he wonders what happened and whether they were victims of some random mechanical failure or something more sinister. But it's all still too foggy and his thoughts loop and fade and trail off without resolution.

He casts his mind back to the preceding weeks, tracing the events that led him to this place. He'd been busy preparing for his first major London exhibition, a showing of his latest collection of black and white oils at The Whitechapel. It'd been a real coup, his American agent, Burnley Welsh, had assured him.

And then he'd got the phone call from Farai, his old friend from his volunteering days in Zimbabwe, later the best man at his wedding, later still recipient of money transfers and care parcels as Zimbabwe's economy had nose-dived, until a year or so ago, when Farai had finally given up on his homeland, taken his accountancy skills across the border to Durban, then Jo'burg. Once settled, he'd brought over his family, Rose and their five children, one of whom, Robbie, had suffered his entire childhood from poorly-managed, haphazardly-treated diabetes.

Twisted irony. There in South Africa, with access at last to better medical care, Robbie's condition had suddenly worsened. Twice he'd been hospitalised, twice brought back from coma. The third time he was not so lucky. He had fallen ill in his own bed one night and was found dead by his sister the following morning. Greg had dropped everything as soon as he'd heard the news, given last-minute instructions to Burnley about the exhibition as he booked a flight, threw some clothes in a bag, said his goodbyes to Nuala and the children. He reckoned to be gone a week, enough time for the funeral and to spend a few days afterwards with his friend.

A bitter-sweet time, shouldering his burden of grief, relishing the time spent with Farai and Rose, neither of whom he'd seen for ten years, their friendship previously limited to texts, emails, the occasional phone call.

He sits by the hut and these memories roll into others, a previous life in Zimbabwe, first in a rural school, later in a township college, images of stifling classrooms, shebeen visits, shared buckets of chibuku beer, church services on Sunday. He remembers Farai's wedding to Rose, the birth of their first child, now a young man.

And from there he's back home in Britain, at the further education college in London where he and Nuala had both found teaching jobs, memories of an early London date, an Oliver Mtukudzi concert, the studio flat they'd shared before the arrival of children, Nuala's pregnancy, their world turned upside-down by parenthood. A second child. A move to Oxford. And then the decision to try and make it as a painter, Nuala selflessly shouldering the main financial responsibilities in the early years, shifting her part-time job teaching asylum-seekers and refugees at the college to full-time to maximise their income.

And then his first exhibition and, from there, the first sale of one of his paintings, a desert landscape bought by a Cotswold farmer for a hundred pounds. He recalls the children's glee when he'd announced the sale, the bottle of cheap fizzy wine he'd bought with some of the proceeds, a tipsy evening of celebration with Nuala.

He wonders whether it is a life he'll ever return to.

Eventually he dozes. He dreams of a weekend he'd spent in Brussels with Nuala before the birth of the children, the Musées Royaux Des Beaux Arts, the Christmas markets and cafés, the attic room in the bed and breakfast, the clean white sheets of the double bed, Nuala's pale skin, her flat stomach.

At dawn, Asrar shakes him awake. The children are already up, yawning and stretching.

We will go to my uncle's village, she says. It's a day's walk. He'll help us. She thinks, but doesn't say, if he's still there.

He looks at her blankly and remains sitting. She mimes walking, points off towards the barren hills, gestures for him to follow. He gets up, rummages in his bag for the last bottle of water, takes a drink and passes it round. Then he repacks his bag and picks up his rifle. He looks around the remains of the village, making a move to leave, but she stops him and points at the bag on his back, gestures for him to give it to her, pointing then at her head.

My bag? You? Oh, no, I wouldn't think of it, he says. She gestures again, this time with a trace of impatience. Reluctantly, he slips it off his shoulders. She hoists it onto her head, spends a moment redistributing the weight, finding the right balance, then says something to the children and they move off, Asrar leading, her offspring at her side, Greg bringing up the rear.

They hike the first two hours at a brisk pace set by

the woman. The children are uncomplaining, Greg dizzy with weakness, with the needling abdominal pain, struggling to keep up but anxious not to show his failings. The water's finished and his throat is parched. As if she can read his mind, Asrar calls a halt. She takes down the backpack and pulls out four of the empty bottles. She hands them to Rasheed, points off towards a ridge to their left and mutters something. He scampers off in the direction she indicated, she replaces the bag, and the three remaining figures continue on their way. Twenty minutes later Rasheed re-appears with the bottles filled. He returns three to his mother, and on her command, passes the fourth to Greg. The liquid inside is a murky brown and he examines it suspiciously. But his thirst is commanding, so he uncaps the bottle and drinks off a quarter of its contents. It's rank and brackish, but welcome nevertheless. The others take it in turns to drink, the children first, then Asrar. Revived, they continue on their way.

Greg notices how Munia collects suitable sticks of wood while they walk, building up a sizeable bundle on her head as the day progresses. He soon sinks into that trance-like daze that comes so easily when trudging through such uniform surroundings. Once, as they are passing between two rocky ridges, Rasheed lets out a whistle, points frantically at Greg's rifle and gestures towards a termite mound. Greg swivels and catches a flash of a small animal, some greyish mammal that he guesses is a type of hare. By the time he raises the rifle, the creature has long disappeared. Rasheed turns away, trying unsuccessfully to hide his disappointment.

Roused from his stupor, Greg keeps the safety catch off and tries to stay alert. An hour later, passing a clump of trees, two large birds suddenly rise up in the air, screeching out warnings in a whirl of flapping panic. Rasheed lets out an excited cry and Greg raises the rifle, aims, closes his eyes and presses the trigger. He fancies that Rasheed's expression has moved from disappointment to mild contempt.

Asrar calls a halt as the day's heat reaches its peak. They settle under a tree. This time, apart from the water, they have nothing with which to sustain themselves. The children whisper together. Asrar is distant, withdrawn. After ten minutes, Rasheed approaches Greg, taps the rifle, points at himself, mimes first an animal running, then him shooting and finally himself eating and smiling.

You want to take the gun? He is vaguely uneasy giving a gun to a child, uncomfortable about being left without protection. He feels robbed of his previous assertiveness and in his present state of alienation it seems no more absurd for this boy to be carrying a firearm than for himself to do so. He passes the gun over, as well as a handful of rounds. The boy checks the magazine, re-loads expertly, rests the firearm on his shoulder and leaves without a further word. Greg looks at Asrar for reassurance, but her face is expressionless.

Greg needs to defecate and searches through the bag for something to use as toilet paper. Out of desperation, he flicks through his sketch pad and tears out an empty page. He disappears behind a bush.

When he returns, he finds Munia flicking through the pad. She seems unimpressed by the sketches, giving them no more than cursory glances, but dwells with interest on the family photographs at the front. He sits down beside her, points to a picture of a tall, angular woman, a shoulder-length brunette with paper-white skin, an aquiline nose, grey-green eyes. She's sitting, playing at a piano.

That's Nuala. My wife.

He feels a sudden spasm of emotion, realises that he's about to cry.

Munia looks up at him, uncomprehending. Struggling, he points at the photo, at himself. Now she understands, nods.

She's a remarkable woman, you know. Played camogie for Wexford as a teenager, could have been an international. Works as a teacher now. All her students adore her, she'd do anything for them. Heart of gold, she has. Brilliant parent, too. God knows what I'd do without her. I just sort of muddle along, she's the expert. I wonder what she's doing now...

He's rambling, he knows, but it has helped him regain

his self-control. And now he's angry at himself, aware that he's been so wrapped up in his own pain that he's hasn't given a thought to what Nuala must be going through. He wonders what she knows, what she's been told. They must have found the crash site by now, he guesses. He thinks of the scattered bodies and vultures, and shudders. He looks back down at the photo.

Look. A piano. It's her passion. Jazz mostly. She does a cracking version of 'God Bless The Child'. You know, Billie Holiday. Munia examines the image silently. Of course Nuala's no stranger to Africa. She did three years in Eritrea, worked as a volunteer teacher for, what was the name... He searches his memory. It's on the tip of his tongue. APSO, that's it. Bit like Peace Corps, you know, but Irish. 'Course that was years ago. Still, that's how we met. I'd been a VSO teacher at the same time in Zimbabwe. Big conference of volunteer NGOs during the Christmas holidays in Nairobi one year. We'd both signed up for it, her for the right reasons, no doubt. Me, just an excuse for a holiday in Kenya, do the beach thing in Mombasa, the Masai Mara. We met in a doctor's surgery, her with cystitis, though she didn't tell me that until much later, me with a chest infection. My smoking days, you know. He smiles and she smiles back. Anyway, we got chatting, went for a drink. Don't think she thought much of me then. I was a bit of a tit, if truth be told. I thought I was the bee's knees. Another smile reciprocated. But God I liked her. That old cliché of an Irish beauty. Great body. And those eyes. You could lose yourself in them.

There's a moment's silence broken by the sound of a distant gunshot. Greg looks around anxiously but neither of the females seems perturbed.

She'd be great in this situation, he continues. Much better than me. She's one cool customer, if you know what I mean. Never gets flustered. Very deadpan sense of humour, quite black really. Some might call her cutting at times. She certainly doesn't bear fools gladly. But she's the kindest person I know. Bit of a contradiction, I suppose. Soft as shite, hard as nails. God, I miss her...

Apart from the picture of Nuala, there are three other photos. The first is a group portrait.

Oh look, that's one of us all together in France outside this weird grotto. We'd been visiting these amazing cave paintings there. I did a whole series of oils based on them, strange spotted horses and hand prints in really deep burnt siennas and vivid cadmium reds. He stops, realises he's wittering.

He picks up the final two photos, individual shots of his children, Sammy armed with a spade on a Mediterranean beach, Beth dressed up as a tiger, face-painted, for some school play. Again, he points at the pictures, at himself.

Those are my kids. That's Beth, he points. And that's Sammy.

Beth, she repeats. Sammy.

That's it. She's the artist, does these amazing poems too. Not the sporty type, head buried in a book all the time. She's twelve now, that awkward stage before womanhood. Munia looks down at the photo, traces Beth's head with a finger. She likes Greg's voice, finds it soothing.

We were so worried about her as a baby. She seemed so floppy, wouldn't walk when she was supposed to, just bum-shuffled everywhere. Again, the smile exchanged. Took her to all these specialists, had her doing physio, funny diet stuff, the works. Anyway, it all seemed to work out in the end.

Away in the distance, another gunshot.

Why is your daughter dressed in animal skins? Is she dancing? Munia asks suddenly, pointing to the face-painted tiger picture. It's the first time she's spoken directly to Greg. He follows her finger, guesses at the gist of her query.

Oh that? Yes, it's funny isn't it? They did 'The Jungle Book' at her school. She was what's-he-called, Shere Khan.

Munia turns her attention to the beach photo and stares intently at the sea.

That was Turkey. Great holiday. Somewhere near Marmaris. That's Sammy building the sand castle. Always big on building is our Sammy. Great at maths, too. Quick with numbers. I can see him as an engineer, though he's not that keen on school. Gets bored easily, I think. He's ten.

It's his turn to reach out, to touch the image of his son. From somewhere in the depths of his memory, he suddenly recalls Tom's bedtime ritual aged five, the glass half-filled with water, his teddy, Harry, tucked in at his side, the demands for one of Greg's own made-up stories, The Magic Fishfinger, Nyoka The Lonely Snake or The Juicy Mango Brothers. He wonders what Sammy's been told about his father's whereabouts, pictures him brushing his teeth at home in Oxford, feels a great well of tenderness. He has an overpowering urge to cry suddenly, fights to hold back the sobs, rubs away his tears. For a few minutes they sit together in silence. He feels embarrassed at his blathering, even though, as he knows, she won't have understood a word of it.

Look at me. Silly old fool. He gets up as much to conceal his distress as to stretch his cramped legs. He hears a whistle and turns to find Rasheed approaching. He's holding the rifle in his hands and has two furry objects slung over his shoulders.

Her son's arrival, and in particular his hunting booty, spurs Asrar into life. She gets up, barks orders at Munia, turns to Greg and mimes cutting. He understands, takes out his penknife and shows her how to open the biggest blade. Munia lays a fire with the sticks she's been collecting, points to it and Greg hands her the waterproof matches. Rasheed, who has been resting all this time, sipping on a bottle of water, produces a handful of large, thick leaves, some small green berries and a hefty bulbous root.

Greg watches as Asrar skins and guts the two creatures. One is definitely some kind of hare, similar to the one they've seen earlier. The other looks a bit like a badger. As the first aroma of roasted meat wafts through the air, Greg suddenly realises how ravenous he is. When the first animal is cooked, Asrar slices it up with the penknife and they chew hungrily on the sinewy flesh. Munia has meanwhile peeled and sliced the tuberous root and he tastes a piece, takes a handful of berries. He catches Rasheed's eye, smiles, giving him the thumbs up.

While they eat, Asrar adds the second animal to the fire. When it's done, she carves it up and wraps the pieces in the leaves.

Asrar seems rejuvenated. As soon as they finished eating, she douses the fire with dust, nods to Greg and the children, and sets off at a lively pace.

The next five hours are gruelling. They barely stop to rest and push on through the hottest part of the day. Greg's companions seem oblivious to the punishing temperature.

Greg is unprepared for their arrival at Asrar's uncle's village. One moment they are trudging through a particularly barren stretch of landscape seemingly far from anywhere, the next he finds himself standing in a clearing surrounded by four huts and a small kraal. He walks under the shade of a tree, waiting as Asrar walks from dwelling to dwelling. She calls out once but there's no response. Though the huts are unscathed, the roofs still intact, the clay pots at each door unbroken and the animal enclosure undamaged, the village is empty.

Greg wonders where they are, who the huts belong to, what connection they have to Asrar. He is relieved to see that whoever was here hasn't been driven out, that there are no signs of violence.

Another dusk. Munia and Rasheed disappear with empty bottles and one of the clay pots. There are some logs stacked behind one of the huts and Asrar builds a fire. She finds an abandoned aluminium pot in the kitchen hut, half fills it with water and adds the meat she's carried in the wrapped leaves. Greg stands around awkwardly, then picks up the rifle, decides to see if he can't shoot something else for the pot.

When he returns empty-handed three-quarters of an hour later, he's met by a scene of relative domestic harmony. The children have returned with more firewood, the pot and bottles filled with water, new stores of roots and berries. Asrar is tending the pot and, to Greg's surprise, he finds her deep in conversation with an elderly man dressed in white robes, a fez-type cap failing to conceal his smoky grey hair. When the man sees Greg, he stands up and shakes his hand solemnly, then gives enough of a smile to reveal the toothless gaps in his mouth.

Hello, says Greg. He points at himself. Greg.

Asrar says something to the old man, who nods.

Husham, he answers, tapping his own chest.

Greg's feet ache and he tries to remove his shoes but one of the laces is so badly knotted he cannot undo it. He decides to cut it but remembers that Asrar has not returned his penknife since she borrowed it to gut the animals Rasheed had shot. He's too exhausted to attempt to ask for it back, too tired even to try and pull off the shoe as it is. Rasheed is calling him over to the backpack and the need to relieve his sore feet passes.

Meanwhile, Husham has been explaining the situation to his niece. Earlier in the week, fearing an attack, Husham instructed two of his wives to pack up their belongings, the children, the goats, and set off on the three-day walk to the nearest displaced persons' camp. The third wife, the eldest, had been visiting her sister, who had just had a baby in a village some sixty kilometres away. He has stayed behind, waiting for her return and had been out collecting some grain from a secret store they kept outside the village when Greg and the others had arrived. He's caught up with Asrar's tragic news, and now sits away from the fire contemplating the best course of action while Asrar busies herself preparing a rudimentary porridge from the grain. Munia stirs the pot of stew and Greg shows Rasheed his compass, explaining with much gesticulation how it works. After they have eaten, as the final minutes of the day fade into darkness, Husham sits down next to Asrar.

It's not safe here now, he says

Yes, Uncle.

We need to follow the family to the camp.

You are right, Uncle

We will leave at sunrise. We'll take the rest of the porridge. We can hunt on the way with the white man's gun.

Yes, Uncle.

Later, when the fire has died down and he tires of his conversation with his niece, Husham gets up and gestures for Greg to follow him. He shows Greg into one of the huts. There's a rush mat laid out on the floor. Greg lies down, wonders how he could possibly get to sleep on such stony ground, then promptly falls into a deep slumber.

⌘

In his dream, he's under attack from Pol Pot and his bandits. They're armed with machetes, coming at him in waves, and he's trying to run away, only he can't move at any speed, it's like he's wading through dough and before he knows it, they're upon him, a vicious band of murdering butchers, and he's flailing, calling for help, but his voice is drowned out by their piercing screams and...

...and he comes around and from nightmare to reality, he's aware in an instant that they are being attacked, that the screaming is real, that it's coming from Asrar, away in her own hut, that two or three men are inside his dwelling, holding him down while they truss him up in ropes, bundle him outside, throw him down by the fire.

AMAN 2

Time here stretches like a languid cat, the facade of idleness concealing the icy menace beneath. Each day is a mirror-image of its predecessor, the same dull routine gradually chipping away at our hopes. A single event – a fight between detainees, an argument with a guard, a letter from a solicitor – can serve to differentiate between one day and the next. Your memory clouds, stupefied by the tedium, so that when a fellow inmate refers to a recent incident, you may recall the event but cannot remember whether it took place the previous day, or week or even month.

My darling, I miss you.

I watch the effects of time on those around me, observe each individual's struggle to survive, the slow decline into lunacy for some, the ability of others to cling on to their sanity. I try and calculate the techniques employed by those who are able to endure, work out which tactics ensure success.

But my research is fruitless. I cannot see any consistency in distinguishing between he who sinks and he who swims in this swamp. Some drown in their own despondency, unable to accept the hopelessness of their situation, yet for others it is only through a deliberate rejection of expectation that they can tolerate their predicament. For them it is anticipation that is too painful to bear.

And there are other contradictions. For some, it is anger – a rage against what life has thrown at them – that fuels their survival and gives them the strength to keep going day after day. Life, for them, is a personal war of attrition, so to allow themselves to become ground down is to admit defeat. For others, this anger is a destructive acid that eats away at their inner strength and poisons their mind.

And our practical approach to filling our days is another source of interest to me. There are those who retain their sanity through organised programmes designed to keep the mind busy and stimulated. They come together with like-minded individuals, arrange courses of instruction. There is Anicet, the Congolese teacher, giving lessons on Political Science, Tendai from Zimbabwe running a creative writing course, Feilong offering T'ai Chi.

And then there are the others who hang on to their mental health by deliberately deadening the mind, who see survival through a stultified existence. They train themselves to sleep for most of the day, kill what time remains in front of the TV on a diet of soap operas and reality shows. A particular favourite is *Big Brother*, and I cannot help but enjoy the irony of inmate watching inmate and wonder what pleasure the compulsory detainees can obtain from observing the voluntarily confined.

And me?

My strategy is simple. The bigger picture – my future, your whereabouts – is a daunting, unwelcoming burden, something to brush over. To focus on this is to invite the pain of despair into my already miserable existence. So I employ a two-fold plan of action.

Firstly, like the Anicets and Tendais of this institution, I concentrate on distracting my mind and filling my hours with mental stimulation. My chosen subjects are English and Islam, my textbook the American donation *Qur'an*, and my fellow student and mental sparring partner is my cell mate, Kalil. I confess that I approach my religious studies with some ignorance – your conversion to Islam was done more to satisfy my family than meet my own religious demands. I have always accepted my religion as a way of life, a characteristic of the community I grew up in, but never paid much attention to the details. Having always adhered to my father's gentle, liberal interpretation of Islam, I fancy myself as an open-minded, critical student. We shall see.

Secondly, I have decided to seek solace and distraction in the details of my existence here and of those of my fellow detainees. After my first interview with the legal aid solicitor, she asked me whether there was anything I needed, and I asked for a pen and some notebooks. She kindly brought them for me on her next visit and I am using them to record what you are now reading. Incarcerated in this prison, marginalised and forgotten by those whose lives are safe and secure, we have lost our status as human beings. We have become shadows and ghouls. In filling the notebooks with our details, I seek to return to us something of our lost stature.

Otherwise I am in good health. I continue to reduce my food intake – plain rice or bread, the occasional apple or banana, though fruit is only rarely available here. I have reacted against the milk in my tea – it bloats my stomach – so now drink it black with three or four spoonfuls of sugar. I believe it is this strong brew above all which sustains me.

⌘

Mamadu comes to see me today. He is Liberian, fled to Ivory Coast to escape the slaughter in his own country. Paid a smuggler to organise a flight to Lebanon. From there moved to Syria, then a series of long lorry rides to the UK via, among other countries, Slovakia and Germany. He tells me that his friend Joachim, an Angolan from Cabinda, has been admitted to the medical unit of the detention centre, having been found with slashed wrists early this morning. Joachim travelled from Germany with Mamadu and has been told he will be deported back there as a safe third country. His mutilation is an attempt to prevent the deportation. Mamadu says his condition is stable. It is lucky he did not cut himself at the weekend as they close the centre's clinic from Friday afternoon to Monday morning, so self-harm during those hours is frowned upon.

⌘

I wake before dawn, rouse my cellmate, Kalil. We carry out our ablutions in silence, then side by side in brotherly union we kneel together in prayer.

While we wait to be called for our morning meal, let me draw you a picture of my place of abode. The centre is divided into three sections, one for administration, one for the prison officers and one for the detainees. The inmates' accommodation is itself divided into three blocks named blue, red and yellow, though underneath the garish primary colours, the buildings are all dour grey breezeblock.

The routine here is unchanging: breakfast from 7.30 to 9.30, lunch between 12.00 and 1.30, dinner between 5.00 and 6.30. Food is poor quality, poorly prepared. Like everything about this place, the menu is designed to make us feel ill at ease and to persuade us that a departure from this country would be desirable. To drive us away.

The facilities are limited: a poorly-stocked and badly-neglected library with two computers, neither of which is connected to the internet. There are four PC games featuring runaway rabbits, car chases and snooker tournaments. The library is open most of the day, as are the three TV rooms, though channels are censored and restricted to sports, music videos and reality TV. The sports hall features a ping pong table and a volleyball net as well as what is grandly called a mini gym – a running machine and set of weights. Outside there is a courtyard used for listless football kickabouts.

Maintenance and upkeep are minimal. The few cleaning staff who are employed seem to be issued with nothing more than a mop and bucket. No bleach is employed in the mopping process, no disinfectant used for lavatories, sinks and showers. When toilets leak or block, weeks pass before repairs are carried out. Their stench is a permanent feature of our existence.

The medical facilities are negligible, a token practitioner offering only two items on his menu, paracetamol or antidepressants.

They craft our pain with one hand, relieve it with the other.

⌘

Yesterday a visit from a Red Cross representative. She is tasked with tracing missing relatives and goes around systematically checking whether any detainee would like her to instigate a search. I am in a quandary. I am desperate to use this service but am unsure what to reveal of my story. The name I am using here is the one indicated on the passport I bought in Libya. To admit to the falsity of my identity would, I feel, be to lose all credibility in the eyes of the authorities. Yet I cannot lose the opportunity to find you, my love, so I obtain an interview with the woman, give her your name, that of the children, tell her you are a cousin, last surviving member of my extended family. I weave a story, half true, to provide a context to our separation. She tells me she will contact me within a fortnight with any news. The feelings of anticipation as I return to my cell are at once exhilarating and terrifying. A sleepless night follows.

⌘

I continue with my Islamic schooling. I remember how studious you were, how seriously you took your responsibility to transform yourself from kafir to Muslim, poring over each Surah, stumbling over the Ayat, then, once you had memorised the *Qur'an*, attempting to master the Hadith. Today Kalil and I work our way through the second Surah, *Al Baqarah*. We read in 2:39:

> ...*those who reject Faith*
> *And belie Our Signs*
> *They shall be Companions of the Fire;*
> *They shall abide therein.*

And then, thinking of you, we reach 2:62 and the passage offering salvation for those unbelievers that convert to Islam. As we talk I notice a streak of impatience in Kalil's attitude.

For him the world is black and white and Islam offers a set of instructions which, if stuck to rigidly, will earn you the prize you seek. I argue that it is less the formalities of religion that count, and more one's faith. He is fixed on the ordinances of Islam, while I focus on attitudes: compassion, charity, patience, integrity and tolerance.

We work our way through the rest of the Surah, read about the torments and humiliation awaiting those who reject Allah. Again, my thoughts turn to you, my flower. I ask myself whether there was any fundamental difference between you as Christian or you as Muslim. Did you change when you converted? Did you become a better person? If you ever rejected your new-found faith, how evil would you become?

We take a break from our studies. Kalil produces an orange, peels it and shares out the segments. As we chew on the sweet-tart fruit, wiping our sticky hands on our sleeves, Kalil tells me that his interest in Islam is also fairly recent, that it has grown while in detention through contact with so many believing detainees.

He tells me of a Somali he met in the medical ward at Dungavel Asylum Prison in Scotland, a young man in his twenties who had broken his spine trying to escape but whose spirit was sustained through his faith. While we talk we are joined by two more detainees, Howar and Zaki. We swap stories of those we have met in detention, some who have shown great resilience, others who have faltered. Zaki tells of a Kenyan he knew in HMP Rochester who endured fifteen months of misery before setting himself on fire. Howar describes the mental decline of an Egyptian he shared a cell with in Great Dunmow, a placid and sweet-natured man who was discovered hanged from the roof early one morning.

When our visitors leave, we return to our studies. The hints of Kalil's inner anger have grown since our talk of our suffering colleagues, and, back in the second Surah, Kalil's eyes fall straight on 2:190:

> *Fight in the cause of Allah*
> *Those who fight you.*

There you are, he says excitedly. They treat us like dogs and we sit around like sheep, not knowing what to do. The answer is here, plain to see.

I shake my head. I ask him whether he really believes that we are all here because our religion has been targeted. He shrugs, says nothing. We read on and when we have finished the next Ayah, I point out that the words do not advocate violence except in self-defence.

> But fight them not
> At the Sacred Mosque,
> Unless they first
> Fight you there;

And even when you are fighting in self-defence, your response should be in moderation, I continue. That Ayah you have just quoted. You only read the first half. Look at the last two lines.

> But do not transgress limits;
> For Allah loveth not transgressors

Yes, he says. But read on. Look at 2:194:

> If then anyone transgresses
> The prohibition against you,
> Transgress ye likewise
> Against him.

Kalil's eyes are bright, his voice animated. Again, I shake my head.

Finish the Ayah, I say, pointing with my finger at the next three lines.

> But fear Allah, and know
> That Allah is with those
> Who restrain themselves.

Yes, but... he starts to argue. I interrupt him.

Read on. Look at 2:195:

> And make not your own hands
> Contribute to your destruction;
> But do good,
> For Allah loveth those
> Who do good.

Sure, he says. But there is more. Keep going.

I read the next Ayah.

Fighting is prescribed
Upon you, and ye dislike it.
But it is possible
That ye dislike a thing
Which is good for you
And that ye love a thing
Which is bad for you
But Allah knoweth
And ye know not.

OK, I say. So all that means is that there may be some situations where, out of self-defence, you may be forced to fight, whether you like it or not.

Maybe we should stop waiting to be attacked, he says. Maybe it is time to go on the offensive. He quotes 2:244, the one about fighting in the cause of Allah.

You are crazy, I say, slapping him on the shoulder. Allah advocates tolerance between peoples, not war. 2:256, I quote back:

Let there be no compulsion
In religion.

Kalil has grown silent. He stares hard at me, his eyes cold and penetrating. I make one last effort. Allah is no bloodthirsty tyrant, my friend, I say with an attempt at levity. Remember the earlier Ayah:

For Allah is to all people
Most surely full of kindness,
Most merciful.

He looks at me for a few moments longer, then nods and smiles. Sure, he says. Of course. And with that, our study period comes to an end.

⌘

I continue to carry out the Salah dutifully, but confess that sometimes when I pray I have a feeling that no one is listening to me. I must rid myself of these negative thoughts.

Every day I wake up in anticipation of a visit from the Red Cross worker. Three weeks have passed, maybe a month. No news. Hope trickles away like sand through my fingers. I grow weaker. My memory is becoming hazy. I sometimes wonder whether my past life was just a dream, a delusion.

⌘

Days turn to weeks. We live in limbo, our lives frozen in time and space. My studies provide the only distraction. Little by little I commit the *Qur'an* to memory.

⌘

Today at breakfast I hear news of Kudzai, a Zimbabwean barely out of his teens who has been sharing a neighbouring cell. He has already spent months in Colnbrook before being transferred here. I am told he tried to commit suicide there by swallowing a whole bottle of shampoo.

I do not know much about his past, what demons haunt his memories, but we have all been aware that his slow slide into depression has recently accelerated with almost daily panic attacks. We have become accustomed to his pain, our nights punctuated with his tortured wailing. Mustafa, his cellmate, tells me his spirit has finally broken, that yesterday he agreed to voluntary deportation, that he has already been whisked out before he comes to his senses and changes his mind.

⌘

Our *Qur'anic* studies continue. Sometimes we work through the book, Surah to Surah, in a linear fashion. Sometimes we pick a theme and research Allah's message within his work as a whole. Always there is the verbal sparring, the contrast between our interpretations: Kalil's dogmatic austerity; my own more relaxed moderation.

⌘

The word has spread among detainees about my record-keeping. They seek me out in ones and twos, sit down awkwardly beside me and, at first with some hesitancy and then with increasing animation, they open up to me with their own personal histories. In one of my notebooks I record everything. I change their names but omit nothing else in their individual journeys. It is all there: war, torture, loss of family and loved ones, flight, arrival, suspicion, rejection, abandonment and neglect. The themes remain the same, only the details differ.

We communicate in whatever lingua franca is appropriate, usually either Arabic or broken English. I never prompt them, never ask questions, seek clarification or explanation. My job is to record, nothing more.

⌘

Sometimes our study group expands as we are joined by fellow detainees. Today I am sitting with Solly, a Nigerian and veteran of UK asylum hospitality. He has been shunted from HMP Rochester, where two wings are set aside for immigration detainees, through Haslar and Belmarsh before ending up here.

We are waiting for Kalil to return from accompanying a Somali neighbour to the showers. The Somali, a fellow named Saleh, complained of a toothache last week and demanded to see a doctor. When his request was refused, he began protesting loudly. He was taken off by guards and given a severe beating. Since then he remains in his cell, too afraid to venture out anywhere unless accompanied by other inmates.

Earlier, I have a funny turn when returning from the library and collapse in the corridor. I am carried back to my cell by Solly and Pierre-Philippe, a Congolese nurse transferred from Harmondsworth last month. I drink some water while Pierre-Philippe checks me over. He asks me what I have eaten over the last couple of days and comments on my skinny physique. It is true that I have lost weight since my arrival here, and I start to tell him about the bloating and nausea I feel when I take food, but the words will not come out properly and I only rally after he leaves and we are joined by another detainee, Soran. He squats down on the floor, asks me to record his story.

Deserting the army to avoid conscription in his country, he hid close to his family's farm and so witnessed the soldiers' revenge torture and abduction of his father. Fearing for her son, his mother then sold the house and her wedding gold and used the money to pay smugglers to traffic him out of the country. The precise details of his journey are, as usual, hazy, but it took him through Turkey and Italy and he entered the UK via the Channel Tunnel. The smugglers charged $9,000.

After agreeing a pseudonym for Soran, I record the details, and when he has re-read my notes he nods and makes to leave. At the cell door, he stops and tells me that he has forgotten something. He points to his mouth and for the first time I see small dark dots, like pin pricks, above his upper lip and below the lower one. He explains that after eight months in detention, he and two other inmates sewed their lips together in protest at the delay in dealing with their cases. I hesitate and wait for him to say more. I try to imagine him preparing the needle and thread, the first stitch. I want to ask how the situation was resolved but have to keep to my role of passive recorder. He asks me to add this new information but offers no further details.

Another visitor arrives, a middle-aged Chinese man from Xinjiang. He is a Muslim Uighur but his English is poor and we have no other shared language, so communication is difficult. He arrives clutching a copy of the *Qur'an*, as always. He never opens it, simply strokes the cover from time to time. I suspect he cannot read it at all. I ask him about his journey to Britain and he mentions Pakistan, Turkey and France. He is unable to explain further but understands that Solly and I are meeting to discuss Islam. He clearly finds that thought soothing, so he remains seated in the corner of my cell as our discussions develop. He contributes nothing, keeps his eyes closed as his hand brushes the cover of his book.

Solly is a recent convert and I am giving him a lesson in the fundamentals of Islam as I understand them. I tell him what I explained to you all those years ago when we first discussed your conversion to my faith.

I draw three circles, each one inside the other. I explain that what is written down in the *Qur'an* is what was remembered of the Prophet's words by his companions, the Ashab. This knowledge is represented by the inner circle and carries most weight in theological discussions.

The next circle represents the testimony given and recorded by the Tabi'un, the next generation of people who had spoken to the Ashab but not personally to the Prophet. I tell him that this evidence, the Hadith, refers to reports about the statements and actions of the Prophet, as well as his approval of something said or done in his presence. Although integral to an understanding of Islam, it is not considered to be direct communication from God.

Finally I show him that the final outer circle represents the Tafsir, a vast quantity of commentary and analysis built up over the centuries by theologians that seeks to explain the true meaning of Islam.

As I reach the end of my explanation, we are interrupted by Kalil's return. He is bristling with anger and the atmosphere in the cell is transformed from calm study to aggressive resentment in an instant. Even the Uighur, who has been dozing in his corner, senses the tension. He sits up clutching his *Qur'an* anxiously.

Bastards, Kalil begins, as soon as he has sat down next to me on the edge of the bed. They treat us like animals, like dogs. But dogs have teeth and by God I will use mine on them one day.

Be calm, brother, I tell him. If the guards have done wrong, God will punish them. Remember yesterday's Surah – *'Allah is swift in calling to account'*.

My words, designed to soothe Kalil, seem to have the opposite effect. He dives for the copy of the *Qur'an*, flicks through the pages furiously searching for the passages I am referring to.

Brother, have you ever thought that maybe Allah wants us to be his tools to call those sinners to account? he suggests. He sighs with satisfaction as he finds what he is looking for. Here you are, Surah 47:4:

...if it
Had been Allah's will
He could certainly have exacted
Retribution from them Himself
But he lets you fight
In order to test you.

I take the Holy Book from him, flick ahead a few pages.

48:14, I begin. Listen well, Brother:
He forgives whom He wills
And he punishes whom He
Wills: but Allah is
Oft-forgiving, Most merciful.

You see, leave the judgement of others to Allah and just concentrate instead on your own behaviour and spiritual health. That is what Allah asks of you, I tell him.

No, no no, you are wrong, Kalil answers excitedly. The *Qur'an* is a manual, a set of instructions, a 'How To' book explaining what constitutes an exemplary life, what rules and regulations need to be upheld. Our job is to fight to implement those rules, to battle those who do not respect them, not to sit around and wait for things to happen.

He finds a page, begins to quote again:
Allah had decreed:
'It is I and My messengers
Who must prevail':
For Allah is One
Full of strength,
Able to enforce His Will.

Don't you see, he says. We are His messengers. He wants us to act for Him, to help Him enforce His will.

I sigh, shake my head. This seems to infuriate Kalil.

Tell me, brother, he asks. What, for you, are the key characteristics of Islam?

I hesitate, give myself time to consider. I think of you and it strikes me how so often during my theological discussions with Kalil, I find that my own ideas only become clear when I ask myself what you would think, what position you would take.

Love, I say. Love and kindness and charity.

It is his turn to shake his head. You are soft and naïve, brother, he begins. The rest of the world has always hated Islam. Allah has called us to fight, we are his soldiers. Read Surah 61, *Al Saff*:

> *Truly Allah loves those*
> *Who fight in His Cause*

You are wrong, brother, I reply. You take these quotes out of context, poison His message. All your talk of jihad is based on the idea of a battle against others. Real jihad is a battle with yourself. A battle against temptation, against avarice and selfishness and aggression. Read Surah 109, *Al Kafirun*, I counter. It is a message of tolerance:

> *To you be your Way*
> *And to me mine*

Be careful, my friend, says Kalil. There is only one true way:

> *It is He Who has sent*
> *His messenger with Guidance*
> *And the Religion of Truth,*
> *That he may proclaim it*
> *Over all religion,*
> *Even though the Pagans*
> *May detest it. 61:9*

There is no middle way, no opting out. Either they are with us or against us. If the kafirs reject our message, Allah's message, there will be no mercy. 63:6, he reads:

> *It is equal to them*
> *Whether thou pray for*
> *Their forgiveness or not.*

Allah will not forgive them.

I feel myself growing dizzy again. I cannot face up to his storm of bile. I want to take Kalil in my arms, draw out his venom and replace it with my vision of tenderness and devotion. But he is like a man possessed, his words spat like gunfire, addressed to me, yet beyond me, a declaration of war. I want it to end, but cannot halt the flow. All I can do is struggle to return fire.

He continues:

First Allah commands us to fight. In 3:151 He says,

Soon shall We cast terror
Into the hearts of the Unbelievers

Then he offers us salvation if we die in the struggle. Read 3:169:

Think not of those
Who are slain in Allah's way
As dead. Nay, they live.

How can I make him see that he has twisted Allah's licence for self-defence into this declaration of war? I return:

If one exhorts to a deed
Of charity or justice
Or conciliation between men...
To him who does this,
Seeking the good pleasure
of Allah. We shall soon give
A reward of the highest value. 4:114

But he is beyond reason, and he counters in a flash, his words like a battering ram:

To him who fighteth
In the cause of Allah
Whether he is slain
Or gets victory
Soon shall we give him
A reward of great value. 4:74

I reply:

Take not life, which Allah
Hath made sacred
Except by way of justice and law. 6:151

But it is no good. I realise that Solly and the Uighar have left but cannot recall their departure. I try to summon your presence, my dear, a vain hope that you can somehow inspire in me the necessary eloquence to turn Kalil away from his poisonous path, but even you have abandoned me for the moment.

I feel myself slipping away, a wave of weakness overwhelms me, and as I slump forward and fall crashing to the concrete floor, all I can hear are Kalil's strident tones:

Fight them, and Allah will
Punish them by your hands,
Cover them with shame
Help you to victory over them.

⌘

I am alone now. The others have gone to dinner but I am too feeble to make the journey to the canteen. Kalil says he is worried about me. He tells me to visit the doctor tomorrow and I tell him I will, if only to keep the peace. He has offered to bring me back some food but I know the guards will refuse – it is against regulations. In any case, I am not hungry. I will finish these notes, then seek escape in sleep.

⌘

No word from the Red Cross lady. My thoughts too bleak to share on this page. What am I becoming?

⌘

Weeks have passed, maybe months. I have returned from breakfast where I used my usual cup of sweet black tea to swallow my medication, the red and green capsules which I have been taking ever since I was dragged to the medical centre by Kalil all those weeks ago.

The first time I took them, I returned to my cell, lay

down, then slept for two days. Now my tolerance has grown. I feel permanently drowsy and find myself dozing off from time to time, but I no longer sleep all day. The pills help smooth the jagged edges of my life here.

I still record the detainees' details. Earlier this morning I have listened to Sayed's story. Having endured five years of poverty and discrimination as a refugee in Iran, this Afghani borrowed enough money from smugglers to buy a tourist's stolen passport and bribe immigration officers to allow him across the Turkish border. The traffickers forced him to agree to allow his uncle to remain a hostage until the debt was paid. Unfortunately he did not apply for asylum at his port of entry in Britain and so spent three months homeless, unable to obtain any financial support from the authorities. He has lost two toes to frostbite. He worries about his uncle and finds escape in the same red and green pills.

⌘

More detainees' details, more misfortune. Tamils, Chechens, Cameroonians, Kurds, Zimbabweans, Chinese, Afghans, Liberians, Sudanese, Guineans and Kashmiris. Misery does not discriminate.

⌘

Kalil takes an interest in the other inmates' stories, but has never volunteered one of his own. It strikes me that I know next to nothing about him, not even where he comes from. His history is a black hole.

⌘

I sit on my bed and browse the *Qur'an*. Today I read Surah 12, *Yusuf*, about this young man and his ten half-brothers who sell him into slavery in Egypt. It is a message of forgiveness and mercy, and I make a mental note to discuss it with Kalil, though in reality I know that I will not. We still have our study sessions, still work our way through the *Qur'an*, but I can no longer muster the strength to counter his warmongering and find myself submitting to his twisted vision of the world. Instead, like a mantra, I recite in my head an Ayah from Surah 22, *Al Hajj*:

> *... establish*
> *Regular prayer and give*
> *Regular charity; enjoin*
> *The right and forbid wrong*

It is a remedy, an antidote to his poison. Lacking the strength to continue with the verbal cut and thrust, I continue my side of the argument within the pages of my notebook, a section at the back I have dedicated to my own vision. Today I add some new quotations:

> *... avert Evil with Good* 28:54

and,

> *Nor can Goodness and Evil*
> *Be equal. Repel Evil*
> *With what is better:*
> *Then will he between whom*
> *And thee was hatred*
> *Become as it were*
> *Thy friend and intimate!* 41:34

and then,

> *And no one will be*
> *Granted such goodness*
> *Except those who exercise*
> *Patience and self-restraint.* 41:35

I close my notebook. What began as a way to improve our English and keep our brains from fossilising has now become a battle of wits that I am too crushed to take any further part in.

When Kalil enters I can see straight away that he is enraged. A fight has broken out between some of his friends and a group of Jamaicans, the only detainees feared by the guards. All those involved have been rounded up, the Jamaicans merely locked up in their cells but his friends given a beating. In Kalil's eyes it is another case of blatant religious persecution.

I listen with half an ear as he rants, until, his voice hoarse, he throws himself dejectedly onto my bed. With weary resignation, I see he is in a combative mood and that he requires my participation, or presence at least, in another bout of sparring.

We need to unite to be strong, he begins. The Ummah brotherhood is what binds Muslim to Muslim. When we forget that, we risk Allah's wrath.

> *Muhammad is the Messenger*
> *Of Allah; and those who are*
> *With him are strong*
> *Against Unbelievers, but*
> *Compassionate amongst each other* 48:29

Allah talks of a brotherhood of Muslims for constructive development, not war, I begin to explain, recalling a discussion we once had together, my sweet. For charity, to help disadvantaged Muslims, to build schools and hospitals where there are none, to share what we have and prevent suffering among our fellow men. That is what Ummah means. Allah's message is one of non-aggression. Read 43:89. He says that when you meet a non-Muslim,

> *But turn away from them,*
> *And say 'Peace!'*

You are too passive, brother, he tells me. You confuse reconciliation and weakness. Listen:

> *Be not weary and*
> *Fainthearted, crying for peace,*
> *When ye should be*
> *Uppermost* 47:35

He is building up a head of steam, but today, feeling your presence at my side, I am steadfast.

As always, you confuse self-defence with all-out war, I tell him. Read Surah 42 – *Al Shura*. Evil is cured by the mercy and guidance of Allah, not by a doubling of evil. The key is patience and negotiation. If you commit acts of aggression, they will return to you with interest. I quote:

> *Whatever misfortune*
> *Happens to you, is because*
> *Of the things your hands*
> *Have wrought.* 42:30

Kalil is silent. He sits on the bed, sullen and bitter, then gets up and stands by the barred window, staring out onto the greasy tarmac courtyard below. It has been raining but the drizzle has stopped and the clouds are now clearing. Between the grey concrete walls and the blue sky above, the razor wire gleams in the weak sunshine. Minutes pass. Then he turns, sweeps past me and out of the cell.

I have to think, he mutters.

⌘

I find an extract from a Surah, 113:1-3:

> *Say: I seek refuge*
> *With the Lord of the Dawn,*
> *From the mischief*
> *Of created things;*
> *From the mischief*
> *Of Darkness as it overspreads*

I am not sure exactly what it means, but it is calming, like a cool cloth placed on my fevered brow.

⌘

I want to tell Kalil that his mistake is to think that his enemy's enemy is his friend. There will always be warped men who not only think that violence is the solution to all problems, but who positively thrive on it. They lust after bloodshed and cruelty. Just because they call themselves Muslim and do not like this or that – whether it be American politics or Hindu discrimination or semi-naked pop singers – and you agree with them on some or all of those things, it does not mean you share a common ideology. Even if there was no Islam, no America, no Hindus or pop princesses, those men would still be full of poison, still find a reason to kill and maim, still find a twisted cause.

It is time for my pills.

⌘

I read Surah 96 *Al Alaq*. I want to tell Kalil that every Muslim's true enemy is himself – his own obstinacy, vanity and insolence. That is the real struggle.

⌘

Kalil sweeps into the cell today. His eyes flash with repressed excitement.

Brother, it has come to me, the true message of the *Qur'an*. I have found the way. Before, I was a fool, stumbling like a baby in a darkened room, but it is as if a blindfold has been removed.

Mmm, I say half-heartedly. I am loathe to embark on further verbal combat, but can sense that he is not to be put off.

You always tell me that that wrong-doers will end up in Hell. You say the *Qur'an* teaches us to be patient, that Fire awaits them in the Hereafter, that sinners will eventually join the Companions of the Fire. What if you are wrong? What if Allah is not advocating patience? What if the Fire is not in the Hereafter? What if it is in the here and now? Don't you see, we are not supposed to wait for sinners to go to the Fire, we are supposed to bring the Fire to the sinners? Read 74:31:

... *we have set none*
But angels as guardians
Of the Fire;

Don't you get it? That's us, we are the angels, the guardians of the Fire.

His voice has risen, strident with authority.

What are you talking about? I protest. You must be...

No, listen, brother. The *Qur'an* teaches two key messages. First, the sinner must be punished. Remember 5:45:

Life for life, eye for eye,
Nose for nose, ear for ear,
Tooth for tooth, and wounds
Equal for equal.

Secondly, his punishment is in our hands. Allah calls on us to carry out his vengeance. It is our duty, our responsibility to deal with the sinner. 96:18:

We will call
On the angels of punishment
To deal with him

That's us, my friend, he concludes, his tone triumphant. We are the angels of punishment. We are the Companions of the Fire.

I shake my head. I don't know where to begin, how to counter his barrage of perverted inspiration.

You must learn to interpret His message to reveal the true meaning, he says with calm self-assurance. It is just a question of interpretation.

No, my friend, I answer wearily. It is a question of corruption.

⌘

I read Surah 94, *Al Sharh*. My eyes fall on Ayah 94:5. I lie on my bed and chant the Ayah over and over again:

With every difficulty
There is relief

If I say it enough times, perhaps it will come true.

⌘

There is no more strength in my bones. I have grown fatalistic. I no longer think 'What should I do?' not even 'What will happen to me?' Now I just bide my time, wait for my fate to be decided. When I pick up the *Qur'an* now, I read only the passages that deal with Judgement Day. I have surrendered. Retribution?

Reward? I will leave it to Allah, it is easier that way.

Some will be
In the Garden, and some
In the Blazing Fire. 42:7

I have made a list in my notebook of those soothing verses that deal with Judgement: *Al Mutaffifin* and *Al Inshiqaq*, *Al Buruj* and *Al Tariq*, *Al Zalzalah* and *Al Qari'ah* and *Al Asr*.

If this notebook ever falls into your hands, my love, read these and think of me. They are my food and drink. I need nothing more.

⌘

I take my pills, read my passages. The future is over. All I have to look forward to is the past.

NUALA 1

The instant she hears the news of the crash, her life divides into a Before and an After. It's mid-morning and she's teaching in a third-floor classroom working through a newspaper article on knife crime in Britain when there's a knock and one of her part-time colleagues, Fran, pushes open the door and enters. Nuala doesn't stop speaking at once, finishes her explanation, but then pauses and smiles at her colleague as if to say, 'OK, over to you.' She's expecting Fran to have a message for the students, a reminder of a lunchtime meeting to sign bus pass forms perhaps, or a request for them to bring in their Home Office documentation. But Fran's still not speaking, and when Nuala looks more closely at her, she can see that she's in some kind of discomfort, that something is not right.

Can I have a word, Nuala? she says. Outside.

Out in the corridor, Fran seems a little more composed.

What's the matter? asks Nuala. If you had asked her at that instant what she was expecting to hear, she'd still have said that it was an everyday message to be delivered, perhaps to one particular student and therefore a little more sensitive, not to be repeated in front of the other class members. The worst scenario she could have imagined would have involved Sammy banging his head in the playground or Beth taken ill in class, a phone message to come and collect one or the other from the school secretary's office.

There are two police officers in the staffroom, Nuala. They want to see you.

Her words are so unexpected that Nuala opens her mouth and stands there gaping for some seconds. Her brain's working frantically, processing the words, trying to make sense of their meaning. When she finally grasps the situation, she takes a few steps forward, remembers her abandoned class, stops and teeters there uncertainly.

It's OK, I'll sit in with your class, says Fran.

Even as she descends the staircase, taking the steps three at a time, the irreversible Before/After process has begun. She feels a little giddy, the beginnings of the sensation that she'll experience in the coming weeks, time out of joint, neither here nor there, an otherworldly dislocation. Her mouth is dry, she experiences a fluttering of panic in her stomach, as if she is about to be tested.

⌘

In the weeks that follow, Nuala experiences a recurring dream, the same knock on the door of her third-floor classroom, but this time she's partially forewarned. She knows that the person outside the door is the bearer of cataclysmic news, that she must avoid allowing the person to enter, must break the chain of events. So she carries on her teaching and pays no attention to the knocking that grows ever more insistent. The students in the class begin to call out, they're pointing at the door, but she knows that to acknowledge the intruder would be fatal, so she raises her voice, ignores their signals, the unrelenting tapping. The scene grows ever more frantic, the students shouting and screaming, some seem greatly alarmed, others highly amused. The hammering at the door is unremitting, part of her knows she'll have to open up, another part would rather die than yield, and she wakes in a cold sweat, feeling the coiled fist of dread in her stomach, a tightness in her chest and throat.

⌘

How much of the next two hours can Nuala remember? As she steps into the staffroom, she glances out of the window and notices first that there is a policewoman out in the courtyard holding a walkie talkie to her ear. She turns back and finds herself face to face with a uniformed constable, middle-aged and burly. She remembers the stubble on the back of his neck, his nasal hair, his soft Oxford intonation. He's understanding, has plenty of experience of dealing with the confusing effects of shock on ordinary folk. He explains what he's been told, repeats it all twice more, patient and calm, as she struggles to take in the news. Little by little the key concepts filter through: plane crash... your husband's name on the passenger list ... uncertain of exact location... no confirmation of casualties... emergency phone number... wait for more news...

Nuala sits down at her desk. The policeman, practised in such situations, leaves her to absorb this information and busies himself with the kettle. Soon Nuala finds a cup of sugary tea on the desk in front of her.

The policeman is considering his next step. He'd like his female colleague to get Nuala home – always best to have a woman on hand in these delicate situations – but they are both due to give evidence at the magistrate's court at twelve, a case of domestic violence. He's done his bit, given the lady the news and she seems to be taking it quite calmly. Ideally, one of her colleagues could take her home and sit with her for a bit while she composes herself, phones her family or sets in motion whatever coping mechanism she chooses. But there are no colleagues around, they all seem to be teaching in their classrooms.

Just then, a solution. There's a growing commotion outside the staffroom as classes stop for the morning coffee break and students make their way out of the building, head for the canteen or the smoking area. First one colleague enters the staffroom, then a second and third. They have not been warned about the policeman's presence and know nothing of the reason for his appearance.

Nuala is holding her cup of tea in her hand absent-mindedly, still trying to process the information she's been handed. The police officer takes the opportunity to draw the other teachers aside, to tell them the news and appeal for a volunteer to take Nuala home. There's no shortage of willing helpers, and after some discussion they decide that Teri will bring Nuala back. She has a car and is probably Nuala's closest work friend.

Nuala is unaware of all of this, still struggling to digest, to formulate a coherent response. As she's led out to Teri's hatchback, her first reaction is to head straight for her children's school, to haul Beth and Sammy out and gather them close to her. But she knows this is silly, that they will have their own Before/After moments to face and that the longer they postpone that experience, the better.

It's only when Nuala gets through her own door that she feels a little more galvanised. At Teri's suggestion, she makes a list of people to contact. At the top of the list are her own parents in Wexford, her sisters in Dublin, the brother in Cork, Greg's father in Leeds, his sister in Bristol and brother in Huddersfield. Teri gets her settled in an armchair, produces another cup of tea and hands her the phone. The next sixty minutes are spent repeating to these people what little information she's been given. She finds it easier to talk about the news than to think about it, and each time she repeats the details they seem more distanced. Everyone's reaction is similar – initial shock, then expressions of hope.

One after the other, her relatives and friends offer to come straight to Oxford, to stay with her, and each time she politely refuses. You're at the end of a phone line, she tells each of them. If I need anything, I'll be sure to ask. In the meantime, she has her children to look after, she explains. She'll have her hands full helping them over the coming days.

She's made six or seven calls and now she stops to take stock. In her trouser pocket she has the card with the emergency number that the policeman gave her. She takes it out. She has a sudden urge to fly out to Africa, to be close to where Greg has gone missing. She dials the number. The female voice that answers is mellifluous, the lilting Geordie tones reassuring. Nuala is asked a number of security questions – names, dates of birth, postcode – before she satisfies the speaker that she is who she claims to be. There's some new information, she's told. They've managed to pinpoint the position of impact using the plane's emergency locator transmitter. The woman tells Nuala the name of the country, of the area too. Nuala scrabbles around for a pen, writes down this detail. Meanwhile the woman is telling her that the story has already broken on national news, so she may be contacted by journalists once they get hold of the passenger list. The speaker advises Nuala to say nothing to the media, then takes Nuala's contact details, promises to call as soon as they learn anything new. It's only when she hangs up that Nuala realises she doesn't even know who she's been talking to.

Nuala checks the time, suddenly panicking that the children will need picking up from school. It's not yet two o'clock. Teri's trying hard to conceal the fact that she needs to be somewhere else, and Nuala feels an abrupt desire to be alone so she puts her out of her misery. She tells her she'd like to lie down, that she'll be fine. Teri promises to call in the evening, then makes her exit.

The phone rings. It's her line manager, Feroza. She'd been away at a meeting when the police had visited the staffroom, is phoning to find out if Nuala has had any further news. She isn't expecting Nuala back at work in the foreseeable future, she tells her, and has already organised cover for her classes. She should, of course, take as much time off as she needs. Nuala thanks her and hangs up.

No sooner has she replaced the phone than it begins chirruping again. This time it's a representative from the airline, a man's voice, a slight drawl, a long-exiled Aussie or Kiwi, she guesses. She tries to take in what he's saying but a paralysing shock is creeping in, it's information overload, and besides, it soon becomes clear that this man knows nothing that she doesn't. He is merely making contact, a supposed reassurance that the company will do all it can to assist the families of all those involved in the accident.

The standard procedure, he tells her, is for all close relatives of the passengers to be brought to a central location in London where they can be fed the news directly by the authorities, shielded from media intrusion. She is invited to join the others.

The thought of imminent travel helps pull Nuala's mind back from paralysis. She considers this offer. She's torn between a desire to protect Beth and Sammy and the urge to fly straight out to the crash site. This proposal seems to satisfy neither of these demands.

She can hear the man's breathing at the other end of the line.

For the first time that day she feels a needling twinge of frustration, a need to rebel. She tells him she wants to stay at home for the time being, asks him to arrange a flight out, that she will ask a relative to take care of the children at her own home. He seems momentarily flummoxed, uncertain how to respond. He promises to talk to his superiors and get back to her as soon as he gets a response. In the meantime, if she is unwilling to come to the central London rendezvous, he asks her to remain at her house and promises that they will contact her as soon as they receive any further news.

This time, when she puts the phone down the silence that descends is prolonged, and Nuala is forced for the first time to face up to the calamity that is unfolding.

She tries to conjure up the last time she saw Greg, her last conversation with him on the phone. He has been gone a week, but she's picked up snippets of his news through texting and hurried calls on his mobile. He's given her a brief description of Robbie's funeral and they've talked about how Farai and Rose are coping.

But now her mind is muddled and she can't even remember for sure where exactly he was flying to from, Cape Town or Johannesburg or one of the other airports. She decides she needs to find out this detail, that her ignorance is a sign of neglect. She logs onto the web, finds a record of his flight on an email sent by the site he'd used to book the ticket. It was to and from Johannesburg that he'd flown.

She's still not satisfied, feels the need for more physical

evidence of where Greg's journey has taken him. She stumbles over to the bookcase, hunts for an atlas. With a large map of Africa open in front of her, she finds Johannesburg and traces a line due north: Botswana, Zambia, Congo, Central African Republic, Sudan, Chad, Libya. It is comforting to sit there, the atlas on her lap, her finger marking out the flight path. It somehow brings her closer to Greg, and makes her even more determined to fly out there, to be nearby.

She recalls the last time she'd seen Greg. His departure time had been at an unseemly hour and he'd been packed and ready the night before. He'd set his alarm for half four in the morning and had left the house just after five, planning to catch the half past coach to Heathrow. She'd stirred as he carried his bag out of the bedroom and had forced herself awake just long enough for a sleepy goodbye kiss.

Safe journey, she'd said. Take care.

I'll phone you when I arrive, he'd answered, anxious to get on the road.

And that had been it. They might as well have been business associates. Pathetic, she thinks, and feels the first cracks in her heart.

And now her last phone call. Again it had been all too brief, early evening, catching Nuala as she spread the mashed potato topping onto a shepherd's pie.

The flight's not 'til tomorrow evening, he'd said. I get in before seven. Should be home for a late breakfast.

I'll be at work, she'd answered, matter-of-fact. I'll see you when I get in.

A few seconds of silence, the gentle purr of long-distance phone line in the background. Then,

The kids OK?

Sure. They're upstairs. Want to say hi?

No, I'd better not. My mobile's playing up so I'm using Farai's. Must be costing him a packet. Just tell them I love them.

OK. Give my love to Farai and Rose. Tell them I'm thinking of them.

Will do.

Another pause. A crackle of static.

Miss you, he'd said.

Get away with you, man.

Those were the roles they played, he affectionate and demonstrative, she dismissive of his sentimentality. They enjoyed the banter and performed their parts with enthusiasm. Their friends and family found it amusing. But today, the scale of the calamity still only partly digested, it just seems foolish, a thousand missed opportunities. Through the fog of confused wretchedness she feels the first twinges of guilt and regret.

She remembers the airline representative and his comments about the news breaking and scrambles to switch on the television in the lounge. She channel-hops between news stations, transfixed by the rolling headline subtitles.

It's not enough, she's impatient for detail, so she logs onto the computer too, navigating her way onto the BBC website. Numbed with shock, she spots the headline as the lead story but struggles to take in the information in the text below it, recognises only after several attempts at reading that the site has as few concrete details as she does.

She tries to concentrate, to pull herself together, but the awareness that her private life is being played out in public is too surreal, renders her dizzy and enfeebled. She transfers her attention back to the TV, brings down a radio from her bedroom, listens to the alternating bulletins. They too describe the incident in only the vaguest detail. The only additional information that she gathers concerns speculation over the cause of the crash. Unconfirmed reports suggest that it may be an act of terrorism rather than an accident.

She wanders from lounge to kitchen and begins tidying up the breakfast things, an unconscious attempt to alleviate the pain, to find distraction through activity. And standing there in front of the sink, washing-up brush in one hand, porridge bowl in the other, it's suddenly too much, the dam is breached, and she surrenders to her self-pity, to her fear. Her face crumples, salty tears stream over flushed cheeks, her sobs break the silence of an empty house. She wipes at her puffy, reddened eyes with her sleeve, brush still in hand, angry at her weakness, in control enough to know that the school pick-up is looming, that she needs to put a lid on these emotions.

She commands herself back into composure and finishes the kitchen chores, letting the sink tap run cold. She splashes water on her face until it is numb. Drying herself with a clean dishcloth, she checks her appearance in the bathroom mirror. The eyes are still puffy, her cheeks ruddy, but otherwise she looks quite normal. She wanders back into the kitchen. The wall clock tells her it is time to collect the children. I am strong, she tells herself. I will be strong.

The rest of the day passes in a blur of childcare. Unable to contemplate sharing her news with the children, terrified that a news bulletin may reveal the tragedy to them, Nuala disconnects the satellite cable. She tells them that the TV is not working properly and suggests a DVD as an alternative.

Both Sammy and Beth have remembered that daddy is due home so Nuala is forced to explain his absence. She tells them the plane has had a problem and that they are waiting for news. The children accept this unhesitatingly as nothing more than an inconvenient delay. Beth has written a poem for his return, Sammy's built a Lego monster in his honour. They're both momentarily annoyed that the handover ceremony has been postponed but are soon distracted by a squabble over which DVD to watch.

The eye of the storm has moved on, she's now slipped into the After era.

A sleepless night. Nuala lies in bed and makes plans. It's only when the school run has been completed the next morning that she can begin to put them into action. She phones her favourite sister, Andrea, the one who has the fewest ties at home, explains her intentions, obtains from her an assurance that she can come without notice and take over the running of the household. Then she phones the information line she's been given and runs through the same security details to confirm her identity.

This time the male voice is officious and impersonal,

though the information is essentially the same. Reconnaissance planes have been sent to look for the aircraft, its location identified through the ELT signalling beacon. Unfortunately the crash site looks to be in the middle of a highly sensitive, extremely dangerous area of territory. This accounts for the delay in carrying out a thorough search for survivors. The British government is working in cooperation with the local authorities and will keep all relatives informed as soon as there are any developments.

Through the numbing shock she's felt since she first heard the news, Nuala experiences a gnawing anger. She interrupts the man's drone and tells him she'd like to make arrangements to fly out to the crash site as soon as possible. She has prepared a pen and pad before making the call and sits poised to note down details of what she will need to organise. She has expected cooperation and encouragement. Instead she hears hesitancy, awkwardness. Surely they must be expecting this, she thinks. The man recovers his poise and begins to repeat his last statement, the promise to inform Nuala of any developments. He checks her landline and mobile numbers, offers a smooth assurance that they'll have some news very soon. In her raw, exposed state, Nuala finds herself allowing the conversation to end.

She paces the house, her fury growing. She cannot wait for the promised updates, her impatience dragging her upstairs to her bedroom where she begins to pack a suitcase. She decides to call every hour until she receives the go-ahead to journey to the crash site. In the meantime, there's a phone call every twenty minutes or so, the electronic tone setting Nuala's nerves jangling, a sense of dread every time she picks up the handset, but it's always a friend or relative. Hours pass. The telephone, with its capacity for relief or ruin, becomes a toying instrument of torture.

⌘

Anger, along with guilt, becomes an essential component of

Nuala's emotional development over the coming weeks. After the initial anesthetising shock comes a restless vacillation in her behaviour, a world rendered meaningless, a suspension of the logical, the rational. The only consistency in Nuala's behaviour is its lack thereof.

And how can it be otherwise? When she receives confirmation, sometime in the spotted blur of the next few days, that the first medical and salvage team has reached the wreckage of the plane at last, she listens but struggles to understand the information that follows. That there are no known survivors. That many of the bodies salvaged are identifiable only by dental records and DNA tests. That there are signs of looting at the site, located in an inhospitable region currently plagued by warring factions. That it is too dangerous to contemplate allowing visits by the victims' families. That it seems almost certain the crash was caused by an explosion on board.

And finally, that Greg's body, like a number of others, has so far not been identified. The police officer who visits to break the news in person, his manner gentle yet firm, is solemnly adamant: Greg should be presumed dead.

Presumed dead? Nuala seethes at the ease of surrender. If her neighbour's car is not parked outside his house, she might presume that he has gone off to work. If the family cat is not prowling around its food bowl, she might presume that it has escaped into the garden. But to presume the death of her husband just because a first scouting at the crash site does not produce his corpse seems the height of irresponsibility, of insanity, a perversion of logic. At this stage, there is no ambiguity for Nuala. Despite the policeman's insistence, the absence of Greg's body is conclusive evidence of his continuing existence.

⌘

Nuala wakes every morning from the anxieties of her sleep world. Often it's the Fran-at-the-door dream but sometimes there are others. At university in Cork Nuala took part in two charity-raising parachute jumps. The first passed without event, the second with slightly more drama, her friend falling awkwardly and suffering a serious leg break. The jumps occurred during that time in her life when she thought herself invulnerable, and she hasn't considered these experiences in years. Now she dreams she's jumping again, the adrenalin squeeze as she leaps from the plane, the liberation of freefall, but then the realisation that she has forgotten the parachute, that she's plunging to certain death, and she wakes up breathless and panicky.

And then, when there are no nightmares, there's still the waking, the few seconds of calm before the vicious kick is delivered, and she remembers.

⌘

When she's not deliberately avoiding her situation, she thinks about loss. Her older brother had died just after Beth's birth, killed in a motorway pileup just outside Dublin on his way to a job interview. She remembers the violence of her reaction, the paroxysm of pain, the mental and physical distress. But looking back she sees few similarities between her feelings now and those at the time. Of course there was an initial sense of denial, but there had been a wake, a body to mourn.

Dwelling on her brother's death, Nuala recalls, above all, its unambiguity, its absolute black-and-whiteness. She pictures the fateful car journey, her brother behind the wheel, a living breathing being, all pumping organs and zapping synapses. And then, an instant later, from white to black, the heart has stopped, the pulse and brain functions have ceased, and all that remains is the cold, still cadaver in the hospital morgue. And Nuala feels again that her present experience is unique, for in her mind the loss of Greg is the most ambiguous possible, neither dead nor alive, an absolute grey.

⌘

In the days that follow, there is no self-scrutiny, only raw, naked experience. Nuala does not yet understand the crucial role that her own children will play in helping her to deal with such emotional upheaval, their status as both bane and boon. All she feels is that there are moments where she resents them deeply, their endless demands, when in fact she craves the opportunity to focus on her own emotional needs. And that at other times she feels grateful for their presence, the very relentlessness of their requirements, as desperate diversions distracting her from her thoughts, a bulwark propping up her fragile state of mind, a barricade between herself and complete mental meltdown.

During the first few days Nuala breaks the news of the air crash gently but continues to maintain to the children that Greg is temporarily missing rather than permanently gone. In their minds, she hopes, he has lost his way. He is wandering around the African bush and will re-appear at some future time, dusty and tanned, with thrilling tales of wild beast encounters.

And as the days pass, the questions about the timing of his return grow less frequent as they accept the length of its delay, and his absence becomes woven into the fabric of their existence. Routines are put on hold 'until daddy gets back'. Plans are made for after his homecoming.

Of course there are moments when emotions erupt, usually close to bedtime when tempers are frayed and the spirit exhausted, when they cry that they miss him, that they want him back. But then Nuala lays aside her own hurting and focuses on restoring morale, first on establishing in their minds a daddy en route home, then on distractions and promises and plans. And it works and the children believe what they are told, what they want to believe, and life goes on.

⌘

Another visit from a government official, a Mr Cartmel, to update Nuala on developments. Again, the insistence that there can be no survivors. She listens politely, then informs him of her plans to travel to Africa. She's already dug out her passport. She has planned in her mind the trip to London for a visa, the purchase of a ticket. She'll make the rest up as she goes along once she's in-country.

Cartmel looks at her, wondering if she's heard correctly what he has just told her about presuming her husband's death. He contemplates repeating himself. There's a steely determination in her flinty eyes that he hadn't noticed before. When she'd first opened the door, she'd worn a look of startled raw vulnerability. It was a look he'd seen before in people facing great mental distress, like a movie-goer emerging from a matinee performance into bright afternoon sunshine, something naked and bewildered, momentarily caught off guard.

He hesitates, then explains that he can't comment about the possibility of travel, that she'll need to talk to his superiors. He promises that someone will get back to her soon.

She waits for a day but having received no call, she phones the information line again. She explains her plans and is put through to a supervisor. By now she's angry, a cold fury that stems from her growing belief that she's being fobbed off. She's aware that her voice is raised. The woman is telling her that political sensitivities make travel to the country difficult. She listens in disbelief. There must be many of us, friends and relatives of the victims, who want to make this journey, she thinks. She interrupts the woman and tells her she'll go to the newspapers if she doesn't receive the necessary cooperation from the authorities. After a long delay she's put through to a third person.

This time the man's voice is placatory, a little oily even. He reiterates how difficult travel would be at the present time. He reassures her that the Foreign Office is nevertheless in delicate negotiations with its counterpart, and that Nuala and the other bereaved (his word, not hers) would be the first to be notified of any progress. He's smooth and persuasive, but Nuala's calm rage fuels her persistence. No, she says, that's not good enough. She wants to fly out to the capital as soon as possible. She will apply for the necessary visa tomorrow. If she does not receive the government's full cooperation, then she'll go to the press.

There's a moment's pause. She can almost hear the man's brain processing her words, calculating his next move. When he speaks his voice has lost some of its sympathetic tone. He will speak to his superior at once, will call back before the end of the day.

The final call of the day is short and to the point. The man introduces himself as a senior something-or-other in the Foreign Office. He invites her to a meeting in London the next day, a briefing on the situation that they are offering to all those directly affected by the incident. She takes down the address and asks him to repeat his name: Rafferty.

Nuala, restless, wanders around the house. Everywhere she looks she sees Greg's ghostly presence. Outside in the back garden is the shed that he constructed, the barbeque pit he built, the fencing he patched up. At the front of the house she strokes the garden gate he'd replaced a fortnight before his departure, had primed but never got round to painting. She looks up at the brickwork and the sprawling wisteria, noting the branch hanging limply across the front bay window. It has always been Greg's job to tie it back.

But it's not only his handiwork that Nuala notices. Since she first learned of the crash, she has seen and heard Greg at every turn. When the phone rings, day or night, her first thought is that it must be him. The doorbell heralds his entrance, the creak of a floorboard signals his proximity. Every tap on the window, every moan of the wind sets her heart racing.

And outside, too, she sees him everywhere. Greg's favourite coat is a brown zip-up jacket and she only has to catch sight of someone wearing something vaguely similar to feel a stab of expectation. Their car is a particular shade of pale blue and no matter how many times she encounters a similar one on the road, she cannot suppress the immediate detonation of hope followed by grim deflation, even when she's driving the very car at the time. Worst of all is the flash of the back of a man's head in a crowded street, the same cut, same shade of hair, a moment of belief she wishes she could stifle.

The following day Nuala ventures outside again and manoeuvres her car out onto the ring road. She remembers little of the drive into London. She parks at a friend's house in Ealing and catches the tube into town. The room she's led into is airy and cold, with white walls, a couple of gold-framed oil paintings and a conference table with steel chairs. There are three men present including Rafferty. She's expecting other victims' relatives to be present but she's alone. The briefings must be individual, she supposes, and wonders whether that's an attempt to keep the families apart.

Rafferty introduces the other men but Nuala scarcely takes in the details. One of them launches straight into a political analysis of the region where Greg has gone missing. He explains about the country's current government, the distance from capital to crash site, the plane brought down in an area of fierce conflict between militia armed by the government and local groups fighting for autonomy. He explains about the roots of the conflict – a fight for land, for ethnic superiority, for natural resources – and its exacerbation by outside interests. He mentions neighbouring countries, names rival warlords, refers to the world price of certain valuable minerals. Nuala can see that he's enjoying the opportunity to lecture on his area of expertise.

The man talks about the foreign government. He mentions its refusal to admit to its role in the conflict or to accept that its faraway province has become a battlefield. He explains that Britain has joined many other countries in applying pressure on the government to end the violence. It has accused the country of genocide, called for international sanctions, and this has made relations between the two countries extremely frosty. It has become almost impossible to get a visa from their embassy, he concludes. As such, travel to and from this country is almost impossible.

Look, I understand exactly how you feel, says Rafferty when the man has finished. If it was me, I'd definitely want to get out there, see the site, pay my respects. It's important for closure, I'm sure. He smiles at Nuala, looking pleased with the sensitivity of his words. She gazes back at him and burns inside with a wrath she doesn't know she is capable of. Closure? She focuses on her right hand resting on her lap and concentrates on controlling its shaking. She doesn't want an outburst. She still hopes to convince them to assist her in her travel plans.

Thank you, she manages, and draws her own lips into an icy smile.

As I say, I do understand your position. He pauses, choosing his words with care. However, I must emphasise the hopelessness of any such plan. First of all, their embassy will not issue you a visa. Through UN pressure, they have allowed the Civil Aviation Authority in to examine and photograph the wreckage, carry out cause-of-crash on-site testing, remove debris and human remains, take away the DNA samples. It's a one-off, an exception after years of growing diplomatic isolation. We've already made enquiries about visas for relatives of victims and they have so far refused. He pauses again to let the words sink in, then picks up the thread. Secondly, even if you were allowed to fly into the capital, you would not be able to travel to the crash site area. Apart from being nearly a thousand miles from the capital, it's in an extremely dangerous region. The government has sealed off the area for several years, and nobody can move to and fro without its say-so. To all intents and purposes it's a war zone.

Look, I'll take my chances, says Nuala. Even if I can just fly into the capital, I'll feel that I'm closer, that I'm doing something. Can you help me do that at least?

Rafferty looks at her sadly and shrugs.

The capital and the site location are both within the same country, but they're a thousand miles apart. Think about those distances. That's like going to Milan to look for something in Wales.

Please, says Nuala, a plea in her voice.

It's out of our hands. I've told you, we've tried. They've said no. I'm sorry.

A temporary dead-end. Nuala leaves the building fuelled by a cold, dark fury, an absolute refusal to accept what, according to these people, fate has dished out to her. She makes her way back to Oxford flanked by her two closest companions, Anger and Denial

⌘

A new phenomenon emerges, a change in Nuala's outlook that manifests itself in her attitude to her children. It begins as a creeping over-protectiveness underpinned by a feeling of impending catastrophe that suffuses her everyday life. Unable as yet to deal rationally with this growing need, she allows it to become an all-consuming obsession, an insatiable urge to check and recheck on her children's welfare.

When she's not with them, her mobile never leaves her person. Five minutes cannot pass without a glance at the display, dreading the confirmation of the calamity she expects at any instant. A running commentary of ghastly what-ifs loops around her brain. When the parents of her children's friends invite them to the park or pool, she finds herself casually suggesting that she accompany them instead. When there are invitations to play at their friends' houses, she makes some excuse to switch the venue to her own. Will something ghastly happen to Sammy and Beth if she's not there to watch over them? Impossible to answer, but for the moment it's a risk she cannot take.

⌘

Meanwhile, Nuala continues to function in a state of suspension. There are better days and worse ones, some where she's barely able to see her way through breakfast for the children, the school pick-up, evening tea, let alone beyond that to the future.

Friends and family have rallied round. Her parents refuse to be put off. They insist on a three-day visit that she can barely remember, an endless round of tea and toast. She talks to Greg's family every day, but they've run out of things to say. They have covered everything except the likelihood of his death. It's too early for that, so they skirt around it carefully.

She's deeply touched by her Oxford friends: the women from her book group, Mary and the other mothers of her children's friends, Teri and her colleagues at work, Joan and the neighbours. They phone and text, drop round cooked meals, offer to shop and sort out laundry as if she is an invalid. She refuses what she can, accepts what she has to. Activity is still the only pain relief, so all these offers of help are appreciated but unwanted.

She feels most calm in the early evening, occupied by cooking and her children's requirements – Lego with Sammy, homework with Beth. She's aware that for the moment the most she can expect is to survive each grim, bloody day. The past has nullified the present, cancelled out the future.

When the children sleep she prowls around the house. This is the time when her stranger urges are given freer rein, those irrational superstitious feelings that come and go in no clear pattern. The CD player in the kitchen still contains the album Greg played the evening before his departure, a Fats Waller compilation beloved by the children and their father alike, and Nuala finds herself unable either to remove it or to play it, so it remains in its slot and she's forced to rely on the radio for distraction. Down in the basement studio Nuala finds a tube of alizarin crimson, its top lying next to it. Greg must have forgotten to screw it back on, but she cannot bear to do it herself. It's a bizarre fear of disturbing the status quo. He's alive until he's dead.

Occasionally, as she passes her piano, she stops and lets her fingers run softly across the keyboard, but she cannot bring herself to play.

She's still not back at work, but plans a return for the following Monday. She needs the distraction, an escape from her self-pity. At night she lies awake in the dark, eyes closed, and imagines her misfortune displayed in front of her like the bright lights used in prison torture, like a neon sign pulsating, its message burning through her eyelids, flashing on and off and on, HE IS GONE, he is gone, YOU ARE ALONE, you are alone.

SEMIRA 2

Dear Kassa

Moving on, moving on, never staying still for long. I feel so bad for Yanit and Abebe, forever bundled from neighbourhood to neighbourhood, school to school, friendship to friendship. But I know in the long-term it is for the best and I hope they will understand that one day.

Yanit will be ten this year, you would hardly recognise her she has stretched so much. You would get on so well with her. She shares your passion for literature, for the ability of words to weave magic worlds in the mind. She would love to be able to get her hands on your book collection, the one you built up so carefully in Asmara, stored so lovingly on the shelves of your room. Mind you, you would be jealous at the treasures she can access in the libraries here, row upon row of tomes at her disposal and all in English, a language she has mastered with an ease that I can only marvel at, despite all my classes in Addis at secondary school and university and now here on my ESOL courses.

So here we are, a new city, a new home, a new life. Armed with my Indefinite Leave To Remain status, I left Bristol a month ago. I arrived in Oxford a total stranger and endured the familiar insanity of temporary emergency accommodation, this time a grim bed and breakfast, before finding the support I needed from a local charity, the Open Arms Project. It was the volunteer here, Jenny, who helped sort out the housing benefit that enabled me to leave the B & B and look for the flat I am now living in. It is a privately-owned two-bedroom place above a shop off a street called Hollow Way. There were also long hours spent working through the application form for council housing, though Jenny tells me not to hold my breath.

I enrol the children at the primary school and register with the GP and the dentist. I know the ropes, I have done it so many times before.

Indefinite Leave To Remain? I hear you ask in disbelief. Yes, it is true, a phone call from the solicitor tells us that we have won the court case. Our status is assured, our position as permanent residents in UK secured. The first step to citizenship...

And it was just the kickstart I needed to make possible our getaway from Bristol, from that house which, at night, became little more than a prison. Yanit suffered again, a daily grind of name-calling, slapping and spitting at school. I too had my share of insults and taunts from some of the neighbours. One family in particular seemed to almost encourage their children to pester us. Hours spent scrubbing paint daubed on the front door, cleaning up the strewn rubbish, the dog waste from the garden path. One occasion when a stone was thrown through a downstairs window. I tried to shield all this venom from Yanit and Abebe, but they were aware of the atmosphere if not of all the particular incidents.

In truth, refugee status or not, I could not have stayed there for long.

And Oxford? Yes, I am sure you are thinking, Oh no, not another history lecture! So I will keep it short and sweet as I have only browsed my source of information, a first acquisition from the local library. The book is full of the city's rich history, its academic heritage of course, as well as its location as the King's court during the Civil War. I read a section on religious aspects of Oxford's history, learn about the Oxford Martyrs five hundred years ago, burnt at the stake, victims of religious intolerance, of the dogma of violence, ignorance, bigotry.

And the city itself? Much smaller than Bristol, less than a third its size. Another split personality, half studious professor, half hard-working businessman. A long-standing influx of migrant labour for the car works and for the hospitals, the growth of the Asian community in east Oxford. And that's not to mention the colourful international student population and the recent arrivals from Eastern Europe. Despite its size, it is truly a city of diversity.

The only down side so far is that this city, lying as it does in the Thames Valley, is damp and wet and foggy. Abebe's chest has been most affected, and he is beginning to develop some signs of asthma. It is nothing too serious, and the GP has been quick to treat him with inhalers and a spacer device.

It is Ramadan and the Cowley Road lamp posts are hung with Eid decorations, the mosque pokes its head above the urban skyline. The school, not far from the library, is friendly and mixed. Through the mosque I have identified a weekly *Qur'anic* class for young girls that Yanit has started attending on Thursday evenings, a boys' youth club for Abebe at the community centre on Sunday afternoons.

The flat is quite comfortable, less spacious than the Hartcliffe property and one of the bedrooms is very damp, but it has the essentials – central heating, cooker, washing machine – so it feels like home. The shop underneath is a typical corner grocer's, owned by my landlord's cousin. He is somewhat creepy. He eyes me up in an odd way, keeps asking about my husband's whereabouts. I buy my milk, smile politely.

Jenny, my volunteer worker, has helped register me for more English classes and I have started my first language course in the community centre. It is a welcoming environment, a morning crèche organised for student mothers, a common room set aside for coffee-break socialising. My class is full of like-minded souls, mothers juggling with their housing, their benefits, their children, their Home Office status, the pain of lives lost or left behind.

Ramadan is hard in Britain. This year we start on the first day of September. Summer has not yet given way to autumn. The sun does not set until late, so the fasting period lasts sixteen hours. I set my alarm for three to cook, the meal over by four thirty, then nothing until dusk at eight. Neither child really needs to fast yet, they are both too young, but Yanit observes the changes to my lifestyle and she wants to copy me, so I let her join in for the odd day. And then of course it is Abebe's turn to declare his intention, and again I do not refuse, allow him to try it once or twice. Many of their friends are Muslim. The children go to their homes and watch their families follow the same rituals, and it feels good, as if we are part of the community, like we finally belong.

I remember those nights of cooking, you and I working side by side in the kitchen, Kassa, to produce cuisine worthy of fast-breaking, pulling out loaf after loaf of qitcha and khobz from the oven, plates piled high with injera, pots of zighni and tsebhi bubbling away on the stove. What a team, my dear, what a team!

It is after midnight. I need a few hours' sleep before the early rise, so I will sign off now.

I have heard nothing from the Red Cross. Tomorrow I will call them and check that they have not lost my contact details.

As always, we think of you in our prayers.

⌘

Dear Kassa

Eid has come and gone, a happy time for Yanit and Abebe though a strain on my purse, what with new clothes for both of them, a mobile phone for Yanit, a games console for Abebe and the main expense, a new computer that now sits on a table in the lounge. Yes, my dear, we are moving up in the world, embracing twenty-first century technology!

I say the computer is new, which is not entirely accurate. In fact it is second-hand, sold to us by a woman I met at the mosque. I know it is not the latest model, but we can write our homework on it, send emails, go on the internet, and the woman threw in her old printer as part of the deal, as she was getting everything brand new herself.

Abebe has been hankering after a computer ever since he started visiting his new friend, Ibrahim, a Sudanese boy who lives next to the health clinic, just five minutes' walk away. Ibrahim, it seems, is something of an expert, has a computer at home and has introduced Abebe to all sorts of PC games and websites. Like Yanit, he has been taught the basics at school and so has an almost intuitive sense of how to manage those infernal machines.

Yanit, too, has mastered the beast, though she uses it for her story-telling, the tales and poems and plays she produces with such ease. Yes, Kassa, you are not the only artist in the family! She is a creative wizard, turning the stories into slide shows or decorating them with illustrations she has come across on the internet.

And don't forget me. Yes, don't die of shock, Kassa! Since January I have been taking a weekly computer class, a government initiative, my first opportunity to wrestle with this piece of satanic apparatus. And what a struggle it has been! As the weeks go by it seems clear to me that here is one new trick that this old dog will never master.

No, I should not be so negative. Let me focus on the positives. With the incredible patience of my teacher and the persistence of Yanit, I can switch the monster on, click on the right icons to allow me to write my assignments, to check my spelling, to save and print. I can open my emails, send and reply. But most of all, I can open the miraculous doors of the internet, sweep through into this world of knowledge. This World Wide Web is my liberator, my magical key. It may not seem like much and these few skills represent many hours of blood, sweat and tears, but I cannot tell you how good it makes me feel, powerful and unfettered. I have been given the password to my own freedom.

Since its arrival in our household, that computer has become the focal point of our lives, and also, unfortunately, the source of many of our arguments. Yanit and Abebe squabble over turn-taking, I complain that it has taken over their lives, that they are neglecting homework and household chores. And, I must confess, my own complaints are tinged with guilt, since my first action once the children are in bed and the house tidied is to log on.

And what a revelation it is! With Google as my comrade, I doubleyoudoubleyou this, dotcom that and, lo! I find myself entering worlds I never thought I could access. Who needs libraries? With the touch of a button I can see train times from Addis to Djibouti, discover the title of Tigist Assefa's latest bolel CD, locate a new recipe for niter qibe, find the contact detail of the Ethiopian Art Centre in London, peruse the academic calendar of Addis Ababa University, even read the online editions of the *Ethiopian Herald* and *Addis Admass*.

And it is not all about trivia. With a wave of my magic mouse, I find the prayer times at the Manzil Way mosque, compare the cost of school uniform at three different retailers or request a repeat prescription with the GP for Abebe's asthma puffers. Oh, Kassa, I just wish you were here to share this with me.

I am not limiting myself to computers either. At the Ethnic Minority Business Service, around the corner from my English language classes, I have enrolled on a Back To Work course. They help me craft a pathetically empty curriculum vitae. They take me through interview techniques, show me how to fill in application forms and draft covering letters. I cannot tell you how exciting it feels, my life on track. The sample application forms we practise on are for supermarket shelf-fillers, shop assistants, cleaners. But I dream of my old life. I have set my sights on a teaching assistant post in one of the primary schools, perhaps one day a fully-fledged classroom teacher. A teacher of history.

With the help of my teachers and the internet, I know what I have to do, the challenge that awaits me. First I must master this language fully, achieve the ease and fluency of a native speaker. Then I hope that my Addis University degree will prove to be my passport onto a part-time teacher training course. I do not know whether it is feasible, what new hurdles I will meet, but that is my dream. And without dreams, Kassa, we are nothing.

During coffee breaks in my classes, I sit in the common

room and listen to my classmates' stories. Some are so sad I end up feeling guilty for my own good fortune. The tales of death and rape and torture that have brought these people here are never talked of, remain unspoken, invisible burdens that we carry. What can be mentioned are our present woes of grinding poverty, bureaucratic nightmare, the fear of deportation hanging over us. And finally the symptoms of these misfortunes, the mental illness, the self-harm, the despair.

Yesterday I asked after a Bangladeshi woman who has stopped attending class. Her friend told me she is at home and refuses to leave the house. She had a car accident last year, lost her front teeth, managed to get a bridge fitted privately. Now the bridge keeps falling out and she cannot find an NHS dentist to take her on. She has no money. Her husband has tried gluing the bridge into place but it no longer holds and she is too embarrassed to be seen in public.

An Iranian friend is distraught. Her fifteen-year-old daughter is being racially abused at school by a gang of girls led by a particularly spiteful bully. This chief tormentor has encouraged her boyfriend and his friends to join in and the daughter's day has become a nightmare. She is called names, has had her bag slashed, her PE kit stolen. They spit in her lunchbox and graffiti obscenities about her on the toilet walls. Teachers tell her they will look into it but do nothing. When she reacts by slapping one of the gang while being hounded by a mob in the playground, she is spotted by the on-duty teacher and hauled off to the head of year. She is then excluded from school for three days for violent behaviour despite her protestations.

Last weekend, a quiet Friday night at home, my friend, her husband, the daughter and their two other children are sitting in front of the television when there is a crash outside. When they open the door they find a pack of fifteen youths, boys and girls, all in masks, calling for the daughter to come out and face the music. The windscreen of the family car has been smashed. My friend is terrified. The children cower in the hall while the husband, furious, runs out to confront the rabble. A few more stones are thrown, the mob scatter. The police are called. They arrive eventually, take some statements and promise to look into it. The masks are a problem, they say with a shrug. Without a positive identification any progress will be difficult.

I have my own troubles, too. When I check my latest bank statement, I notice that my benefits have been cut. I make an appointment and am told I have failed to supply the necessary information about my husband's circumstances. They explain that they need to ensure that he is not in a position to contribute to the children's financial upkeep. Until such information is supplied, they tell me, the appropriate sum will be deducted from what I am given. I have supplied all the information when I first applied for benefits, but when I tell them this, they say they have no record of the details.

The next day I go to see Jenny. She sorts out an appointment with another solicitor. He promises to write to the benefits office and to supply the Home Office documentation to authenticate my claim. Until then, I am living on a fraction of my usual income.

I continue to harass my case worker at the Red Cross. The same response as always: no contact established. I tell myself that no news is good news, but sometimes my spirit falls and I fear the worst. I tell myself, I will be strong! I am strong!

It is not always easy, but I think of you and Gadissa, your own journey that I have lived and relived in my imagination a hundred thousand times, a spiralling loop of tortured speculation, so many alternating worlds of conjecture, so many maybes and what ifs, and I feel as always the icy whiplash of sorrow and shame, shame and sorrow, backwards and forwards, and between these worlds I find I have no excuse not to be strong.

Our love to you, to Gadissa.

⌘

Dear Kassa

Outside the house, things are going well, my dear. Yanit is a star at school, Abebe popular with teachers and schoolmates. My studies too are a success. You will be amazed to learn that I have been 'promoted' to a higher level, now travel to the further education college in Blackbird Leys, another edge-of-city estate. The classes now run every morning. Another step closer.

Things have become more difficult at home, however. My landlord is an elderly fellow with a hawk-like expression. He reminds me of Mr Faisal, one of my lecturers in Addis. Our initial contract for this flat was for six months and imagine my shock when I told him we wished to extend our tenancy, and he announced that he wanted us out as soon as possible. I asked him whether we had done something wrong and pleaded with him to reconsider, but he was adamant. It was nothing that we had done, he insisted, just that his nephew and his family were coming down from Leeds to live in Oxford and he had promised them the flat.

Back to the Open Arms Project for advice. Jenny arranges an appointment with a legal aid solicitor. Another appointment at the council with a housing officer. I get told to stay put, to wait for the landlord to go through the legal proceedings for a compulsory eviction. Only if I am forcibly evicted will the council take any responsibility for our accommodation.

A fortnight ago I checked on my position on the council housing list. To my dismay I found that they have no record of the application form I so painstakingly filled in with Jenny on my arrival in Oxford. It seems that the address on my application form is the old bed-and-breakfast. After submitting it, I moved to the new flat without telling the council. When their letter confirming receipt of the application was returned to them, they simply took me straight off the housing list.

The housing officer I speak to shows me the small print in their documentation explaining that failure to notify the council of a change of address renders the application void. She cheerfully hands me another copy of the form. For every thorn I pull from my foot, another two lie waiting in my path.

The officer explains how my claim will be dealt with, how my circumstances are weighed up, how my demand is ranked against all the other current applications. There is now an online bidding system, houses and flats displayed on the website with a procedure for applicants to submit requests for particular homes, the candidate with the highest ranking securing the accommodation. I log on and see that I am ranked seventy-four. My heart sinks.

Sleepless nights.

Red Cross are silent.

I love you.

⌘

Dear Kassa

Relations with Faisal have deteriorated. He wants us gone and I cannot oblige. Jenny's solicitor tells me plainly that if I leave of my own free will, I will have technically made myself homeless and so would forfeit any council assistance. Faisal has been here several times to show his nephew around the property. They peer into the kitchen, check the bedrooms, avoid eye contact as if we do not exist.

Some weeks ago he brought me a piece of paper, a notice to leave that he had signed. He told me he hopes I will leave peacefully, that it would distress my children if he has to call in bailiffs, if they are forced to witness our physical eviction, our belongings spread out on the pavement outside. It would not be good for me, he insists.

So I phone the legal practice. I manage to persuade the reluctant receptionist to give me an emergency appointment. The solicitor scans the letter. He tells me to stay put, to let the landlord's legal proceedings take their course. It is an expensive process, he tells me. The landlord wants me to go quietly in order to save himself the court costs.

Last week Faisal's next bombshell. The meter for my electricity is downstairs in the store room of the shop. Up until now I have been paying him a flat fee for power, but now he tells me this has not been enough, that it was a miscalculation, that I owe a lot of money in arrears. He hands me a document, a bill for over a thousand pounds. He tells me I have a week to pay. I take the letter, look at him and he stares back, unblinking. We have gone past the stage of reasoning, of negotiating, so I say nothing.

I spend the next few nights lying awake wondering what to do. The solicitor had been brusque and made it clear that I should contact him only when I received the court summons from Faisal. This latest development is unforeseen. Eventually I make an appointment to see Jenny, but by this time it is too late. I return home on Friday afternoon, having collected the children from school, to find my electricity supply disconnected.

A wretched weekend. On Monday I go to the council. I have no appointment at the housing department but the receptionist listens to my tale. She lets me take a seat and goes off to whisper to one of the housing officers on duty. I wait for two hours but am eventually seen. I am referred to the environmental health department. Another office, another waiting room. The frustration mounts. I am supposed to be in class. Since the landlord began his campaign of intimidation and harassment, I have been too occupied to concentrate on my studies and have missed a number of lessons.

My ruminations are interrupted by a piercing scream from one of the interview cubicles. No! No! I don't believe it! Do you see what you've done! You've broken them! It is a white woman, not even thirty but ageing prematurely, her face lined with strain. Her hair is the same texture as mine, bushy and wiry, the same length, but faded rusty red. She has her two children propped up on the cubicle bench, a pair of boys aged five and seven, I would guess.

Her wailing continues. She is utterly distraught. She is holding something in her hands, and it emerges through the tears that one of the boys has taken her glasses and has snapped off one of the arms. She is beside herself, unable to control her emotions. It is obviously the final straw. As I look on, I wonder what trail of misfortune has led to this despair. How could you do this? she wails. They're brand new. Brand new. I can't see without them. I'm completely blind. Why did you do this? Why? Why? Her voice is jagged, the scene harrowing.

I am sitting next to a teenager, hollow-cheeked, grey-skinned with ragged hair and baggy clothes. I hear mumbling and glance sideways at the person but cannot make out its gender, think probably that it is female. There is something damaged in its gaunt expression. It is watching the wailing mother, its mouth twisted with contempt. She's no right to have kids, it mutters. Look at her. She's not fit to be a parent.

The screaming continues. People look away, bury themselves in council leaflets, trying not to catch each other's eyes. Where am I? I think. Am I in hell?

A council officer appears, a middle-aged woman. She bends over the hysterical woman and puts an arm around her. She is talking to her, her voice low and soothing, and gradually the howling subsides, then the sobs turn to damp, defeated whimpering. They examine the glasses together. The officer goes off and returns with a roll of sellotape and begins to stick the spectacles back together. I catch sight of the boys' faces, blank and pale. They watch as the woman bends over their mother, as she offers her aid package of sympathy and stickytape. I try to interpret their expressions but can read only a controlled void.

When it is my turn to be seen, I am told that the landlord should not have disconnected my electric supply. Phone calls are made. I am told to go home and wait, that I should have the power back on by the end of the day. But it is not until the following afternoon that the electricity is reconnected.

Now between the landlord and myself there is an uneasy truce. Yanit and Abebe are perceptive. They know something is wrong. I have told them of the landlord's plans and I can see it worries them.

Today I check my housing list ranking. Last week I had moved up to thirty-six, then forty-two. Now I am back in the sixties. I scour the letting pages of the local newspaper. I have registered with four different agencies. I know how much my housing benefit is, what I can afford, but the cheapest two-bedroom property in the area is two hundred pounds more than I am receiving. The letting agent tells me that landlords avoid tenants on benefits. The housing officer suggests I move area, look beyond Oxford itself. She is not unsympathetic, but explains that there just isn't enough accommodation to go round in this safe, comfortable, sought-after city. I go around in circles, dizzy and despondent.

I must remain positive. I think of you and it gives me strength.

All my love.

⌘

Dear Kassa

Things have gone from bad to worse. Whereas before we were threatened with eviction, living in an uneasy state of uncertainty, today we are looking at the prospect of our first experiences of sleeping rough. We are in a bed-and-breakfast but only have enough money for one more night.

So how did we get here?

Well, as always, one thing seems to lead to another, but at the heart of the matter is the latest development in Faisal's campaign to rid himself of his unwanted tenants. After failing with his extortionate electricity bill, he comes up with something more subtle. Appearing at my door around five weeks ago, he announces that he has installed a new meter in the shop below. He brings me downstairs and shows me the new machine, explaining how it works, where to put the pound coins. He tells me that as a gesture of apology for the invoice episode he has put in an initial five pounds. Still, he does not waste the opportunity to advise me to leave. He informs me that the court case is progressing, that bailiffs have been contacted. He does not want things to get nasty for me, he says. I should just go, if only for the sake of the children.

Upstairs I log onto the internet and check my ranking. Sixty-one. I google properties to rent in Oxford and come across a local information website that carries private advertisements. My eye is caught by an advert for a flat near Cowley shopping centre. It is the rent that draws my attention, a figure covered by my housing benefit. There are photos of the property. It looks neat, cosy, well-maintained. I email back, expressing interest and asking to arrange a viewing.

The next morning, at six thirty, the electricity supply cuts off. I wait an hour until the shop opens downstairs. The meter is empty, the LCD display flashing a row of zeros. I change a five pound note and re-load the machine. Power returns. I think, there must be a mistake with the supply. Five pounds cannot have been eaten up so quickly. I make a mental note to keep a supply of coins handy.

The five pounds last until the following morning. The next day I run the washing machine and have to put in seven coins. I decide to keep a note of expenses and find that by the end of the first week I have spent forty-five pounds. I stop using the washing machine and take to soaking the clothes in buckets, washing them by hand.

I wait another week. By now I am in dire financial straits. Twice I am cut off during the night and so cannot re-connect until the morning. It is late October and still quite mild. I think about the coming winter and what it will cost me.

I arrange an appointment with the council and am shunted from the housing department to environmental health. A tenancy relations officer tells me that what she calls secondary metering, the installation of private meters and the setting of electricity tariffs by the landlord, is not something the council can deal with. They will, however, come and inspect the property to check whether or not I have access to the meter at night. Only that issue, she tells me, lies within her remit. She advises me to see a solicitor. I go and see Jenny. She is outraged, says she will contact the legal aid law practice to arrange an appointment.

I return home to check my emails for a reply from the Cowley flat landlord. Nothing.

Days turn to weeks. No progress. The council officer

fails to appear, phones to re-arrange the inspection for the following week. Jenny calls to tell me that the solicitor is away on holiday. She has tried to get someone else to see me, she will call as soon as she has any luck. I try to phone Faisal myself but he does not pick up and ignores my voicemails. I send a follow-up email to the Cowley landlord but there is still no response.

A difficult fortnight. The temperature drops and I run out of money. At night we climb into bed together, the children and I, to keep warm. Damp has spread from the bedroom through to the bathroom and kitchen. The walls are pockmarked with spores, the air dank with mould. The solicitor has flu. The council officer has inspected and tells me she has written to Faisal requesting that he moves the meter to a more accessible location, but otherwise washes her hands of the matter.

And then, just as I grow desperate, there is unexpected progress.

First of all, an email from the Cowley landlord. Apologies for the delay in responding. A faulty server, an administrative oversight. By chance, the flat is still available but a number of people are interested. There is no time for a viewing. The first person to send the four hundred pounds deposit secures the tenancy.

Could it be my salvation? I do not have the money and run through the possible ways to raise it. Sell what belongings I have, my washing machine, the computer? See whether the council can arrange a loan? Talk to Jenny?

And then, before I have had a chance to consider my options, Faisal appears. He is unapologetic about the meter. He tells me he has spoken to the council, told them that his metering rate was fair, that I must be squandering electricity to be spending so much each week. But he is also conciliatory, and for the first time he offers me money to go. I think of the Cowley deposit and hesitate for only a second. Then tell him we will leave for four hundred. He agrees to pay me half on the spot, the rest on our departure in three days' time.

I email the Cowley landlord back to confirm I want the

tenancy. Life becomes a blur. I have forced myself to return to my classes at the Blackbird Leys campus, still have the usual to-ing and fro-ing between home and school, but have to find time to pack. Two days pass. I get a phone call from the Cowley landlord. He wants to come over the following day to sign contracts, sort out the inventory and collect the deposit. It is also the day of our departure. We agree to meet at my present address at half past ten.

The father of one of Abebe's friends, a Kenyan boy, is a decorator by trade and owns a van. His name is Tom, he is a kind fellow and has offered to help us move. The following day I have arranged for him to help drive my belongings over to the new place. Faisal shows up early. He watches us load up, takes possession of the flat keys and hands over my final payoff. I ask Tom to take my belongings and the children to his house and tell him I will phone him with the new address once I have the keys.

I wait on the pavement for an hour until the landlord shows up. He is out of breath, clearly in between important appointments. We run through the paperwork and sign copies of the tenancy agreement. Finally I hand over the four hundred pounds. He counts out the money, writes a receipt and gives me the set of keys. He offers me his card and tells me to get in touch if there are any problems. I ask him if we cannot both go together to the flat to check that everything is satisfactory. He looks at his watch, sighs, tells me to go over to the property, that he will cut short his next meeting and meet me there within the hour.

The property is just ten minutes' walk away. I decide to go alone, to call Tom when I arrive at the address. It is a ground floor flat, part of a small two-storey block. I check the address and try the key in the lock. I find it does not fit. I go through all the keys in the bunch. It is only when I check the address again and have made a second attempt with all the keys, that it dawns on me that something is wrong. I feel the first butterflies of panic. I fumble in my bag for the landlord's card and ring the number. The line is dead.

He must have given me the wrong keys, I tell myself. A simple mistake. I sit on the front door step and wait. An hour and a half later, an elderly lady pulling a trolley arrives at the next-door flat and gets out her front door key. When I approach and ask her about the flat next door, she looks surprised. She tells me the same couple have lived there for fifteen years. He works for the post office, she for the Co-op. They are both at work at the moment.

Blind with mounting dread, I stumble back to the library and wait in turn for a computer. I log on, go to the local information webpage. The Cowley landlord's details are gone.

I feel sick, make my way to the ladies, lock myself into a cubicle. I lift the seat just in time. My stomach erupts and I hurl my breakfast into the bowl. Wiping my mouth, I sit on the toilet and give in to the hot tears. Soon self-pity gives way to anger. I scold myself for my stupidity, then think of Yanit and Abebe and bully myself into a positive state of mind. I will be strong! I am strong!

I make my way to Tom's house. I cannot bear to tell him the truth, so I explain that the flat is being decorated and ask him to store our stuff in his garage for a few days. He is polite but restless, keen to get off to work. Before he goes, he allows me a few minutes to pack a small holdall – toothbrushes, toiletries, Abebe's asthma medication, a change of clothes for all.

I gather up the children and we walk back towards the library. Opposite, across the main road, is the police station. I go in and wait to be seen. A duty sergeant listens to my story and takes down my details. When I tell him about the deposit he raises his eyebrows. I can see he thinks I am an idiot. Who am I to disagree?

We walk over to the library. It is somewhere warm to rest and think. On the outside I suppose I look quite calm – the children certainly do not suspect a problem – but inside I am icy with fear. It is a Saturday, we have an emergency supply of a hundred pounds and are effectively homeless.

That day, yesterday, was the worst for me. We found

a bed-and-breakfast on the Cowley Road last night and have enough money for tonight, too, but after that we are on the streets.

The children ask when we will be moving into the new place. I have kept to my decorating story and tell them to be patient for a few more days. For Abebe this 'camping' is still a novelty. I think Yanit suspects all is not well but she has not confronted me yet.

Am I failing again? I feel I am fumbling blindly, out of control, towards another disaster. I feel your gaze on me, you who are uniquely placed to judge my deficiencies. Please God, let me succeed, I have lost too much already. Any more, I fear, would kill me.

I must be strong. I will not let this setback harm the children. I will not let it affect our well-being. I am not bowed. I have a plan.

Yours in love, yours in strength.

GREG 3

He spends the early hours between dead-of-night and dawn face down with his cheek pressed to the sandy ground. His wrists have been bound together, his arms raised above his head in a diving position. Once, when Asrar's screams become unbearable, he lifts his head to see what cruelty could be generating such pain. At once a foot presses down on his spine and a gun barrel prods the back of his neck. He closes his eyes and wills himself elsewhere.

When he is finally raised into a sitting position, he finds Rasheed and Munia on either side, also tied up, both dazed and terrified. He tries to catch their eye, to offer a weak smile of reassurance, but their expressions are distant, impenetrable.

There are eight or nine armed men milling around the village, two guarding Greg and the children, a couple tending the horses tied up near the kraal. He spots Husham outside one of the huts surrounded by several more militiamen. They seem to be questioning him, firing sharp questions to which he mutters muted responses. His head is bowed, his eyes averted.

Two more men squat outside the hut nearest the kitchen. They are smoking, their rifles leaning against the mud wall. There's a shout from inside the hut that causes the interrogators to pause in their questioning. The others look up from their silent musing, their smoking, their idle chat. From the door of the hut, a bearded soldier emerges dragging Asrar behind him. Her hands are tied together like the others, but her clothes have been stripped off her. Greg takes in her nakedness, flushes with anger and shame and pity, immediately raises his gaze. Her face is expressionless, her eyes devoid of life.

⌘

Munia's hands are numb, her wrists so tightly bound that the circulation has been cut off. She has spent the previous hours sitting next to her brother as her initial panic and fear has turned to a seething, icy fury. The white man had been lying motionless on his front and for a while she thought perhaps he had been killed, but he tried to raise himself once and eventually was hauled up into a sitting position. Now he sits quietly by her side as helpless as herself.

She hasn't seen her mother since the raid, but knows that she is in the hut across from the fire. She has watched the armed men take it in turns to enter the hut, heard the screams of pain and misery.

She watches the men question her uncle. Every so often, when one of his answers displeases them, they bend down casually, swing a lazy fist in his face, slap his cheeks, grab a handful of hair and pull back his head sharply. Now his head is averted, his answers mumbled, but the last time he looked up, she saw that his face was almost unrecognisable, puffy eyes peeping through the swelling, his nose bloody and broken. The men are relaxed. They crack jokes, smoke, toy with their guns. She hates them with a passion she did not know she possessed.

There's a shout from her mother's hut and one of the soldiers pulls her out. Her hands are tied together and he has her by the arm, yanks her so hard she stumbles and falls onto the dusty ground by the fire. With horror, she sees that her mother is naked.

The man, bearded like a billy goat, dressed in army khaki with a pistol holster and hunting knife strapped to his waist belt, is laughing. He's telling her mother that she is a black bitch, a worthless slave, less valuable than a goat, for a goat can provide tasty milk and delicious meat, less valuable than a dog, for a dog can stand as a guard and help when hunting. As he makes each point, he reaches down and slaps her face. Pow. Pow. Pow. Now, he is telling her, at last she has a use, a purpose, as a vessel for his fine, pure-bred seed. He reaches down and gives her a careless cuff. Pow. Now she will carry the child of a pure-bred, not a filthy insignificant slave. Pow.

There's a scuffle to Munia's right and she sees that her uncle has roused himself and is struggling to stand. His interrogators, momentarily absorbed in the entertainment, have not noticed his movement and by the time they realise what has happened, Husham is on his feet and has launched himself towards Goatman.

Despite his beating, he is moving fast, screaming curses, scrabbling across the dust. His arms are still bound together and Munia wonders what he will do when he reaches Goatman. Bite his opponent like a rabid dog? Kick him like an angry camel? Or launch himself through the air like an arrow?

But Goatman has stopped abusing Asrar and watches Husham's approach with a half smile. He unholsters his pistol with a casual indifference, and shoots Husham in the head from a distance of two metres or so. There is a moment of stunned silence and then the soldiers break into laughter, cheers, excited chatter.

Munia has no time to absorb this act of obscene brutality. Now, she sees with alarm, it is Rasheed's turn to lose his self control, to struggle to his feet, cursing and shouting that he will avenge his great uncle's death. Rasheed is on the other side of Greg, out of her reach. She shoves Greg in the ribs, barks an urgent command to hold Rasheed back. Greg looks confused for a few seconds but to Munia's immense relief he seems to understand, reaches out with his bound hands, catches hold of Rasheed's sleeve, and pulls him back down to the ground. The young boy struggles but is no match for the adult's grip.

The soldiers watch the struggle with interest, hoping that the boy will break free and provide more sport for their leader. But the spectacle is over. Goatman puts his firearm away and drags Asrar to her feet. She stands swaying by the fire, a pitiful figure as she tries unsuccessfully to hide her nakedness with her bound arms. Munia's wrath is tight, suppressed, entirely concealed. She keeps her face perfectly vacant.

Now the Goatman is speaking.

There, bitch. You see what happens to slaves who become rebellious. He gestures towards the prone figure of Asrar's uncle lying face down in the dust at his feet. This dog tried to bite his master, so he paid with his life. Then his face softens. But these child slaves will not be foolish enough to try the same thing. He gestures to Munia and her brother. We'll take them back home with us. They will learn to serve their superiors obediently. His smile is thin. The white man, too, may be valuable. He gives Greg a searching look, still unsure quite what to make of his presence here. As for you, bitch, you've served your purpose. We have no more use for you.

With that, Munia watches him unsheath the hunting knife, move towards her teetering mother

No! she screams.

Goatman smiles again. Her reaches for Asrar's wrists, slices through the cord. Asrar's hands fall apart, still bunched into fists. She continues to try and cover her nakedness.

You think I'm going to kill your mother? he says to Munia. No, her only value is as a warning to other black slaves. She's free to go now, to find her fellow dogs and warn them what will happen to them if they remain on this land. Tell them to run away, to head south to the jungles where they can live like monkeys. He laughs at his own wit.

For the first time that day, Asrar speaks. Her voice is hoarse, barely a whisper.

I can't leave my children. Don't make me leave my children. They are all I have left. My family...

Family? Ha! What do you people know about families. You go around opening your legs like a dirty animal, you daughter of a whore! Now get away with you. Go and spread your filth elsewhere!

Please, she says, her voice low, imploring. Let me stay.

Goatman looks at her for an instant, sighs, shrugs almost sadly, and begins to unholster his gun.

Looks like I will have to kill you after all, he says.

No, wait, says Asrar. At least let me say goodbye to my

children.

She makes a dash for Munia, launches herself at her feet, clasps her hands over those of her daughter.

Listen, daughter, she rasps, breathless with fear. You must forget about me now, I am already dead. You must save Rasheed, bring him to safety. That is my command. Do you understand?

Munia feels her mother's hands grasp her own. There's a moment of confusion and then she realises that her mother's drama has been a ruse, that she's pressing something small and heavy into her bound hands. In an instant Goatman is on them. He reaches down, clasps a handful of her mother's hair and yanks her away from Munia. Now it's Munia's turn to keep her hands bunched into fists to keep the object concealed. Without looking, she knows what her mother has passed to her. It's the white man's penknife, the one her mother had used to skin Rasheed's hunting booty. While Goatman drags her mother away, Munia casually transfers the knife to the pocket of her dress.

Go on, slave bitch, get out of my sight, goat man says coolly. He gives her a final slap that almost detaches her head from her shoulders. If I can still see you by the time I count to twenty, you are dead.

No, please, no, she pleads.

One, two, three...

I can't.

Four, five, six...

You can't...

Seven, eight, nine...

Please...

Ten, eleven, oh what the hell. He shrugs, bored with his game. He looks over to the men who have been smoking by the hut door. Arkou, Hossein, take this mangy dog away and get rid of her.

No! scream Rasheed and Munia at the same time. Unable to contain themselves any longer, the children struggle to their feet, make to hurl themselves in the direction of their mother. Before they have taken a single step, the armed men are on them, forcing them down to the ground. They struggle, curse, twist their bodies to escape, but are pinned down by their captors. Asrar, seeing her children manhandled, attempts to throw herself at the soldiers but is intercepted by the two guards nominated by Goatman. They grab an arm each and start pulling her away from her children. She screams, her cries mingling with those of the young ones.

Greg looks around, his eyes revealing the alarm and confusion he feels. He has followed the action without much understanding, but even he can recognise that the horrific events are building to a climax. On either side, the soldiers are assaulting the children. One is kneeling on Rasheed, another holding down his shoulders as he thrashes around as if convulsed by some monstrous epileptic fit. Munia, too, is pinned to the ground by two of the men, her legs and arms held fast. Her mouth is open, lips drawn back, teeth bared in a snarl as she weaves her head backwards and forwards in an effort to bite the hands that hold down her shoulders.

Greg looks up, sees the terror in Asrar's eyes as the two soldiers drag her away.

Since the bearded man shot Husham with such casual nonchalance Greg's state of mind has moved into a kind of terrorised submission, too shocked to do more than witness the surrounding events in numbed detachment.

Asrar's ordeal and the subsequent attack on the children bring him back out of himself. This is the last supreme outrage, the culmination of all that he has suffered since the crash: his own physical trauma, the vultures' feasting, his shooting of the militiaman, the rape and murder he has been forced to witness. Galvanised by the children's screams, by their mother's struggles, he is spurred into action. His guard has been co-opted into dealing with Rasheed's struggles. He edges backwards so that he's out of the guards' line of vision, gets to his feet, then charges at the two men holding Munia down. His first kick catches one of the guard's squarely in the belly, the second catches the other guard under his chin. He turns to Rasheed's captors, kicks one of them in the kidneys, picks his spot on the other's torso and is about to launch another kick when he feels a sharp pain in the small of his back. As he swivels to face his attacker, he sees for an instant in the corner of his eye a rifle butt arc down towards his face, a dark fleeting blur, and then it makes contact with the side of his head and from one instant to another he's plunged into darkness.

⌘

Rasheed guesses they've been riding for two or three hours when they stop next to a wadi. He is sitting on one of the horses wedged behind a soldier with a lazy eye. His hands, like those of his sister, are still tied in front of him. His mind is a fog of fear and misery. He won't cry, mostly because his sister's eyes have remained dry and he refuses to appear weaker than her, but he has never felt so at a loss, will not even bring himself to consider the fate of his mother. When she was frogmarched out of his uncle's village by the two men, when they returned thirty minutes later without her, his mind simply saw her absence, their separation, as temporary. They will meet up again later, he keeps telling himself.

In front of him, sitting behind another of the militiamen, is his sister. Further on, the white man, Greg, lies face down across one of the horses like the carcass of a beast. The militia are taking no chances with him since his attack. They have trussed him up with snaking coils of thick rope and blindfolded him with a length of cloth torn from Asrar's discarded dress.

The soldiers dismount under a clump of trees, tie up the horses, drag Rasheed and his sister down and leave them in the shade. They throw Greg down beside Munia and one of them hands Rasheed a canteen of water. He holds it clumsily in his bound hands, drinks, passes it to Munia, then splashes some on the white man's face. Greg stirs, licks his lips, groans. Rasheed puts the bottle to the white man's mouth and Greg sucks down the liquid greedily.

Meanwhile, Goatman is giving orders. Rasheed watches one of the men tend to the horses, two others saunter off to collect firewood. A campfire is lit. When the jobs are done, the men sit around laughing, smoking, chewing on hunks of dried meat they unwrap from their saddles.

Rasheed looks at Greg. Beneath the blindfold, his complexion is chalky, the gash he's been carrying on his temple since they first met has reopened and the blood has dried almost black down one side of his face. Unable to read his eyes, Rasheed can only guess what is going through his mind.

An hour passes. The soldiers grow sleepy and their conversation ebbs. Rasheed is just beginning to wonder whether they have camped down for the day when he hears the low drone of vehicle engines. The militiamen rouse themselves and pick up their semi-automatic weapons and RPG launchers. One of them is carrying the white man's hunting rifle. He has attached a rope to the barrel and stock and has slung it over his shoulder. Rasheed notes the soldiers' lack of haste and speculates that the new arrivals must be anticipated friends rather than unexpected foe.

Two jeeps pull into the clearing, one full of soldiers, the other occupied by driver and front passenger only. The passenger seems to be the commanding officer. He has a smarter uniform and a holstered pistol. He waits for the driver to open his door for him before stepping down onto the dusty ground. Rasheed watches the soldiers snap to attention and salute. Goatman emerges from his troops, shakes the man's hand and they walk away from the clearing in deep conversation. Meanwhile the new arrivals mingle with the other soldiers. They shake hands, slap backs, offer cigarettes. There's laughter and excitement as news is exchanged. For something to do, Rasheed starts to count the militiamen.

One, two, three, four...

The soldiers keep shifting around and he has to start again. He tries to remember whether all the firewood-collectors have returned. There is too much movement and so, frustrated, he gives up the count.

Rasheed turns his head. His sister is obscured by the white man's body but he knows she is there.

Munia, are you well?

I am fine, she answers. There's a steeliness in her voice he's never heard before.

What should we do? he asks. As always, he defers to her when it matters.

Be patient, brother. Be patient.

Rasheed starts to count the soldiers again.

⌘

The second blow to Greg's head seems to have done more damage than the first. He lies on his side where he was thrown down on the ground, his hands tied together in front of him, his arms roped to his sides. The combination of the battering and blindfold render him dazed and disorientated, a passive bystander.

Since the moment he regained consciousness amongst the crash debris, he's been feeling strangely anaesthetised, blanketed in an odd glow of self-perceived invulnerability despite the moments of terror as he fled from Pol Pot's men. After all, he'd fallen out of the sky from several thousand feet and survived.

Now, having witnessed the casual shooting of the old man and the treatment meted out to Asrar, he's suddenly and painfully aware of the infinitesimal margins that separate life from death, the precariousness of the tightrope he walks. That comforting sense of invincibility has disappeared.

When Munia surreptitiously tugs on his sleeve, pokes and prods to get his attention, he makes an effort to regain his senses.

Greg, she whispers. She pronounces his name well, just like he taught her.

Take off my blindfold, he says. And then, to explain, I need to urinate.

Sshh, she answers, unwilling to draw attention to

themselves, to arouse their captors' wrath. She wants only to know that no permanent damage has been done, that Greg can still function.

So Greg remains blindfolded. He can hear but not observe Goatman's return with the other leader, the assembling of troops, the barked orders and hasty departure of the two vehicles, both packed this time with armed men. He is unaware that he and his fellow captives have been left with just two guards.

Munia knows that their fate is in her hands, that it is time to act. The two militiamen are busy attending to the horses. She watches them, waiting for her moment. One of them, she observes, has got the white man's hunting rifle slung over his shoulder. When they have finished, they squat under an adjacent tree. Hunting Rifle produces some playing cards and begins dealing out a game. Munia recognises the other militiaman as the Hossein who marched her mother away from her uncle's village. She feels a surge of energy, knowing that she will not rest until she has exacted vengeance from this man. This knowledge soothes her fury, tempering it with a chilled serenity.

She's still sitting on the ground, her hands fastened with cord. Slowly, carefully, with the most imperceptible of movements, she begins to shuffle on her backside, past the sightless figure of Greg, towards her brother.

⌘

Rasheed only becomes aware of her approach when he turns and finds her squatting behind him. He smiles at her uncertainly, opens his mouth to say something, then shuts it quickly when he sees the look in her eyes, the slight shake of her head. He waits while she manoeuvres herself to his side, then turns slightly in towards him. She turns once to check that the soldiers are still absorbed in their card game, then edges closer and extends her bound arms towards her brother. For a moment he is confused and wonders why she is offering him her two hands, tied together and bunched into fists. Then she slowly opens her right hand and he sees the penknife she has been concealing. He looks up into her eyes and understands.

Manipulating the slippery penknife between them to prise open the longest blade with their hands secured with rope is a tricky and painfully slow process made worse by the need to conceal it from their captors. It takes twenty minutes to get the blade open, Munia holding the knife handle while Rasheed works to open up the cutting edge. When they finally succeed, Munia allows herself a tight smile. Rasheed, seeing it, feels fortified.

Now they begin the next stage of the process. Munia holds the knife steady as Rasheed works the rope around his hands across the blade, back and forth, trying to minimise his movements, to draw no attention. He keeps one eye on his sawing work, the other on the two soldiers. At one stage Hossein throws down a card and cries out in triumph. While the other guard picks up the deck of cards and begins to shuffle, Hossein looks over at his captives and sees that they have bunched together since he last looked at them. Rasheed freezes, closes his eyes and pretends to doze. Munia, who has her back to Hossein now, senses the danger, slips the knife into her dress and awaits the guard's approach with dread. But Hossein sees nothing amiss, or more likely cannot summon the energy to get up and investigate, and the moment passes.

The card game resumes in silence. Munia and Rasheed continue their surreptitious work. A horse whinnies and its comrade responds.

Greg's discomfort is growing. His blindfold, soggy with sweat, is itching madly. He's tried to distract himself, to let his mind drift to a more peaceful place, but he's become aware that his need to urinate is growing and the pressing ache in his bladder keeps bringing him back to reality.

I need to pee, he says to no one in particular.

Munia jumps, surprised by Greg's proximity and his breaking of the silence. She looks up from the knife she's holding, aware that he's drawing attention to their presence.

She whips the weapon back into her pocket.

Ssshhh.

I need to piss, he says. Can't hold it in much longer.

Shut up! Munia hisses.

Greg turns his head towards her, senses that his talking is unwanted and lapses again into silence. Munia waits for a nod from Rasheed and takes out the knife. She sees with satisfaction that they are making progress on Rasheed's rope.

For five minutes they work in silence, but then their progress is again interrupted by Greg. The tightness in his bladder has developed into a sharp stabbing sensation. It's all he can think about. This time, despite his vulnerable state, the ropes and blindfold, he stirs and gets to his feet.

He takes two tentative steps forward, teeters there for a few seconds, uncertain where to relieve himself.

Can somebody help? he asks, raising his voice a little.

One of the guards notices his movements.

Hey, he shouts, temporarily abandoning his cards. What are you doing?

Need to piss, Greg repeats. His bound hands rest just above his groin and he manoeuvres them down to his fly, unzips and takes out his penis.

Sit down, the guard calls out, his initial confusion giving way to annoyance. There's a trace of menace in his voice now, but Greg's need is too powerful. With a sigh, the pee begins to flow, an angry stream that is instantly absorbed by the sandy soil.

The guard has grabbed his rifle, is rising to his feet when he realises what Greg is doing. He looks at his colleague, they exchange a few words, laugh, shrug their shoulders and he resumes his seat. They watch Greg as he relieves himself, zips himself up, takes a few hesitant steps backwards and sits down again. Hossein cracks another joke, the other guard guffaws. They put their guns down and pick up their discarded cards.

Meanwhile, Munia and Rasheed have used the distraction to cut through the last few strands of the cord binding the young boy's hands. Careful to keep their movements measured and unhurried, Munia passes the knife to Rasheed who sets to work on her ropes. This time he has full use of his hands so his cutting actions are far more efficient. Within a few minutes, both children are free.

Now Munia takes back possession of the knife. She indicates to Rasheed that he should hide the severed ropes in his shorts. She bunches her hands together in front of her as if they are still fastened together, holds the penknife in her closed fist, the blade facing downwards, concealed between her legs. She's ready to proceed.

Munia, whispers Rasheed. What are we going to do?

Listen carefully and do exactly what I say, she answers, her voice low and calm. We need to find a moment when one of them moves away. To relieve himself, perhaps. Or fetch firewood. You must watch them carefully. When it happens, you call out to the remaining one that there's something wrong with me, that I'm very sick. Make it sound convincing. After that, I'll do the rest. OK, Rasheed? You understand?

Rasheed nods.

They stay like that, afraid to move, aware of the guards' every movement, every utterance. Munia wills Greg to stay silent, wills one of the soldiers to get up. Finally, after what seems like time without end, she hears a slapping of cards, a jeer of victory. She holds her breath and then, just as she resigns herself to another hand of cards, Rasheed nudges her. Slowly, ever so slowly, she turns her head a full ninety degrees and sees that Hossein is still sitting down, is fiddling with a cigarette, while the other guard is heading away towards a termite hill beyond where the horses are corralled.

He must be defecating, she thinks. It's now or never. She watches the man disappear behind the mound, checks that her hands still look tied, that the knife is concealed, then nudges Rasheed.

Hey! Help! My sister's dying! Help me, please. For the love of God, help me!

Munia was worried that Rasheed's acting might be feeble, that they would see through the ruse easily. Or that he might make such a racket that he'd send the absent guard hurrying back to investigate. But he's pitched his appeal perfectly. It's authentic-sounding but not too loud. She tenses herself.

Hossein drops his cigarette when he hears Rasheed's cries. He gets to his feet, picks up the hunting rifle the other guard has left and walks towards the children. If he has any suspicions, they aren't strong enough to worry him. After all, their hands are bound, he has the firearm, he is in control.

Rasheed is looking up at him with imploring eyes as he approaches. Munia, her back to him, squats between him and the young boy. He drops to his knees, puts his left hand on her shoulder, pulls her round to face him. His right hand is still holding the stock of the hunting rifle. There's a slight smile on his lips.

What's wrong, monkey? he begins. He's turned her round now and looking down at her face for the first time is momentarily confused to see that she, too, is smiling broadly. But before he has time to appreciate that something is amiss, she has spun round fully.

There's a blurred movement as her arm arcs up towards his midriff. He feels a blow to his chest, a moment of irritation bordering on anger. The thought flashes through his mind that he will punish this girl for hitting him, and then he looks down and sees the handle of a knife sticking out from above his belly, angled upwards, entering just below the bottom of his ribcage. It takes a few moments for him to grasp what has happened, for uncertainty to turn into terror.

God have mercy on me, what have you done, you daughter of a whore? he screams. He realises he's dropped his rifle, that the young boy is scrabbling forward to grab the weapon. It comes to him only now that the children's hands are no longer tied. Too late. He clasps his hands over the handle of the knife. Instinct forces him to pull the blade out. As the flow of blood immediately increases, he regrets his hasty action.

Bitch! he screams. Whore! He reaches out for the girl, still strong enough to react with violence. He makes a grab for her throat but she ducks and he flails. She's still sitting on the ground, an easy target, he thinks, as he snatches at her a second time. But he hasn't seen that the boy has risen to his feet, is swinging the butt of the rifle. There's a loud crack as it makes contact with his knees. He tumbles down onto the ground, his front now soaked with blood. A gradual wave of sleepiness is creeping over him as shock and blood loss set in. His anger has dissipated as quickly as it appeared. He feels calm, almost radiant.

Hey, what's going on?!

Rasheed, who has been watching Hossein with grim satisfaction, spins round. The other guard has heard his colleague's cries. Emerging from behind the termite mound, he is hastily buckling his belt as he runs towards them.

Rasheed is frozen with fear. He is aware that he's holding the hunting rifle but seems powerless to act. The guard is closing in fast. Munia's still on the ground. Greg has frozen, aware of some critical drama unfolding, unable to see or understand. As the guard passes the spot where he had been playing cards earlier, he registers that the second firearm, an assault rifle, is still there lying on the ground next to the discarded cards. He stops in mid-pace and bends to retrieve the weapon.

Rasheed hesitates for one long second. Then he acts. He hoists the hunting rifle, slides the safety catch off and raises the gun. The soldier has collected his weapon and lifts it into place with a fluid efficiency born out of experience. They point and aim together. There is a single retort, shockingly loud to Rasheed's ears. He has closed his eyes and when he opens them, he sees the guard lying in the dust.

For five seconds, nobody moves. Hossein stirs and groans. Munia gets to her feet. She takes the hunting rifle from Rasheed, goes over to the stricken soldier and bends to check that he is no longer a threat. Then she rummages in his pockets for spare bullets, pocketing a handful.

Come on, she says. There's no time. The others may come back any moment.

As if on cue, they hear in the distance the low hum of an engine.

The horses, says Munia.

The two children take a few steps towards the animals, then remember their travelling companion. He's still sitting in exactly the same position, seemingly oblivious to the bloody incident that has taken place. Rasheed retrieves the knife from Hossein and squats down in front of the white man. The young boy removes the blindfold and cuts his bonds. Greg is momentarily dazzled by the blinding light. His wrists are rubbed raw, his hands bluish from cut-off circulation.

Come, Greg, he says, his gentle tone failing to conceal the sense of urgency that he feels. We must go now.

What the fuck...? Greg responds, surveying the corpses in front of him, the pools of blood and severed ropes. Despite his disorientation, he is quick to understand what has occurred. He has recognised the panic in Rasheed's voice.

Munia knows she needs to prepare the horses. Before she sets to work, however, she returns to Hossein and kneels down next to his prone figure. He's moaning gently, his eyes closed. She shakes him, slaps his face. Her earlier desire to enjoy a drawn-out revenge has given way to an anxious wish to escape, to protect her brother.

Hey, Hossein, Hossein, wake up! She slaps him again and he stirs. His eyes flutter open. Tell me, where is the nearest camp? Where's the nearest camp for displaced people? Since the shoot-out, her mind has been racing. Her first instinct, to retrace their steps to Husham's village and search for their mother, has been quashed by the realisation that she could not find her way back. She remembers her mother's last words to her, that her priority must be to save her younger brother.

Water, he answers, his voice a weak croak.

Answer me first, then I'll give you water.

The soldier closes his eyes. For a moment, she fears he is slipping away. Then he swallows, opens his eyes again, and with great effort manages a faint whisper.

North, about thirty kilometres, he mutters. Beyond the

hills. He adds something else that she cannot catch, the name of the camp, she guesses.

She turns to Greg, about to say something to him, then decides that it will take too long. Instead, she squats down and dips a hand into his pockets. He flinches at the unexpected gesture but allows her to fish around. She brings out the compass she has seen him play with, knows he has explained to Rasheed. She passes it to her brother.

You understand this thing. You will be our guide. You heard the soldier. We must head north.

While Rasheed studies the compass, Munia gets busy with the horses. She releases all but three of the beasts and climbs up on her chosen ride, the rifle slung over her shoulder.

Be quick, Greg, she shouts breathlessly. Get on. She gestures to the horse, the largest of the remaining three.

What? he says in panic. A childhood fear of horses has carried through to adulthood and he shakes his head, the phobia compounded by his dazed state of mind. I'm not getting up on that. I can't. I don't know how.

Munia watches him, understands nothing of his words but reads the refusal in his tone. There's no time to argue.

Little brother, she calls to Rasheed. Greg cannot ride alone. You will ride with him. Hurry.

As always, Rasheed obeys. He drops the reins of the horse, leads Greg over to the imposing animal and signals that the two of them will ride together. He beckons to Greg to slide his left foot into the rudimentary stirrup and to haul himself up into the saddle. Greg looks mutinous, but the whine of the approaching engine cuts through the silence and Rasheed gestures to him, mimes the returning vehicle, the angry soldiers, draws a finger across his throat. The message is all too clear.

Sweet Jesus, Greg says. He lifts his foot into the stirrup and pulls himself into the saddle. Rasheed holds the bridle steady, then yanks himself up in front of Greg. He picks up the reins, kicks the horse into motion, then steers it out of the clearing. Checking the compass, he adjusts the horse's direction and looks round to check that his sister is following. In the distance the low drone of the motor engine grows in volume. He flicks the reins to urge the horse into a trot, kicks again to move into a canter.

⌘

The sudden transformation from confinement to escape has a salutary effect on Greg's mind. The disequilibrium brought about by his head trauma is clearing. He feels as if jolted out of a cloying dream, less reverie than hallucination. Physically, he knows some serious damage has been done. The side of his face is painful, his head pounding. He tries to remember whether there has ever been a time since the crash when he has not experienced this all-consuming hammering.

Still, the panic of their flight, the fear of capture has sent his adrenalin soaring, dispelled the terror he'd felt at the prospect of horse-riding. Rasheed has the reins. His own passenger status and lack of responsibility for overall control make the ordeal tolerable. He begins again to hope.

Greg scans the horizon to get his bearings. Ahead is a flat plain, in the distance a jagged range of hills. It looks so similar to the crash site, minus the wreckage of course, that for a few moments, Greg believes that he has somehow found his way back there.

For over an hour they make good progress, but the animals have not been properly fed and watered, and gradually their strength is exhausted. Galloping has given way to trotting, then to a steady walk. Every few minutes Munia twists around in her saddle, expecting to see the jeeps approaching at high speed.

Rasheed examines the compass. As they approach the hills, he can see that the track they are on must take them through a gorge between two particularly prominent peaks and that according to the compass, the camp must lie just beyond. He realises that riding due north across the plain must make them very exposed and does his best to zigzag along concealed wadis where possible. But knows that the three of them cannot be difficult to spot.

Munia is just wondering how long the horses can continue without rest or sustenance when, turning in her saddle, she sees what she has been dreading. Away in the distance, the jeep, a cloud of dust rising in its wake, is heading straight for them at some speed. She pictures Goatman gazing at them through his binoculars and shudders, her feelings torn between revulsion, fear and anger.

She looks at her brother and sees that both he and Greg have observed the approaching danger. Without a word, the siblings urge their horses on, flicking the reins across the animals' necks, kicking them on in a last desperate effort to reach safety.

The final few kilometres before they cut through the gorge seem to stretch on for an eternity. The horses somehow sense their riders' terror and find a second wind, but even so, the jeep seems to eat up the distance between them effortlessly.

As they get closer, the three riders hear a series of loud cracks and simultaneously realise that their pursuers are shooting at them even though they must still be some distance out of range. Nevertheless, Greg finds himself braced for the deadly impact of these bursts of gunfire. With no control over the horse, it is he who feels most powerless.

As they draw nearer to the gorge, their route takes them around a modest hillock and the vehicle, still some way behind, temporarily disappears from view. Ahead is the gully and in the distance, across the flat, arid plain, he can see the camp, the ragged armada of makeshift tents scattered haphazardly across the landscape. Shabby and chaotic as it evidently is, he nevertheless recognises it as a place of sanctuary. The desire to be transported there at once is so powerful that he feels it like a twist in his stomach, an instant of lurching nausea.

The ravine is narrow and short, a flat corridor of some hundred or so metres with sloping rock on either side. A minute or two and they'll be through, and after that it's just the home stretch to safety.

But then Greg's horse stumbles, a hoof caught in a treacherous crack in the baked ground. It all happens in a blur, the horse buckling, lurching, head over heels, folding and rolling, Greg and Rasheed tumbling off, spinning through space, the force of impact on the sandy soil, the air knocked out of them. Munia sees at once what has happened, pulls her horse up and is down on her feet and racing towards them in a matter of seconds.

Dragging the two figures to their feet, Munia unslings the rifle. Rasheed clutches his arm to his side, grits his teeth. He has heard a snapping noise when he fell and knows something is broken. As yet the adrenaline keeps the pain at bay. Munia hears the drone of the vehicle engine revving. It is still out of view but any minute it will sweep around the bend. With bitter rage, Munia sees defeat looming.

After the long period bound and blindfolded, his back-seat role on horseback, Greg feels as if his fate has been in the hands of others, spiralling out of control. But this tumble has now given him back his independence, galvanised his spirit of resolve. He is calm, composed.

It takes him a few seconds to take stock of the situation, to estimate the distance between themselves and safety, themselves and the jeep, to assess the effect of Rasheed's injury on their progress, to weigh up their options. In an instant he sees what has to be done.

The horse that he and Rasheed have been riding is clearly out of action, one of its front legs broken. It lies in the dust, its body trembling uncontrollably. Greg gestures to Munia to pass him the hunting rifle and motions for her to fetch their remaining beast. While she collects the animal, he takes off his belt and straps Rasheed's injured arm to his torso. He helps him climb up onto the horse's back and signals for Munia to follow. There is no time for words. He simply points off in the direction of the camp.

Munia gazes down at the man and understands what he is doing. Her overwhelming urge is to protect her brother, so she looks him in the eye and nods. Before she pulls on the reins, she remembers what she has in her pocket, salvaged from the shot soldier. She hands Greg the handful of shells.

Precious seconds have passed. A burst of gunfire throws them into action. The jeep has appeared from around the bend, is bearing down on them at speed. Munia turns the horse, kicks out and sets off at a gallop. Greg looks up at the rocky slope to his right, grasps his rifle tightly and makes a run for cover.

It takes him a couple of minutes to scramble up to a suitable ledge. He crouches down behind a boulder, checks the magazine, slips off the safety catch, aims through the telescopic sight and pulls the trigger.

The jeep is twenty yards from the entrance to the corridor when the bullet strikes. Greg had aimed for the driver, misses, hits Goatman in the chest. The driver panics momentarily, the jeep skids, swerves, then pulls to a stop. The soldiers, all except Goatman, pile out and throw themselves behind the jeep or run for cover behind bushes, trees, termite mounds.

One of the soldiers has seen the horse gallop off and thinks that perhaps the danger has passed. He emerges from behind a thorny shrub. Greg understands that to buy time for the children he must keep the soldiers pinned down for as long as possible. He raises the rifle, aims and fires. Again a wobbly shot, the bullet just grazing the man's shoulder. But the sound is loud and his action has the intended effect. The soldiers poke their rifles out from their hiding places, letting off volley after volley of gunfire in Greg's general direction, but remain concealed behind their protective cover. Every few minutes, Greg raises his head and fires off a shot. For the moment, they have reached a stalemate.

Behind his boulder, Greg closes his eyes to visualise the jeep as it was before he fired his first shot and tries to calculate how many soldiers he's up against. Six, seven, eight, he guesses. He raises the gun and pulls the trigger, but is rewarded with nothing more than a click. He slides out the magazine and checks his pockets for the bullets Munia gave him. He counts them out. Six, seven, eight. He reloads the rifle.

When he looks up next, he realises that he needs to be more vigilant. He catches a glimpse of a soldier throwing himself behind a rock directly below him. He strains to see where else the advancing militiamen have moved to, but ducks down as a shower of bullets crack against the rocks just above him. It dawns on him that it is he who is now pinned down. The tables have turned.

He needs to keep moving, so he squats down, shuffles along the ledge, then scrambles up as quickly as his exhausted legs can carry him, zigzagging his way between a series of boulders. There's an angry salvo of gunfire, bullets smash against the rocks, ricochet off at random angles. My God, he thinks. That was close.

Now he has a line of cover he can use to add an element of surprise to his counterattack. He turns and looks northwards and sees the dot of the horse drawing ever closer to the encampment in the distance. He knows that he has almost succeeded.

He turns back and looks down towards his attackers, catching glimpses of the last of the soldiers finding cover among the boulders on the slope below. They're getting closer, he thinks. He notices that he's dropped his rifle, reaches down to pick it up, and is puzzled when his arm refuses to obey the instruction. He looks down and sees for the first time that he's been hit, that a bullet has passed through where his arm meets his shoulder. The stain of blood is spreading but he feels lightheaded, unruffled, almost serene.

He lifts the gun with his good right hand, wedges it between two rocks, looks down and spots a soldier making his way along a ridge to his left. He aims, fires, the bullet hits home. A lucky shot, the soldier cries out, spins and falls. His movements are now slow, laboured. He ducks back behind the rock, edges over to a new position ten metres to his right as another salvo of bullets strikes the boulders around him. A few more minutes bought.

Focus, Greg, focus, he tells himself. The giddy feeling is growing, as is his sense of peaceful composure. He notices that the gunfire has stopped, reasons that his shooting of the last soldier may have made them more cautious, that knowing that he cannot escape, they have perhaps dug in to wait it out. Suits me, he thinks as he drops down to the ground, turns and rests his back against a rock. The rifle slips from his grasp and he's suddenly too tired to pick it up. Suits me fine.

NUALA 2

To grieve is to abandon hope, to abandon Greg. So for those first months after the event, Nuala concentrates on Not Grieving.

With no body to mourn, her fury towards the world at large burns unabated. But despite the intensity of her inner turmoil, if Nuala were to ask herself, during those first months, what she was doing with herself, she would shrug and think, 'I'm not grieving'. And it is this Not Grieving that is characterised by the vacillation in her emotions, the illogical fluctuations, the irrational switching between courses of action, feelings and attitudes relating to Greg's absence.

Not Grieving, for instance, means at times wanting to tell the world about Greg's disappearance – after all it consumes her every waking moment so why pretend to want to discuss anything else? – but at other times an inability to address this unspeakable event, an almost superstitious feeling that by maintaining silence she can prevent confirmation of her loss. When Greg's agent, Burnley, calls to discuss cooperating with the media on Greg's obituary, she point-blank refuses.

Not Grieving means at times an obsessive researching of every facet of Greg's disappearance, a need to peel back and reveal the truth behind the events. The media have speculated on which terrorist group was responsible, and she spends hours googling the names of the alleged perpetrators, researching details of the air crash, the regional conflict, then aviation accidents in general.

She goes over every moment she can claw back from her memory of Greg's final days in Oxford, of their transcontinental phone calls. She phones Farai twenty, thirty times to ask him about the details of that last week in South Africa, the minutiae of their daily conversations, what Greg ate and drank, his sketching, the funeral, the visits to town, the market, the pub.

But then at other times she refuses to allow herself to explore what has happened and banishes such thoughts from her mind. It's a painful area, of course. And after all, he'll walk back through the door any day, so why waste time on an episode that they can soon put behind them? To allocate time to the contemplation of Greg's disappearance is to concede to its significance.

So Not Grieving means an ebb and flow, an initial tendency followed up by some contradictory manifestation. Driving to London to meet a Foreign Office official, drugged by a feeling of utter recklessness, she finds herself hitting over a hundred miles an hour on the motorway; the next day, consumed by acute anxiety, she cannot sleep for fear that the washing machine will leak and flood the house.

She oscillates between lethargy and sleeplessness, between razor-sharp concentration and cognitive deficiency, between an inability to leave the house and a desire to flee.

And most of all, in her process of Not Grieving, she shifts between anger and guilt. How could she have let him go? How could he have allowed himself to take such risks? How can she blame him? How can he allow her to feel such guilt? Why don't the authorities do more? Why are her friends and relatives so insensitive? So oversensitive? How can people carry on as if nothing has happened, as if the world hadn't stopped, a cataclysmic permanent time-out, when Fran first knocked on her classroom door?   So the months pass, and Nuala concentrates on Not Grieving.

⌘

Despite the best efforts of the government officials she meets, Nuala does not give up her plans to visit the crash site. As she threatened, she does go to the newspapers, as do many of the other victims' families. Through one national paper, she meets a number of the bereaved. They swap details and begin communicating by phone and email. There are profiles and interviews in magazines, a petition to Downing Street, a demonstration outside the foreign embassy. There is no shift in diplomatic positioning, but she doesn't give up.

Still, though, she feels apart from these grieving relatives. She suffers a secret guilt for the loss that they have suffered and which she, in her mind, has not. The DNA testing process is near to completion and almost all the other people she campaigns with have received conclusive confirmation of their loved ones' demise. The officials continue to insist Greg must be presumed dead. According to them there's no reasonable scenario that can explain his status as alive but unaccounted for. But without a body, Nuala remains unconvinced.

⌘

When the children were younger, they were inseparable, due partly at least to a natural pleasure they found in each other's company, a genuine lack of sibling rivalry. In recent years, though, as their different characters have developed, they've grown apart. Their interests have sent them in different directions.

Now, through the fog of her own self-obsession, Nuala realises that she's in danger of damaging her relationship with her children. It's another example of unhealthy vacillation, a tendency to switch between smothering and neglect. She's aware that she needs to nurture each one on their own, to seek opportunities to share their individual passions separately. Her instinct now, though, tells her to corral the children. It's a kind of misguided laager mentality. Sammy doesn't mind this. He is used to a working mum with a hectic lifestyle and enjoys the extra attention. He hasn't yet seen that although he finds himself in close proximity to his mother more frequently, she is, for the most part, incapable of engaging with him at any meaningful level. She seems permanently distracted, absorbed in a world apart.

Beth, two years older, is more astute. At first she feels a natural empathy for her preoccupied mother. She accepts the periods of absent-mindedness, the erratic displays of emotional warmth, the lack of connectedness. But she grows increasingly frustrated and without any conscious rejection of her mother, she begins to look elsewhere for a maternal figure.

It is Nuala's friend, Mary, who recognises the early onset of puberty. She buys Beth a stock of sanitary pads in preparation for the first loss of blood. And so it is to Mary that Beth goes to ask for help shopping for her first set of bras, one pink, one white, one patterned with pale blue and yellow forget-me-nots.

Does Nuala notice these significant landmarks in Beth's development? She puts the bras through the wash every week, sees the box of pads in Beth's drawer each time she puts away her clean, folded knickers. When she finds out from Beth about where they came from, she smiles and nods, but there's something a little robotic in her response. Beth sighs, shrugs, small signs of a growing impatience

⌘

As she had suspected, work does bring some relief, though there are a number of early setbacks beginning with a panic attack during her first day back when she is forced to flee the classroom for the shelter of the ladies' loo.

The autumn term is demanding, with students preparing for speaking exams and teachers gearing up for a spring inspection. Nevertheless, she looks ahead to the Christmas break with a sense of dread.

The children have never known a Christmas without Greg. How many of the rituals are associated with him? His practice of taking Sammy to choose a tree at the sea scouts' hut; his habit of baking three Christmas cakes with Beth the Sunday after she breaks up from school; his custom of taking both kids off to the Ashmolean one afternoon in the pre-Christmas run-up to give Nuala a chance to get on top of her own preparations;

his penchant for filling the children's stockings with practical jokes – stink bombs, snap-shut gum, itching powder and fake turds – and Nuala's with a single piece of jewellery, always silver, always featuring a green or blue semi-precious stone. To match your eyes, he'd say, and wink seductively. She'd tut and groan disapprovingly, feel secretly thrilled, then punch him on the shoulder.

And of course it's not just Christmas that lays bare the pain of Greg's absence. The longer that he is gone, the more Nuala finds the present begging a comparison with how things used to be. So many routines are either no longer possible or else soured and therefore undesirable. So much, once taken for granted, she deems priceless now that it has become unobtainable. In identifying the extent of her misfortune, Nuala makes new discoveries every day.

It's too daunting to gauge her loss in such terms as 'widow' or 'single parent', even though increasingly she feels pressure from those around to accept one or other of these as her newly-acquired status. At the moment, the most she can manage is to measure her loss according to the number of small practices that have changed.

Greg made up the fourth player, along with Nuala, Mary and Phil, for a regular Sunday afternoon tennis match. Now she will not contemplate the recruitment of a replacement.

He used to take Sammy to the Sunday morning football matches, shouting out support from the touchline as the boy and his team mates fought for midfield supremacy on the pitch. This habit allowed Nuala time to take Beth off for two hours of swimming, followed by hot chocolate and cake and mother-daughter bonding. Now Nuala takes Sammy to football, determined that he should receive no less support than before. She switches Beth's swimming to Thursday afternoons, while Sammy is at karate, but it's not as relaxed and she knows that Beth is disappointed.

In bed, when the kids are asleep, she misses his touch, the intimacy but, almost as painfully, the nightly attempt at the quick crossword. Since his disappearance, she hasn't even bought a newspaper, let alone tried to resurrect the evening tradition.

A piece of her jigsaw is missing.

She feels her whole identity altered, her social status transformed. Greg's disappearance teaches her how far she had gone in the journey from individual to team member. And now, returned to her original standing, it becomes clear very quickly which roles she took on in the team, and which ones, previously delegated to Greg, now leave her clueless.

DIY work is the clearest example. Greg had always been a natural around the house – it was only his ability that had allowed them to buy the Divinity Road house in the first place and had given them the courage to take on the challenge of a complete modernisation on such a shoestring budget. It'd been her idea: buy something bigger than they could afford, but cheap because of its state of disrepair, then he'd do it up with his builder brother, Ian. They'd spent months house-hunting, determined to find the perfect balance between ruin and affordability. They had finally found it in the Divinity Road place, on the market after the death of the owner, a woman in her eighties who'd lived there alone for many years.

It was a wreck. There was no central heating, the kitchen and bathrooms needed replacing, the roof was in poor condition, the exterior needed re-pointing, the plaster in many of the rooms had blown. There were problems with floorboards, skirting, insulation, damp-proofing.

But underneath the neglect were some promising gems – original fireplaces, beautiful ceiling roses, an elegant staircase. It had taken five years of hard work, each stage postponed until they'd saved enough for the materials, the rental of the floor sander, the scaffolding hire, the new boiler. She'd done what she could, but it was superficial, her input limited to the initial design and later the painting and decorating. But the nitty-gritty was down to Greg.

And now, in his absence, it starts with minor inconveniences – the towel rack comes off in the bathroom and the holes need filling, new screwholes drilled. She opens the door to the tool cupboard, aware that she's never rummaged inside before and fumbles with drill bits and rawlplugs. Eventually she asks Phil to help and vows to buy herself a book on DIY.

She sees the flaking paintwork on the outside of the windows and remembers that they'd agreed to get the exterior of the house repainted. In the past it was Greg who either carried out the work himself or identified firms, chased up quotes, made the final choice and supervised the work. It's too daunting to contemplate for the moment, so she ignores the problem.

More worryingly, there are numerous on-line accounts she needs access to – internet banking, insurance, road tax, something new every week – and she realises not only how much of their financial and administrative affairs Greg dealt with, but also how many of these dealings require passwords that only he knew. She recalls one or two of them, always the names of artists he admired. She's forced to experiment each time a password is demanded, trial and error, hours spent punching in combinations of Kiefer, Raedecker, Freud, Magritte and Lautrec.

So at every turn, there are reminders of her loss. Broken habits, new responsibilities, she meets each new problem unprepared, aware that she's winging it, that she has no strategy to cope beyond day-to-day survival.

Financially, Nuala finds that her head is still above water. There will be an eventual compensation package from the airline, a complicated insurance matter that Nuala leaves in the hands of her solicitor. In the meantime her own salary pays the mortgage and meets their basic needs. And she continues to receive the income from the occasional sale of Greg's paintings, though she grows increasingly unwilling to lose a single one. She feels a need to keep them close to her, to cherish them.

In fact the publicity surrounding Greg's demise (for that is how his disappearance is now perceived by the media) has only served to heighten interest in his work, that macabre phenomenon that equates death with popularity and success.

His agent presses her to sell. She demurs at first but financial fears eventually hold sway and she sanctions the sale of three or four paintings, works that she knows Greg was not overly fond of.

⌘

As Christmas looms, Nuala's parents push for her to bring the children over to their farm for ten days over the festive period. She recognises the opportunity for a change of environment as a way of cheating the gloom that would inevitably descend if they spent it in their own house, however maniacally she tried to establish an atmosphere of jollity.

They drive to Wales, catch the ferry from Fishguard to Rosslare, then it's another couple of hours in the car to the farm. The days pass in a blur of farmyard games, drizzle and fog, steaming plates of mashed potato with stew or chops, endless cups of tea and cake. They make the tour of relatives, more tea and ham sandwiches, then sherry or whisky. They are taken to the pub, rounds of white wine for Nuala, red lemonade and crisps for the children. Nuala's parents encourage the kids to get out of the house and explore the farm. There are hay barns and stables, an old smithy and a kitchen garden, meadows full of indolent cattle. But Nuala, overly anxious, worries about silage pits, kicking horses and unguarded machinery. She can only relax when the kids are in sight.

When Nuala gets back to Oxford, she accepts that although she may need to drop routines that serve as the most painful reminders of the past, she will also need to create new ones to fill the void. She signs up for an evening course in Urdu, but she cannot concentrate away from the children and begins to skip classes. After the crash she had dropped her old yoga class but now finds a martial arts school offering two evening classes a week at one of the local secondary schools. Joan, her neighbour, agrees to babysit for one session. She pays a neighbour's daughter to sit in for the other. The training is physically hard but she relishes the escape and the opportunity to vent her anger and frustration in acts of controlled aggression.

Nuala's over-protectiveness, her reluctance to let the children out of her sight, continues to be a problem. She has been vaguely aware of this irrational tendency since she learned of the crash, but her state of mental imbalance does not allow her to face it head on. She negotiates with her line manager to drop her teaching hours to three-and-a half days a week. She volunteers to help Sammy's teacher in class every Thursday morning, signs up to accompany Beth's class on all their school excursions.

Sammy positively relishes the extra time spent in her company, but his older sister becomes increasingly exasperated by her omnipresence. Her natural desire for her own independence is growing, and this control begins to feel intolerable. When her mother insists that Debbie comes to their house for a sleepover, rather than the other way round, or when she offers to accompany Beth and Charlotte to the park, her daughter grinds her teeth and decides to cancel the arrangements rather than put up with her mother's company. And at that stage still, Nuala remains oblivious, unable yet to pick up the signals, to recognise the scope of her own madness.

⌘

A further change in Nuala's behaviour since the tragedy is a growing introspection. She is unable to take part in group social events with the same assurance and enthusiasm as in the past. She's not sure whether to put it down to a loss of confidence or whether she now simply finds such occasions trivial and tiresome.

She remembers her monthly book club get-togethers in the past. Over cava, cheese, olives and French bread, the women would talk about their frustrations over errant or disobliging husbands, their worries about underperforming or wayward children, their commentaries on school admissions and house prices, on interior decoration and residents' parking, on foreign holidays and frail parents, on irregular sex and disappointing after-school clubs. She remembers that she too would join in. But the events now appear alien. The Nuala who took part seems a remote stranger.

It's been six months. Tonight, the first Friday of the month, is supposed to be book group night, her first attendance back since Fran's knock at the door. She'd thought she would go and had even organised Joan's babysitting services, but had panicked at tea-time, a crisis of confidence. Instead, she has allowed both children to invite friends over for sleepovers. She turns a blind eye as they turn the lounge into a bombsite with pillow fights, crisps, sticky juice and popcorn.

Now the children have been asleep for hours, she's been dozing in front of the TV, but she stirs and gets to her feet. She surveys the wreckage of her lounge and begins piling up the dirty plates onto a tray, collecting the half-empty bowls of snacks, gathering the empty juice cartons for the recycling bin. She checks on the children in their bedrooms for the umpteenth time that evening, then returns to the kitchen to stack cutlery and crockery into the dishwasher. The oven clock tells her that it's one o'clock but sleep still feels out of reach, so she takes out the hoover to run over the rug in the lounge.

It's been a difficult day to get through. That afternoon, a long conversation with the police liaison officer to bring her up to date with the latest investigations. As usual, little new to report. The officer is honest and direct, which Nuala appreciates. A final confirmation that DNA testing on all human remains has been completed and there are now only a couple of passengers unaccounted for. It is thought most likely that they've either been vaporised in the explosion or carried off by wild animals. Highly unlikely, but still considered a faint possibility, is that they've survived and left the crash site under their own steam. However, the question then arises: why have they not re-appeared in the interval? No, this seems almost beyond belief. The official position is that there are no survivors. Of course, for Nuala, without a body to mourn, beyond belief lies the limbo of doubt. Despite the officer's candour and conviction, Nuala feels as if she's been left marooned on an island of uncertainty.

And so Nuala switches on the dishwasher, puts on a load of laundry while she's at it, reluctantly makes her way up to bed. Tomorrow she has a day of child-ferrying, a shopping run and lesson preparation. She's still not ready to sleep but knows she must try. She leaves the landing light on and undresses in the semi-darkness of her bedroom. Naked, she stares at herself in the full-length mirror, traces the outline of her face, the shadows where her eyes should be, below her breasts, between her legs.

She remembers years before, Greg's one and only attempt to paint her nude one evening in the flat they'd first lived in. She'd been six months' pregnant with Beth, heavy but voluptuous, her libido on overdrive, and after forty minutes she'd grown bored, had coaxed him away from his brushes and they'd ended up coupling on the sofa where she'd been posing. That was as far as he'd got with her painting – no more than a half-finished charcoal outline – but they'd had the sketch framed and it hung, an anonymous souvenir of sensual abandonment, next to the medicine cabinet in the upstairs bathroom.

But in the darkness of her bedroom, she feels a different kind of abandonment. She climbs into bed and buries herself under her duvet. A few minutes' later she gets up again and moves to the chest of drawers. She pulls open the bottom one that Greg had used for his clothes and takes out the green v-neck tee-shirt that he'd worn in bed on their last night together, the one he'd thrown on the floor in his hurry to be on his way.

With an almost guilty air, she carries it back to bed, slides back under the covers and puts her face to the cotton garment and breathes in deeply. Though his scent has faded, it's still unmistakably of him. She takes in his musty odour, a slightly sour combination of sweat and soap and white spirit. It's the most powerful reminder she has of him and sometimes, clutching it to her breasts, burying her face in it, it's the only way she can get to sleep.

⌘

From the sixth month of Greg's disappearance, Nuala hits a number of important milestones, the first of which is the memorial service. Friends and family, those who have accepted Greg's demise, have been pushing for it for months. They dig out the usual clichés. It is a celebration of his life, a paying of respects, even that dreaded word, closure. So why does Nuala eventually agree?

Part of it, of course, is her vulnerable state, She's caught at a weak moment and bows to the pressure. Those around her are pleased, see it as an important part of the grieving process – they call it acceptance – which began with denial.

Nuala doesn't contradict them, but inside an illogical half-hope that the ritual of the service will somehow conjure up a miraculous return of the prodigal husband. In her more lucid moments she recognises the lunacy of her idea but keeps her thoughts locked up inside like a guilty secret.

In the end the service passes relatively painlessly. She immerses herself in the preparations, the on-the-day organisation, in dealing with the children, so the experience passes in a numbing fog. It's an unreal day, and so easier to get through. It's the other days, the ones before and after, where she has to live with her reality.

Another milestone, her return to the book club. It's at Mary's house, usually a place of refuge for Nuala, but tonight the atmosphere's strained. Too much effort is made by the women to behave 'normally'. Too much thought is given before speaking to avoid a ghastly faux pas. Nuala knows from Mary's gossip that one member, Amanda, has only recently been told by her spouse that he is moving in with his lover, the inevitable younger work colleague. She is still distraught and in normal circumstances, much of the evening would be given over to her, the others listening while she vents her feelings. Tonight, though, there's an understanding that even such a domestic upheaval as this cannot compare to Nuala's ordeal. Aware of the story, watching her friends skirt around it, only adds to Nuala's sense of isolation.

Another member of the group, Tamsin, has been single for over a year following the discovery of her husband's adultery and her subsequent move for divorce. Part of book club nights are usually given over to the other members listening to Tamsin's latest escapades. It's a brief moment of vicarious excitement for the other middle-aged women, mostly settled into long-term partnerships or permanent single status.

One night she'll be showing off her recently-acquired tattoo, a shooting star on her shoulder, another narrating a hilarious episode speed dating. Oiled with alcohol, she'll describe her new life of liberation and danger – tales of dubious lovers and disastrous liaisons.

She's a good story-teller, her timing sharp and punchy, her delivery usually inspiring a mixed reaction of hilarity and incredulity. The others will listen intently, their unspoken thoughts vacillating between pity and envy.

Then she'll come to the end of an anecdote and somebody will mention their daughter's request for a tummy piercing, a recent experience of hair removal laser treatment, a son's disastrous school report, and they'll shift back to safer territory – families, children, domestic conflict.

But tonight it's different. Stilted conversation, Nuala's friends are desperate to avoid anything at either end of the emotional scale.

Nuala knows they mean well. They've all done their best over the past months. And she knows the atmosphere is partly her fault. She's become increasingly aware how many of her social skills she's lost since Before became After.

At the end of the evening, Mary asks Nuala to stay on.

You OK, love? she'd asked earlier on. Finding it hard?

A bit, she'd admitted. I'll be alright.

Now Mary makes tea for Nuala and they sit on the sofa their mugs on the table amongst the shrapnel of cava corks and olive stones.

I'm sorry, says Nuala. I really killed the evening, didn't I?

It's not you, it was us. We were pussyfooting around. God it must have been awful for you. It was excruciating for me at times.

Yeah, well, says Nuala, smiling. It does things to her face muscles that feel very unfamiliar. I'm not much fun to be around.

But that's your right, your privilege. You can act any bloody way you want. There are no rules for how to behave, you can make them up. Our culture's so bound up in suppressing our feelings, avoiding outward displays of emotion. You look at other cultures, they don't bottle things up.

Yeah, well, Nuala repeats.

Whatever you feel, say, do, it's OK by us, Nuala. We know what you're going through and we know what sort of person you are, however hard you're finding it at the moment. Don't forget, we've all known you for years. Everyone loves you, Nuala, we all admire you. You give so much, you never expect anything in return.

Oh for God's sake...

No, let me finish. You're in a hole at the moment so deep that you've forgotten what you're really like. But we haven't forgotten. If there's a favour that you can do anyone, you jump at the chance. Nothing's ever too much trouble. I don't know whether it's Catholic guilt, sweetheart genes or a damn good upbringing but you've always been that way. You don't wait to be asked, you look for ways to help. You're thoughtful, caring, loyal.

Please, Nuala protests.

When Tanya's father had that fall and she had to go up to Scotland to sort him out, it was you who took her kids in for a fortnight while she was away.

Look...

No, hear me out. When Cassie had the gall bladder op, it was you who visited every day, looked after her dogs. Mary's building up a head of steam now. Who makes the soup for the school winter fair every year? Who does the cash and carry runs for its summer fete? Nuala shrugs. Whenever there's a birthday party for a child, it's always you who offers to help with the food, the ferrying. And you're always the last one to leave, mucking in with the cleaning up afterwards.

Everyone helps out.

Tell me, Nuala, how many kids are you godmother to?

Oh, come on...

No, it's true. And that's not all. You're damn good fun, too. Remember all those girlie weekends we used to go on. Whenever we were planning them, the question we'd all be asking each other was always, 'Will Nuala be coming?'. Why? Because your presence was a guarantee of a bloody good laugh.

You're embarrassing me now, says Nuala.

It's true. Remember Ingrid's hen party? The boozy ferry crossing to Calais, the gourmet restaurant booked? An evening of fun with a dawn return crossing to recover? Remember what happened?

Nuala smiles ruefully.

Yeah, I screwed up, forgot my passport. They wouldn't let me off the boat at Calais.

And what did we do? Bugger off to the posh nosh, the clubbing? No, we stayed on the boat with you, all sixteen of us, lost our deposits on the restaurant meal, spent the evening drinking in the ferry bar, lasagne and salad for all in the canteen, made our own bloody entertainment. Bloody fantastic, it was, too. Remember the dancing on that silly cabaret stage, the girl band routine we did with Carrie and Linda and Martina? And you know what? We didn't stay out of pity for you, there wasn't an ounce of resentment amongst the lot of us. We stayed because we knew damn well that you'd be the life and soul, the one to make the party as memorable as it was. We stayed because we loved you. And you were embarrassed out of your skin, kept saying Ingrid would never forgive you. Well, you know what? When you owned up about the passport, she was the first to suggest we bin the restaurant and stay on the boat. Everyone else wanted to, but felt too awkward to propose it, not without Ingrid's say-so. When she made the suggestion, we all felt such relief.

Nuala listens, starts to say something, but she's welling up and her face crumples. Now there are tears for her loss, not only of Greg but of herself, of who she once was. And of who she will never again be. As she heaves great sobs, Mary shifts up to her, puts an arm round her shoulders.

There you go, says Mary. You have a bloody good cry. You do whatever you want. Remember, you make up the rules.

⌘

A further milestone. Nuala starts seeing a counsellor, a referral by her GP. She has her first experience of the professionalisation of death and bereavement. Dr Ahmad talks about the grief cycle, the mental and physical effects of bereavement.

It's from him that she learns about 'complicated' or prolonged grief. A reaction to the loss of someone on whom the bereaved is particularly dependent for happiness or well-being such as a partner or, for a parent, one's child. He explains that this more complex version of grief can also stem from a situation where there are other circumstantial factors (like no body to grieve for, no definite confirmation? Nuala wonders). In this version, according to Dr Ahmad, the bereaved becomes locked into the ordeal and cannot move through the cycle. The transient trauma becomes permanent.

From Dr Ahmad, too, she learns the formal names for the 'symptoms' she has been experiencing, the tell-tale signs of grief which, with his help, she can now skim through, apply to herself and wryly tick off. A sense of unreality? Check. Emotional anaesthesia? Check. Depersonalisation and withdrawal? Check. Feelings of anger, terror, resentment, jealousy and depression? Check, check, check, check, and fucking hellish check.

And then there are the physical symptoms that, once formalised by him, she can now identify. Since the initial shock of the crash, the first days of adrenalin overload, she has found herself overcome by periods of lassitude. Her nights are frozen in timeless insomnia. She develops palpitations, breathlessness, a chest so tight she would be at the doctor's in a flash if she didn't recognise in the back of her mind that what she was suffering from was mindfuck not body sickness. As Dr Ahmad reassures her that these indicators are entirely normal, she feels a sweeping sense of relief.

In one session, Dr Ahmad gives Nuala a writing task, to produce three texts about herself. The first one must describe a past pre-Greg event where Nuala felt strong and happy and powerful. The second is to describe a significant episode in Nuala's life that occurred sometime around the beginning of her relationship with Greg. The final text has to describe a more recent episode involving Greg and herself, a time of intimacy.

For the first episode she writes about the second of her parachute jumps and fills two sides of A4. She tells the counsellor about her jump dream, finds herself describing the pleasure she now finds in her martial arts class as if the two activities are somehow connected.

For the second text she writes about the holiday she took to Tunisia some twelve years before, and in so doing notices that she's attempting to re-discover her old self. The process sets off a stream of memories of those early days. She begins:

> I'd planned the trip with a college friend, Liz, a chance to enjoy my independence, discover a new culture, kick back from the stresses of teaching and London. I'd met Greg three years before at an NGO conference in Nairobi, me an English language teacher in Eritrea, he an art teacher in Zimbabwe. At first I'd viewed Greg as a bit lightweight, an enjoyable holiday romance, but probably no more. But he'd been persistent in his attentions, producing a regular stream of letters from Zimbabwe, sent first to my Asmara home and then, when I left Africa a year after our Nairobi encounter, to the flat in London I'd shared with three other girls. That was my first job on the mainland, teaching English to French au pairs, Japanese teenagers and young Spanish

business graduates at a north London college of further education.

Despite his apparent interest, I hadn't expected our relationship to develop. Not that anyone else had taken his place. Between graduating in French from Trinity College Dublin and my overseas volunteering, I'd spent three years teaching English to foreign students in a private language school in Cork. Arriving in London after Cork and Asmara felt like being thrown from a paddling pool into an ocean. There was so much to discover and the girls I was living with were more interested in partying than romantic relationships. Clubs, concerts, museums, pubs, badminton and tennis, but always as a female gang. True, I'd got drunk at a party in Camden Town and enjoyed a one-night stand with an American who did something in insurance. I can scarcely remember anything about him apart from his magnificent mane of hair. And I'd been on a couple of dates with a colleague from work, a rather uptight Mancunian with a barking laugh and receding hairline. But that was all, and for the time being, this single status suited me.

Why should I have thought that my fling with Greg had meant anything significant? After all we'd only been together a week in Nairobi before heading back to our respective postings. When my contract had come to an end, he'd already extended his. He made it clear he was enjoying a footloose life in Harare and was in no hurry to return to the gloom of insipid Britain. But the letters had continued, and when he'd finally headed home a year after my departure, he'd made straight for London. He'd called me up a few days later, we'd met up in a pub on the Archway Road and I'd surprised myself when, catching sight of him standing at the bar as I'd walked in, I'd felt a kick of pleasure, of tenderness, as if he already belonged to me.

He was looking for a teaching job and I'd kept

an eye on vacancies at my college. I found a post for him covering someone's maternity leave that was soon upgraded to permanent. So without quite knowing how, I discovered that my temporary overseas fling had become a more serious domestic relationship. Three months later, when my tenancy came to an end, I found myself setting up home with Greg in a studio flat in Willesden.

And just before my departure for Tunisia, he threw a bombshell, an out-of-the-blue marriage proposal. When he put the question to me, I experienced a curious sensation, something between nausea and a spasm in my gut, like the first sign of dysentery. It was an awkward moment to propose, just as I was about to take pleasure in a period of independence. So the exhilaration I felt I ought to be enjoying seemed soured by traces of resentment. It was supposed to be three weeks of personal time, an opportunity to show the world, and myself, that I was still a cool, reflective, adventurous individual: back-packing, sightseeing, a blend of culture-vulture and beach bum, but what I hadn't planned for was to have Greg's proposal hanging over me. If truth be told, though a little inopportune, the proposal was exciting, and I felt genuinely stirred. It was just bad timing, I felt.

At the time I wondered why he couldn't have waited until my return. Now, in hindsight, I suspect that perhaps Greg's action was deliberate. His choice of timing was probably a reaction to his own insecurities, an attempt to tie me down before I headed for the liberating and, in his mind, inhibition-loosening sunshine.

Not that I was looking at the holiday as a means of escape. Even before my departure, I knew in my heart of hearts that I would say yes to Greg. Still, in the meantime, there was an adventure to be had, and it's this that I want to write about.

She describes the disastrous beginning to the holiday – her bout of diarrhoea and vomiting a day after arriving in Tunis, the falling-out with Liz, their decision to go their separate ways, meet up again only on the eve of their return to Britain. Then she writes about her tourist experiences, the sweeping circle she'd made through the country, her growing confidence travelling alone, using the local minibuses and coaches, staying in cheap hotels, haggling for food in the markets, coping with the daily irritations she'd been subjected to as a lone foreign female.

And she describes her life-changing experience towards the end of the three weeks, an episode she's never shared with anyone, not even Greg to whom she told everything. She describes her meeting with a young Algerian, hardly more than a boy, broken in spirit by the civil war in Algeria, by the damage it had done to him. She describes their fleeting friendship, a night of comfort shared in her bed.

When she returns to Britain, she has changed. She writes about the after-effects of that encounter, her self-politicisation. It's a process over the following months in which she educates herself on development issues, commits herself to various left-wing causes, shifts her job from teaching affluent Europeans and Japanese to more vulnerable asylum seekers and refugees.

And when she returns home, another development: she says yes to Greg. Within six months they are married. Less than a year later, Beth is born.

She tells the counsellor about the postcard she'd sent Greg from Tunisia, the one of the Grand Erg Oriental. She tells him of its effect on Greg, the inspiration for his first exhibition.

And then she's talking about Greg, his character, his habits, an odd assortment of details that pop into her head, that she shares without editing: his special names for the kids, Bethanina and Sammalamadingdong; the emails he'd send to her at her work, sometimes silly, sometimes rude; his habit of breaking into song at the drop of a hat, *Dirty Old Town* as he washed the car, *The Bare Necessities* on country walks, *Food Glorious Food* as he made bread; the way fluff would always gather in his tummy button, the times she'd scoop it out, hold it up like a magician, and he'd laugh and kiss her on the mouth. And soon there are tears and more tears, and she can no longer speak, the session is over.

For the third text she tries to write about a week's trip they'd made to San Francisco, the longest time away from the kids. But as soon as she gets to their departure, the flight from Heathrow, she finds it too painful. She remembers how Greg always used to say how he hated flying with her and the kids, the fear that something would happen to them, but that when he flew alone he loved it, the terror giving way to exhilaration, a momentary liberating celebration of his own mortality. She wonders whether this was a premonition. A thought process germinates, a question in her mind about how Greg must have felt in those seconds between bomb blast and crash landing, but she cuts it off before it's fully-formed.

And then she's telling the doctor about the thousand daily traps she has to avoid – his favourite radio station, the programme he always watched on TV, the music he loved, the recipe he used to cook, the shop they always went to together, the restaurant and pub. All designed to ambush her, to ensnare her when she least expects it

This referral to Greg plagues her life. How many times a day does she get the urge to share a piece of news with him, to ask his advice? Imaginary conversations are a bitter-sweet habit she fails to kick, exercises in exquisite masochism.

⌘

One day she arrives at Dr Ahmad's house in a particularly awful mood. She'd been ill-prepared for a lesson at college and had been short with her colleagues in a meeting. At home Beth had asked her if she could go shopping in town with a couple of friends, her first independent excursion into the city centre. She'd got it all planned, had been saving her money, researched the bus number to catch, the stops to board at and descend. Her friends often travelled in groups to town and were careful to stay together at all times, and besides, they all had mobile phones.

But Nuala dismisses the idea out of hand, and instead offers to accompany the girls, promising to allow them a long rein. Beth says nothing, but the look of loathing on her face is a shock to Nuala, a look that seems to scream, You're a crazy suffocating bitch and I hate you! Nuala carries the image with her into Dr Ahmad's room. She describes her day, ending with her daughter's furious contempt.

I'm going to damage something permanently in our relationship if I don't snap out of it soon. I'm going to lose her, she says. Jesus, since Greg went, things have never been worse for me.

Dr Ahmad gives her a long look and smiles.

I don't agree, he says. If you ask me, things have never been better.

You must be joking!

No, I'm not. Think about it. For the first time since you've been coming to me, you're talking about how other people feel. Up to now, you've been living in a bubble, oblivious to your impact on their lives. That's only natural, of course, part of the process. It may not feel like it, but I think this is real progress.

Nuala considers his words in silence. She recognises the accuracy of his revelation, the madness she's been living with these past months. She nods and talks to him for the first time about what she has named her Doomsday Theory, that compulsive overprotectiveness towards her children that has been growing since she first heard the news of the crash.

At the time, befuddled by the rawness of her emotions, she had understood little of what she felt, but over the months that followed, as she has begun to make sense of her calamity, she has started to formulate an explanation for her obsession. Today, at the end of her session with the counsellor, he asks her to go home and draft a summary of her side of the conversation. She writes:

What happened to Greg was one of those One in a Billion events. For most of us, for most of our lives, One in a Billion events actually mean Never events – they may happen, but not to us. If we do worry about them, the anxiety is buried deep in our subconscious. When the One in a Billion event does indeed happen to me, those odds change radically. Henceforth, in my mind, One in a Billion is transformed from Never to Quite Likely. So if the odds of Greg plunging out of the sky become Quite Likely, then so too does the odds of my daughter drowning at the swimming pool, my son falling out of a tree in the park and snapping his neck, one of them being abducted by a psychopathic child killer somewhere between the house and the shop at the end of the street. Faulty plugs, dodgy toasters, lightning storms and rabid dogs. The dangers are everywhere.

Like the crash that robbed me of Greg, there's only a One in a Billion chance of something happening to the children when I'm not around to protect them. But those odds are no longer worth taking.

Even as she scribbles these words she realises that in identifying and analysing her Doomsday Theory, she has begun to move beyond it.

⌘

There are days when she makes a conscious effort to 'progress'. Sometimes it's a step forward, sometimes a step back.

A day off, the children at school. Nuala wanders around the house aimlessly, eventually finds herself in the utility room off the kitchen. She opens the cupboard above the washing machine. The breadmaker sits on the top shelf, its cable coiled around its body like the tail of a contented tomcat.

She reaches up, brings it down and carries it into the kitchen. She puts it on the table and surveys the appliance with a mixture of pain and nostalgia. The machine hasn't been used since Before. It'd always been Greg's thing, the breadmaking, a mid-morning ritual, a break from his painting, the mixing and measuring carried out while the kettle boiled for coffee.

She roots around again in the cupboard, finds some powdered yeast, two half packets of flour. The weighing scales are on the shelf next to the CD player. Amongst the recipe books she finds the breadmaking guide and flicks through until she finds a basic recipe. Flour, yeast, sugar, salt, olive oil, water. She props the guide up on the table and begins to weigh out the ingredients. There's something comforting in resurrecting one of Greg's old practices.

The phone rings. It's Mary checking that it's her turn to do the school pick-up. On the way back to her baking, Nuala stops at the radio, flicks it on and surfs the stations looking for something of interest. There's an extended news broadcast on one of the national stations, and she listens to the stories with growing gloom: a tanker spillage off the coast of Alaska; hundreds killed by a series of car bomb attacks in the Middle East; ethnic clashes on the Indian subcontinent; new figures showing an increase in malaria deaths, a rise in HIV infections.

When she reaches over to flip the off switch, she hits the radio with such force that the shelf judders and two cookery books fall to the floor. With her one flour-free hand, she selects a CD, an Ella Fitzgerald compilation, and for the first time removes the one inserted by Greg those months before.

At four o'clock Mary drops both Beth and Sammy home as arranged.

I'm starving, says Sammy. What's for tea?

Look, says Nuala. Look what I've made.

She's put the loaf on a grill to cool down. The aroma of fresh baking still fills the kitchen. The children gaze at the bread. There's a long pause as the associations are made.

What about some nice toast? Nuala begins brightly. She's already sensing the depth of her error. Beth, you'll have peanut butter, won't you? she adds, though in her mind she's saying, Please don't think badly of me. This is meant to be a good thing. I'm not trying to usurp him.

OK, says Beth, finally. Is that an accusatory look that Nuala reads in her expression?

Sammy?

Jam please, says Sammy. Nuala detects in his tone a combination of reluctance and hesitation and doubt.

She cuts the loaf, slides slices into the toaster. When it pops, she spreads butter, passes around the plates. The appearance of food silences the children. Nuala busies herself microwaving a jug of milk for hot chocolate

Is it OK? asks Nuala as Beth swallows a mouthful. Of course she means, but doesn't say, Is it OK to have done this?

Mmm, it's good, Beth answers. Nuala tries to read between the lines but fails.

Sammy?

Mmm, great, he manages. Nuala is certain she can detect the but...

Not too brown? Greg always used to bake a mixture of plain white and coarse wholemeal flour and she's tried to get the correct blend. Greg's loaves would be the colour of toasted pecan, the inside a creamy caramel flecked with wheatgerm.

Just right, answers Beth. She doesn't say, Just like dad's.

I could make it for your lunch boxes if you like, Nuala suggests. It's what Greg used to do. To outsiders, the conversation would be innocuous, but Nuala feels she's teetering on the brink. Beth and Sammy have still not responded. She's about to repeat her suggestion, then realises that in their own way they have expressed themselves perfectly. In her mind, she has already returned the breadmaker to its place in the cupboard above the washing machine.

Still, it's not all stalemate. In other ways, Nuala feels a lifting of some unnameable burden. In the first few months after the crash, in conversation with friends and family, when talking about Greg, she'd hate to hear any information about him that she didn't already know, stories of times spent with him in her absence, anecdotes of episodes she'd not shared, details of events she'd not been present at, things he'd said and done without her. She'd felt a deep resentment, a crazy sense of betrayal. But that seems to have lifted. She now welcomes these snippets and encourages such revelations. She understands that between the two of them there can be no treason.

Has she started to forgive Greg? Has she started to believe that he's forgiven her? These are questions that she knows have to be answered but that she's not yet ready to face.

AMAN 3

With *every difficulty*
There is relief
Yes, it is true, my love. I still cannot quite believe it, but here I am, some six weeks since my last entry, and I find myself a free man, sitting in this semi-detached house in leafy Levenshulme.

How did this happen? Who can tell exactly why my luck changed, what caused that faceless Home Office bureaucrat, leafing through my case file, to make the decision to set me free pending the result of my court hearing?

I will never know what chain of events led to my release, just that one morning I was told to pack my things, was handed a train ticket and an address in Manchester, told to make my way there. I was given clear instructions as part of my release conditions to report to the local police station once a week, had to sign endless papers, promise not to seek paid employment and then, with just a few minutes to say goodbye to my friends and neighbours, I found myself standing in front of the centre's high steel gates, blinking in the late spring sunshine. Kalil wrote down my new address carefully, promised to look me up if, insh' Allah, he ever got let out, and we embraced on the threshold of our shared cell.

Despite our ideological differences, I recognised my debt to my fellow inmate, that whatever was left of my sanity I owed to him.

I remember little of the journey north and the following few days as I negotiated my way through the bureaucracy of setting up a new life. I recall how colourful my surroundings seemed after the drab greys of the detention centre, how healthy everyone looked, ruddy and vibrant from mental and physical stimulation. And how green and lush the environment appeared, even in the city with its carefully maintained gardens and parks.

At the beginning of the second week, I had to make a trip south, to my solicitor's office in London. Under her relentless probing, I found myself unable to continue with my original story of half-truth and deception, and although I felt a great relief to be able to tell my real story, the car accident and the family's subsequent blood feud, the solicitor's reaction was not encouraging.

Though she could make a good case out of fear of injury or death from such a feud, she said, it did not fit into the usual categories of political or religious or ethnic persecution. More importantly, the essential key to success with the Home Office, she explained, was to convince them of your credibility. One small discrepancy, a tiny detail of your story confused or changed, and however plausible your suffering, however real the danger awaiting you should you be deported, your case was doomed to failure.

To help me understand, she gave the example of a Rwandan woman, traumatised after witnessing the slaughter of her family. After experiencing rape and torture at the hands of the same murderers, her case was rejected because, over the course of several interviews, there was some uncertainty over the colour of the tee-shirt of one of her rapists. If such a minor issue could lead to dismissal of a case, then to change one's whole story in mid-process was to positively invite disbelief and, consequently, rejection. Still, she wrote down my statement and promised to do what she could.

Back in Manchester, these first weeks were eventful, a hectic to-ing and fro-ing between social services, doctor's surgery, housing department and all the other institutions and offices that were now taking an interest in my existence.

I had been given the address of a local charity organisation, Refugee Welcome, and the elderly volunteer counsellor, a short squat woman with a body like a bullet and a head of tight, white curls, assisted me through some of the more arduous hurdles in setting up my new home and life in Levenshulme.

Doreen, that is her name, helped me register at a doctor's surgery, sorted out an eye test at an opticians and my first pair of spectacles, organised a grant to buy a bed, table and chair for the room in the shared house I had moved into and showed me how to enrol on an English language course at the local further education college. This hectic schedule was therapeutic after the months of enforced idleness in the detention centre, and within a week I had reduced my anti-depressants consumption to a single daily dose.

Most importantly, Doreen put me in touch with a number of other Eritreans and, for the first time since my flight from home, I have found myself integrated into a small community of my compatriots.

We are a close-knit circle, all at various stages of the asylum process, from those awaiting the outcome of their initial court case to the lucky few who have been granted indefinite leave to remain in UK. Many are caught in limbo, their cases turned down, appeals rejected, emergency payments cut, reliant on help from those receiving benefits or paid paltry wages by exploitative employers within the black economy.

My benefits after housing amount to a handful of notes and a few coins, most of which I use for basic groceries to split with my hungry countrymen. We cook together sometimes, sharing information on everything from where to buy cheap international phone cards to which private landlords to avoid. From one man I inherited an unwanted mobile phone. Another took me to the public library and helped me take out my first books, both architectural in content, one entitled *A Dictionary of Architecture & Building Construction*, the other *An Outline of European Architecture*. I cannot really make much sense of these texts yet, but I leaf through the dictionary and the task of mastering them gives me a challenge to work towards.

So I now have contact with some of my fellow expatriates.

Still, however welcome this is, my recent experiences have turned me inwards, and I find myself unable to endure these group occasions for too long, and so I seek my own company as soon as I can. Once I am alone again in my room, I still look for the protective shield of the *Qur'an*, but I have also taken up my drawing pad and pencils again after a long lay-off. I have begun sketching out some building designs, towering and ornate fantasy edifices, sunny and airy, created as an escape from melancholic suburban Manchester.

When I am not sketching or reading, I like to sit in the kitchen of this house, a messy but welcoming room filled with warm cooking smells. I sit at the large pine table and sip my sugary black tea and watch my housemates chop onions and dice carrots. Or I simply stare out of the grimy sash window at the street scene outside, the bus shelter, the zebra crossing, the traffic, boisterous children returning home from school.

The house belongs to a Pakistani landlord who has a social contract with the council to provide accommodation for those on benefits. My housemates, eight or nine in total, are a mixed bunch, mostly asylum seekers with one or two 'natives'. For the most part, we keep to ourselves, guarding our own privacy as carefully as we respect that of our fellow tenants. Only two of my co-residents talk to me at length, a Zimbabwean in his mid- twenties called Mahanya, and Derek from Scotland. They both address me in what I can only guess is fluent English, though I struggle to follow their conversation. Still, their loneliness is tangible. I can offer them no more than a sympathetic ear but that seems enough for the moment.

So all in all, I suppose you could say that I am on something of a high. I have my own room in this shared house. I am about to resume my studies and have established a circle of friends. Things are looking up, my darling. Now all that remains is for me to succeed in my quest to locate you. Tomorrow I will ask Doreen about re-establishing contact with the Red Cross.

⌘

I discover a copy of the Bible lying abandoned on top of the wardrobe in my bedroom. Who did it belong to? Why was it left behind? My thoughts turn to you and I wonder what comfort you are finding in your faith at this time. Ramadan is approaching and I shall find a sweet pleasure in my fasting, knowing that somewhere (close?) you are doing the same.

⌘

Just when I thought it was safe to relax, the axe comes swinging back, catching me unawares. The call from my solicitor came this morning as I was preparing for my first English class at college. I had finished my prayers and was washing up my dirty crockery from last night, my first hot meal in a week, rice and lamb, the return of my appetite a real sign that I was on the road to recovery. She sounded tired, her voice low and dull. The court hearing had taken place and my case had been rejected. I felt my stomach tighten, my spirits plunge with fear and uncertainty. I did not know what to say. The line remained silent while she waited for a response. After a long pause she explained about the appeal process, that all was not yet lost. I listened, thanked her, hung up. My hands were shaking, so I left the sink full of greasy pots and returned to my room where I fumbled in my drawers for my medication. I swallowed two of the pills and lay back down on the recently vacated bed. I pulled my duvet over my head.

I think of Doreen. She has given me her mobile number. She has told me on many occasions to call her if I ever have a problem, if I ever need to talk. But I feel overwhelmed by a dejection that renders me too apathetic to act.

A little later I get up. I am in no mood for college so I stare listlessly at my architectural books, then the *Qur'an*, but find solace nowhere. Eventually I pick up this notebook and add these lines.

I have never felt more rejected. I remember something my father used to tell me. In the jungle, he would often say, the lion is the most dominant creature, strong and powerful.

The antelope, on the other hand, is the most harmless, weak and vulnerable. The test for the lion is to be tolerant. For the antelope, the challenge is to be courageous.

Where is this country's tolerance? Where is my courage?

⌘

More bad news. I received a letter in the post this morning informing me that I am being given notice to leave my accommodation at the end of the month. I show the letter to Mahanya and he tells me that the landlord has sent similar letters to all the tenants, that he has decided to end his contract with the council. Mahanya explains that there is more money to be made in housing young single eastern Europeans, cramming three to a room, rather than putting up with the bureaucracy and delays of a social housing contract.

My despondency grows, but Mahanya is upbeat. He has lived in Manchester for two years and been moved five times already. He reassures me that the council has a responsibility to find alternative accommodation for us.

Don't worry, my friend. They will sort something out for you. For all of us.

He smiles and I try to respond. We are in the kitchen. He has been cooking, has produced a thick stiff maize porridge and a sauce made of green leaves and peanut butter. It smells good and he offers to share his bowl with me but my appetite has disappeared again so I shake my head and return to my room. My bedroom window looks down on our neglected back garden, a jungle of brambles and bindweed. I consider going for a walk but cannot summon up the will.

I think: I was in a detention centre and they set me free. But I am still a prisoner now, it is just that my cell has got bigger.

⌘

Weeks have passed. I am now in new accommodation,

another shared house, another private landlord. I appear to have moved down in the world. The house is more cramped, a shabby terraced property sandwiched between two boarded up homes. This is Longsight and the streets are dirtier. There is an air of neglect and it makes sense that this is where I have ended up. The house is damp. The bathroom walls are flecked with mould and the kitchen is musty and dank. There are two other bedrooms, one taken by a skinny, taciturn Somali with delicate hands and eyes that avoid my own. The other room is occupied by a seemingly endless sequence of Chinese men, never the same ones, it seems to me, who come and go at odd hours, sleeping on the mattress-strewn floor, then emerging to our clammy kitchen to cook rice and slurp green tea. When I left the old house in Levenshulme, Derek shook my hand and told me to take it easy. I forgot to ask him how.

⌘

The walls of my bedroom have been painted a deep blood red. As soon as I entered the room for the first time, I felt something slipping away. I began to tremble with weakness. I am sleeping in someone's open wound.

⌘

My first sortie from the house for a week. I collect my repeat prescription, then attend the interview with the Red Cross worker. I repeat all the details I had once before given, list your names and dates of birth. I tell her about the blood feud, about my hunted status, and receive her assurance that my own details will be kept confidential. She takes copious notes and promises to contact me as soon as they have any information.

⌘

Ramadan is upon us but I have got into the habit of eating so little that I am hardly aware that I am supposed to be fasting.

I spend my time sleeping and working my way through my scant collection of books, to which I have added my rescued Bible and an English dictionary. Yesterday I made a start on the Old Testament.

⌘

I begin to harbour suspicions that my Somali housemate may be out to do me harm. It is nothing that he has said – indeed we have still exchanged fewer than a dozen words – more the way he avoids eye contact and seems to be concealing something from me. This morning I enter the kitchen to find him rummaging in the cupboard in which I keep my black tea supply. As soon as he becomes aware of me, he slams the cupboard door shut, mumbles something about an appointment and leaves the kitchen and then, shortly after, the house. I examine the tin in which I keep my tea. It seems untampered with, but when I brew up and sample the drink, I detect a slightly bitter aftertaste. As a precaution, I throw what remains of my supply into the bin and make a rare trip outside to buy a fresh packet at the corner shop.

Later I begin to worry that he will see my discarded tea supply in the bin, evidence that I am on to him, so I collect up what I can in a dustpan, take it out into the back garden and scatter it among the beds of tangled weeds.

⌘

Another week gone. I rarely leave my room, let alone the house. Having missed my first English language class, my place has been given to someone else and I am now relegated to a waiting list. Doreen tried to organise some voluntary work for me at a charity shop, then to recruit me as a counsellor for young people at the Refugee Welcome centre, but I oversleep for the interview for the former and say no to the latter. Directionless, indifferent and befuddled as I am at the moment, I do not feel qualified to act as mentor for anyone.

I collect my repeat prescription tablets, the only event to distinguish today from yesterday and tomorrow.

No news from the Red Cross.

⌘

My stomach is perpetually swollen, aching with suppressed tension. I go one, two days without eating, then, at sunset on the third, I walk down to the Indian takeaway on the corner and buy a lamb methi and naan, eat slowly at my bedroom window. Often I have barely finished half before my throat tightens and I abandon the meal, toss the silver tray into the bin, stinking and overflowing, and throw out the naan for the birds in that cheerless back garden.

⌘

Doreen still calls me on my mobile but I do not answer. She leaves messages that I delete without listening to. I know she means well but I have no strength to deal with her cheerful enthusiasm.

My Eritrean contacts still phone, leave voice mails, but I have not spoken to any of them for a long time, and the calls are becoming less frequent.

I stare at my bedroom walls and hear the blood seeping through the wallpaper. When I close my eyes it stops.

⌘

My Somali housemate and myself are engaged in a game of casual nonchalance towards each other, though beneath the façade we both know what is at stake. We exchange pleasantries and pretend indifference, but I watch his every move and presume he too watches mine.

My tin of tea has become a decoy that I reduce spoonful by spoonful each day but never drink. I keep an untainted supply safe in my room.

I spend the evening of Eid ul-Fitr in bed. At midnight I dress and walk through chilly autumnal Manchester. An icy wind picks up as I kick my way through pavements thick with fallen leaves. At a street corner an Asian minicab driver is arguing with two scantily clad white girls and I have to fight the urge to shake him by his jacket lapels and order him home to his wife and children. I want to tell him what is at stake, how transitory and delicate his happiness could be. The women, too, seem unaware that their contentment hangs perilously on a tightrope, that the slightest unforeseen event could shatter their hopes.

The cabbie is standing in front of his car and I walk up between him and the women. They notice me at once and break off from their loud accusations of overcharging and dodged fares. They look at me expectantly, but I cannot express the enormity of what I am feeling and in the split second that I hesitate, struggling to formulate the right words, their curiosity turns to impatience.

What the fuck are you looking at? he says

Yeah, piss off, adds one of the girls.

Oh fucking hell, look at him. He's blubbing like a fucking baby, says the other, and I realise that I am weeping, that I cannot stop the tears, that only I know what they mean. That I have failed to save these people. I turn round and retrace my footsteps, leaving them to their fate.

Inside my bedroom, the walls are still bleeding.

⌘

No news from the Red Cross.

⌘

I have started on the Old Testament. The tone is angry and frightening. I read in *Exodus* that The Lord is a man of war.

I follow the stories of God-ordained massacres, the genocide against the Canaanites and Amorites in *Numbers*, Moses' slaughter of the Medianites, the butchery in *Deuteronomy*, the carnage in *Joshua*, the command in *Samuel* to kill Amalek and his people, in *Psalms* to deal harshly with all non-believers:

> *Thou shalt break them with a rod of iron; thou shalt dash them in pieces like a potter's vessel.*

And then,

> *Blessed be the Lord my strength which teacheth my hands to war, and my fingers to fight.*

Now where have I heard those self-same sentiments before?

⌘

Winter is upon us.

The first frosts coincide with the boiler breaking down. On Tuesday the Somali man told me he would report it to the council. He left three days ago but has not returned.

The Chinese continue to come and go, to cook and sleep in shifts. They rarely speak to each other, rendered mute by fatigue and cold.

Ice forms patterns of cruel beauty on the inside of my bedroom window panes.

I seek escape in my drawings, sketching desert edifices from the warmth of my quilt. My room is littered with drafts of my Sahel citadels, my Arabian fortresses, my Turkish castles, my ksour and mosques and palaces.

When I check my mobile I find sixteen missed calls, from my Eritrean friends, from Doreen, from the college where I am supposed to be studying. Working on my drawings, I hear nothing, see nothing, feel nothing except what is in front of me. The temporary relief of oblivion.

⌘

Sometimes my walls seem scarlet, sometimes crimson. Always menacing.

⌘

Doreen appears at my bedside.

At first I think it is a dream. She is shaking me awake, telling me to get up. She draws the curtain and I see that it is the middle of the day. She disappears, returns with a mug of tea. She has added milk so I cannot drink it, but she insists so I pretend to take a sip. I stumble out of bed, my breath a cloud of condensation. I head for the toilet, urinate, swallow two pills.

When I get back, I see that Doreen has not stopped speaking since she arrived, her tone by turns outraged and sympathetic, though I am finding it difficult to pick out the individual words and am not sure whether she is talking to me or to herself. She tells me to dress, that she is taking me back to the Centre to get warm. She stands outside my door talking on her mobile, in the same indignant voice. I want to tell her not to trouble herself, that I am perfectly well, but my tongue lies heavy and leaden, an alien body squatting in my mouth.

I get dressed. When she comes back into the room, she looks at me sadly and points at my chest. I look down and see that I have forgotten to put on a shirt. I am naked beneath my jacket. When I rummage around for a tee-shirt, I realise how neglected my room is, the presence of a stranger helping me to see it through new eyes. My floor is several inches thick with soiled underwear, dirty cups, stinking curry trays, stale blankets, half-finished sketches, discarded books.

Doreen pokes around amongst the detritus and emerges with a pair of socks which she hands to me. I am suddenly aware that she is holding herself in. She finding it hard to contain her disgust, and I am overcome with shame.

When I finish putting on my shoes and socks, she takes my arm and leads me away. On the threshold, I stop and run my fingers along the cold, damp wallpaper. I peer at my open palm, expecting to see fresh wet blood, but my hand, like my heart, is dry and empty.

⌘

Back in my room, discharged from hospital. The first few days I am alone in a single room, attached to a drip, days and nights a foggy blur of dozing and pills. They have changed my antidepressants and these ones make me even sleepier. I am also on antibiotics for a chest infection. The drip feeds me, bypassing my obstinate throat and disobliging stomach.

After a few days I am moved to a ward, a corner bed. Fortunately this requires interaction with only one other patient, a retired postman from Birmingham with ill-fitting dentures and mottled cheeks. He spends his days studying the horse racing section of *The Mirror*. He occasionally asks me to choose a winner, says I look like I have a lucky touch. His name is Terry and I find his accent too thick to pick up more than the gist of his conversations, though I understand enough to recognise the underlying loneliness.

He receives no visits.

Doreen comes to see me every other day. She brings me oranges and bars of chocolate, both of which I pass on to Terry after she has gone.

She sits by my bedside and tells me gossip about people I do not know, anecdotes about places I have never been to, comments on television programmes I have never watched. Her voice is gentle and soothing and I take in little of what she says, though the overall effect is comforting.

I ask her about the Somali, but she has heard nothing. She tells me the house is empty following a police raid on the Chinese. It appears that most of them were illegals and are now facing deportation.

One day a doctor appears with a clipboard of questions. I keep my answers short and simple, give nothing away.

My Eritrean brothers continue to call. They want to see me but I tell them I cannot have visitors at the moment, that my infection is considered a risk to others. Their voices are bright and positive, and we make plans to meet up when I am discharged. We promise each other trips to London, evenings on the town. I agree to everything, anxious not to arouse suspicion.

Terry asks me to choose a horse for his betting hobby. He hands me the page of names from the newspaper and I point at one without looking. He makes a note of my choice, a beast called Loita Hills. Later he tells me the horse has won and tries to make me accept a couple of grubby banknotes, my share of the winnings, but I tell him my religion prohibits me from gambling. He looks offended and does not speak to me again.

Doreen tells me about her eldest son, her only unmarried child. He has always worked in a supermarket warehouse and was reversed over by a delivery lorry twenty years ago. Initially presumed dead, he was saved after a number of cranial operations. According to Doreen, he has never been the same since, transformed from a bright, happy-go-lucky clown to a moody, workaholic loner. Now in his forties, he lives alone in a two-bedroom house ten minutes' drive from Doreen but, as she tells me with an awkward blend of sadness, pride and maternal love, he still calls in every morning for his lunchbox.

I want to hug her, for herself, for him and for me, but I say nothing.

Eventually, I am discharged.

When I get home, the boiler is fixed and the house is warm, stifling almost. They must have put the heating on override to get rid of the previous month's dampness. I would like to turn the temperature down, off even for a time, but I am afraid of disturbing the thermostat's programming, so I leave it as it is.

The house is empty, the Chinese room open but bare, the Somali's door locked.

I make tea in the kitchen. The bin is still full, stinking of rotting waste, and the fridge, though almost empty, smells of sour decay. I make to start cleaning up but decide to leave it for the morning. I sit at the kitchen table, its surface sticky with grime, and let my mind wander.

Hours pass.

Later, I feel sufficient courage to face my room. It seems smaller than I remember, the crimson walls pressing in, suffocating.

Someone (Doreen?) has tidied up, disposed of the decomposing curries, put away the soiled clothing and stacked my drawings into a pile on the chest of drawers. I have a sudden urge to cover my walls with these sketches, to conceal with my art the red menace beneath. I walk down to the corner shop to buy some tape to stick up my pictures. Outside it is dark and when I get to the shop I find it closed. I have lost track of time and my mobile tells me it is past midnight. I know I won't be able to sleep with those bleeding walls, so I walk on to the all-night garage and buy a supply of chewing gum to use as adhesive.

It takes me half an hour to display my illustrations. They cover a large enough area to take the edge off the bloody walls and when I crawl into bed having swallowed my tablets, I fall asleep quickly.

⌘

When I wake up this morning and survey my decorating handiwork, I feel a great sense of satisfaction, as if something significant has happened, as if we have turned a corner.

Today when I pray, I sense for the first time in a long while that I have a direct line to God. I feel certain that this is connected to the Somali's absence, as if previously he had found a way to block my prayers.

Outside it is icy though clear, the weak sun making no inroads into the night frost. The garden seems in sterile limbo between death and a new dawn and I take my tea out and stand on the lawn in the arctic sunshine. I wander down to the bottom of the garden and admire an ivy-clad tree that towers over the fencing. I spot a bird's nest in one of the lower branches and climb up to retrieve it. It is empty of course, but a beautiful piece of engineering and I carry it into the house with me, lay it down gently on the table in my room.

My mind is buzzing, full of newly-hatched plans. I make a second pot of tea, fetch a scrap of paper and a pencil, then sit down to begin a 'to-do' list.

Before I can start, I become aware of the state of the kitchen. I find bottles of cleaner and bleach under the sink, a bucket and mop outside the back door, and set to work on the table, the floor and bin.

As I scour the sink, I feel the therapeutic benefits of cleaning, enjoying the sweat on my brow, the strain on my arm muscles. Still not satisfied, I fetch a black bin bag and begin removing all the packets and tins from the shelves. I toss everything out, half-empty jars of coffee, old cereal boxes, packets of instant noodles, cans of peas, herbs, stock cubes, pasta and rice. I am ruthless, sparing nothing except my tea tin, sugar, the cutlery, pots and pans.

I remember the fridge and attack it with bleach after emptying it of its contents. A second bag is required for the margarine and eggs, the mouldy cheese and curdled milk carton. I hardly notice the foul stench and work in a frenzy of concentration until, finally pleased with my efforts, I stand back and admire the naked simplicity of my kitchen.

Only now can I relax enough to make a start on my project list. My first action, I think, should be to buy a gift for Doreen to express my gratitude. My second to contact my Eritrean friends to set up a get together to celebrate my release from hospital and my new-found dynamism.

I have a marvellous idea. I will purchase some Ethiopian jazz CDs, those produced by your favourite artists, and a CD player. I have a strong sense of certainty that if I commence playing your music, it will act as a kind of aural beacon, signalling to you my whereabouts, helping to bring closer the moment of our sweet reunion.

I make another decision. I can no longer abide the appearance of my room, even with my display of sketches, so I add a tin of paint to my shopping list. I check my room for cash and am relieved to find my savings intact, hidden inside a pair of socks in my wardrobe, then make haste for the city centre.

I burn with impatience on the bus ride into town, buy a portable CD player, visit three different music shops in order to locate an initial collection of four disks, collections by Tesegue-Maryam Guebrou, Getatchew Adamassu, Alemayehu Eshete and Lemma Demissew. I sense your approval. I feel sure that this will hasten your return.

I cannot think what to buy for Doreen. After nearly an hour of searching, I settle on a ladies quartz three-piece set consisting of a watch, matching bracelet and heart-shaped pendant.

I get off the bus at the retail park a mile from my home, stand in front of the paint aisle in a DIY superstore, unable to choose a suitable colour to paint my walls. Eventually I pick an unassuming, soothing eggshell blue. I add a brush to my basket, then struggle home with my purchases eager to start broadcasting your music and to set to work on my bedroom walls.

As soon as I get through the front door, I sense that someone has been inside the house. The kitchen looks as scrubbed as I had left it, but something is altered, the angle of a chair perhaps, or the position of a dishcloth. I approach the Somali's locked bedroom door and put my ear to the smooth surface. Silence. I realise with a jolt that I have left my own bedroom unlocked. I open the door with dread and survey the mess with my senses attuned for the slightest signs of disturbance. How could I have been so careless?

It is impossible to assess the damage, he is far too clever for that, and I realise that I will have to take drastic measures. I fetch a black bag from the kitchen and begin the same process of ruthless cleaning that I carried out earlier. Out go most of my possessions, gifts and cast-offs from my Eritrean friends: the handful of DVDs, the portable television I seldom watch, a Hand of Fatima key ring and several novels. They all feel tainted.

I collect up armfuls of soiled clothes. The washing

machine in the kitchen has long-since stopped working and I cannot summon the patience to seek out a launderette, so I fill a bath with hot water, add detergent from the kitchen, then heave the clothes into the soapsuds to soak.

Back in my bedroom, I cannot relax. I fetch the hoover from under the stairs and run it around the filthy carpet. I strip my bed, add the bedclothes to the bath, wipe my table, scrub the skirting. I yank off my sketches from the wall, but before I start the re-decorating, I need to finish the room's purification.

It is almost bare now, nothing remaining except the *Qur'an*, my architectural works, the Bible and the bird's nest. I cannot bring myself to throw these out but I have left my mobile on the table, and I know he will have tampered with it, so reluctantly I add it to my bin bag.

Before it goes, I check it one last time for messages. I see that there is a voicemail from my solicitor. The message is short and to the point – my appeal has been heard in court and rejected. There is the possibility of a further appeal, but she would need to see me before that to discuss how we could build on our current case. I have nothing more to add, I think. Nothing more to give. I put the phone into the bin.

At the bottom of the wardrobe, I have kept my case file, all the documents I have collected from my solicitor and the Home Office, and this too I decide to dispense with. Then I remember the bathroom. My bathbag lies where I have left it on the shelf above the basin. It looks untouched but how can I take any chances? Out goes my toothbrush and toothpaste, the soap and paracetamol. With the greatest unwillingness I add my medication to the rubbish. It is too great a risk to take.

Now, for the first time since my return, I feel some relief. My bedroom is now bare, and before I open the paint pot and dip my brush in, I set up my new music player, and slip on the Alemayehu Eshete CD. The music is fluid, tantalising. I hum along as I slap paint onto the walls. Everything is getting better, I think, and I am convinced that these are more than vacuous words. It feels like a golden beginning.

It is now evening and I stand in my room surveying

my work. The blue reminds me of the sky at home and, by extension, of you, my flower. Together with the music, which I have not stopped broadcasting since midday, I feel I have everything in place to make contact with you. I am waiting, my sweet...

⌘

Two days have passed. Yesterday I had just finished my early morning prayers and was filling the kettle when two of my Eritrean acquaintances called in. They have been trying to phone me. I do not tell them what I have done with my mobile. I lead them into my kitchen. They comment on its tidiness with, I suspect, a note of envy.

I fix the tea and we make idle conversation. I am careful to listen vigilantly to everything they say, to comment on their stories and even add one or two of my own.

I borrow a mobile and text Doreen. I tell her I am going on a short holiday with some of my friends, a two-week tour visiting compatriots in Birmingham, London and Cardiff. I tell her I will contact her when I return. When my visitors leave I agree to meet up today at a café in town run by a sympathetic Sudanese family.

It is odd, but since I stopped taking the pills, I have felt more vibrant, more full of energy than ever in my life. I am aglow, riding a wave of positive vitality. I feel I can do anything if I put my mind to it. Oh, my darling, I know you are so very close.

It is a beautiful afternoon, chilly but bright. I have been playing your music on a loop since I first bought it. I have left the Tesegue-Maryam Guebrou CD playing in my bedroom and hum a refrain as I wait at the bus stop. The guitar plays like fingers down my spine, the drum caresses the nape of my neck, the saxophone whispers lewd suggestions in my ear. A middle-aged woman in fur-lined boots and a red anorak sits next to me nursing her shopping trolley and I have to fight off an urge to break into song, to tell her about its significance, about you.

At the café we are served tea and chickpea cakes. I eat a little out of politeness. There are ten of us, fellow Eritreans I have not seen for months. They have all heard of my hospitalisation. They are solicitous in their enquiries, and I find their consideration touching.

I question them about their latest news, making a point of asking after their families and then, shortly before I make my apologies and leave, I tell them that my friend Derek, has invited me to his home in Scotland for a few weeks, that I will get in touch on my return. I tell them about my misplaced mobile and promise to text them my new number once I buy a replacement. Walking down the street towards the bus stop, I feel an enormous sense of release.

Back at my house, I am busy changing the CD when I notice that the blue of my walls is changing, that it is darkening, becoming more intense. I stand up, back off, then move in close, run my fingers over the surface. There is no doubt in my mind. The red underneath is pushing through to the surface. It is seeping out of the pores of the wallpaper, tainting the purity of my soft pale azure.

I run through to the kitchen where I have stored the paint pot and brush. I haul them into my room and begin slapping on a fresh coat. I do not stop until every surface is glistening wet.

I clear up, return my room to its bare simplicity and sit at the table with a cup of black tea and this notebook. I am restless with excitement. I have cleared the decks in every way, tied up all my loose ends. Now all I have to do is wait.

⌘

A month has passed since my last entry. A month of killing time. For what? Of course, I thought I was waiting for you, but perhaps in all honesty I knew that this was just a fantasy, that actually I was waiting for something else. For some other, more realistic conclusion.

I have never felt anything more exciting, more

addictive, more all-consuming, than that sweet rush of hope I was experiencing. It superseded all my more trivial needs, hopes and aspirations. Its raucous screams of delight drowned out all the humdrum voices around me. Its dazzling explosions of colour blinded me to the scenes of everyday life. I closed my eyes and clung on as I was taken for a glorious, devil-may-care ride. I accelerated and felt as if I was travelling upwards at the speed of light. And then, the inevitable, I peaked, then faltered and finally began the free-falling plunge towards reality.

That, my dear, is what I have been through. Two weeks of frenzied mania. During the day, consumed by a need for action, but unable to leave the house for fear of missing your arrival, I sought out projects to burn off the excess energy.

I sketched the towers and castles of my fantasies, copied out lists of English vocabulary, made copious notes from my architecture books and my Bible. I discovered a bag of abandoned tools in a shed, a pile of timber, and built a tree house for the horse chestnut at the bottom of the garden. I stripped off the grimy, cracked lino in the bathroom and sanded the floorboards below by hand.

The only dark cloud on my horizon was the red seeping through my paintwork, and time and again I felt compelled to apply another coat of paint, then another, racing off twice more to buy extra tins.

At night I could not rest and did not even attempt to sleep. When I could not contain myself in the confines of the house, I hurried onto the streets of Manchester for hours at a time, returning only at dawn. These were the occasions when I would eat, lamb curries or kebabs from all-night takeaways.

Eventually, after several days of this frenzied agitation, I would find myself able to doze on and off in the early hours of the morning. Then, my energy recharged, the cycle would begin again.

I can remember little of these weeks beyond a sense of urgency, of impatience, of restless anxiety.

When the crash came, it was sudden and brutal. It seems to me that there was no single event that prompted it, no clear-cut trigger, just, perhaps, an accumulation of despondency. A clash between hope and helplessness, my imagination fertile with thoughts of you and the children, my reality barren and desolate.

This time, when I woke from my light doze, I found myself unable to rise, to wash for prayers, to brew my tea and play my CDs. This time I was struck down, bereft, crippled. All my anxieties, my loneliness, my fears seemed to gang up on me. It was a complete mental and physical paralysis.

I stared up at the ceiling. My plans to read two chapters of my architectural textbook, to wash my laundry in the bath, to clear some of the flowerbeds of weeds, now seemed ludicrous, the madcap projects of an eccentric stranger. I needed to urinate yet even carrying out that action seemed overambitious.

And so from dynamism to lethargy. I found myself straitjacketed by my exhaustion, my depression, this stupor of lassitude. I did eventually crawl to the toilet to relieve myself and managed to repeat this several times a day, but that was more or less the sum total of my productivity over the following fortnight. By the time help arrived, I was a stinking, unwashed, unshaven sloth cocooned in a nest of my own fetid squalor.

The end to my suffering, my rescue from this paralysing despondency, occurred yesterday. And my rescuer, the eagle swooping down to liberate me from the flames of my own personal hell? None other than my cellmate from Glynbourne House, Kalil.

Later on, he tells me how he traced me through Refugee Welcome. He was given the name and number of one of my compatriots who passed my address on to him. The first I know of this, though, is when he knocks at my bedroom door. I cannot muster the strength to call out, can barely turn my head on the pillow to face the door.

He pokes his head inside my room, sees me, smiles then frowns as he realises that all is not well. He squats down beside me.

Your front door was open, he says. You should be careful.

He bends down, lifts my feeble head. I feel his breath on my cheek.

How are you? he asks in Arabic, his voice barely a whisper.

I am well, thanks be to God, I answer. For some reason, my reply is met with a rich chuckle. Despite my weakened state, I feel a stab of irritation.

Where is your medication? he asks. Your tablets?

Gone, I say, and shrug. I cannot summon the strength to explain.

Would you like some more? he asks. Shall I get you some more?

Yes, I croak. Please.

Before he goes, he cradles me in his arms. I hold on to him with all my strength, hold on to my brother, my saviour, and I cry myself dry.

When he returns it is late afternoon. I have not moved. I do not know how he has managed it, but he is holding a paper bag from which he pulls out a box of pills. He removes two of the red and green capsules.

Here, he says. These were the ones, eh? I remembered, see? He passes me the tablets and goes off to fetch a glass of water, but by the time he returns I have swallowed them dry. As he fills me in on his release from detention, temporary freedom until his case comes to court, and tells me about his successful hunt for me, I lie back and wait for the chemicals to take away the here and now.

When he finishes his story, Kalil tells me he has been shopping for food. He is going to cook for us. I drift off to sleep with the smell of roasted chicken and rosemary in my nostrils, sleep straight through to the following afternoon, today, when I write this extract.

⌘

Another month gone. The return to my medicated existence has ended the rush and brought back my old befogged and sluggish self. I idle away my days in bed, carried over the hurdles of daily existence and cushioned from harsh reality by Kalil, my protector. In the early days he carts me from bedroom to bath, soaps away the grime, towels me dry before dressing me in freshly laundered clothes. When my skin erupts in an eczema-like rash, he buys ointments and ensures they are applied three times daily. He sorts out my repeat prescriptions, cooks fragrant dishes of chicken or lamb, comes around every day to check on me, to tell me stories, to read to me from the *Qur'an* and to join me in my daily prayers.

I remain in bed for the first week, rising only for physical needs. I sleep all night, most of the day. Sometimes I lie on the bed, waiting for the knock at the door, the arrival of immigration officers to take me off. The pills help to turn this fear from acute terror to mild anxiety, but it is nevertheless now an ever-present possibility.

During the second week, I venture around the house. My projects, boldly planned and professionally executed in my mind, now appear shoddy and wretched. The bathroom floor is uneven and splintered. The tree house, an arborial palace in my imagination, is a pathetic, slapdash piece of workmanship. Never before have I felt so pitiable, so shameful. I deserve no more, no less than what I have got. I hide the Ethiopian CDs at the bottom of my wardrobe and disconnect the music player. I prefer the lifeless melody of silence. It offers no false hopes.

At first Kalil comes and goes using my front door key. By the third week I notice that he has made up a bed in the Chinese room. He continues in his attempts to turn this sterile house into a home, there is an ever-present aroma of roasting meats and appetising spices. The place remains spotless. There is toilet paper in the bathroom, fruit in the kitchen. He has brought in two combined TV and DVD players, a large-screen one in the kitchen, a smaller one for my bedroom. I thank him for his kindness but as soon as he leaves the room, I switch it off.

This week, there has been a change. I notice it first one late morning. Coming round from my sleep, I hear the sound of people talking. I think initially it is the TV in the kitchen, then recognise first the rhythm and intonation of Arabic, then the tone and tenor of Kalil's own voice interacting with another lower-pitched one. A little while later, Kalil enters with a cup of tea, followed by a burly fellow with cropped hair and a week-old beard who Kalil introduces as Tariq.

And this is Aman, he adds. He has not been well recently, he continues. But we have high hopes for him.

This visit sets the pattern for the time being. First Tariq, then Iqbal and Lazar and Asif and the others. They sit in the kitchen drinking tea and sharing meals. I hear their voices, usually a quiet hubbub, occasionally raised, but I seldom join them. I suspect some of them may stay overnight. They may even have moved in permanently, as I find them present whenever I emerge from my bedroom whatever the time of day or night. I know that being alone for those previous weeks was not good for me, so I suppose I should be grateful for the company.

Kalil continues to care for me, though my needs are minimal. I feel like a machine on power off, on physical and emotional standby. My appetite remains irregular, a hot meal once every two or three days. Other than that I require nothing more than black tea and tablets. On Kalil's insistence I bathe every day. He has cut my nails and hair, has bought me a toothbrush and supervises my ablutions.

Occasionally my emotions break through the ice. Today I receive a letter from the Red Cross. They have made no progress in locating you. They tell me my case will be kept on file, that it will continue to be monitored in the future. But I can see that they are giving up.

I am standing by my bed as I read the words. I let the letter fall, feel myself crumple inside, cannot control the heaving sobs, the hot wet tears. Kalil must have heard my anguish. He comes to me, puts his arms around me. He is talking to me now, his voice is soothing.

A little later, as I begin to regain control over my emotions, I am able to hear what he is saying. He is mumbling, his words of comfort little more than murmurings, but I can just about make out his words.

The Garden or the Fire? he is saying over and over again. What is it to be, brother? The Garden or the Fire?

⌘

I am regaining a little strength, enough to resume my reading. I have abandoned the anger of the Old Testament, have made a start on the New Testament. I read in *Matthew*:

Think not that I am come to send peace on earth: I come not to send peace, but a sword.

Then in *Luke*:

He that hath no sword, let him sell his garment and buy one.

As if on cue, Kalil enters. When he sees what I am reading, his eyebrows rise and he frowns.

Do you know what that is? he says. He does not wait for an answer. His voice is hard, tight with an anger I have forgotten but instantly recognise. It is an instruction manual for a war against Islam, for the crusades. Have you heard of the 'Milites Christi', the Warriors of Christ? Soldiers dedicated to destroying the followers of Allah? They are nothing new. Did you know that the idea of a 'bellum sacrum', a so-called sacred war against Islam, was first ordained as long ago as 1095 by none other than a Pope, Urban II? Kill a Muslim and your sins are forgiven. And of course these attacks on our faith, on our brothers are still going on today.

I say nothing but this seems to add fuel to Kalil's rage.

You have been too unwell to play a part, my brother, he says, eyeing me with a mixture of contempt and pity. But you are getting better now. It is time to show a little bit of commitment. Principles are something to fight for, not just to live by. He continues to stare for a few seconds, then the door bell goes and he has gone.

⌘

Kalil still takes responsibility for my wellbeing, overseas my healing. He encourages me to get out of bed, to join him and his friends in the kitchen. The men speak sometimes in Arabic, sometimes in English, usually a hybrid combination of the two. They discuss their families, their jobs, everyday matters. They tell each other about cheap insurance deals, give each other advice about where to buy second-hand cars, swap tips on how to climb council housing lists. We read the *Qur'an* and pray together.

But when I return to my room, the conversation at these meetings changes. Sometimes the door is left ajar and I eavesdrop. There is a trial going on in London, eight men accused of conspiracy to set off bombs on flights to America, explosives hidden in soft drink containers. They follow the course of the case with enormous interest. Every aspect is analysed and discussed at length. Someone has brought a DVD of the defendants' martyrdom videos, and they play it over and over again.

⌘

The Bible has been taken from my room.

⌘

My skin condition has worsened. Blisters that I scratch have become infected and now leak an angry, foul secretion. Kalil continues to treat them with tender care.

My sores remind me of the Surah called *Al Fil* and the story that it refers to, the one set in Yemen when it was ruled by Abyssinian Christians. Do you remember the tale, how the governor, a man named Abrahah Ashram, led an expedition to target the Ka'bah at Makkah? It was a mighty force that included elephants, an army that many thought invincible. But just when it seemed that defeat was inevitable, a flock of birds rose miraculously into the sky and showered the invading troops with stones. As they hit their targets, sores and pustules appeared on the soldiers' skin, and these spread like pestilence.

I recall how fond Kalil was of this Surah in our old detention centre days. He would argue that we should all see ourselves as birds of such a flock, ready to rain destruction down upon the enemy.

⌘

I sit at the table as Kalil feeds me day-old stew and bread. He fills me in on some of our fellow Glynbourne detainees. He has already washed and dressed me. Iqbal is present, and a new arrival named Hamid. From my room earlier I'd eavesdropped on another court case discussion, this time a group of men accused of organising terrorist training camps in Britain. I overhear fragments of the conversation, half-sentences and words, ummah, and kafir and shaheed, the language of conflict, of division. One of the accused, it seems, has dismissed killing fifty of the enemy as less than a decent breakfast for him. Iqbal finds this wonderfully witty. He repeats it three or four times.

I re-read my notebook and find sections of nonsense, incomprehensible gibberish that I have no recollection of writing. One section, written last week, begins 'His Excellence is camping in Gabon. Ow Ow sugar'. Whenever I find such passages I scrub them out, but they continue to reappear.

⌘

Kalil has stepped up the pressure. Today he forces me to accompany him to the chemist to collect my prescription. We make slow progress. My muscles are uncooperative, weakened from lack of use.

When we return, I find one of the others has worked on my room. Gone are my architectural books, my sketches. My notebook, hidden beneath my mattress, is still there, but the room is more naked than ever. The only additions are new handmade posters arranged around the walls, quotes from the

Qur'an in handwriting I recognise as Kalil's. The tone, too, is
familiar. I read one:

> *Allah hath purchased of the Believers*
> *Their persons and their goods;*
> *For theirs in return*
> *Is the Garden of Paradise:*
> *They fight in His cause,*
> *And slay and are slain:*
> *A promise binding on Him*
> *In Truth, through the Law*
> *The Gospel, and the Qur'an*

And another:

> *I will instill terror*
> *Into the hearts of the Unbelievers:*
> *Smite ye above their necks*
> *And smite all their*
> *Finger tips off them*

And a third:

> *O ye who believe!*
> *When ye meet*
> *The Unbelievers*
> *In hostile array,*
> *Never turn your backs*
> *To them*
> *If any do turn his back*
> *To them on such a day*
> *...*
> *He draws on himself*
> *The wrath of Allah.*
> *And his abode is Hell*
> *An evil refuge indeed!*

There are two shorter ones, both pinned above my bed:

> *O Prophet! Rouse the Believers*
> *To the fight.*

And

> *Fight and slay*
> *The Pagans wherever ye find them*

The red walls have gone, but the room is still haemorrhaging.

⌘

Another step closer.

Homemade DVDs have been left in my room, a pile on top of my television, looped images of torture and carnage. Women, children, helpless civilians brutalised by invaders in uniform, the bloody aftermath of aerial bombardment. The Arabic subtitles detail each location, each context – Chechnya, Kashmir, Al Fallujah, Helmand, Ramallah, Mogadishu – but the pain and loss is identical.

Another DVD consists of a compilation of martyrdom speech videos. Their messages, too, are unvarying, the same validation I have always had from Kalil, violence justified by divine instruction.

⌘

I still dream about the accident, about the boy. I still dream about you, the children, our old life.

The past is the motherland from which you can never escape.

⌘

Kalil comes to me again. He has brought my latest repeat prescription, but before he hands it over, he looks at me quizzically.

Well, brother? It is time to decide. What is it to be? The Garden or the Fire?

And this time he waits for an answer.

⌘

Without my noticing, winter has made way for spring.

The endgame commences. An unannounced dawn rise, a few clothes thrown into a holdall, a bus into town, then a coach to Gatwick. Kalil shows me my new passport, takes me to the check-in desk, leads me through immigration and security.

Ours is a direct flight to Cape Town. Kalil has given me extra tablets and I am already dozing in the departure lounge. The journey passes in a foggy haze.

⌘

I am writing this from my bed. Kalil tells me we are in a house in Chatsworth, a township suburb of Durban.

We move from place to place every few days. He has hired a car, and we drive across the country following an itinerary that only he understands. I sit beside him, his passenger, as he points out landmarks, exclaims at the outside world. I nod but I have no idea where I am.

Today I read with a stab of recognition the Surah *Al A'la* in which hell is depicted as a place in which you neither die nor live.

When I was in Britain, I memorised a verse from the Bible:

> *There is no fear in love; but perfect love casteth out fear: because fear hath torment. He that feareth is not made perfect in love.*

I try to make sense of the words, to identify a course of action that will stop the fear, end the torment. I do not know what to do. It is no longer in my hands.

The only love I feel is for you, but is it enough?

I am so sorry, my flower. Forgive me.

SEMIRA 3

Dear Kassa

The last few weeks have been difficult, with neither the time nor opportunity to write to you. Now, however, we seem to be enjoying a temporary respite from the threat of homelessness, so let me update you on this latest episode in our topsy-turvy lives.

I should start from where I left off and explain the nature of my plan. Since my class switch from Union Street, I have become familiar with the campus layout at Blackbird Leys, and in particular the comfortable English department staffroom. The campus itself is divided up into several large buildings – one for the construction department, another for motor mechanics, others for carpentry, for the canteen, for the reception and library.

The English language department, housed in a separate two-storey building, is based at the back of the college campus. The staffroom is on the ground floor. My form teacher, a woman named Nuala, has on several occasions sent me there to collect dictionaries or the class register, or make extra photocopies of class worksheets, and in so doing has revealed to me the door code for the security lock. The first time I go there, I note how warm the room is, take in the soft, electric blue carpet, the WC with toilet and basin, the tiny kitchen area with sink, mini fridge and microwave. I think already then the seeds have been sewn in my mind, if only as a vague and fanciful 'what if?'

This idea is further crystallised one lunchtime some

weeks before my crisis as I am standing beside Nuala's desk. I am waiting for her to return from the photocopier where she has been making a copy of some homework I missed the previous week.

Two workmen in overalls are rolling up wheels of cable and folding up their stepladders. As they return their screwdrivers to their toolboxes and replace some ceiling tiles, they explain to one of the other teachers that they have just been told to stop the job they are doing – a much needed rewiring of the old burglar alarm system – and get straight up to the main city centre campus, where a serious fault with the system has been reported. Security there is considered a priority, so they will be postponing this job until it is completed. That could take up to six weeks, and in the meantime they have already stripped out some of the essential wiring, so the alarm system in the English language building will be out of order.

There are jokes about tipping off someone to break in and steal the staffroom paper clips, some moaning about how the city centre campus is always prioritised over the Blackbird Leys one. From me, though, there are no complaints or laughter, just a vital nugget of information to store away.

And it all comes together on that first Monday. Checked out of the bed-and-breakfast, the children dropped off at school, arriving at college with no guarantee of where we will be sleeping that night, I am galvanised into action.

I take the bus into college and make my way through the campus to the English department building. As I pass through the main doors, I notice that they too have a security lock, though it is now on the latch. Have they been programmed with the same code as the staffroom door? I flick off the catch, punch in the numbers and pull back the lever. It clicks open smoothly. So far, so good.

On the way out, I take stock of the college grounds. I examine them the way a burglar surveys a likely target. I know that in the evening the security guards will lock the two sets of college gates, front and rear. I have noticed that the fencing close to the back gates is poorly maintained. At one point it serves as a border between the college grounds and a concrete playground, an area used by the apprentice plumbers for impromptu lunchtime football matches. There are a series of holes in the fence there made by these footballers to retrieve poorly placed shots that sail over into the college grounds.

Class finishes at one. I buy a cup of tea in the college canteen and sit amongst the rowdy apprentices with their fry-ups and pie-and-chips, and sketch out a plan of action.

By three thirty I am back at school to pick up the children. We walk around to the library, look at the books and toy with the computers until it closes at five thirty. We stroll up to the Cowley shopping centre, buy chips at the takeaway and sit on a bench to eat. It is as much to kill time as to satisfy our appetites. The children are unsettled and demand to know what is happening. I tell them to be patient.

Now it is back to Blackbird Leys, only this time we walk so as to waste more time. There is a sick feeling in my stomach – too much to go wrong.

It is half past seven, eight by the time we get to the front entrance, and I note that the gates are padlocked.

Ahead I can see the main building with the reception and, next to it, the cramped control room used by the on-duty security guard, little more than a cupboard equipped with desk, chair and the CCTV screens. The whole area is dark. I breathe a sigh of relief. I had presumed – prayed – that the college would not have night security but here was the confirmation.

We walk around to the rear entrance and skirt across the concrete playground. I find a big enough hole in the fencing. The children are confused but not afraid. I make light of our illegal entry, turning it into an adventure. Once inside the college grounds we head straight for the English building. I am aware of the CCTV cameras but figure no one will re-run the film unless there is a reported incident.

My memorised security codes get us through the main doors and into the staffroom. Inside I take out my holdall. I have brought books for the children, some fruit, teabags and sugar, a torch and two blankets. The heating has gone off but there is still the residual warmth from the day. It is our first night as squatters.

The following morning I get the children up. I make tea in the kitchen area and we eat a little fruit. I am restless, unsure what time the security guards go on duty, when the cleaners will arrive. This is information that I need, so after hiding my bag on the top shelf of a store cupboard, we make our escape through the damaged fencing. I take the children across the road to the row of shops, wait until the bakery opens and buy them warm rolls for breakfast. While we wait, we take our seats on the bench facing the main gates of the campus.

The security officer arrives at seven o'clock, the cleaners soon after. The first teacher arrives at eight. Ninety minutes later I have dropped the children at school and am back for my first class. We have a routine. We have a new home.

And so it continues. I return to Tom's house every couple of days, to fetch clean clothes and dump the dirty laundry. I still don't tell him what has happened. I have fabricated some friends with whom we are now staying, friends who do not have space to store our things. His wife, Gloria, is sympathetic. She insists they will keep my goods for as long as I want. I have also sworn Yanit and Abebe to secrecy. I promise them we will soon find better accommodation.

The following weeks feel hazardous and disorientating, a crazy mixture of the normal and the bizarre. There are moments, lost in some classroom writing exercise or picking up the children from school, when I forget that I sleep between a photocopier and a filing cabinet, that I wash in a kitchen sink, dry myself with a towel that stays hidden between archived student records.

The routine does not change. After classes, I kill the afternoon in the college library completing homework tasks or scouring the internet for properties to let while all around the boisterous plumbing apprentices and pimply motor vehicle trainees sit at their computer terminals and banter over music videos and gaming websites. Then it is the school pick-up, the local library where I supervise any homework jobs, the takeaway for tea, and finally the long haul to Blackbird Leys.

Anxious not to arouse suspicion, I draw the staffroom blinds and we lie on the floor and read by torchlight. I keep a supply of blankets in the first aid cupboard, and have divided up our other belongings and have them secreted around the building.

At the end of the second week I have to take a trip to the launderette. I realise Tom and Gloria must find it strange that we cannot even store our clothes at our present accommodation, but they say nothing. And me, I keep up the cheerful façade.

Still, by the beginning of the fourth week, the strain is beginning to show. My routine visits to the letting agencies are fruitless, I check my bidding rank for council properties and find I am still up there in the fifties. Worse, though, I have not informed the council about my 'change of address', I am sure that quite apart from my squatting, I am breaking any number of other housing and benefit regulations. It is too much to deal with, a mountain on my feeble shoulders, so I mentally shelve my responsibilities and bury myself in the present.

Of course I know it cannot last, am only unclear how long I can get away with it, how it will end. All I know is that I have no options.

And the end comes sooner than expected. The day after checking my bidding rank, a Tuesday, it is one o'clock and I am about to leave my classroom when Nuala calls me back, says she would like to have a word with me. I am used to these private chats. Sometimes they are to discuss progress or set learning goals, sometimes they are to deal with some other aspect of college administration, to enrol for an exam or update records. Occasionally they are just an opportunity for her to offer help with any personal issues.

We sit opposite each other in an interview room. Nuala gets straight to the point. I am re-constructing from memory, but the conversation that follows goes something like this:

So tell me, Semira. How long have you been sleeping in the staffroom?

I am dumbfounded. My first instinct is to bluff. I gulp,

search for the right words, the right expression to convey my outrage. Nuala just smiles at me.

It's OK. I know it's true. Don't try to deny it. You can trust me.

I hesitate. Nuala is a good teacher, kind and patient, and her lessons are interesting and funny and useful. She is caring and considerate, but I have never got beyond our 'professional' relationship.

Let me explain, before you say anything, she says. I left my debit card in my desk drawer on Friday, and I only realised it after I got home that evening. I needed it the next day, so I came back here at half eight hoping that someone on security might let me in. The whole campus was locked up but I came round the back and found the hole in the fencing. I guess that's how you get in. She pauses, but does not wait for a response. I was just about to come in when I saw flickering lights through one of the windows. The blinds hadn't been closed properly and I could see in. I saw you there, you and your children. You were reading together with torches. I didn't want to disturb you. I thought I'd frighten you, so I just turned back.

I look at her, weigh up her words. Her eyes are beautiful, a greeny-grey, flecked with blue, like nothing I have seen before in Africa. I examine them carefully, think I read in them honesty and sympathy and compassion and sadness. But I still don't know what to say, where to start.

Look, you can't stay here. It's, it's...

Why not? I say, breaking my silence. I do not know why I say that, perhaps I am just playing for time.

Well, it's... it's... you... Nuala bursts out laughing. Christ almighty, where do I start? You're not stupid, you must realise what you're doing's wrong. I say nothing. The point is, she continues, as much to herself as to me, that you wouldn't be doing it unless you had to. She looks at me with those powerful, flinty eyes. Things are bad, eh?

I nod, I take a deep breath, and then I tell her everything. I tell her about the council housing lists, my problems with the meter, the Cowley landlord, Tom and Gloria. When I finish she purses her lips and gives a low whistle.

Jesus Christ, that's some story, she says with a hollow laugh. She continues to stare at me and we remain like that, in silence, for a long minute. Finally she speaks.

Well, you can't stay here. You can stay at my place for a few days. Just until you get yourself sorted. We can go round to your friends this afternoon to collect your stuff. I've got some paperwork to do but I should be free in an hour or so. I'll meet you in the canteen.

I start to protest. I certainly appreciate the generosity behind Nuala's offer, it feels in some ways like a miraculous answer to our prayers. But I hardly know this woman...

Look, Semira. I can see you're hesitating, but let me put it this way. If you stay here and are caught, the college could prosecute you. You could be arrested and that might even mean a spell in custody. If you're locked up, your kids would be taken into care. Come on, don't be stubborn. You know it makes sense.

And of course, she is right. I hesitate for only a few more seconds, long enough to consider, then dismiss the idea that Nuala might be a crazed child killer, a dealer in human body parts. What is the worst that can happen? I think. If it turns out to be an awful mistake, we can always leave. And in the meantime, this buys us a bit more time.

So that is what I remember of our conversation, and that is how I come to be here in this spare bedroom, sitting at a small pine desk, finishing off this letter, dear Kassa. It is late, nearly two o'clock. Tom drove around with his van this evening to drop off our belongings. Yanit and Abebe are both on put-me-up beds in the basement, the house is silent, and I am dropping with fatigue.

All my love to you and Gadissa.

⌘

Dear Kassa

I thought of you today with your love of stories, as I bought my copy of the local newspaper. Yanit has won a short story competition for schoolchildren and the prize is publication of the tale in the paper and a hundred pounds in book tokens. She is so proud of herself, as I am too. She told me nothing about it and submitted her entry secretly. It was not until they announced the winners that she allowed me to read it. It is about a young girl who is made homeless and breaks into her school classroom every night to sleep there. My eyes nearly popped out of my head when I read it! I have cut out the story and enclose the clipping for you to read. I know you would be proud of her.

Our new home is large, a tall handsome terraced house half-way up Divinity Road. It is closer to the mosque and to the Asian shops that sell some of the herbs and spices I like to cook with. It is a little further from the children's school, from the library and my classes, but the bus to Blackbird Leys passes the bottom of the road, and everything else is still within walking distance.

And what a handsome road it is, a thoroughfare whose life begins up at the top of a park, and which then meanders lazily down the hill bursting forth onto Cowley Road, from source to estuary a good quarter mile of tarmac.

In many ways the road is typical of this part of the world, residential urban comfort, a mixture of professionals and students. I could be in London or Bristol. There are the green dustbins, the blue recycling boxes full of empty beer tins and cardboard, the posters in the bay windows advertising school fetes or political meetings. At any one time three or four of the houses are being worked on, their front gardens filled with rubble or bags of cement. Cars are parked from top to bottom, enough space on the road for only a single vehicle to pass at one time, so manoeuvring up and down the hill demands patience and politeness – the English are good at that.

For me, though, the road is unique. It is our temporary safe haven from life's storms, so I have studied it at some length. In my mind, I divide the road into three parts. The first stretches from the top to the first bend, where the road veers to the right. On this section, as you head down the hill, your eyes travel above the houses and you can see a rising area of greenery in the distance, a mile or two away perhaps. Then, if you raise your eyes, you see beyond the first ridge a proper hill, far out in the country, a patchwork of fields and woods, and you understand that Oxford is a small urban island in a rural ocean.

When you reach that first bend, you are into the hundred-and-twenties where we live. From here you are too low to see the country landscape beyond the buildings. Instead, rising above the houses, the view is dominated by the curved roof of the mosque, matt or gleaming depending on the time of day, the lighting and weather, and the minaret, tall and stately. It is a beautiful sight, the first thing I look for when I leave the house, a warming, welcome presence and yet exotic, too, in its setting.

The bend is short, from the one-twenties to the nineties, and then you are in the home stretch, the road sweeps down the final section to the insurance firm and manicure bar facing you on the main road at the bottom.

And what of our sanctuary itself? It is a four bedroom house with a large basement converted into some kind of art studio. Nuala has the master bedroom and both of her children, Sammy and Bethany, have their own rooms. I am in the fourth bedroom, with Yanit and Abebe on camp beds sharing the basement.

At first I protest and offer to share my bedroom with the children, but Nuala insists that the studio is temporarily not in use, and both Yanit and Abebe plead to be allowed to stay there. The piles of canvases, tubes of paints, jars of brushes, the haphazard stains and smears on every surface, all make it seem like some exciting playroom. Together with Nuala, we hoover the room, tidy up the worst of the mess, scrub and dust so that it can serve as a place to sleep.

Settling in has not been straightforward. At first everything is awkward. Sammy, aged nine, and Bethany, eleven, seem like sweet, funny children. They are obviously confused by our arrival, but they are polite and helpful as they go about showing Yanit and Abebe around the house. They explain how to use their playstation, which cupboard holds the biscuit tin, what password you must use to log onto the computer.

I hate those first weeks. Perhaps I have just grown unaccustomed to sharing a life with anyone. All those uncomfortable episodes: opening the toilet door before realising that someone is already inside. Having to ask a hundred times a day where such-and-such lives, how to switch it on, why it will not work. Always wanting to help, to put on the laundry, do the dishes, cook the meal, but worried that you are being too pushy.

But gradually things have got better. Nuala has a knack for putting people at ease – I have seen it often enough with new students in the classroom – and little by little we work out a routine that seems to satisfy us both.

First of all she announces that henceforth she will be buying her meat halal from a Cowley Road butcher. She likes to do the weekday cooking – great saucepans of beef stew, chicken curry, tomato and red pepper sauce, which she throws together with rice or pasta or mashed potatoes. I help out with the peeling and dicing. For my taste it is wholesome but one-dimensional and rather bland. Still, it is food her children are used to, and Yanit and Abebe, sick of takeaway chips, approve heartily.

At weekends, we feed the children on pizza and I make them mountains of falafel, which everybody seems to love. Then, once the little ones are fed, I cook my own dishes, lamb and lentil wat, kitfo and tibs and gored gored. I introduce Nuala to berbere and niter kibbeh. The familiar cooking smells draw Yanit and Abebe away from the television and computer, bring them into the kitchen for a second sitting. And then Sammy and Bethany appear, anxious not to miss out, and even they will sniff the plates, break off a hunk of injera and dip it into one of the stews.

My studies are going very well. Nuala says I have a gift for languages. She says it is almost miraculous how quickly I pick things up. I don't know about that, but it is pleasing to be moved up classes regularly, to see my hard work reflected in certificates and qualifications. I am now in the top English language class, a pre-access course called Pathways for Adult Learners. Every week I inch closer to my goal.

Money is difficult. At first I have nothing. My housing benefit is going straight to my ex-landlord, I guess, and I still cannot face the council with my tale of foolish misfortune. I want to contribute to household expenses but am unable.

I try to explain this to Nuala and she waves away my embarrassment. Still, she tells me I need to sort out the bureaucracy for the council if I want to avoid losing my housing ranking for the second time. She helps me make an appointment with a housing officer and accompanies me to the meeting. We have already agreed to turn her landlady status into something more formal so that I will remain on housing benefits and can keep my place on the housing list. We fill in the paperwork to transfer my benefits payment to her. It is a huge relief to have all that sorted out, and I feel better handing over some rent. There is still some awkwardness. I keep telling her all this is only temporary, that we will be out of her hair soon. She tells me we can stay as long as we like, but I cannot help feeling a little uneasy.

Nuala's two children are interesting characters. When they are tired or frustrated, they squabble and fight constantly, are insolent towards their mother and lose all sense of boundaries. In other words, they show that lack of respect that we find so scandalous when we observe family relationships here. At these times I look over at my own children observing the scene with shock and awe, and I think, Now don't you get any ideas...

Most of the time, though, Nuala's children are bright and funny and thoughtful. Bethany is a year younger than Yanit but similar in many ways, a book-lover, a sketcher, a scribbler of poems, an actress. She has introduced Yanit to a computer game that involves designing and building your own virtual home and lifestyle and they spend hours choosing colour schemes and furnishings. Sammy is nine, the same age as Abebe. His passion is Lego and his bedroom is little more than an on-going construction site. His interest has brushed off on Abebe, a good thing since it keeps him off the computer.

Despite their occasional tantrums, the 'paddies' as Nuala calls them, there is something admirable about these children. It is difficult to explain, Kassa, but as I watch them, I begin to understand that the freedom they enjoy, the lack of boundaries and respect, is both a curse and a blessing.

Of course it is shocking to see children abuse each other and show so little respect for authority. But as I watch them pushing those boundaries, flourishing in the freedom they have to experiment, to learn from their mistakes, I see that there is a healthy side to this way of bringing up children, that it makes these young ones strong-willed independent-minded and creative, and this must be a good thing too.

In the meantime, though, there are times when Nuala's children are playing up, where I have to fight the urge to deliver a few choice slaps...

On the kitchen wall, there is a framed collage of photos of family and friends. It is easy to identify the children's father, a gentle-looking man with a long face and thin, mousy hair, greying at the temples. He appears in many of the pictures and I study his features for glimpses of his children – the shape of Sammy's mouth, the humour in Bethany's eyes. I scrutinise his profile, occasionally reflective, caught off guard, but usually smiling, pulling a silly face, playing up to the camera. I wonder where he is, what his story is, but of course I do not ask Nuala.

And I am not the only one who is curious about the lives of others. Nuala digs around for my past, not in a bad way, not aggressively, just a gentle but dogged grilling for information. Since my arrival here, I have opened up to no-one about my history, save for the minimal account necessary to persuade the Red Cross officer to commit himself to my cause.

It is not only that I still feel a danger, the long claws of the Asmara family. Much more than that it is an act of self-preservation – I need to survive here, to flourish even, if only for the sake of Yanit and Abebe. To do that I have to be focused, to deal ruthlessly with my memories. To open the lid, to allow my past out, would be to risk the mental equilibrium that I currently maintain. My history buried, I remain strong. My family, my friends, my lost life in Africa, you are all needles in my heart, Kassa, but I cannot afford to give you my attention, must work to push you out to the edge. That is how I survive. That is how it must be.

But Nuala is persistent, and from time to time I feel strong enough to open the door a crack. Yesterday she asks me about my family. I have rarely spoken to anyone about the early years of my life, not even to you and Gadissa, but on this occasion I find some relief in revealing my past. Here is the conversation as I remember it. You may find it illuminating.

I am an only child, I begin. My mother nearly died in childbirth, she could not have any more children after that.

And were you close? Do you keep in touch? I mean, are your parents both still alive? She realises she is being pushy, looks a little sheepish.

Yes, no, and I believe so, in that order, I reply, and allow her time to digest my answers. She waits for me to go on. I come from a wealthy family. My father had a car dealership in Addis Ababa. My parents were brought up as strict members of the Ethiopian Orthodox Tewahedo Church. My mother's uncle was a bishop, as was my father's youngest brother. I grew up steeped in that culture, but I reacted against it, and although I loved my parents deeply I think from an early age I was questioning the doctrines. Why do we have to do this? Why can't we do that? I used to drive them mad. I suppose I was spoiled, you know, an only child and all that. I studied hard at school and went to university. In my final year at college I met a man. We fell in love and decided to get married. But there were problems. He wasn't Christian, wasn't well-off, wasn't even Ethiopian for that matter.

Go on, she says.

My parents were devastated. My boyfriend was a Muslim from Eritrea, a country we had been at war with until recently. If I wanted to marry him and get his family's blessing,

I would have to convert to Islam. I must admit I had my doubts about this at first, but I loved him and felt, to be honest, that it did not really matter which religion I signed up to – I believed in God, had a clear understanding of where I stood with Him, so why did it matter what I called him. That is how I looked at it. Well, my parents did not share my point of view. It was too much for them to bear. They told me in no uncertain terms that I would have to choose between my family and my fiancé. They were ashamed of me, of course.

So what happened? she asks.

I was in love, I could not give him up. The last time I saw them, I had already moved my things out, I was staying with university friends. I went round to our house to say goodbye. They were devastated, I could tell, but equally adamant that they could not accept my marriage, my conversion. They saw me to the garden gate and promised that if I came back a Christian, the door would always be open for me. We embraced and I walked away. A week later I left Addis for Asmara. A month later I was married.

Wow, says Nuala, impressed. Wow.

It was awful being cut off by my parents, but I felt they gave me no choice. Being in a new country with a new life made it easier, I suppose. They were physically distanced, as well as emotionally, so it wasn't as if I kept expecting to bump into them at the market.

And now? Why don't you contact them now? Nuala asks tentatively. I think about this. Of course she does not know about my situation, about the accident, about prison, the blood feud, our flight. I think about what she is suggesting. Could I re-establish contact? Of course not. Our separation has not affected the sanctity of our marriage. My Muslim status has not changed. The same conditions still apply. And of course there is another reason to remain silent. While my whereabouts are a mystery to everyone, I remain safe from the clutches of the Asmara boy's family. Anonymity brings protection.

It is complicated, I say.

Nuala knows she has taken it as far as she can. She

attempts to lighten the mood by changing tack.

I didn't know you lived in Asmara. So did I. Three years I was there. Back in the early nineties. Small world, eh? Maybe we bumped into each other! That's a weird thought.

I do know this. She has mentioned it several times in the classroom, but I feign surprise, and we spend a few minutes reminiscing about familiar Asmara landmarks and institutions. Nuala tries out a few words of Tigrinya she had picked up and I compliment her on her pronunciation, which makes us both laugh. Then the doorbell rings. Yanit is back with Abebe, and before we know it the conversation is forgotten and we are plunged into dinner preparations, the dicing and peeling, the warm homely aroma of frying onions and garlic.

I leave you with those appetising smells wafting through your imagination.

As always, you and Gadissa are never out of our thoughts and prayers.

⌘

Dear Kassa

A welcome period of calm. I continue to search for a suitable home, to check my council ranking, despite Nuala's insistence that there is no hurry, but in the meantime we are comfortable here. It is a relief to feel safe and secure and the children delight in the stability of their lives.

A period of discovery, too. Through Nuala, Sammy and Bethany, through the steady stream of their friends and playmates, I pick up facets of modern British culture and language from which in the past, with nobody to provide an explanation, I was excluded. I learn the difference between a wii and an ipod, between lol and omg, between a twit and a twat.

And through the innocent remarks of Sammy and Bethany, I learn about their family history. About their father.

First, last week, I overhear Abebe asking Sammy why there are paints and brushes in his bedroom.

That's daddy's room, answers Sammy. That's where he does his pictures. But daddy's lost in Africa now. And we don't know when he's coming back.

Then, a couple of days later, a Saturday morning, I eavesdrop on a conversation between Yanit and Bethany. They have just come back from town laden with new books. Nuala has taken them to a bookshop so that Yanit can spend some of her prize book tokens. Nuala leaves straight away to drop some shopping off for a neighbour and the girls spread out their new purchases on the kitchen table. Bethany has helped choose some of the books and, faced with such lucrative rewards, she is obviously working on her own creative inspiration. I am in the lounge on the computer searching for properties but the door is open and they are unaware of my presence.

I'm going to write my own stories, she begins. About my dad. About somebody putting a bomb in his airplane. About how it crashes in Africa and he has lots of adventures. It's going to be a series, lots of different episodes. They'll make a TV series, too, and a Hollywood film. There'll be sequels. They'll pay me millions.

Can I help you write it? asks Yanit. She sounds very impressed.

Sure. You can be in charge of spelling.

Come on then.

And the next thing I know they are at my side, clamouring for me to log off and abandon the computer. Back in the kitchen, I try and recall a terrorist attack that matches their description. I vaguely remember one or two such incidents, the most recent about seven or eight months ago. I make a mental note to google it later.

In fact, there is no need. Perhaps my willingness to open up to Nuala has helped her find the courage to speak about her own. One night last week, drinking mint tea after the children had been seen to, she opens up. She fills in the details of the air crash and her husband's disappearance, or at least what few details she has grasped, for in truth her situation, like my own, is a kind of hellish limbo, her life suspended by uncertainty.

She is matter-of-fact and just tells me the bare facts. She avoids any mention of feelings and emotions.

For a few brief moments I consider telling her about the extent of my own loss. It is a natural reaction born out of belief that in exchanging our stories we might perhaps be providing relief, a reduction of the hurt. But as these thoughts flash across my mind, they are at once dismissed. I cannot speak for her, but I know that for me now, the process of sharing would neither halve nor double my pain, would only serve to underline the loneliness of my journey, so I continue to listen and nod, to murmur trite words of sympathy. The conversation drifts and finally draws to a halt.

I worry about our stay in Divinity Road. Every so often I bring up my awkwardness about abusing her hospitality but Nuala tells me not to worry. Recently I am offered a flat by a Sudanese couple I met at the mosque. They are moving to Coventry and have spoken to their landlord about me. When I mention this to Nuala, she offers to drive me over to the place to check it out. The flat is in Wood Farm. It is cold and cramped and gloomy, the second bedroom little more than a cupboard, the kitchen hardly bigger. We look around and I make positive noises, though I am silently dreading the prospect of a move to this place. Outside, back in the car, Nuala is emphatic. The property is just not suitable, she says. It is dingy and damp, a health hazard for the children. Something better will come up soon, she adds. We just need to be patient.

Nuala's insistence sets me thinking. I begin to wonder whether my presence in her life is in fact more of a benefit than a burden. Perhaps that is the definition of friendship.

We continue to probe each other's minds. She tells me about her childhood, growing up on a farm in Ireland. She describes how her brother used to milk the cows straight into her cupped hands, the warm creamy velvet slipping down her throat. In exchange I tell her about my dream of teaching and sketch out my career path from classroom learning assistant to fully-fledged teacher via a teacher training course.

One evening we are sitting together in the lounge.

The children are in bed, the evening battle with baths and bedtime stories eventually won, and Nuala has collapsed on the sofa with her newspaper. She is grappling with a sudoku, a passion of hers, but has made a mistake and is cursing, about to surrender. Finally she throws down the paper and looks up at me. I am reading the *Qur'an*. Yanit and Abebe have been told by their *Qur'anic* class teacher to learn a passage and I am trying to locate the right Surah. She breaks the silence.

Tell me about your faith, she begins. How did it change when you converted?

I consider the question carefully.

I don't think it changed much, you know. God remained God. Just the details were dissimilar. Not just the obvious rule changes, but the different character, the colour and texture, the taste of the religion. It is difficult to explain.

Was it a big change? A big shock?

Not really. You know, if you study theological history, how religions began, how they developed in their early days, how they relate to each other, you see that Ethiopia holds a special place in the heart of the matter.

What do you mean?

History, of course, is my passion, and I soon warm to the task. Yes, Kassa, I can picture you now, rolling your eyes and groaning! Anyway, I tell her about the birth of Ethiopia, the reign of Menelik I in 1000 BC. I tell her that one of the Egyptian pharaohs, Taharga, was Ethiopian, that at the time that Christianity began, there were four great global powers – Rome, Persia, China and Aksum. I tell her that the Aksumite Kingdom was centred in what is now Ethiopia but its control spread to parts of Yemen, Somalia, Sudan, Egypt, Eritrea, Djibouti, even Saudi Arabia. I point out that emperors right up to the modern era have traced their lineage to that kingdom, to Solomon and the Queen of Sheba.

I look carefully at Nuala, try to assess her reaction. She does not appear too bored so I plough on.

I tell her that Christianity came to Aksum in 316 AD when a Christian theologian called Meropius was shipwrecked off the Ethiopian coast. He was taken to the royal court, along with two Syro-Greek brothers, Frumentius and Aedesius, both also Christians. Frumentius converted the queen, went back to Alexandria, and, when he later returned as Bishop of Aksum, he baptised her son, King Ezana. I inform her that after that, Christianity became the official state religion. That after Armenia, Ethiopia is the second-oldest nation to adopt Christianity. That references to Ethiopian Christianity go back as far as the New Testament. I instruct her to read *Acts* 8:26 to 39, tell her they refer to an Ethiopian baptised by Philip the Evangelist.

Nuala laughs, a gesture of surprise, I think, and tells me she never knew that Ethiopia was such a Christian heartland. I shake my head and tell her no, it is not just Christianity, that traditionally Ethiopia has always opened its doors to any religion. That is what makes it so special. I tell her that in 615 AD Muslims fleeing from persecution by the Quraysh tribe in Mecca found refuge in the court of the Christian king, a man named Ashama ibn Abjar. He offered them a settlement in Negash which became one of the first Muslim communities in Africa. Did you know, I ask her, that the very first muezzin, one of Muhammad's key followers, was an Ethiopian, a man named Bilal?

I have warmed to my theme now, so I move onto the Ethiopian Jewish community, I mention the Beta Israel, though point out that most of them were taken to Israel during the 1980s to escape the famine. I tell her that some Jewish scholars believe they were the Biblical 'Lost Tribe of Israel'.

Nuala nods and tells me she remembers reading about that, so I soldier on. I say that even though Christianity is supposed to be the majority religion in Ethiopia, we have got our own version, the Ethiopian Orthodox Tewahedo Church. I tell her that it shares some characteristics with the other religions and their doctrines.

Nuala frowns, asks me what I mean, so I explain that our Bible is more like the Jewish *Torah*. Our Old Testament includes some of the original Jewish books. *Enoch* and *Jubilees*, for instance, which have survived in our ancient Ge'ez script.

Then I talk about our religious architecture, too, and how it differs from other Christian buildings, that our churches are monolithic, constructed from a single block of stone. I ask her if she has seen a picture of the Church of Saint George in Lalibela, tell her that we believe the original Ark of the Covenant is kept concealed in the Church of Our Lady Mary of Zion. I tell her that a new church cannot be consecrated unless a replica of the tablets of the Ark is placed in it by a bishop. It is a bit like the Jews and their Aron Kodesh, the special place in each synagogue where they keep the *Torah*.

Nuala stirs and asks me if I would like some tea. I am thinking that she must be growing bored but when she comes back she says it is fascinating, asks me to tell her more, so I explain that like Muslims and Jews, the Ethiopian Christians have set rituals that cover the way they slaughter animals. They cannot eat pork. Women cannot enter a church if they are menstruating. When they enter the church, they must cover their hair with a scarf. Even the way they sit is like in a mosque or synagogue – men to one side, women to the other.

And that, in a way, brings us back to the beginning of our discussion, the nature of my own personal faith.

So you see, in my mind, there was no great contradiction in my conversion, I tell her. It is difficult to explain, but it was just like swapping one blanket for another. They are both warm, comforting, fulfil their function. So converting was no big deal.

And now you still consider yourself a Muslim?

Of course. Not just out of loyalty to my husband. Like I said, Islam gives me what I want from a faith. What I want for my children, too.

What about all those accusations of Islam oppressing women?

Well, part of the problem is that outside the *Qur'an* itself there is what we call the Hadith. Those are the secondary, oral traditions relating to Muhammad's words and deeds. They are sometimes contradictory and vague and can obscure the *Qur'an*'s original message. Also, this message can be corrupted by cultural influences. All this burkha business, for example. There is nothing in the *Qur'an* that says women have to cover up completely. There are one or two parts dealing with how women dress, Surah 24:31, I believe, and 33:59. They say that women should behave with modesty and cover their bosoms in public, nothing more. Well, I don't have a problem with that.

Wow, you really know your *Qur'an*, eh?

Bible, too. I spent my childhood learning it by heart to please my parents. Then I had to do the same with the *Qur'an* to satisfy my in-laws.

One thing people are always talking about is how harsh Islam is to Muslims who leave the faith. Isn't the punishment death, or amputation or something equally gruesome according to Shariah?

For apostasy? Well, it depends who you listen to. Me, I always go back to the *Qur'an*. Let me see, it is *Al Nisa*, 4:115:

> *If anyone contends with*
> *The Messenger even after*
> *Guidance has been plainly*
> *Conveyed to him, and follows*
> *A path other than that*
> *Becoming to men of Faith,*
> *We shall leave him*
> *In the path he has chosen,*
> *And land him in Hell –*
> *What an evil refuge!*

Now to me that doesn't sound like Allah telling us to go out and punish an apostate ourselves. Sounds to me like He is just telling us to leave him to his fate. That call to violence is down to the interpretations of individual scholars fuelled on poison, urged on by a lust for power. But my faith is between me and God, so to hell with whatever anyone else says!

What about that stuff about the different values put on men and women? Someone once told me that there's something in the *Qur'an* about how in a law court, one male witness is worth two women.

Surah 2:282. Yes, it is true. Just like *Peter* 3:7 describes a woman as the 'weaker vessel' in relation to her husband. And of course I can't agree that women are inferior. Both books are old, they were written at times in the past when people saw some things a little differently, so maybe we have to see them in some kind of context. I believe that any healthy religion must be open to a certain amount of adaptation, that any religion whose every facet is a hundred percent prescribed must be unhealthy, insecure, and can only survive through blind adherence, or brainwashing, or force. A mature, secure religion must allow for some dissent, for discussion. And that is what Islam means to me.

But there must be some key differences between Christianity and Islam? Nuala asks.

I consider the question.

Look, I am not a theologian. All I can do is read the books and make my judgment. I certainly think there are more similarities than differences. For both it is basically the carrot-and-stick approach.

What do you mean?

Both of them start off with the promise that if you adhere to them, if you behave well, treat others with mercy and care and respect, then you will be rewarded. On the other hand, if you don't do what is prescribed, then you will be punished. Both books have their positive messages of peace and tolerance and harmony. And their negative ones of hell and damnation, of war against the enemy. But at the end of the day both are about mercy and love. Surah 7:199 goes:

Hold to forgiveness;
Command what is right;
But turn away from the ignorant

Micah 6:8 says:

What doth the Lord require of thee, but to do justly, and
to love mercy, and to walk humbly with thy God.

Two books, one message, eh?

Nuala is looking at me oddly and I feel a little embarrassed at my discourse. To cover my feelings I put her on the back foot.

What about you? I ask. Where do you stand on religion?

She laughs a little awkwardly.

Well, it'd break my mother's heart to say it, but I suppose I'm against any organised religion, whatever that's called. I don't know if there's a name for it. I was brought up a strict Catholic, mass every Sunday, Easter like a permanent camp-out in church. That's what put me off first. Later I suppose it was seeing the effects of religion around the world that made me so negative. Not just the Christian versus Muslim thing that seems to have been going on since the Crusades, but all the other conflicts, the Protestants and Catholics in northern Ireland, Singhalese Buddhists against Tamil Hindus in Sri Lanka, Hindu fascists persecuting Muslims in India, the violence in northern Nigeria, Sunnis and Shiites in Iraq. All that brutality committed in the name of one doctrine or another.

Yes, but that is not the religion. That is the people interpreting the message, twisting it, using it for their own pursuit of power or wealth, or because their minds are poisoned and weak. That is human nature. You cannot blame the religion.

Maybe. I mean, if the religion leads you to be kind to others, to do unto them as you'd have them do unto you as it were, then I haven't got a problem with it. If your *Qur'an* or Bible or *Torah* or whatever leads you to behave in the right way, then good for you. In that sense, when it's just a means to an end, I have no problem with it. It's just that I don't believe you need to sign up to a set organised faith to get that. I mean to me it's common sense. Personally I'm just cutting out the middle man.

We both laugh.

What about your mother? I ask. What does she say?

Well, I'm sure she disapproves of the way the kids have been brought up. They've been baptised all right, but I don't manage to get them to church more than twice a year, I suppose. And that's really just to appease their grandma. Of course, I still feel the guilt. Once a Catholic, always a Catholic...

The conversation peters out, we reflect on each other's words. Then Nuala breaks the silence.

I've never heard the *Qur'an* read, she says. But I like the sound of Arabic. It's kind of soothing but powerful. Read me something from the book.

Really, I say, caught off guard by her unexpected request. What do you want to hear?

I don't know. Anything. You choose.

I consider this, flick through the Surahs, finally pick on 41:34 and 35. I begin to read the Ayat off the page, but I know them well and soon I close my eyes and let the words flow from my heart:

> *Nor can Goodness and Evil*
> *Be equal. Repel Evil*
> *With what is better:*
> *Then will be between whom*
> *And thee was hatred*
> *Become as it were*
> *Thy friend and intimate!*
> *And no one will be*
> *Granted such goodness*
> *Except those who exercise*
> *Patience and self-restraint –*
> *None but persons of*
> *The greatest good fortune.*

When I finish she smiles and sighs. It sounds nice, she says. Like a song. And then, Fancy another cup of tea?

And with that, our theological debate comes to an end.

It is late now, my love, and I must get up early to revise for a classroom test.

My purest love to you, to Gadissa. You are my food, my drink, the air that I breathe. You are my waking and my sleep, my dreams and my prayers. You are inside and out. You are everywhere. And you are nowhere.

NUALA 3

When she invites Semira to stay it is almost in spite of herself. She's already told herself that it wouldn't be a good idea. She treasures her own privacy too much. When she reveals to her friend Mary what she has done, the older woman shakes her head in amazement.

You must be mad, Nuala. You spend your working day dealing with all those problems. Surely you need that time at home to protect your own sanity.

What could I do? She had nowhere else to go.

Yeah, but you've got enough on your plate. You're your own worst enemy.

Enough on her plate? She knew Mary would say something like that. It isn't the first time she's come across the idea that her loss is some kind of time-consuming burden, an activity to prioritise, as if she needs to set aside a certain number of hours for it each day. And yet nothing could be further from the truth. What she fears most since After is an enforced idleness that gives her time to dwell. On the contrary, her coping mechanism is based solely on the creation of activity, of bustle and commotion. The children's needs provide a great deal of distraction, of course. But there are still gaps to be plugged, especially after bedtime, when reality comes hurtling down on her. There's a part of her, then, that sees Semira's arrival as an opportunity. She's not sure whether this is a sign of weakness, though, so she says nothing of it to Mary.

And anyway, her decision to invite Semira is not taken blindly. After all, she's been her tutor for some months, certainly enough time to gauge her personality and conclude that she has a good heart.

And of course there are other benefits. Like an end to the organisational headache and financial burden of babysitters. Semira rarely goes out in the evening, and makes it clear she considers it perfectly acceptable to take responsibility for Sammy and Beth when Nuala is bullied into a trip to the cinema with Mary or Linda, an after-work drink with colleagues on the Cowley Road, or an evening at the monthly book club get-togethers she has now resumed.

A further advantage, less easily measurable, is the positive effect of Semira's children on her own. Helpful and obedient, no fights, no stroppiness, no sibling combat. Nuala watches and marvels and prays that just a tiny bit of that magic might rub off on her own two.

Semira's arrival also allows Nuala to get to grips with her overprotective neurosis, to come to terms with her Doomsday Theory. Watching Yanit and Abebe's independence – Semira now permits them to walk to and from school and often sends them to the shops on errands – gives Nuala the strength to hand some back to her own children. She returns to full-time teaching and gives up her role as voluntary classroom assistant for Sammy and Beth. She forces herself to take a step back from their lives.

Her job is fine. It provides all the escape she needs. From the moment she arrives at college she's thrown into a frantic cycle of administrative and bureaucratic activity as well as the classroom teaching itself. There are termly schemes of work to complete, weekly class records, syllabus design and materials development, registers and student files, lesson plans and photocopying.

But it is her interaction with the students that inspires Nuala and prevents her jumping ship when the bureaucracy seems too oppressive. When people ask her where her students come from typically, she always tells them to pick up a newspaper and identify where there has been recent conflict. Today they are Afghans and Kurds, Somalis, Sudanese and Congolese, East Timorese and Burundians, Chinese, Palestinians, Rwandans and Kosovars. Tomorrow, of course, it might be different. At any given time she has, within a single classroom, a snapshot of global upheaval, whether social, economic or environmental. Contemporary politics in a nutshell.

A week has passed since Semira's arrival. She spends her lunchbreak giving individual tutorials, an extended trouble-shooting session that she timetables in once a week, an opportunity for her students to bring her their problems. Today one student is uncertain how to get a place for his daughter at primary school. Nuala drafts a job reference for another, helps a third one to fill in her passport application form, a fourth to obtain a free bus pass. She helps decipher a court summons letter, refers a young girl for counselling, runs through the procedure for claiming back income tax. One student asks her how she can apply to a British university, another how to deal with council tax.

Nuala's not timetabled to teach that afternoon but she's agreed to accompany one of her students to the town hall for her daughter's local education authority appeal hearing. Having endured months of bullying by a gang in her school including a night attack on her home, the daughter has refused to return to class and so they have applied for a transfer to another school further from her home. The new school has refused and they have appealed.

Nuala has helped her student fill in the appeal paperwork. She feels nervous before the meeting but at the hearing it becomes clear that those adjudicating have read the daughter's account, are sympathetic, and that the onus is clearly on the school representative to justify the refusal rather than for her student to plead her case.

The wait in the reception area takes longer than the appeal itself, and when they emerge, triumphant, twenty-five minutes later, Nuala's student invites her for a celebratory coffee. They find a small café and eat sticky cakes with their cappuccinos.

The student's daughter is no weak-willed wall flower, she's feisty and sassy and droll – not at all how Nuala had expected. Nuala can see how her strength might well have infuriated a bully. She's a natural mimic, providing cutting impersonations of the appeal panel members, the school representative and her own mother, and she keeps the two adults amused as they finish their snack.

Back at home Nuala finds Semira, Yanit and Abebe absent – some meeting or class at the mosque, she recalls – and her own children in front of the television.

As she'd arranged the previous day, her neighbour Joan is watching the children. She's a sprightly octogenarian, a pumpkin face, wiry close-curled hair, a generous smile revealing the stumps of her few remaining teeth. Resident of the street for over fifty years, to Nuala she's as much a fixture as the postbox on the corner. Nuala knows something of her past, that she's watched her husband succumb to cancer and her children grow up and move out – one to Australia, one to Canada, the third to the Potteries. In the absence of blood relations she has adopted many of the other residents, including Nuala and her offspring, as family.

Nuala has mixed, mostly positive feelings for Joan. She's warm and caring though displays an odd quirk, a penchant for the non sequitur and an ability to generate her own logic, which can be endearing or hilarious or infuriating depending on the circumstances.

Joan often talks about the old people's home in Headington where she worked for forty years. Nuala knows that they allowed her to continue working until well into her seventies, and even after her retirement she has continued to return there once or twice a week to visit the residents, as much for her own benefit as for theirs, Nuala believes.

Hello, dear, she begins when she sees Nuala. Your phone's just rung but it's one of them cordless ones, so I didn't touch it.

That's OK, Joan. Will you have a cup of tea?

No thanks, dear. I had one earlier. The kids have had a snack.

How are the legs?

Joan's health has taken a turn for the worse recently after a decade of relative stability. Despite their tree-trunk appearance, both her legs are frail and her latest problem involves the left one. In addition, both ankles are permanently swollen and she has never fully recovered from a hip injury following a fall on the icy pavement the previous winter. Nuala's unclear about the precise details of the on-going problem – Joan's always vague about her doctor's diagnoses – but she knows it involves tablets as she went herself to collect the prescription for Joan the previous day.

Nuala sticks her head into the lounge, notes that Beth and Sammy are installed in front of the television, and, with a sigh, that the snack consisted of a two-litre bottle of cola, a family pack of crisps and an assortment of sweets. They'll be buzzing all night, she thinks.

... he's very good at football, too. Plays for the county.

Nuala realises that Joan's been talking, that she's not been listening. This inability to concentrate has been a bane since Greg's disappearance, a kind of delayed symptom of the shock. She wonders who Joan is talking about and decides it's probably a neighbour's son, another of her adopted 'grandchildren'.

... mind you, he's very cocky, is that one. He's always poking his sister, sets her off screaming. And she's got a terrible scream. Ooh, it goes right through you. You know, she's coloured, she is, so it goes right through you. She's got that, what's it called... celebrity palsy. Her brain stopped working for a bit when she was born...

Mm, says Nuala, distracted. The story of the cocky boy has reminded her that she was supposed to chase up one of her students, a young Kurd, seventeen years old, who has been absent from college for over a week. She has been leaving voicemail messages on his mobile for the past four days without success, but has been told by another student, the Kurd's friend, that he is on holiday.

According to the classmate, two or three times a year the boy gets itchy feet and decides to do see his many scattered friends. He'll head for Glasgow, Sunderland, Leeds, Sheffield. When caught out in between his friends' homes, his modus operandi is to head for the nearest police station, show them his Home Office documentation, tell them he's penniless and under eighteen and throw himself at their mercy. Invariably he gets offered a hot meal and a cell for the night. In this way he's been all over the country without paying for a bed. His friend has provided Nuala with a new mobile number, but she's unsure what she'll say when she tracks him down, whether to reprimand him for missing classes or congratulate him on his ingenuity.

... and I had to ring three times to get someone to take her to the toilet, Joan is telling her. And you should have seen the state of the room. We used to get down on our knees and scrub the skirting boards. Now it's all sub-contracted out, they just give it a quick once over. It went downhill when they got rid of the matrons...

Mmm, says Nuala. She wonders whether there's any point cooking for her kids, realises she'll have to organise something for Semira and the others anyway, opens the fridge door to check what the possibilities are.

... when I saw them in Lidl. Ooh he's a horrible man. The way he talks to her. 'Do this!', 'Stand over there!' It's not right.

Nuala tuts in sympathy. Bolognese, she thinks. That's nice and easy. She busies herself with onions, tomato puree, mince, garlic.

... Market Rasen, I think. Or Musselburgh. Worth an each way flutter, that's what he said...

Nuala's slicing onions now. She waits for an appropriate pause in Joan's monologue.

You'll stay for tea, won't you, Joan? she says. She's seen Joan's bare kitchen and wonders what she lives on, how often she eats a hot meal.

Thank you but no, dear. I'm not a great one for foreign food. It tends to repeat on me. I've got a nice piece of gammon at home. I'll have that with a slice of pineapple. That was always John's favourite.

Joan's husband, John. Thirty years dead and buried but still her point of reference for everything from politics to pub food. Nuala smiles, recognising how often she, too, uses the image of her spouse as a kind of moral compass on the journey she's been taking since his disappearance.

Joan has started off on a new story, something about a hot-air balloon during the war. Nuala sees that she's in a particularly garrulous mood and that's she's settled in for the foreseeable future. She opens the fridge door again, pulls out a bottle of white wine, pulls open the cutlery drawer and takes out the corkscrew. It's going to be a long evening, she thinks.

⌘

A thousand triggers a day call up reminders of Greg, a thousand traps sprung. A casual remark, a glance, a few bars of music takes her back from now to then, to the life she lived with him. But sometimes she considers not the things that happened, but the things that did not – the places not visited, the ideas not shared, the tales never told – and these thoughts in their own way are just as painful.

⌘

Some weeks after Semira moves in, a Wednesday afternoon, Nuala finds her sitting at the kitchen table, toiling over a notepad. Neither woman has classes and Nuala's taken her marking home with her. At first she thinks Semira must be doing some of her language homework. She peers over her shoulder to see if she can help (once a teacher, always a teacher, she thinks with a wince as she does so). But it's not homework that Semira's working on, it's a letter. She scans it momentarily, notes the unfamiliar script, then backs off. At Semira's side there's an envelope already addressed in English with a single name.

Who are you writing to? she asks. She knows she's being nosy, can't help it. Who's Kassa?

Semira looks up, startled. She's completely absorbed in the task at hand, hasn't noticed she's being watched.

Kassa? Oh, she's... she's a friend. A friend from home.

Right. What's she doing now? It's a simple question, a good opportunity for Nuala to glean a little more information about Semira. She'd like to have a clearer picture of her guest, but somehow the moments for those intimacies never come. Semira pauses for the briefest instant. Nuala notes that she's already swept up her notebook and pen, is poised to stand up.

I've got to go into town in a minute. Do you need anything? It's a smooth swerve, artfully done. Nuala doesn't answer at once. She feels a stab of irritation. Part of her feels that Semira has an obligation to answer her questions. Totally unfair of course, she tells herself. After all, there were no conditions attached to their friendship, and her past history is nobody's business but her own.

No, don't worry. I don't need anything.

You will be here to let the children in?

Sure.

When Semira has gone, Nuala sits down at the computer. She has emails to write, college work to complete, but she's still feeling a sense of frustration. Aware of Semira's Ethiopian background and of her stay in Eritrea, she googles first one country, then the other. She ignores the guilty feeling that she's engaging in a cross between stalking and espionage.

Her investigations are interrupted by the door bell and she is forced to abandon the computer. From the hallway she can hear her children's voices, Beth strident and authoritarian, Sammy whining in protest.

Yanit and Abebe also make their own way home from school together, though theirs is further away. It's only since their arrival that Nuala, in the face of her own children's insistence, has allowed Sammy and Beth to make the return journey alone. Even so, she still feels uneasy, but understands that it is progress of sorts. It is another milestone reached, a further step towards her letting go.

Inside, the children continue their squabble while Nuala produces mugs of hot chocolate and biscuits. She asks Sammy about his swimming lesson, Beth about the current supply teacher, and successfully distracts them from their argument. When they finish their snack, Sammy goes off to his room to play with his Lego while Beth announces she has English homework and needs the computer. Nuala is still standing in the kitchen, the remnants of the snack in front of her on the table, next to them the work she's taken home from the staffroom. She looks at the pile of exam papers that she has been trying to ignore. Can't put it off much longer, she thinks, and picks up her pen with a sigh.

⌘

A half-term Monday. Nuala has booked the time off as holiday, vaguely planning to take the children on an excursion.

When Greg was around, the Before time of her life, they'd often jump on the London coach and head for the Tate Modern. The children were younger then, so entertainment could be as simple as running helter skelter across the Millennium Bridge screaming at the top of their voices, or ambling alongside the Thames waving at the tourist pleasure boats.

For Greg, it was a question of mixing business with pleasure. He'd usually call his agent in advance, and after an hour or so perusing the paintings, Nuala and Greg would take Beth and Sammy up to the café on the fourth floor. Burnley Welsh would be up there already, sitting at a corner table nursing a black coffee, dressed in his trademark charcoal suit and white tee-shirt, stylish and urbane.

While Nuala bought the food and supervised the children, Greg and Burnley would sit aside and update each other on developments. Nuala knew Greg felt a little guilty about this, but he disliked his professional trips to London, so it was a way of killing two birds with a single stone.

After thirty minutes or so, Burnley would stand up, shake hands with Greg, nod at Nuala and leave. He never acknowledged the children and seemed only vaguely aware of Nuala's existence. Once, when Nuala commented on this to Greg, she told him that frankly she found the man decidedly creepy. Greg had laughed, then shrugged. Maybe he's just a bit shy, he'd suggested. Anyway, he's very good at his job. But Nuala has always seen reserve as a lame excuse for bad manners, so she distrusts him.

Today, though, there's no Greg and no children, and so no Tate trip. It's been eight, nine months since the crash. The initial gagging, ghastly shock has gone. It's no longer a violent punch in the stomach, a long, internalised scream. That's the best part of it, she supposes, the fact that it's now just a steady, dull ache.

Still, what she's also losing is that minuscule glint of hope, that unsaid but ever-present possibility that at any moment her phone would ring and she'd be told that he'd been found, that he was alive, that everything would be OK. That expectation is fading, and though she'd never admit it, there's a part of her now that would be more capable of absorbing the news of a body.

So no Greg. But no children, either. Semira's friends, the Kenyan ones, have arrived an hour before in their van to collect them all for a trip to the Cotswold Wildlife Park. Nuala and Semira have prepared a picnic, and they've all bundled into the back of the vehicle, wrapped in raincoats and clutching umbrellas. Nuala has turned down her own invitation after Semira made it clear that she'd be happy to take responsibility for all four children. Nuala's excuse is lesson planning, but really she just wants a day on her own. For so long she's sought distraction in company, but today she feels strong enough to face up to herself.

So the van doors slam. Nuala makes one last effort to

give Semira some money for the trip and again Semira refuses. Her friends Tom and Gloria have somehow acquired a free entry ticket for the park, she tells Nuala, so the only expense will be ice creams at the end. Nuala sees that she's beaten so she shrugs and smiles and the van moves off in a cloud of acrid exhaust.

Her reminiscences about Burnley and the Tate have reminded her that there is a week-old message from him on her answer machine. He's remembered Greg mentioning a set of animal sketches he'd done, charcoal on paper, and wondered whether Nuala had seen them around.

She's been meaning to have a root in the studio, to let him know if she finds anything. Since Greg's disappearance, Burnley's continued to represent his art. He has been scrupulous in providing Nuala with detailed records of revenue and with every penny of earned income, minus his commission of course. She feels a little guilty for her previous mistrust, though she still finds dealing with him a strain. Even after Greg's disappearance he has never thawed out, never shown much warmth. Not that he has been offensive or rude, just avoided the slightest intimacy. There is never any hint that their relationship is anything other than professional

Before she begins the hunt, she decides to make coffee. In the old days she would snatch at such moments of freedom, slide herself onto the piano stool and lose herself in her music. But she still cannot bring herself to play. Instead, mug in hand, she wanders vaguely towards the basement studio.

The room is well lit, the ceiling fitted with rows of spotlights. She remembers people's surprise when they learned that Greg painted in a basement. Even she knew that painters normally sought as much natural light as possible. But he'd always maintained that paintings were designed to live indoors, so good artificial light was acceptable for his work. Still, whenever the weather permitted, he'd haul his easel out to the back garden and set up shop there.

The room's been transformed since Yanit and Abebe's arrival. Gone are the easels – Greg often had three or four pictures on the go at one time – and the stacked up canvases.

Gone, too, the wooden table strewn with tubes of oil paint, brushes, rags and bottles of white spirit. There are two built-in cupboards in the basement, and one of these now contains all of the paints and brushes. The easels have been folded up and are stored for the moment in a cupboard in the spare room. Any finished canvases have long since been collected by Burnley. The unused and unfinished ones are secreted around the house, one or two still in the basement cupboard, others in the loft, the spare room, even Nuala's own bedroom.

The white walls are now decorated with posters – different species of snakes and the Chelsea squad for Abebe, a boy band and a map of Africa for Yanit – and the table has been moved into a corner. The two camp beds now dominate the room.

Nuala looks around distractedly for the charcoal sketches. She thinks she would have noticed them all those months back when she first went through Greg's things. She doesn't recall any such artwork, but is aware that she had been in a terrible state at the time, oblivious to much of what was going on around her. She opens the cupboard and checks under the table.

She can't face the loft, but tries the other possible hiding places – her bedroom, the airing cupboard in the bathroom, the bookcase on the landing. Finally, and with a twinge of guilt at the invasion of privacy, she pushes open Semira's door and enters what was once the spare bedroom.

She hasn't been inside this room since Semira moved in. It's almost unchanged, no photos on display, no pictures or posters to personalise the space. On the desk is a pile of books. There's an English grammar, a heavy dictionary, a history of Oxford, a text on computers, a prospectus for Oxford Brookes University. Next to these lie a copy of the *Qur'an* and a notebook. Pens and pencils are stacked inside a coffee cup. There's an electronic dictionary beside the cup.

Next to the lamp on the bedside table is a hand mirror and bathbag full of make-up, its zipper open and contents displayed. Nuala recognises the bright scarlet lipstick Semira tends to use most days, the eyeliner and mascara.

The bed's been made, a spare blanket neatly folded on the duvet. The room's stuffy, the window shut, Semira's scent – half perfume, half human odour – hanging in the air. Nuala opens the window.

She's about to leave when she remembers why she came, pulls open the door of the wardrobe. It's full of Semira's clothes, padded jackets and dark baggy skirt suits and colourful dresses, three or four pairs of shoes. Nuala closes the door, then as an afterthought, reaches up on top of the wardrobe and runs her hand along the surface. She's hoping to feel a pile of loose leaf sheets, or perhaps a large thin sketch book. Instead, her fingers brush against something much more solid. She drags it across to the edge of the surface and pulls it down – a shoebox.

It feels full but not heavy. Nuala takes off the lid. Inside are a pile of envelopes, each addressed with a single name in English: Kassa. She takes out the first envelope and turns it over in her hand. It's sealed. She pulls out more, all identical. Carefully she returns the letters to the box, the box to its original location.

Back in the kitchen, she sees that the cat's food bowl is empty, the water bowl dry. She tops them both up, hears the metallic click of the catflap and feels the soft sensation of the tabby as she rubs herself against her legs.

Nuala's restless. She opens the sliding doors that lead out into the garden and stands on the lawn amongst the bats and balls, the plastic wheelbarrow and overturned see-saw. She hasn't worked outside for months but even in the Before time, she'd been a reluctant gardener, enthusiastic for only about three days a year, usually in early summer, when she'd bully Greg into mowing the lawn. She'd hack away viciously at any overgrowth in an attempt to get all the pruning over in a single hasty session, then pull up handfuls of weeds that would lie where they were thrown until the following autumn.

Nuala goes back inside. She contemplates a spot of spring cleaning. Fortunately the floor tiles are a zesty yellow, good for concealing the dirt, but even she can see that they need a scrub. The fridge, too, hasn't been cleaned for some time, nor has the microwave. The book shelf opposite the table is dusty, a mess of unsheathed CDs and piled cookery books. She sighs, knowing that the chores need doing while yearning for some more meaningful act. She's about to set to work, rummaging under the sink for cleaning fluid and scouring cloths, when she has a better idea, a moment of inspiration that falls somewhere between raging rebellion and reckless desperation.

She phones everyone she knows in Oxford, the book group women, the school mums and neighbours, her old friends from yoga, Cassie and Angie and Ingrid and Mary, and tells them of her plan, an impromptu party. They all say yes, they'll be there, what can they bring? And they don't tell her, of course, of their own arrangements that they'll cancel, postpone. Their loyalty and love for Nuala make it an automatic response.

So she gathers her purse and shopping bags, spends an hour at the supermarket filling her trolley with cheeses and snacks, baguette and olives, the ingredients for a great pot of chilli con carne, a green salad, bottles of wine, cartons of juice and fizzy drinks. And back home, she sets to work so that by the time the children return with Semira, the chilli is simmering on the hob, the snacks laid out in the lounge.

It's early evening when the van rolls up outside the house and Semira and the four children bustle into the hall, kicking off muddy shoes and throwing their jackets in the general direction of the coat stand. Semira heads for the toilet while the children invade the recently peaceful kitchen.

What's going on? asks Beth when she sees the festive preparations. Are we having a party?

Nuala explains that it's a Thank You party, that there's no time to lose, that it's all hands on deck. The children are swept along in the excitement, put to work blowing up balloons and organising party games. Nuala won't let herself stop and consider her actions, fears that she'll abandon the project if left to her own thoughts. Semira, sensing the significance of the event, takes her place in the kitchen and begins preparing a batch of falafel.

And the party's some way towards a success. It's too chaotic for pussy-footing, for inhibitions and stilted self-consciousness. The guests arrive in threes and fours, adults and children. There's music – Beatles and Beach Boys and The Pogues, the children's latest pop chart favourites, then later Tom Waits and Ry Cooder, the *Jungle Book* soundtrack and Billie Holiday, Greg's music as much as Nuala's, but tonight it's OK, the pain is tolerable.

The adults mingle and drink and dance. The children shriek and scream in an atmosphere of hilarity, of abandonment. For Nuala, there's still no letting go. She's disappointed to admit that it is an evening to endure as much as enjoy. But many hours later, when the kids have been put to bed and Nuala clears up with Mary and Semira, she feels a sense of relief, an important rite of passage successfully navigated.

⌘

It's six months since Semira first moved in. The two women have grown closer. Semira is no longer irritated by Nuala's gentle inquisitiveness, Nuala willing to let Semira's past remain a mystery. Acceptance, thinks Nuala. Another essential component of friendship.

Although she no longer expects revelations from Semira, Nuala nevertheless still dwells on why she felt such a need for this intimacy and tries to analyse her own impulses. As you make someone's acquaintance, she reflects, you learn details of their past, and these help explain their personality, become like the pegs on which you hang their present characteristics. Deprived of this background, she feels cheated, somehow vulnerable. But perhaps what her relationship with Semira is teaching her, she wonders, is that history counts for nothing. It's a luxury and when all the frills are torn away, the present is the only thing that counts.

Nuala no longer thinks about Semira's departure. There's a silent agreement that her residence has acquired a greater permanency. The routine of their lives is soothing.

Time is marked only by occasional celebrations – Easter, the children's birthday parties, the school holidays.

One evening, Nuala, Beth and Yanit are in the lounge, spread out on the sofa and beanbags, watching a tepid romcom on DVD. Beth asks Nuala whether Yanit can move into her bedroom.

Is that what you want, Yanit? Nuala asks. She nods eagerly. On a number of occasions, there have been 'sleepovers' involving the girls sharing Beth's bed. Nuala considers the request. Both of her children have spacious bedrooms, plenty of room for second single beds.

Well, it's OK by me, but we'll have to check with Semira, make sure she's happy with Abebe being left on his own.

That problem is solved as soon as Sammy hears about Beth's scheme. Not to be outdone, he demands that Abebe moves in with him. Abebe has slept top-to-toe with Sammy several times in the past, too tired to make his way downstairs after mammoth Lego-building sessions.

When the request is put to Semira, she feels a little awkward, an irrational fear that her family are playing cuckoo in Nuala's nest. Still, when she tries to raise this unease with Nuala, she is told that she's being silly.

So the camp beds in the basement are folded away. One of Nuala's colleagues offers her an unwanted single bed, Kenyan Tom comes up with a second, and within the week, the change has been made. The basement is now free.

And, most unexpectedly, this begins a new chapter in Nuala's life. It starts one Tuesday during the October half term. Semira's taken the children ice skating and Nuala finds herself wandering down to the basement. She stands at the doorway and casts her eyes around the room.

The old table's still there, pushed up against the wall, its paint-stained surface concealed beneath a floral cloth. There's a chair, there, too, tucked beneath the table, a solid piece of pine also smeared with dried oil paint. Nuala remembers it as Greg's thinking chair, the throne from which he'd contemplate his latest creation or plan out a future project. She stares at the chair and, despite herself, conjures up his presence.

There he is, leaning back, one leg crossed over the other, a hand resting on his ankle, the other cradling his head, locked in fierce concentration. She remembers what he used to say – that he did ninety-nine per cent of his painting in his head, the initial inspiration of a vision perceived, then the process of mapping out in his mind the dimensions, the perspective, the lighting and colours. Only then, sometimes days after, would he prepare the canvas and pick up his brushes and oils.

There he is, dressed in his scruffy jeans, the grubby tee-shirt beneath the baggy long-sleeve shirt, collar frayed, cuffs rolled-up. He's so wrapped up in his thoughts he hasn't seen Nuala. She coughs and he looks up and his face breaks into a smile and Nuala steps forward. And then – poof! – he's gone and the room's as stripped and empty as it was when she first walked in.

Nuala rubs her eyes. She's been doing this conjuring trick ever since the crash, hating herself for it, the ritual of masochistic scab-picking. It's like plunging her leg into a scalding bath, the first time excruciating, each time thereafter less painful as her tolerance grows. And today, for the first time, it's actually almost pain-free, almost soothing. Even the moment when he disappears and she realises she's on her own again, that she's lost him forever.

She pulls out the table, removes the tablecloth and runs her hands over the rough surface. She can pick out the acrid tang of oils and with it all the memories and associations. Without thinking, she heads for the cupboard and begins to unpack the equipment so carefully stored away. Before she knows it, she's set up an easel and propped a blank canvas on its lip. She pulls out the toolbox that Greg had used to store his oils and brushes, grabs a bottle of turps and a handful of rags.

Nuala selects a half-used tube of oil, a scarlet, and unscrews the cap. She lifts the paint to her nose and breaths in deeply. She's set out a palette and she begins squeezing out her colours.

First she covers most of the canvas in a grey hue leaving

the left hand edge untouched. Then she uses vivid reds and yellows and oranges dabbed onto this edge in an arc. She paints in thick blobs, merges the different shades with her brush, then uses a palette knife to scratch lines through the colours so that they shoot out like fierce hot sparks. The effect is like the rim of a sun or fiery star.

Nuala is utterly absorbed. With the background and sun completed, she starts on the central detail. She begins to sketch out a large black figure, a sort of naked silhouette kneeling in supplication, its arms held out towards the sun's burning heat, an image of worshipful surrender. She works away in silence, oblivious to the smears of paint she has inadvertently transferred to her jersey, the black trousers she is wearing, even her left cheek.

When she finishes, she steps back and surveys the product. She feels breathless, shaking with excitement. Her watch tells her she's been working for almost two hours, and for that period she's been entirely lost in herself, a giddy exhilarating escape. And yet, at the same time, since the crash she's never felt closer to Greg, never felt more aware of his absence.

She leaves the painting to dry on the easel, puts away the oils and cleans the brushes. When she leaves the basement, twenty minutes later, she's still on a high.

⌘

Nuala remembers the moment of revelation with that strange mixture of alien dislocation and absolute clarity that is the hallmark of life-turning shocks.

It's late afternoon. Mary has called in to collect Joe, who has come back to play with Sammy after school. Nuala comes into the kitchen together with Mary and the boys. She's making small talk but is focused on her next chore, to get a chicken stew on the go. Semira's sitting at the table filling in a form. Nuala remembers Semira's comment earlier in the week that her permanent resident application had arrived from the

Home Office. As she passes the kitchen table, she glances down at the form just as Semira has finished filling in a section.

Oh, look, she says brightly. You've filled that bit in wrong. You've put that you've got four kids. She points at the appropriate box. Look, you've put four, not two.

She looks up into Semira's face. As she does so, her mind searches for a joke, a witty comment, perhaps something about doubling your troubles, two being enough for anyone, or wishful thinking.

But as soon as her eyes meet Semira's, these witticisms seem pathetic, are banished from her mind. Semira's glance is only momentary, a fleeting instant of contact, but a split second afterwards Nuala feels as if she's been slapped in the face, so potent a cocktail of emotions does it stir. Nuala experiences within it a tremendous maelstrom, a confusion of raging pain and tender longing. And then, a moment later, it's gone, Semira's face is a blank.

She gets to her feet, form in hand, and leaves the room in silence. Mary, who has witnessed the exchange but not the full force of Semira's gaze, is sidetracked by a squawking Joe and is soon engrossed in locating his schoolbag, his shoes, supervising his preparations to leave.

As soon as Mary's gone, Nuala heads for Semira's room, the chicken stew entirely forgotten. She knocks at the door, waits, knocks again, then pushes the door open tentatively.

Semira's standing at the window, her back to Nuala and the door.

Look, I'm sorry, love. Really, I didn't mean anything, I shouldn't have been so nosy. It's nothing to do with me.

There's a long pause. Nuala waits for a response, considers saying something else, then shrugs. She's about to turn around and leave when Semira speaks. She remains facing away from Nuala. Her voice is low, almost inaudible, as if she's really talking to herself, to someone inside her head, someone absent.

We were in Turkey when it happened. I remember it like it was yesterday. I play it over and over in my mind until it feels as if my brain is rubbed so raw it bleeds. I don't even know which town it was, somewhere on the south coast I'm sure, because it was close to where we'd docked after the crossing from Alexandria. Talking to the Turks was difficult. We spoke a broken English together, but one of the men said we were near Antalya. I don't know for sure. I'd paid the traffickers in dollars, I'd been waiting for weeks in the cramped room, trying to keep my spirits up, the spirits of the children.

She breaks off. Nuala can still only see the back of her head, peers at it for clues.

It happened early one morning. We'd been woken at dawn, they told us to get dressed and gather our things together. Today was the day. We were taken to the meeting spot in the back of a pickup. We pulled up in a dusty car park in an industrial zone of the town, deserted, just our pickup and a lorry waiting. It's back doors were open, its engine was running. I remember the stinky smell of the exhaust fumes.

Another pause. Nuala has the impression that Semira is gathering her strength.

We got out of the pickup. They ushered us over to the lorry. Two traffickers had brought us over, the driver and our Egyptian contact, the only Arabic-speaker. There were another three waiting, five in total. They were all different, different clothes, features, hair, but the one who brought us over to the lorry was a bear of a man, barrel-chested, black leather jacket, thick moustache, stubble, greasy black hair. It's his face that's etched in my mind. When it all runs through my head, they somehow all look like him, they're all identical.

Nuala waits. It feels like she hasn't drawn breath since Semira began speaking.

They took us over to the lorry. I asked the Egyptian if we were going straight away and he said yes, that we should fetch our baggage from the pickup. There were two bags so I sent back the older children and made sure the younger ones were close by. I was frightened, you know that feeling when things are out of your control.

Seconds pass. When Semira resumes, her tone is flat,

distanced, almost dreamy.

So I am standing by the back flaps of the lorry. I've got one hand on Yanit's shoulders, another placed on Abebe's head, as if to touch them is to protect them. The Bear is behind me, the Egyptian to my right. Some thirty metres away, next to the pick-up are the older children. They are bent over the back of the vehicle, hauling down the baggage. Close to them are two of the other men, the fifth one up in the cab of the truck. I am feeling anxious. I want to get safely hidden away in the lorry with the children. These thoughts are interrupted when I feel something hard pressed into my back. I turn and find the Bear pointing a gun at my chest. 'Gold,' he says, and points the barrel at my necklace, my earrings. When I sold up my life in Addis, I converted everything into US dollars as well as one or two small pieces of gold jewellery. I sewed the dollars into Yanit's jacket and wore the gold about my person as discreetly as I could. Now I am about to lose it. I start to argue, plead, but the Bear doesn't hesitate. With the gun levelled at me in his right hand, he pulls back his left and slaps me hard across the face. It's a backhanded cuff that catches me completely by surprise. His knuckles split my lip and I'm already stripping off the jewellery before the first splash of my blood has hit the ground.

For the first time since she began speaking, Semira makes a movement, a slight shaking of the head, as if denying what was coming next.

So that's when it happens. That's when everything becomes confusing. I have got my earrings off, the bangle on my wrist, the thin necklace and my wedding ring. I'm not looking up. I haven't been aware of the wailing in the distance and only take notice as the police car shoots around the corner and skids to a halt fifteen metres or so in front of the pickup. One moment we're all frozen, caught like hares in a headlight, the next the police officers are out, guns drawn, barking out orders. And then the traffickers pull out their own pistols and open fire.

The words continue to flow and Nuala takes in the meaning, the raw facts, but it's only afterwards, later that night alone in bed, that Semira's words start to sink in, that she begins to understand what it must have felt like. She closes her eyes and takes herself back to the car park, to the pandemonium of fear and panic. Semira is caught in two minds, the desire to guard the younger children she is holding, and the desperate need to protect her older ones caught up in the fighting. Amidst the roar and screams of the men, the crack and hammer of gunfire, she's dimly aware that the Egyptian next to her has fallen to her feet in a heap, that one of the traffickers at the pickup has been shot, that two officers are also down.

Across the courtyard, she sees that the third trafficker has pushed the two older children in front of him as a shield and is edging round the pickup, manoeuvring himself out of the two remaining officers' line of fire. Meanwhile the lorry driver has stuck his head around the side of the truck and is screaming at the Bear to get into the vehicle, gesturing to him to get the back doors closed so they can be off. The Bear turns to Semira, waves his gun at her and growls a command to get herself inside with the younger children she is still holding. Semira can still see the trafficker hunched behind the pickup, her two older ones crouched down beside him as he lets off shot after shot at the remaining officers who have, by now, retreated to positions behind their own vehicle. She begins to scream.

She can no more get into the lorry voluntarily and leave behind her older children than split her own heart in two.

She looks into the Bear's face praying that he'll see sense but he's in no mood to compromise. He whips his pistol across her cheek, punches her hard in the face, then pushes her into the back of the lorry. The younger children, too shocked to protest, scramble into the hold behind her. She has fallen to the floor, lies dazed, spitting tooth and blood. She looks out of the darkness of the lorry, her last few seconds of light for the next twelve hours. The trafficker behind the pickup is shooting at the officers. The Bear too is emptying his pistol, the officers are returning fire. Then there's a roar, a flash of fire as the police car explodes in a ball of flame and smoke, a final glimpse of the huddled youngsters at the pickup, and the Bear swings the doors across her line of vision.

Kassa! She screams as the doors slam into place and the bolts are pulled across. Kassa! Gadissa!

She's still screaming their names as the lorry pulls out with a shrieking of tyres and grinding of protesting gears.

⌘

Nothing has changed for Nuala, there's no light at the end of the tunnel, no journey completed. But as she remembers Semira's voice, the dyke is breached, the tears begin to flow. And she discovers, as the minutes pass, that the tears which began as a lament for her friend Semira, for the loss of her two children, soon begin to alter in nature, to become in time tears for her own loss. For Greg and the fifteen years of Nuala-and-Greg, the fifteen years Before the After. And with the tears comes not healing, and end to the meaninglessness, but at least a kind of recognition that henceforth Greg to her may be a memory of breadmaking, a half-finished sketch on the bathroom wall, a flashback of soggy walks in Shotover Park, a photo in her purse of him posing with Beth and Sammy on their Marmaris holiday. All this, but nothing more. Ever.

EPILOGUE

Dear Kassa

You'll never guess what happened today! The letter was waiting for me when I got back from class, brown manila with the familiar school postmark. I opened it, scanned the contents and let out a scream. The house was empty, so I screamed again, then put the kettle on for a steadying cup of tea.

It was Nuala who spotted the advertisement in the *Oxford Times* a fortnight ago. She circled it in red ink and left it open on my bed: Learning Support Assistant Required for East Oxford Primary School, it said. I had scanned the rest of the information as a froth of panic and excitement began to churn in my stomach. I had found Nuala in Sammy's bedroom, piling Lego bricks back into his toy chest. When I showed her the advertisement, she smiled.

Well, it's what you wanted, isn't it? she told me. It sounds perfect.

But I'm not ready. My English is so bad. I don't know anything.

Rubbish, she said. Your English is fine. You're ready, Semira. As ready as you'll ever be.

And it's Nuala who phoned for an application form, who helped me fill it in, supplied the reference.

And today, the letter. The offer of an interview. Nine thirty next Thursday. So soon! Nuala is the first home, just a half day on Wednesdays. I show her the letter and she lets out her own scream, even louder than mine. She insists on going down to the shop at the bottom of the road and returns with cakes and lemonade and sweets and crisps, a bottle of fizzy wine for herself, for me a carton of my favourite mango juice. Then the children arrive and she's put some music on the CD player and the children are jumping up and down. Yanit and Beth are performing some complicated dance routine, Sammy is leaping about on the sofa and Abebe's head is buried in a family-sized pack of cheese curls. The cork pops and Nuala slops the fizzy wine into her glass. I look around at the flushed faces, at the roomful of screaming, twisting, gyrating bodies, and I think, Maybe, just maybe, it's going to be alright.